THE ARBITRARY SWORD

A NOVEL

BY

DIANE GOSHGARIAN

Vision Press
2000

Library of Congress Catalog Number: 00-090933

International Standard Book Number: 0-9665742-0-6

PUBLISHER'S NOTE
This is a work of fiction. Names, characters, places, and incidents either are the
products of the author's imagination or are used fictitiously, and any resemblance
to actual persons, living or dead, events, or locales is entirely coincidental.

Printed in the United States of America

VISION PRESS

Brookline, MA 02446

Dedication

This book is dedicated to:

Margaret Zakarian Ovoian

Koren Ovoian

Paul (Boghos) Goshgarian

Angel Kalousdian (Balian) Goshgarian

My Grandparents, whose strength and instinct

for survival are part of this story and

who I am today.

ACKNOWLEDGMENT

There are many people I would like to thank for their help in this book getting to print. First, my family, my husband Ron, my stepchildren John and Candice, and my children Rachael and Sarah. My writing often took me away from them and I appreciate their understanding. My best friend Libby Sanderson, whose enthusiastic support was her immediate and lasting response to my writing this book. She filled in the gaps in child care and let my know that she believed in my ability to tell this story. Rosalyn Minassian who, with no thoughts of personal gain, gave generously of her time, making phone calls and setting up interviews to promote the book. She is a giving spirit and a true friend. My sister, Sue McGrew, who painted the beautiful cover design. My other sisters, Joan Goshgarian, Paula Patrick and their families who were all unconditionally supportive when I finally came out of my writer's closet and told them about the book. My parents, Jack Goshgarian and Lucy Ovoian Goshgarian, whose stunned pleasure and pride made me feel so gratified. Chaitanya Kanopia, who generously let me benefit from his computer expertise. He helped set up my new computer, converted and loaded the manuscript onto it and answered my stressed phone calls with good humor and understanding. Tracy Longman, whose expert legal advise was invaluable. I am deeply grateful for her help and friendship. The members of my twenty-five year old women's group, Gail Grady, Susan StClair, and Emily Tucker, whose altogether positive feedback gave me the confidence to push this project to the end. Zab Russian whose helpful comments told me that I had met the goals I set out to accomplish. My good friend Marianna Gracey, who among her many ways of giving support, taught me to use a computer and lent me her apartment when I needed a quiet place to work. My other relatives and friends, too numerous to name, but to whom I am grateful for their support. Finally I would like to thank the Armenian community who provided me with the culture and values that served as a background to this book.

CHAPTER ONE

The province of Kharpert,
Ottoman Turkey, November 1895

A seven-year-old can feel the presence of danger even when she doesn't understand it. The moment Victoria set foot in the village square, she knew something was wrong.

She turned to face her best friend, Margaret Damadian. Her own fear was mirrored in Margaret's wide-eyed stare.

Margaret raised a shaky finger and pointed.

That was it. The shops were all locked and barred. And for the Armenians of her village to close their shops in the middle of the day could only mean that something bad was going to happen.

She looked around and saw men in loose, baggy clothing striding up and down the streets as though they owned them. The Turks walked about freely, but she and Margaret were the only Armenians. And they were just children.

One of the men stopped and looked in her direction. His eyes narrowed.

Victoria felt her heart begin to pound. She headed for the road. With each step, she quickened her pace. Soon she was running. Margaret remained at her side.

At the edge of the village, Margaret grabbed her arm. "Come into my house. We'll be safe there."

"No, no, I want to go home."

Margaret ran for the gate in the stone wall that surrounded her house. "Are you sure?"

Victoria nodded without stopping and flew off down the dirt road, leaving a cloud of dust in her wake.

Fifteen minutes ago, school had recessed for lunch. She had grabbed her books and flounced out into the frosty courtyard.

She had been angry because her neighbor, Martin Halabian, who was one of her classmates, had teased her about the books. Hateful Martin. But smart. It was their second year of school and already she knew. He was the one to watch. The one who would try to keep her from first place.

No, she wouldn't let that happen. Her father had allowed her to go to school though a lot of people had told him he shouldn't. She could just hear Aunt Rose's voice now. "Why would you let a *girl* go to school? How will you ever find a husband for her?" While her mother had stood, red-faced but smiling, at her husband's side.

Her father even told her that he might send her to college some day. That was a secret from everyone. Even her mother. "Until she's had time to grow used to the idea," her father had said. So she would not let her father down by being anything short of best.

But none of that mattered now.

Now something was wrong. And she had to get to the safety of home. She began to pant for air. She wanted to stop, but she hugged her books to her chest and ran faster.

Ahead, over the rise, a figure ran toward her.

She stopped and stood still. Then she let out her breath. "Papa."

Koren Adanalian waved his arm to his chest. "Victoria, come here."

She hurried into his warm embrace. "Papa. I was so scared." She told him about the locked shops in the village.

"But who told you?"

Koren pointed in the direction of their neighbor's house. "John Halabian stopped on his way home from the village and told me."

"But what does it mean, Papa? Are the Turks going to hurt us?"

"No, I won't let them." Koren laid his hand on his daughter's shoulder. "Let's go home."

Victoria sighed in relief. Whatever was wrong, Papa would protect her. She handed him her books and they ran, side by side, until they reached the foothills of home.

She looked up. In the distance, her father's cows and sheep meandered in slow circles around their pastures, as they ripped blades of grass from the ground. Further up, nestled into the hillside, stood her sturdy stone house. Seta, her mother, stood in the open doorway shading her eyes with her hand.

"What happened?" Seta said, when they reached her. Her face was set in a worried frown. "Koren, I saw John Halabian talking to you, then you dropped your shovel and started running down the road."

Victoria told her mother what she had seen. Seta's hands flew to her face in alarm. She looked at Koren. "What do you think it means?"

Koren nodded in Victoria's direction.

Seta's hands dropped to her side. Her lips turned up in a strained smile. She put her arm around Victoria.

Koren headed for the door. "I'm going to round up as many of the animals as I can, and get them into the stable."

"Do you..." Seta glanced down at Victoria and lightened her tone. "Do you think you should go out there right now?"

Koren and Seta exchanged a look. "Yes, I think it necessary. Lock the door and don't open it until I come back."

Victoria helped her mother slide the bar across the front door.

"Mother, what does it all mean?"

Seta looked away. "Darling, you're really too young to understand but...oh how can I explain this? The shop owners would only close up in the middle of the day if they thought that trouble was coming our way."

Victoria frowned. "Trouble? You mean from the Turks?"

Seta played with the tie on her apron. "Oh dear, well--" She drew in a deep breath. "Sometimes the Turks...Oh , they become angry with the Armenians and they, well, we have to be careful not to make them more angry."

"Angry with all of us? But we've done nothing wrong."

"No, of course not. And you needn't worry. Papa will keep us safe."

Victoria nodded and picked up her books. Of course, Papa would keep them safe. There was nothing he was afraid of, nothing he couldn't handle.

She marched to the low table that stood in the middle of their one-room house, sat on a cushion and began to study.

Seta picked up her knitting but pulled out as many stitches as she put in, until Koren rapped on the door thirty minutes later.

She threw open the door and scanned his face. "Is everything all right?"

He nodded. "It's quiet right now."

Koren waited until late that night. Then, when he was sure Victoria was asleep, he said, "I'm going into the village to find out what's going on."

Seta paled. "Oh Koren, do you think it's safe?"

Koren brushed her cheek with his hand. "Don't worry,

darling. It's dark. No one will spot me. And I must find out what the shopkeepers know."

Seta paced the floor until he returned.

"What did you find out?"

Koren's jaw was set and he frowned. "Massacres. The Turks have turned against us again. They say that in some cities, thousands of Armenians have been slaughtered."

"And here? In our province?"

"In the city of Mezireh, five hundred people were killed yesterday and many of their shops were looted. When the news of it reached our village late this morning, the shopkeepers locked up. They had to. If their shops get looted, that will be the end of them and their families."

Seta drew in a shaky breath and looked in the direction of their slumbering daughter. She kept her voice low. "What started it this time?"

"It began in the capitol, in Constantinople. As best we can tell, a group of our people had gathered there to present a list of demands to the sultan. They went there in peace."

Koren stopped and gave a short derisive laugh. "Peace, what does that mean to the Turks?" He went on. "The police pulled out bayonets and clubs and went after the demonstrators. Of course, once they started, they let any Turkish riffraff who wanted to join in, go with them. And I'm sure there was no shortage."

Koren clenched his hands into fists. "They began by cutting down any Armenian in their path. Soon they were dragging people from their homes. Thousands are dead in the capitol. Now the violence is headed our way. Whether it will reach our village here, I just don't know, but we'll have to stay inside until it passes."

"Oh Koren, when I think of it, you could have been in Mezireh on business yesterday."

"You mustn't think that way. I wasn't. I was here, with you."

"But still, your business is so dangerous. Can't you give it up? We have the farm. We don't really need it."

"My courier business is what would keep us from ruin, if our wheat crop failed. Look at the Papazians. One year their fields caught fire, and," Koren snapped his fingers, "Next, they were begging from relatives. So you see, don't you my dear?"

Seta sighed and nodded.

Koren put his arm around his pretty wife and tried to kiss the color back into her cheeks. "You mustn't worry. You know I will protect you."

Seta laid her head on his shoulder. "I know, darling."

Koren stroked her hair. He had taken one look at her when she was a girl of fifteen, and known she was the one for him. And he had never had to question his faith. Seta was a simple, guileless person who had brought her gifts of stability, dependability and complete devotion to their marriage. He would die before he let anything happen to her or their daughter.

Koren kept his family in the house, venturing out himself each day, only to tend to the animals in the stable. But one day, he looked out the door and said, "Tonight I'm going to go to Michael Damadian's house. He will know what the news is."

"Can Mother and I go, too? I want to see Margaret."

"No, Victoria. You cannot go out until I know that it is safe."

Late that night, Koren slipped into the village and made his way to his friend's house, where several other men from the village had gathered.

"No one has traveled into or out of our village. We have to assume that means the violence is still going on," Michael said.

Koren ran his hand through his hair. "Has anyone here been hurt?"

Michael shook his head. "No, no one has been killed, if that's what you mean, but the Turks are getting stirred up. Who knows what it will lead to? They've been stealing animals. I heard John Halabian lost over half his sheep."

Koren's eyes widened. "My neighbor, John?"

Michael nodded.

Koren frowned. "That must mean that I lost some of my sheep too, the ones in the far pastures. Thank God, I got the closer ones in. Well, I can afford it but John, I don't know."

"And when this is all over, what can we do about it?" Levon Kalustian, another of the men, said.

Michael shook his head. "John will never get his sheep back, nor will you Koren, or any of the other men who lost their animals. Thank God, everyone harvested their wheat already. Half of our families would be ruined if they lost their crop."

"To think, the Turks who are stealing from us are our neighbors. Men who grew up right here in our village. They kill and rob us. No one does anything. And why? We are citizens of Turkey the same as they are."

"Citizens, yes. The same rights, no," Michael said.

Koren thought about what Michael had just said. Equal rights were what the group in the capitol had been petitioning the sultan for. There was a highly secret, revolutionary group of Armenian men he had heard of recently. The *Dashnak*s, they called themselves. The *Dashnak*s were dedicated to winning freedom for the Armenian people. Freedom from the abuse of the Turks. He hadn't really given serious thought to joining the *Dashnak*s before this. But now, perhaps he should. Perhaps they all should.

Victoria awoke and heard her parents talking, but didn't open her eyes. If they knew she wasn't asleep, they would stop. And she wanted to know what was going on, what secrets her parents were keeping from her. They kept walking around smiling, but they didn't look happy. She listened to the murmur of voices. Papa was saying they still had to stay indoors, that the danger wasn't over yet.

Was Papa scared? No, no. She smiled at the thought.

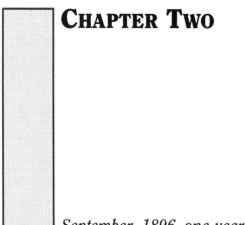

CHAPTER TWO

September, 1896, one year later

From her perch on the crest of the hill, Victoria stretched and glanced at the surrounding landscape. The late afternoon sun dipped low in the sky setting the fields aglow and toasting her back to a comfortable warmth. She lay on her stomach, propped up on her elbows with an open book in front of her. Her lips moved silently as her fingers trailed the words. Nearby, in front of her house, her parents chatted with each other under the shelter of a tree. At their side, sparkling glasses of water, freshly pumped from the earth's cool under-ground stood waiting to quench their thirst.

The air around her was heavy with the scent of newly cropped wheat.

For three days, she and her parents had risen at dawn

and labored until dark to harvest their crop. Her father had insisted that they get it done in a hurry, reminding them of the trouble last year and the importance of getting their food safely stored. She had earned this hour of rest. They all had. And it was all the sweeter to her, knowing that the wheat they ate every day, was now piled in tightly sewn sacks, on their pantry floor.

Victoria twirled a strand of hair as she read. She was a fortunate girl. Every night she sat down to a table filled with food. But many other children did not. She knew because of her trick of pretending to be asleep at night so she could listen to her parents talk. Last year they had told terrible stories. Stories about the Turks and what they did to people from villages not so far away. And some about the Turks from her own village, who stole animals from her friends and made them hungry all winter long.

She flipped to the next page. Her muscles, aching from the three days of labor, protested the simple movement. She stopped to appease them. She let her head become a free-falling weight and her chin dropped to her chest. She sighed and lifted it and again her vision swept across the landscape below.

What was that?

A raised patch of dust far down the dirt road. Something, or someone was coming their way. Friend or foe--Armenian or Turk?

Had her parents noticed?

She glanced their way. Her mother's tall, willowy frame still reclined against the tree; her head was tipped back and her eyelids closed over her soft blue eyes. But Papa was sitting tall and stiff. His eyes were trained on what they could both now see was the lone figure of a man.

His neck ached. He knew he shouldn't keep looking over his shoulder. No one could possibly have followed him this far.

Or could they?

If they caught him, his life was over. He was weary. How much longer could he manage to keep two steps ahead of the law? *No, no*, he said to himself, *don't think that way. You got out of Constantinople. You got away from the trouble. You're in Kharpert now. The police never would have pursued you this far.*

Or would they?

He looked over his shoulder again.

And what was to become of him even here? He'd been all right so far, sleeping in fields at night. But it was fall now, and in the interior of Turkey, fall turned to winter abruptly. What would he do when it got cold?

How far was Mezireh? He had been walking and walking. In busy Mezireh he would be safe. He could lose himself among the city's people and he would find work, any work. But where was Mezireh?

His feet hurt. He just couldn't make his legs take another step. *You must be strong*, he said to himself again. Then he sniffed. Something familiar was in the air. Against his will, his eyes brimmed with tears, which he instantly brushed away. He knew that smell, the autumn smell of wheat. The smell of home.

He slowed his pace and scanned the horizon, his gaze roaming the fields and nearby hills. As he looked to his right, his eyes narrowed and his heart beat faster. A man and woman lounged in the shade. The man was looking at him.

He stiffened. Then he noticed the woman's uncovered head and the man's tailored pants, and he knew that they too were Armenian.

For the first time in weeks, he relaxed.

The stranger turned off the road and began climbing toward them. Victoria's wariness turned into pity, as he came close enough for her to see his wrinkled, threadbare clothes. Why he was just a boy. Only a few years older than herself. Without looking, she knew that her father's hand was in his pocket, fishing for a coin. Her mother would insist that he stay for a meal.

She tucked her legs under her and stood. She brushed yellowed blades of grass from her white muslin dress and went to stand behind her father.

Koren rose to his feet. "*Parev*," he said in greeting. "What can I do for you?"

"I'm looking for directions to the city. How many day's

travel is it from here?"

"I will tell you. But first you must tell me why you want to go there."

"I'm looking for work."

Koren studied the boy. Then he said, "You needn't go to the city to find work. I could use your help right here on the farm."

Victoria's brown eyes widened in surprise. He had always been generous, but this? She turned to stare at him. Her father seemed unconcerned by either her or her mother's surprised faces. But he never worried what other people thought. And he always said that he knew everything he needed to know about a person just by looking at him.

Seta looked at her husband. "Are you sure, dear?"

"Yes," Koren said.

At her father's words, relief washed over the young man's features. His shoulders relaxed, his brow smoothed and he looked like the boy that he was. But the transformation lasted only a moment. Again, he tensed. "If you are going to take me in, you need to know something. My name is Nikol. Nikol Balian."

Balian. Why did he think his name would matter to them? Victoria used the gentle breeze to gather a loose strand of thick dark hair behind her ear. She studied the boy's alert face. *Handsome face*, she thought, then colored.

Nikol did not look in Victoria's direction. He raised his chin and met Koren's eyes.

Balian. Koren's expression did not change, though he recognized the name. A Balian was the leader of Constantinople's contingent of the *Dashnak* revolutionary group. Koren, Michael, and a few of the men from the village had joined the Armenian revolutionaries after the violence last year, galled by the knowledge that its perpetrators walked free and that as Christians in a Muslim society, they lived as second-class citizens. In a meeting last week, they had heard about a big incident in the capitol engineered by the *Dashnak*s there. Clearly this boy was too young to be *that* Balian, but was he related?

"We know that name. The police will know it, too. Are you sure you want to continue to go by it?"

Nikol took out a handkerchief and wiped his forehead. "Yes."

Koren paused. This name could be dangerous for all of them. He looked at Nikol. Nikol stared him straight in the eye. Koren thought about it. Well, the police didn't have to know the boy's name, did they? He looked at Nikol again. Yes, he was sure. He would let the boy stay.

He smiled. "If you're going to stay with us, let me introduce myself and my family. I am Koren Adanalian. This is my wife, Seta, and my daughter, Victoria."

Nikol smiled and nodded at the two. Then he looked back at Koren.

"Have you ever worked on a farm?"

"Yes, I grew up in a village here in Kharpert. My father had land, although we never had anything like what you have here."

His arm swept in an arc outlining the reddened vista of fields rising and falling around them.

Koren gestured to Nikol to sit. "I'll show you around in a few minutes. First, let me tell you a little about what I do in addition to farming this land."

Nikol squatted down on one knee.

"I am a courier. Most of the papers and money I transport for my customers have to be brought to Mezireh. In fact, I must go there again in another week. I'll feel better leaving this time knowing a man will be here to protect my family."

Nikol raised his chin. "You can count on me. I will not let you down."

There was a hard edge to the boy's tone. Koren believed him. He went on to explain what he wanted done. When he finished, Seta spoke.

"Why don't we go inside? I'll put out bread and cheese."

Victoria, who had gone back to her book, closed it around her finger and got up again.

Nikol walked beside her, as the four headed for the house. He craned his neck to scan the title of Victoria's book.

"You can read that?"

"Sure, I go to school."

Nikol raised his brows.

Koren tensed, remembering the criticism he had taken

for allowing his daughter to go to school. Even his dear wife worried about it. But Victoria, his precious treasure. Victoria was like him. She read her books as if they were a meal set out in front of her. If this boy didn't like it, well...Koren kept his face neutral.

Nikol said, "I...I think that's great."

Koren let out his breath.

Nikol went on. "I have a brother and sister in an orphanage that has a school, too. I hope they're learning as much as you are. I think about them all the time. My sister, Anna, is probably around your age."

Nikol's expression saddened. He looked at the ground.

Koren and Seta exchanged sympathetic glances. Silently, they walked into the house and settled on cushions around a low table in the center of the room. Koren looked at Nikol.

Nikol's lip quivered. "My father died two years ago of pneumonia."

Koren nodded in sympathy. Nikol went on.

"I wandered around like a part of me was missing when I lost my father. I just couldn't believe it. One week he was laughing, talking, eating, the next-gone. We all prayed by his bed that week he lay dying. At the end, we were there."

Nikol stopped. He dropped his forehead to his hand. When he looked up, he was glaring.

"My father's death shattered us all, but eventually we went on. My mother, though--what happened to her I'll never forget or forgive." His voice took on the hard edge again. "Do you remember that demonstration in Constantinople last year?"

Koren leaned forward. "Oh yes, we remember. We've learned since that the sultan told the police to get the Armenians out of the capitol any way they chose. Why they refused to go, I don't know. We all know that you should never anger the Turks. Even Victoria knows that."

"And you know, of course, what followed."

Koren nodded. "We didn't go out of the house for three weeks. No one in our village was killed, thank God, but many were hurt in other ways. Every day we waited, wondering if we were next."

"Well," Nikol said, "in my village it was worse. Far worse."

Seta suddenly interrupted. "Victoria, I want you to go outside and pick some apples."

"No, Seta. She's eight years old now. She's not a child anymore. I want her to hear this."

Nikol went on. "We were all in school. My mother was home alone."

Koren felt a sudden chill. He exchanged looks with Seta. It had been so close. So many people had died. The Massacre of 1895, people now called it.

Nikol hugged his chest. "The priest locked the gates and hid us all in the basement. I wanted to go home. I could have protected my mother, but the priest wouldn't let me go. He told me if he unlocked the gates to let me out, the Turkish villagers would come pouring in and all the children would be in danger.

"We stayed in that basement for two days. At last, it grew quiet. I took my sister and brother, Anna and Stephen, and went home. I'll never forget that walk home. The street was red with blood. Dead, mutilated bodies were strewn everywhere. I hid Anna and Stephen's faces in my shirt so they wouldn't see. When we got home, the door to the house was splintered on its hinges and hanging wide open. I made Stephen and Anna wait outside. I went in. She was there. She had died all alone. I can only pray that it was quick. But I should have been there. I should have been there." Nikol's voice broke and he stopped.

Seta jumped up and threw her arms around him. She looked into his face with concern.

Koren said, "You couldn't have done anything. Armenians aren't allowed to own weapons. You had no way of defending her." He put his hand on Nikol's arm. "You were just a boy."

Nikol shook his head. "No, I was twelve years old. I could have done something. After it was over, I tried to find work, so that I could take care of my brother and sister. I really tried hard. But everyone who was alive had been ruined by the looting. The entire village was starving. After a few weeks we were, too, so I took my brother and sister to an orphanage. I was too old for the orphanage, but Anna and Stephan weren't. I didn't want to leave them but what else could I do? I knew the people there would feed and care for them, but I know I let my parents down by leaving them. When I was walking away, I looked back and saw something I still see at night when I am trying to sleep--Anna crying in the window.

"That was last fall. I left and joined the *Dashnak*s. Since then, I've wandered around from place to place. Now I need to settle somewhere. I'll work hard for you. You can trust me on that."

Koren waited. Waited for Nikol to tell him what he had been doing that gave a thirteen-year-old that edge to his voice. What made him keep looking over his shoulder the way he did?

Nikol said nothing more.

So that was the way it would be.

Koren rose. "Come, I'll take you out to the stable and show you around the property." He placed his arm around Nikol's shoulder. The two walked out the door.

Seta turned to the business of dinner. The hem of her long skirt brushed the fibers of the thick oriental carpet that covered the floor of their one-room house. Within minutes, she had a fire lit in the stove and a pot of cracked wheat steaming away.

Victoria grasped a thick wooden bucket by its handle. "I'm going out to the well to get..." Her voice broke. She set the pail down.

Seta drew her daughter close in an embrace. "Darling, I'm sorry. I wish you didn't have to know that the world is the way it is. But your father is right. We can't keep it from you, however much we want to."

Victoria nodded. She drew back, picked up her burden and left.

"Why don't you go on back outside and pick enough apples for dessert?" Seta said, when she returned with the water.

Victoria grabbed a collecting basket and headed for the orchard. On the way, she stopped and took a deep breath of the sweet evening breeze. She reminded herself of how much they were helping Nikol. How long would he be with them? Stay, her father had said. It sounded as though he meant for a long time. That might be nice.

Victoria reached for an apple from one of the tree's laden branches. If only there were something she could do to help all the people who had been hurt in the massacre. Her father had told her she might go to college some day. She could become a teacher. Wouldn't that be a way of helping? Her father always said that education brought opportunity. Look at him and all he could give them because of his education. She felt much better.

Victoria returned to the house at the same time as Koren and Nikol. They had stabled and milked the cows, and carried with them a pail of fresh warm milk. The two chatted easily with each other.

Seta placed a large ceramic serving plate on the table. "Everyone sit."

They ate their cracked wheat with yogurt spooned over the top, yogurt which Seta prepared at night, mixing a starter saved from the previous batch into scalded milk cooled to room temperature, then covering it to sit and culture. Spoilage in the summer was a constant worry, so they seldom had meat with their meals. During the colder seasons of autumn and winter, perishables were easily preserved in the unheated stable attached to the house.

Koren set down his spoon when they finished eating and said, "I'm taking Nikol into the village tonight." He gave Seta a look. She nodded. When it grew dark, the two left.

The *Dashnak*s met in secret, late at night. When they arrived at the meeting, Koren introduced Nikol around. He was pleased at the acceptance Nikol gained from the men of the village, despite his youth. Nikol participated actively, talking about what had led him to become involved with the *Dashnak*s, though he said nothing about his activities of the last year. Koren could see from the men's expressions that they noted the gap in his story and had caught the significance of his surname. They probably had their suspicions, but like Koren, seemed willing to wait and let him explain it in his own time.

They stayed at the meeting late that night, returning home long after dark. Seta and Victoria had taken the mattresses from the shelf where they were kept during the day and spread them on the floor. They were already fast asleep.

The men tiptoed in and slipped quietly under their blankets.

As sleep overcame him, Nikol marveled at all that had happened to him that day. In this little house, on the outskirts of this tiny village, he was safe from the suspicious eyes of the police. And for the first time in months, he was sleeping under the comfortable protection of a roof. He wondered now at the wisdom of his insistence that he be known by his real name. But that name was his last link to his father and the family he had once had. He could not give it up. Now that the men of the village knew it, it was too late, anyway.

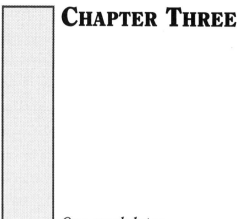

CHAPTER THREE

One week later

"**W**here is Nikol? I have to leave in–" Koren flipped the gold cover of his pocket watch open. "In twenty minutes."

"He's out in the stable, getting the horse ready for you." Seta emerged from the pantry. "Now sit down and eat. You can't go off to Mezireh without something in your stomach."

Koren stuck a foot in his boot and hopped toward the table as he pulled it on. "The animals. Has he–"

"He said to tell you he would tend to them as soon as you left." Seta gave a mock frown. "I suppose you are riding all that way with one boot on."

Koren looked down. He limped across the room and wedged his other foot into his knee-high riding boot.

"Papa, look." Victoria held up a slab of cumin-scented dried meat. "Mother said we could have some and it's not even Sunday."

Koren smacked his lips. *Basterma*. His mouth would burn all the way to the city.

He buttoned his jacket as he hurried to the table. He picked up a knife and pulled the *basterma* toward him. Ouch. He had nicked his finger shaving off a slice of the homemade sausage.

"For heaven's sake, slow down." Seta's frown was real this time. "Eat while I go see what I want you to bring back for the pantry."

The sound of horse's hoofs clopped around the side of the house. Koren devoured his *basterma* with *choereg*s--buttery yeasted rolls. He jumped up and slung his worn leather saddle bag over his shoulder. What was taking Seta so long? He peeked his head around the pantry door.

"Nikol's out front with the horse... Seta, what's the matter?"

His wife's face was pale. Dark circles outlined her wide eyes.

She sighed, peered out at Victoria sitting at the table and said, "Come in here."

Koren stepped into the pantry's spicy interior.

"I had the dream again. The one where something happened to you. Promise me you'll be careful."

Koren brushed a strand of hair from his wife's face. "No,

Seta, don't worry about me. I know these roads. I know the danger. I will keep watch of the roadside every minute of the way, as I always do." Unconsciously, his arm tightened against the hard metal object under his vest. Illegal. A secret even to his wife.

Arm in arm, they stepped out into the sun-dappled main room of their house.

"Your lunch." Seta hurried back to the pantry and returned with a cloth-wrapped package. "Cracker bread and cheese."

Koren tucked the meal into his bag and strode on outside, where Nikol stood with his reins in hand.

Koren slid his foot into the stirrup, gave a hop and swung his other leg up and around. He looked back.

Seta stood in the doorway, her arm around Victoria. Victoria lifted her chin, put her fingers to her lips and kissed them.

He waved to all of them and trotted off.

Seta sighed, turned and headed into the house with Victoria at her side. They might as well get started.

"Victoria, sweep the carpet while I clean up from breakfast," she said. "Make sure you get all the grains of sand out, otherwise they'll grind against the fibers and ruin it."

Victoria nodded. She grabbed a broom and began industriously brushing through its interlocking patterns of deep maroons and rich blues. She hummed to herself while she worked.

Autumn left little chance to rest. The apples needed to be packed into crates and stored in the barn. The grapes needed to be picked. Some they dried in the sun to make raisins, others they processed into jelly and dried candy. Last spring, they had picked grape leaves from the tender shoots of their vines and stored them in brine. All winter long they would pull dripping, salty clumps of the preserved leaves from the storage crocks and use them as an ingredient in several delicious dishes.

Berries grew wild on their land. Victoria would pluck them from the thorny branches and Seta would make them into jam.

Seta and Victoria moved from one chore to the other. Morning turned to afternoon.

Victoria was darning a pair of socks under the light of a lantern, when Nikol came stumbling in. His face was dirt-streaked and his hands raw, but he wore a smile on his face. He sank into a wool-stuffed cushion across the table from Victoria.

"You've been busy all day, too. When do you start school?"

"Next week." Her beautiful brown eyes shined with anticipation. "I'm going to do well this year. There's a boy I hate. His name is Martin Halabian. Last year he came out at the top of the class, but this year I'm going to beat him. He's such a show-off."

"Victoria!" Seta said. "Shame on you. Martin and his family are our friends. You were in second place. Your father was very proud of your grades."

"I know, but you don't know what Martin's like. He's a big tease."

"I'm sure he's not as bad as all that. Don't forget, some day you'll be getting married, and no boy likes a girl who's smarter than he is."

"Oh, I'm not getting married," Victoria said. "I'm going to college."

Seta looked at her in surprise.

Her eyes widened. She clapped her hand over her mouth.

"To college," Seta said. "Who told you that? Armenian girls don't go to college."

She wasn't supposed to have told. But what could she do now? "Some do. Papa said I could, if I study hard."

"*Ouff*, your father fills your head with such nonsense." Seta stomped away.

Victoria looked at her mother's rigid back. She turned to Nikol, pleading with her eyes. "Say something," she mouthed.

"You know, there were almost no schools for Armenians forty or fifty years ago," Nikol said. "And when they first opened, no one was used to the idea of their children going to them. Many thought it was a waste of time."

"No schools at all?" Victoria's needle stopped its criss-cross motion through the threads in the sock's gaping hole. "How did people learn to read and write?"

"Most didn't. Only the sons of the very wealthy went to school. They had to leave Turkey and go to Europe for their education."

"How awful. Why didn't the churches open their schools sooner?"

"They were too poor. Then the wealthy Armenians in Constantinople started donating money to the churches to set up schools. Slowly, more teachers were trained so that more schools could be opened. Eventually, we got them here in the provinces."

"Yes, that's right." Seta came back to the table with her knitting. "In my day, we had a few schools, but there weren't enough places in them for everybody, so only the boys went."

"That's not fair!" Victoria dropped her half-mended sock.

Seta smiled. "Boys take care of their families and run businesses. When schools don't have room for everyone, their education is more important. And," she looked at Victoria, "they certainly need a college education more than a girl does."

Victoria frowned. There was something wrong with that logic, something she couldn't put into words. She frowned again, picked up her darning, and didn't stop until she had woven a puckered new square of fabric into the worn space.

Over the next two days, Victoria and Seta continued to preserve and store their summer's crops. They scooped out the insides of squashes and laid them in the sun to dry. Later, during the winter, Seta would either stuff these with meat and rice or simmer them in stews. They also dried some of their tomatoes in the sun and boiled the rest down in huge bubbling pots on the stove.

Saturday dawned with bright clear skies and sun-studded fields. The morning air held a hint of coolness. They were busy but the morning was long. An air of expectancy hung in the room. Victoria watched her mother open the door and peer down the road for the fifth time that hour.

"Mother, let's go sit in the sun and wait for Papa. We've really done all we need to for today."

Seta smiled wanly and followed Victoria outside.

Victoria sat beside her mother in silence. Had he said he'd be back in the morning or afternoon? Two years ago, her friend's father had gone off to the city and never returned. Her friend had to leave the village with her mother and go live with her uncle.

But how could anyone hurt her strong Papa?

"Is that him?" Victoria shaded her eyes and squinted down the road. In the distance, a horse plodded toward them carrying a solitary figure laden with packs.

"It certainly is!" Seta jumped up. She folded her hands and mouthed a quick silent prayer.

Nikol had also seen Koren approach and met them at the road, as Koren rode up.

"Thank God, you're back!" Seta said. "How was your trip?"

"Fine, fine," Koren said. His eyes darted in Victoria's

direction. His jaw was set, his clothes disheveled.

Victoria's outstretched arms dropped to her side.

Nikol grabbed the reins and led the tired horse off to the barn. Koren marched into the house without waiting for Seta or Victoria. But by the time they caught up with him, the comfort of home seemed to have restored his good humor.

"Victoria, bring the bags over here so I can sort them," he ordered. He added with a twinkle, "Don't bother to look through them, because I didn't bring anything back for you."

Victoria grinned. She knew he always hid something special in his pack.

After the midday meal, it was time for their weekly trip to the baths. Seta packed clean dresses, thick white towels, a pitcher for rinsing and slices of oranges for refreshment. She glanced at Koren, who lingered at the table with a thoughtful expression on his face. She opened her mouth, looked at Victoria, then closed it again.

At the *hamam* entrance, Seta exchanged polite greetings with the manager before leading Victoria into the humid, dark interior. They went directly to the curtained dressing area reserved for their family. After shedding their clothes, they felt their way into the large tiled room, where other women and children had already gathered. Victoria peered through the steam-clouded air and spotted Margaret stretching her toes under a tap, where hot water gushed into a copper basin. Victoria scurried over to her, sat down and whispered in her ear, "Look at Mrs. Nersesian sitting there like a queen on a throne with all her rolls of fat. And she's so mean to her son's new wife. I'm glad I'm not that girl. See how she orders her around? The girl has to do everything she says. Mrs. Nersesian is her new mother now."

Margaret grinned, then whispered something back to Victoria. Victoria's laugh echoed against the ceiling. Margaret's mother, Araxie, glanced at the two in disapproval.

Seta sat up straight. "Victoria, come over here and start washing."

Victoria reddened. "I'm coming, Mother." She scrambled up and returned to Seta.

Seta leaned close to Victoria and said, "Victoria, remember, you are not a child anymore and you can't sit there acting like one. You must be a lady when you're out in public.

Victoria nodded and took up a rough stone. She began to scrub herself all over, repeating the entire process until her skin glowed. When she finished washing, Seta worked her long hair into a lather. Then she rinsed it with pitchers of hot water that ran pleasantly down Victoria's back.

The two paused at the *hamam* door to look for someone with whom to complete the final ritual of washing their feet. Margaret and her mother were leaving at the same time so Seta and Araxie performed this task for each other.

"Let this be the water of health," Seta said, employing the traditional blessing.

"Health be yours," Araxie recited back.

The two girls mimicked the older women's actions.

Seta linked arms with Araxie and they began walking toward the Damadian's house in the Armenian quarter of town.

Like Victoria and Margaret, Seta and Araxie had adored each other, since they were young girls growing up in the same village. They had parted when Seta married and moved to her husband's village. As a new bride, away from home for the first time, fifteen-year-old Seta had secretly cried into her pillow for an entire year. But her homesickness had abated the day she learned that Araxie's father had arranged for her to marry Koren's friend, Michael Damadian.

Michael owned a thriving business, growing poppies. All spring and summer, his fields shimmered in a swaying cloud of reds, yellows and violets. Each fall he sold the sap from them to make opium.

Seta and Victoria arrived home to an empty house. Fifteen minutes later, the freshly scrubbed men stepped through the door.

Koren dropped his damp towels on top of the others.

"There's another hour of daylight left." He looked at Victoria and Nikol. "Why don't you both go to the orchard and finish picking the apricots?"

The two left. Koren settled on his cushion at the table. He picked up a steaming cup of coffee and waited. Seta knelt at the table near him chopping onions. She was preparing a special meal for him, *Kufta* — a ground lamb dish. He looked at her tense and troubled face. Finally, she spoke.

"What happened in Mezireh?"

Koren sighed. "I had a problem coming home, when I was passing through Kezma."

Seta paled. She scraped the onions into the bowl of ground lamb and looked at him.

"What sort of problem?"

He had to tell her, but the story was going to make her nervous. "I was riding down a narrow street, when a Turk stepped in front of me and grabbed my horse's bridle."

Seta's hand shook, as she tossed a handful of toasted pine nuts into the mixture. Koren continued. "A crowd started to gather. No one would help me. I asked the man to let go, but he wouldn't. He looked at my bag and demanded I give him my money."

Koren watched Seta gather a bunch of parsley in her trembling fingers and pick up a knife. He had been scared too, though he wouldn't tell her that. Scared and angry, too. He would have liked to have punched the Turk who was demanding his money. But Koren remembered the massacre last year. One Armenian fighting a Turk could soon turn into an attack on the entire Armenian quarter of a city. And it could spread to other villages just as easily.

He took the knife from Seta. "Here, let me chop that for you. I'm afraid you're going to cut yourself." He continued. "Finally, a policeman came over and asked what was going on. The man told him that I owed him money."

"But you had never met the man before. Did you tell the

officer that?"

"Yes." Koren frowned. "When have policemen ever taken the word of an Armenian over a Turk's? He told me to pay the man or he would arrest me."

Seta began to knead cracked wheat, cumin and other spices into the meat mixture with vigor. The muscles of her slender upper arms rippled with effort. "How much did you have to pay that, that, donkey?"

"Just a few coins. But I was worried about the rest of the crowd. One minute you're fighting one man, the next it's a whole mob. I ran the horse all the way home." Koren felt his knife. Out in the open, one-on-one, he could have taken the Turk, cut him down to the worm he was. But what could one man do against a dozen or more? He had his wife and daughter to think about. Without him, where would they be?

"Thank God, you weren't hurt." Seta pressed the mixture into an earthenware pan and lowered it into a stone-lined baking pit.

Koren watched her. No, he wasn't hurt, but fear and anger had turned into humiliation. And what could he do about it? Nothing, really. Then he thought about his work with the *Dashnak*s and realized there were other ways to fight the Turks.

Nikol and Victoria walked in the door just then. Koren looked at Nikol. He had met with his brother *Dashnak*s in Mezireh and learned something more about the incident in the capitol.

The *Dashnak*s there had taken over a large European bank in protest of Armenian's inferior status. They were led by a tough seventeen-year-old, Abraham Balian. Abraham had a younger brother and agents from the government were in Mezireh asking questions. Koren decided he wouldn't tell Nikol what he had learned about the bank incident. Maybe someday, if he waited, the boy would trust him enough to tell him himself.

Nikol sat down at the table and sniffed. The air was heavy with the combined aromas emanating from the baked meat.

"Mmm, I'm hungry." Nikol looked at the plate of food and patted his stomach.

Seta smiled and cut him an extra large portion.

When they had all eaten their fill, Koren rose and went to his saddle bag. Victoria's eyes gleamed with excitement.

"For you," Koren said. He smiled and handed her a length of the most beautiful, soft blue fabric she had ever seen.

"Oh, thank you, Papa." She rubbed the velvety cotton across her face. Someday she would make a lovely spring dress out of it.

For Seta, Koren had an exquisite silk scarf, which she immediately modeled.

Koren managed to put his thoughts aside about the trip home from Mezireh and enjoy the rest of the evening.

He opened his eyes the next morning and roused his family. It was Sunday, their day of worship and ease.

Seta and Victoria packed food for a picnic after church, while he and Nikol did only their most essential farm chores. Then the four set off, Koren and Nikol sharing the weight of the picnic basket between them.

Curious eyes focused on the newcomer, as Koren led his family through the massive, carved doors of the village church. Koren noticed the looks and thought about Nikol. The young man got up in the morning and worked until dinnertime with never a complaint. He could turn over half a field in a day. Koren had only to show him how to dig a post one day, then the next, he had a whole fence built. He thought about the fate that would have awaited Nikol in Mezireh. Yes, for many reasons, his decision to take the boy in had been the right one.

Koren and Nikol went to stand with the men. Seta and Victoria with the women. The service began. Victoria turned and stole a look at Margaret, who was standing with her mother a few rows back. She quickly faced the front and paid attention, after Seta tapped her on the shoulder and looked at her sternly.

The priest delivered his message from the pulpit. The fine gold threads of his scarlet robe flickered in the light of the candles that surrounded the altar. The air around them was thick with the scent of smoky incense, wafting from brass holders. Teenage boys dangled the shiny burners from chains and marched up and down the aisles, shaking them to release the aromatic fumes.

At the conclusion of the service, the congregation gathered on the stone steps of the church.

Koren stepped forward to greet the priest, who was holding court with his wife and children. "*Paree looys*, Father Mikayelian."

"Good morning, Mr. Adanalian." The priest said. Then he looked at Nikol with curiosity.

"This is Nikol Balian. He's staying with us and working on the farm."

The priest raised his brow slightly, but said only, "I hope you'll be happy in our village."

"I–" Another family, vying for their chance to speak to Father Mikayelian, jostled Nikol aside.

He would have no further opportunity to speak to the priest, who was hidden now by a crowd of parishioners. Koren nodded in the direction of the road. Victoria found Margaret and the two skipped off ahead.

Koren came up behind Margaret's father and grasped his shoulder. "How's business been, Michael?"

"Fine." Michael stopped, until he and Koren were side-by-side. "I thank God every day for my good fortune. Since the massacre last year, I've traveled through entire villages, where the only Armenians alive are begging and in rags. You and I have a lot to be grateful for."

Koren's ride from Mezireh was fresh in his mind. "We do, but for how long? You know, I've been thinking. We were right when we decided to fight the persecution of our brothers. Their troubles today, could be ours tomorrow."

Michael leaned forward and spoke softly. "Be careful, Koren. Not all among us think as we do."

What was he thinking? The *Dashnak* meetings had to remain a secret. If the police found out about them, they were all done for. He glanced around. Armenians never informed against one another but they were not yet out of the village where Turks lived too.

"It's all right," Michael said. "I think we are alone."

Koren nodded. He would have to be more careful.

Koren rounded a corner and saw children chasing each other across the grassy flat, where the community picnicked. He tilted his head and heard water gurgling from a natural spring. Victoria stood in a cluster with Margaret and her other friends. He waved to her, then turned to help Seta spread their blanket beside the Damadians.

Seta and Araxie went off to get water, leaving the men to chat with each other.

Koren stopped in the middle of a sentence. His smile faded. Cousin Rose was approaching his blanket with her daughter, her son and her husband. What complaints would she have today?

The quadruplet stopped.

"I heard rumors that you'd taken someone in to help on your farm, Koren." Rose glared at Nikol.

Koren spoke into the icy-cold void. "Yes, Cousin Rose. I need someone to help with the farm work and manage things while I'm away."

"Help? You went to a stranger for help? I've told you over and over, Alexan," she waved her arm in her son's direction, "would help you any time you needed."

At what price? Koren thought.

"I know. It's very kind of you to offer and I appreciate it." Rose's dark eyes narrowed. "I–"

"Cousin Rose. Good morning." Seta set down the heavy jug she was carrying and wiped her damp hands on her dress. She reached for her husband's cousin's hand, but found only her departing back.

Koren turned to Nikol. "Everyone else here knows, you may as well, too. She's my cousin and her land borders mine. We each got our land as wedding gifts from our grandfather. Unfortunately, there's been bad blood between us since then. Rose thinks the soil on my farm is more fertile than hers and she wants it for herself. She once came to me with some crazy idea of marrying Victoria to Alexan when she's of age because, she knows I have no son to pass my land on to. But I said, no. Alexan was not the problem; Rose was. She would make Victoria's life miserable, if she were her mother-in-law. I want a better life for Victoria than that."

And college. Though he did not mention that in front of Seta. Nor did he believe Rose's scheming for his land had ended with his refusal to promise his daughter's hand in marriage.

Victoria and Margaret dashed up to the blankets and fell

together laughing. Victoria looked at the blanket piled high with food.

"What, nothing to eat?" She collapsed against Margaret giggling again.

"Girls!"

When they had all eaten their fill, Koren wiped his mouth with a napkin and pulled a backgammon case from the bottom of his picnic basket.

"Michael, shall we have a game?" Koren ran his hand along the wooden box's inlaid ivory surface.

"Sure." Michael grinned. "Nikol can play the winner."

"Araxie, let's go over and talk to Lucin." Seta was already on her feet. "I can see we won't be getting any more attention from these men." She rolled her eyes in mock annoyance.

Victoria announced that she and Margaret were going back to their schoolmates.

"Don't go far, and remember to stay together."

"We will." Victoria shook her head. Of course, they would remember. How could they forget? They had been hearing that warning since they were babies.

The other girls were already at the springs, when the two arrived. Victoria knelt and splashed handfuls of cool water over her face. The spring formed a natural pool, before it overflowed into a stream that gently trickled downward toward the surrounding forest.

"Let's walk along the stream," Rebecca, one of Victoria's

friends, said.

Victoria stood. "We can't go far."

"I know. We'll just go a little way. We can pick some of those pretty pink wildflowers and give them to our teacher tomorrow on the first day of school."

The girls set off down the stream, stopping when they spotted one of the flowers that grew scantily along the way. As they walked, they began to separate, so gradually that none of them noticed.

Victoria knelt and plucked a dainty sprig from its roots. Her long thick hair cascaded over her shoulders. Suddenly, her back tingled and she knew someone was watching her. She looked up. Hasan, the son of one of the local Kurdish *beys*, or landowners, was staring at her from where he sat atop his horse.

She looked from side to side. Where were her friends? She felt cold and her gently pointed chin quivered. She stared back at Hasan with wide brown eyes.

He smiled softly.

Victoria was silent. Her ability to speak had fled.

A bird chirped. Hasan looked up. Suddenly he shook himself, as if he were awakening from a sleep. Abruptly, he turned his horse and rode away.

Victoria's heart was thudding in her chest. She jumped to her feet and stumbled back to her friends.

"Victoria, where did you go? We were looking for you." Margaret's face was ghostly.

Victoria gripped her friend's arm. "I was lost, but don't tell." She looked at all her friends. "Please don't tell anyone. We'll all get in trouble."

The girls all nodded, their faces serious. Silently, they began winding their way back to the picnic area.

Had she been in danger? She had no idea. The Kurds weren't as bad as the Turks. Or at least she hadn't heard anything bad about the Kurds in her village. But one of the times she had been pretending to be asleep, she'd heard her parents talking about some Kurds who lived in the mountains. These Kurds had attacked the Armenians in another village. So you never knew. She shivered. Margaret squeezed her arm.

By the time they returned, the sun was beginning to set and the families were getting ready to go home. Victoria was less talkative than usual, but she was grateful that her parents did not seem to notice.

CHAPTER FOUR

Late September, 1896

*V*ictoria opened her eyes. Her nose was cold. She snuggled deeper into the comfortable warmth of her thick quilt. Then she remembered: Today was the first day of school. What was she doing still lying in bed?

Her bare feet met the icy floor. *Brrr.* Fall had arrived overnight. Today she would wear her stockings, those itchy black woolen leggings that she had spent weeks knitting.

She pulled the stockings from the wooden trunk where they lay compressed into a wrinkled ball at the bottom. She turned and the lid fell shut with a heavy thump.

"Victoria, please." Koren sat up in bed.

"I'm sorry, Papa."

The family roused and pulled on their clothes. Nikol

slipped a worn sweater over his head, grabbed a handful of *choereg*s and hurried out the door, chewing as he walked.

Fifteen minutes later, Victoria was ready. She stepped out onto the frosted grass.

"Study hard and use your time well." Nikol leaned on his shovel. A wistful smile played at the corners of his lips.

Victoria touched his arm and walked off.

She marched rapidly down the road to Margaret's house, passing other children who were bound for school as well. When she neared the heart of the village, Margaret fell into step with her.

"We can't be late meeting the other girls." Margaret panted as she walked.

"I know. We'll be there before you know it. I hope Rebecca remembered to bring the flowers. But I'm sure she did. We're so lucky that we have Miss Abovian. She's the nicest teacher in the whole school."

"Isn't that what you said last year about Miss Casian?"

"Well, they're all nice. And anyway--oh, never mind, there's Rebecca and Grace waiting for us. And Miriam is right behind us."

The great iron gate creaked open on its hinges, as the girls ran into the crowded church courtyard.

Martin Halabian crouched on the ground around a line of smooth glass marbles. Four other boys sat with him.

Victoria's eyes narrowed. Chin high, she led her entourage in his direction.

She stopped close enough to be heard. "Come on, girls, *we* don't have time for games."

Martin spun a marble and knocked another one from its place. He looked up.

"No, you don't have time. *You* need to study more."

Victoria's lips tightened.

Martin turned to the marble's owner. "What are you going to give me to get it back?"

The boy handed him a walnut. Then all the boys jumped up and ran into the school ahead of the girls.

Victoria rolled her eyes, tossed her hair over her shoulder and proceeded into the foyer with her friends. Their footsteps echoed, as they clambered up the stairs and down the hall to their classroom. The school year had begun.

Seta inspected the lace she had spent an hour tatting. It would all have to come out. The rows were uneven and she had dropped stitches along the way. Nearby, a broom leaned against the wall, a pile of swept-up dirt trapped under its bristles. She sighed into the empty stillness of the house.

She should not have been lonely. Her mother and father-in-law, brothers and their wives, perhaps a grandparent or two, should have been under this roof. And children. Her children, should have been banging in and out of the door, while she hurried to prepare a meal for her brood. But early in her marriage, her life had taken an unexpected turn, when Koren's father had been struck with pneumonia and died suddenly. His mother, brokenhearted, lost her will to live and followed three months later. Koren's grandfather could not bear to be reminded of the son he had lost and sold the house. He went off to live with his oldest daughter in another province. Before he left, he divided up another piece of property he owned and gave it to Koren and Rose, as belated wedding gifts.

Seta, pregnant at the time, had miscarried. It was the circumstances that had brought it on, everyone had told her. She had wanted to believe this. Oh, how both she and Koren had wanted to believe it. But over the next three years, two other pregnancies ended the same way, each time leaving her exhausted and distraught. At last, she had tenuously hung on to one pregnancy, gladly putting up with the nausea and vomiting that continued for nine long months. She had panicked whenever spots of blood had appeared and prayed that the baby would survive to maturity. The birth had been so difficult that a doctor was called in to help the midwife. She had never known anyone who had a doctor attend a birth. But in the end, her prayers were answered when the doctor handed her a screaming, red-faced baby girl. He forewarned Koren that Seta would not be able to have any more children. Koren had taken the news stoically, but Seta had known how disappointed he was that he would never have a son. The doctor's prediction turned out to be true, and Victoria was all the more precious to both of them because of it.

"Mother, I'm home."

Seta looked up with a start. How long had Victoria been standing in the doorway? "Come on in, darling. How was your first morning of school?"

"Wonderful! We worked on our arithmetic and writing this morning, and this afternoon our teacher is going to read to us."

Koren and Nikol marched in the door, and the four began to eat their noon meal.

"Did you finish digging the hole?" Seta spooned yogurt over her serving of steaming bulgur. "If you did, I'll start filling it with water this afternoon."

The men had labored all morning digging a deep, narrow hole outside the house. They did this every fall when the temperature dropped, but before the ground froze solid. Seta then dumped bucketful after bucketful of water into the hole until it was filled. After it froze, she packed it with straw, leaving it like this until the intense heat of summer hit. Then, on slow hot days, she sparingly chiseled off shards of it to make iced fruit drinks for her delighted guests.

"Yes, it's finished. Nikol is going into the village after lunch, so Victoria can walk back with him."

"I'm ready now." Victoria jumped up, and grabbed her satchel.

Koren laughed. "Hold on. Can he finish eating first?"

Seta watched her exuberant daughter dash off a few minutes later with Nikol. She shook her head. Victoria was so devoted to school and her studies. One would think she was out to solve the problems of the world. Well, Koren may have some crazy dream of a college education, but she was Victoria's mother. And she would see to it that Victoria continued to learn what every girl from a good family should know. Already, Victoria had half-filled her trousseau with lace-bordered pillow cases, table scarves and neatly embroidered napkins. Eventually, she would settle down to a marriage like other girls. When she did, she would be prepared.

Seta had not told Koren that she knew about his plan and she didn't intend to. Why have words with her husband over something that time was likely to take care of on its own? She looked at him and smiled.

He patted Seta's cushion. "Come sit down, my dear. I want to talk with you about Nikol."

Seta nodded and sat down. "Yes, he's been with us for a few weeks now, but really most of the heavy work has been done. Isn't it time to send him on?"

"Well, in a way, yes. But the next season is always coming and I've gotten used to having him here. I like the boy."

"I like him, too, but if you mean permanently, I don't know." Seta stared at Nikol's empty cushion.

Koren leaned forward. "You know, every year I get busier and busier with my courier business. I like having him here, when I'm away. Maybe I can even train him someday to take over the business."

Seta thought. Pass the business on to him like a son? Oh,

now she understood. She reached across the table and gently laid her hand on his. "You know, Koren, you're not his father."

A sadness passed over Koren's face. "No, but neither is anyone else. And I want him here with me. I'm not saying forever, but for now."

Seta thought for a moment. "Well, he is a lot of help and a nice boy, too." She sighed. "I don't know. Sometimes, its almost as if, as if...there is something he's not telling us."

Koren looked at Seta, smiled and shook his head. "There you are, my dear, right as usual. There is something he is hiding, but you must leave that to me. It's nothing that concerns you."

Seta nodded and smiled. "If you're sure then. I'll leave it to you."

Victoria slowly became aware of her cramped legs. It was nighttime and she was crouched over the table immersed in her homework. She flung her pencil down, got up and stretched.

"Are you finished with your homework?" Seta's knitting needles clicked and a ball of yarn bumped along the floor as it unwound. The kerosene lamp on the table in front of her glowed softly on her still-beautiful face.

"Yes. What are you working on?"

"A sweater for Nikol. The poor boy has nothing but rags to wear. And if he's going to stay with us, he might as well have something decent to put on."

Victoria pulled the sweater's draping ends into the gentle radiance flowing from the lantern. She rubbed her cheek with a sleeve. "So soft. It will be more than decent. It will be warm and beautiful." She leaned her head affectionately on Seta's shoulder. "You are so nice. No wonder Papa loves you so much. Mother, tell me the story again of how you and Papa met. It's so romantic."

Seta's face melted into a smile.

Victoria shivered with pleasure. She loved this story.

Seta had stepped out the door to the baths and noticed a tall young man in trim riding pants and shiny leather boots, staring at her. He was not handsome, not really, but his distinctive nose and prominent cheekbones gave him a look of eminence. Who was he? Surely not someone from her village.

He had smiled when he saw her looking at him. She had blushed and immediately lowered her lashes. Her mother and sisters stepped in and blocked her line of vision, but she could feel his head turn to watch her as she walked on.

Until today, she had been tired of being noticed. She was fifteen. Wherever she went, mothers, who were looking for a bride for their sons, studied her. She had begun to hate the baths, because these mothers always managed to find out when she would be there. She would have to bathe, knowing that they were all pointing to her and talking behind their hands.

But now she was glad that people thought her beautiful and remarked on the exotic, unconventional blue of her eyes. Glad that she came from a good family. And all those years of her mother insisting that she behave like a lady suddenly made sense.

She had waited three days. Three long days, before hearing her father announce that the following Sunday they were having company.

"Papa, who is coming?"

Her father had looked at her with something next to sadness in his gaze. "A young man came to me a few days ago and said that he had a friend who wants to meet you."

Seta's mother, Lilyan, had been instantly alert. "Who is this boy? What sort of family does he come from?"

"Naturally, I checked on that before I gave my answer. His name is Koren. He's from a very respected family and he has a good business as a courier.

On Sunday, five minutes before the appointed hour, Seta heard a knock at the door.

"Go to the back room until he's seated," Lilyan, said.

Lilyan floated serenely to the door, while Seta scurried out of the room, her heart pounding. She peeked out from behind the curtain that separated her from the others.

Koren stepped in and glanced around. He and his friend went to sit on cushions beside Seta's father, Paul, who greeted them. Koren glanced around again.

Lilyan disappeared into the pantry and reappeared with

her silver serving tray piled high with apricots, nuts, and dried chickpeas. She passed it around, then sat down herself and signaled to Seta.

Seta tried to move, but her legs no longer worked. Tears sprang to her eyes. She retreated into a corner, where she slid down to sit and buried her head in her knees. She remained where she was, until she felt the warm familiar hand of her mother who took her arm and led her into the room.

"Did you love Papa right away?"

"No, not love. That comes with time, dear. But when I saw him that first day standing outside the baths, I hoped my parents would let me meet him. When I did meet him, I couldn't even talk to him. But later, after we were engaged, we got to know each other. By the time we married, I knew I loved him."

"What if you hadn't liked him?"

"My parents would not have forced me to marry someone I didn't like. Marriage is for a lifetime. A good parent wants their child to be happy."

Seta looked up when the door opened and a cold draft of air blew across the room. The men came in, stamping their feet and rubbing their hands together. But tonight they could not warm themselves.

There had been another massacre.

It had followed the failed *Dashnak* terrorist attack on the

Ottoman bank in the capitol. The revolutionaries had escaped, but the Turkish government had decided to make the rest of the Armenian community pay for their disobedience. They sent Muslim extremists and fanatics into the Armenian quarters of the city with clubs and iron bars. More than five thousand Armenians had been killed, while the police quietly encouraged it.

News of this violence had already reached Europe and the Europeans had written articles and given speeches protesting it. As if in answer, Turkish soldiers attacked two more cities and, with the help of local citizens, killed another two thousand people.

"We are meeting again tomorrow to discuss it," Koren said. "The European powers are calling for reforms. We are going to come up with some plans of our own."

The following night, twelve men huddled together in a barn under the meager light of a lantern. Another kept watch at the door.

"Yes, the British are giving speeches about forcing reforms on the empire, but they did this after the massacres last year and what do we have to show for it?"

"What do you propose we do?" Michael Damadian said.

Koren cast a glance at the shaded faces of his comrades. "We must think of something that will force the Europeans to use their power on the Turkish government. This time we want to see the results of the reforms they make."

"I know what we can do."

Every head turned to Nikol. His young eyes scanned the corners of the stable. "We can threaten to blow up one of the embassies in the capitol."

Koren felt his chest tighten. This out of the mouth of a thirteen-year-old boy.

The other men's jaws dropped. The man guarding the door quickly peered out into the black night, then turned back. Finally, a voice spoke.

"He's right. We've been patient long enough."

"I can write the letter," Nikol said. "We can take it to the *Dashnak*s in the capitol. If they agree with it, they will know how to deliver it to the palace."

Michael stood. "If you write it, I'll deliver it." He looked at Nikol. "Any of the *Dashnak*s in the capitol would die, before they revealed its source to the authorities. And we would here, too."

Nikol was the first one up the next morning. The fences in the far pasture were in need of mending — a project that would take him all day. He was glad for the solitude it would bring him.

He threw a shovel over his shoulder, grabbed an ax and began walking. Last night he had lain awake, worrying over the suggestion he had made. Would it draw the police to their village? But he had promised his brother that he would continue the work they had begun. He would write the letter, then he would leave. Begin running again. No, Michael had said the men here and the *Dashnak*s in the capitol would protect him. And he felt safe here on Koren's property. Safe from the dangerous eyes of the Turkish officials.

He thought about the massacre and the lives that had been lost and the businesses ruined. How had his people come to this position of second class citizenship? Centuries ago, they had ruled over the very ground he walked on. All this land and more had been theirs. Then had come the Ottoman Turks...

By 1534 AD. the entire Armenian plateau had been conquered by the Ottoman Turks.

The Ottoman government set up local governments in the defeated territories by dividing all non-Muslims into groups called *millets*. Each *millet* was composed of people who practiced the same religion. Internally, they ruled over their own. The Armenian archbishop was granted the title of "Patriarch" and supreme authority over all the non-Orthodox Christians. The *millets* were expected to pay taxes and remain peaceful.

Among the system's many flaws was that Muslims and non-Muslims had separate court systems, but cases of dispute between the two were heard in the Muslim court. Initially non-Muslim testimony was prohibited, later it was allowed but routinely disregarded. A Muslim was thus guaranteed to win any civil suit, no matter what the circumstances were or how unfair the decision was and the Armenian had no other recourse.

Taxes were another problem. Local *pasha*s or governors, always Turks or Kurds, set the taxes and collected them by any means they chose. The amount set depended entirely on the *pasha*'s greed. Families were often ruined, when exorbitant taxes were more than they could pay.

Religion was the prime factor that separated the Armenians from the Turks and Kurds. The Turks were Muslims, the Armenians, Christians — infidels. Riots against the non-believers could break out at any time and its perpetrators went unpunished. The Armenians lived their lives never knowing when the arbitrary sword of violence would swing their way.

The Europeans came sorrowfully close to resolving the matter of the Armenian's plight in Ottoman Turkey in 1878, following the Russo-Turkish war.

The Russian Tsar, Alexander II, had declared war on the Ottoman empire on April 24, 1877. Russia was a Christian nation, which found the treatment of the Christian populations in Turkey unacceptable. Russia intended to improve their brethren's lot by detaching their territories from Turkish rule.

Within a year, the Russians had advanced across Turkey and reached the capitol. The Ottoman empire was on the verge of collapse. The Russians agreed to stop only when the Ottoman government consented to a preliminary peace agreement in which they granted some territories independence and others autonomous administrations. Bulgaria,

Montenegro, Romania and Serbia were given their independence. Bonsnia and Herzegovina were allowed autonomous administrations. But Armenians, one of Turkey's largest Christian groups, were about to be forgotten. The Armenians realized their mistake and sent a delegation to the Russian ambassador, who was negotiating the peace agreement. The ambassador added a clause that guaranteed local self-government to the Armenian provinces. Then the British realized that if the treaty passed, Russia would acquire huge territories in Asia, which could jeopardize British trade routes to India. Britain opposed it and the peace agreement came to a stalemate.

To resolve the deadlock, a conference was scheduled in Berlin. This time the Armenians sent a delegation to represent their interests. But, despite their efforts, the delegation returned deeply disappointed. The British, still wary of Russia's power, insisted on deleting a clause that stated the evacuation of the occupying Russian troops was conditional on Turkish *implementation* of reforms. The final article concerning the Armenians, Article 61 of the Treaty of Berlin, merely stated that the Ottoman government agreed to carry out certain reforms and improvements in the areas inhabited by Armenians. Nothing in the article compelled the government to actually carry out these reforms, and it carried with it no repercussions if the government chose to ignore its agreement, which, for the last twenty years, it had.

Lost in thought, Nikol worked on the decaying fence without a break. Late in the afternoon, Victoria appeared over the rise. Sweet Victoria. Her face was a knot of concern.

"Mother sent me up here to get you. She said you missed lunch."

"Yes, I'm afraid I was busy working and thinking today."

"The massacre?"

"Yes." He put his arm around her. "It makes me remember what happened to my family and I feel angry all over again. But I remind myself that God has given me something too — a wonderful new sister to worry about me."

Victoria's face relaxed into a smile and the two walked home.

Victoria worked beside her mother in a comfortable silence. It was early Saturday evening. Tomorrow, her friend Rebecca was coming to visit with her family. Victoria was excited. The Kalustians were one of her favorite families. She and her mother were making *derevi sarma* for their favored guests in preparation. Victoria hummed a tune to herself as deftly folded the ends of a tender young grape leaf over a spoonful of rice, mixed with olive oil and seasoned with onions, lemons, and pepper. She rolled the other ends of the leaf around it like a cigarette and laid the finished product alongside the others in a baking dish lined with more grape leaves. Seta would simmer them over a low fire for the next hour and a half, then chill them overnight and serve them cold.

"Make sure you are stirring the rice mixture from the bottom to mix in the spices as you take each spoonful."

"I am, Mother. Will Rebecca's brother, Leon, bring his banjo tomorrow?"

Koren looked up from the backgammon board, where he sat across from Nikol. "When has Leon ever gone anywhere without at least one of his instruments? Let's see, he plays the guitar, mandolin, violin, and about any other instrument he can get his hands on." He shook his head and threw the dice. "Amazing. Never even had a lesson."

Victoria rolled her last grape leaf. "Can I play the winner?"

"Before you play anything, let me see the embroidery you worked on this afternoon," Seta said.

Victoria bought the piece to her mother. Her fingertips were rough and pinpricked from the hours she had spent on it. Seta held it under the lantern's light. She smiled and handed it back.

"The stitches are nice and even. *Shad lav.*" Seta nodded her head in approval.

Victoria let out her breath and went to watch her father and Nikol finish their game. She loved backgammon. She loved it more, knowing that she was the only girl in her circle of friends who was allowed to play. Her mother always said it was not ladylike, but her father had taught her, anyway. Sometimes, she made him sorry that he had.

She took Nikol's place, when her turn came and matched

wits with her father.

"I won." Victoria snatched her last piece from the board and kissed its cool ivory surface.

"I don't know anyone who has as much luck throwing doubles as this *moog* does." Koren's voice was a mixture of pride and annoyance. "Four times she threw doubles!"

Victoria turned to him with a teasing, show-off grin. "Luck and skill," she said.

"Well, it's time you put that away and got ready for bed," Seta said. "It's getting late. We have a busy day tomorrow."

"Oh, please play just one more song," Victoria begged. "Rebecca and I aren't hungry yet anyway." The Sunday gathering was in full swing.

"Well, Leon is." Seta smiled and frowned at the same time. She inched forward under the weight of a tray piled high with stuffed grape leaves, string cheese and other traditional guest offerings. "Let the poor boy get something in his stomach. There's plenty of time after you eat to sing and maybe dance, too."

Seta paused in front of each of her guests and lowered the tray of delectable goodies. Then she set it on the table and went to get the coffee. She returned carefully balancing a tray of small demitasse cups filled with steaming Armenian coffee. The adults drank the thick brew black and strong. Victoria and Rebecca both loaded theirs with spoonfuls of sugar and thick rich cream.

Rebecca's father, Levon, turned to Koren. "I understand Charles Halabian, your neighbor's oldest son, is about to leave for America."

"Yes, the passage is thirty-four dollars. After his father lost half his sheep last year, he didn't think he'd be able to go. But the entire family pooled their money so he could, because they said it's the only way they are going to improve their situation. Charles can work in America for a few years and put away enough to start a business when he comes back. Then he'll be able to help his whole family."

"I hear the factories there pay seven or eight dollars a week."

"Yes, imagine that. No wonder all the people in America are so rich."

"I talked to Charles," Nikol said. "He told me he wishes he didn't have to go to America to earn money. But there's no opportunity for him here, and his parents could barely keep food on the table before the trouble. Now..." Nikol shook his head.

"It's a shame. His parents have two other sons, too. Well, who knows, maybe Charles will be able to send enough money back for one of his other brothers to go, too? Maybe the whole family will emigrate from here."

"No, Charles was definite. He picked up a handful of dirt and said, 'This is why I am going, and this is why I am coming back.'"

"Well, a lot of our people have given up. They don't

believe the Turkish government will ever change the way it treats us."

Koren set his half-eaten stuffed grape leaf on the table in front of him. "The Turkish government will change because we will force it to change."

Victoria looked at Rebecca and rolled her eyes. An argument. This was sure to delay their singing and dancing.

"How? How do you think you can stop them?" Levon gestured and a long stemmed glass teetered. Seta grabbed for it and caught it before it hit the table.

Koren straightened his spine. "One man alone can't change them, but many men together, can."

"No, Koren, there you are wrong. You *Dashnak*s think you can change the world. But just look at what happened in the capitol. Do you think the men who took over that bank changed anything?" Levon's voice rose. "Well, I'll tell you something. They didn't. And a lot of people suffered because of them." He looked around the circle of faces.

Nikol took out a handkerchief and wiped his forehead.

Koren banged his fist on the table. The cups rattled in their saucers. "People suffered because of the Turks, not the *Dashnak*s. They treat us like dogs. They're the ones we should be fighting."

"Maybe, but I don't think the *Dashnak*s are the answer to our battle. The Europeans — they're the ones with the power to help us. I heard that England is negotiating with the Turks now for reforms."

"We will not listen to any more empty promises of reforms from the same government who orders our massacre. We've been doing that for years and where has it gotten us? Reforms, reforms, and more reforms, all of which the Turks ignore."

The men continued to argue back and forth. Victoria looked at Leon's banjo with longing. When would their party resume? She sighed. Gradually, the men quieted down. The discussion ended with Koren saying in a gentle voice, "Join us, Levon. We need good men like you."

Levon hesitated. Then he shook his head. "No, I don't believe that is the way to solve our problems, but we are all brothers in the same struggle, Koren."

The look on Levon's face seemed to communicate something to Koren, because he said, "I understand."

The adults went on to chat about other matters.

Nikol, who had not said a word throughout the argument, wore a strange expression and remained quiet.

Soon Levon signaled to his son, Leon. Leon snatched up his banjo and began to strum. Victoria and Rebecca joined hands and began to dance. Everyone except Nikol followed. As the afternoon shadows grew long, Seta drew steaming cauldrons of lamb and vegetable stew from her oven pit.

The guests devoured Seta's feast with broad loaves of fresh bread and chattered with excitement as they ate. After dinner, Koren disappeared into the pantry and reemerged with a crystal decanter of *raki* in hand. Seta and Koren brewed the potent liquor from distilled raisins. The process was a secret. Seta had learned the secret as a child watching her parents make it every year. Now her own child watched her and one day would make it herself. But first, Seta would teach her what she needed to know to be a wife and mother.

Three weeks after Koren and Nikol's late night meeting, an Armenian man in the capitol was nabbed in front of his house by the police. He was dragged off to jail and questioned about a letter that had been delivered to the palace. The man was beaten, tortured and killed. For their efforts, the police learned only that the letter had come from a village in one of the provinces.

CHAPTER FIVE

Winter, 1899

*V*ictoria listened to the dark winter wind pelt the stone house with fine loess. She shivered and rose from the table, where she sat with her parents and Nikol. She wandered over to the stove and held out her hands, letting them absorb the heat from the cozy fire inside.

"Victoria, have you finished your homework already?" Koren said.

"Yes, Papa. The teachers are busy planning the Christmas pageant, so they've given us very little."

"Well, then you wouldn't mind my beating you at a game of backgammon, would you?" Nikol peered over the edge of the newspaper he was reading and grinned.

Victoria eyed the wooden case sitting on the table in

front of him, tempting her with its polished, gleaming presence. She grinned back. "I'll have a game with you, but don't count on winning until the last set of doubles is thrown."

Nikol raised his brow, stared at her, and opened the cover to the board.

"Remember the luck she has with those dice." Koren shot Nikol a warning glance.

"Really, Victoria shouldn't be playing at all. She's almost eleven years old now. Young ladies should not be rolling dice like boys." Seta frowned.

"Let the child have a game. What's the harm here, in our own home? It's not as though she plays in coffeehouses, the way Nikol and I do."

"I should hope not."

Koren slid closer to Victoria and Nikol. "I'll play the winner."

Victoria grinned. "Then you'll play me."

The low table was draped as it usually was on bitter winter nights with a *koursey*, a big, quilt-like blanket. Burning coals radiated heat from a pit under the table. The quilt, draped to the floor, trapped the heat in. Each person at the table pulled the cover over their laps and benefited from the trapped warmth emanating from beneath.

An hour later, Victoria emerged as the champion. Her famous luck with throwing doubles had held.

Koren smacked the dice down on the table. "That's it, I quit." He looked at Victoria, then at Seta. "Maybe you're

right. It's not very ladylike for her to play. I think we should
forbid it."

"You wouldn't be saying that if you were the winner,"
Victoria said. "Admit it, Papa, you don't like to lose."

"How dare you accuse me of being a bad loser?" He
paused and grinned. "And anyway, who likes to lose?"

Nikol basked in the warmth of the family. So many
changes. Just three years ago he and his brother had struggled every day to stay alive. Now he lived in the comfort of
this house, where he could still continue his work. And
Koren had said nothing about Nikol leaving. He seemed to
need his help more each year.

Nikol studied how the lantern light played on Victoria's
face. She was another reason why he was glad he was here.
He would miss her terribly, if he were to go. She looked up
to him, came to him now to talk about things that bothered
her. Massacres. She wanted to know. Why? Why did things
like that happen? He answered her, too. It seemed that every
time he told her about another injustice, she studied harder.
She studied every night, until Seta insisted she stop before
she ruined her eyes. She would just look at her mother, close
her book, and the next night be right back at it.

It hurt him to see the pained look on her face, when he
explained how the Turks despised the Armenians for being
Christians. But what else could he do? She trusted him to
tell the truth. And pretending that hatred wasn't there did

not negate its existence.

At the heart of their difficulties with the Turks lay their religion, yet they would not give it up. Their faith was what held them together, as a community and as a culture.

The Armenians had adopted Christianity nearly sixteen hundred years earlier in 300AD. Over the centuries, they had resolutely clung to their religion, even after the Ottomans conquered their land. The Armenians maintained their faith, knowing that it brought the disfavor of the sultan who, as Ottoman leader, was the highest person in the Muslim religion.

Islam, the Muslim religion, means submitting oneself to God. The Prophet Muhammad, who named this religion, believed that in their purest forms, Christianity and Judaism were Islam, but both had been corrupted by its followers. The basis of Islam is the Koran and the Hadith. The Koran is a record of the specific messages Muhammad believed had been divinely imparted to him. The Hadith is an account of Mohammed's actions in various situations and is used by Muslims to guide them in their own behavior in similar situations.

In his day, Muhammad had negotiated pacts with the Jews and Christians that allowed them to continue to practice their religion and keep their possessions. He required only that they pay a tax. Non-Muslims were exempted from military service, too, since only a Muslim was allowed to draw his sword in defense of Islam. Philosophically, Mohammed's treaties had continued as the model for the treatment of non-Muslims in the Ottoman Empire.

In theory, then, any non-Muslim need only be given the choice of adopting Islam or paying taxes. But, in practice, the treatment of non-Muslims varied greatly, depending on who was sultan.

The present ruler, Abdul Hamid, was a corrupt, self-indulgent leader who had already bankrupted his empire by squandering money borrowed from foreign powers. He used the animosity of the Muslim population to blame the country's poverty on Armenian bankers. Since his reign had begun, Abdul Hamid's troops had sporadically attacked Armenians. The outbreak of violence in Constantinople nearly three years ago was one such attack.

In spite of treatment such as this, the Armenians had steadfastly refused to convert to the Muslim religion. Christianity was central to who they were as a people. Their daily lives revolved around their system of beliefs and their loyalty to it had persevered through centuries of violence and discrimination. Holidays, therefore, had a special importance to them.

Nikol sighed and thought about Christmas. The sacred event celebrated by the entire community, would soon be upon them. Now he was a part of it again. He went to sleep that night grateful for the sense of belonging that Koren had given back to him, when he had taken him in almost three years ago.

The next few days sped by. Victoria's school was putting on a Christmas pageant and she, Margaret and Rebecca had been given the parts of the angels. Every afternoon after school, the three friends labored together at Victoria's house on their costumes. Then Victoria stayed up late every night working on her schoolwork.

When Saturday arrived, Seta was tempted to let Victoria sneak a few extra minutes in bed, but they had work to do. They cleaned all morning, then prepared yeasted dough to make their breakfast *choereg*s. Seta took the first turn, kneading the dough until her arms ached. When Victoria took over, Seta took a handful of sesame seeds and spread them on top of the stove to toast for the top of her *choereg*s. She walked away from the stove, preoccupied with Christmas plans. A few minutes later, a burning odor reached her nostrils. Annoyed with herself, she rushed back to the stove. Blackened seeds. She hated to waste even the smallest amount of food, but what could she do? She shrugged, lifted the lid of the stove with one hand, and brushed the seeds into the fire with the other. She went back to the pantry to get more raw seeds to toast. Just as she reached the pantry door, there was a loud explosion. She flew back into the room. Victoria looked shocked, but was not hurt. Koren and Nikol rushed in, their eyes wide with alarm.

"What happened?"

"I don't know. I just threw some burnt sesame seeds into the fire, went to the pantry, and heard a loud boom."

Koren stared at her. "You threw sesame seeds in the fire? What's the matter with you? Don't you know they explode?"

Koren sank onto a stool. His knees were trembling and he glared at Seta.

She shouldn't laugh. She had scared everyone badly. The corners of her mouth began to turn up, despite her resolve. She looked at Victoria. Victoria covered her mouth and giggled.

The upper half of Nikol's face maintained a frown, while the lower half twitched. He turned away.

Koren still scowled. "It's a good thing we don't live closer to the village. What would the police think? They would think that we, we..." He began to laugh. "That we were making bombs."

Soon all four were laughing, the relief from fear adding to their hilarity.

Nikol rolled his eyes. "Imagine trying to explain that one to them. Exploding sesame seeds."

Suddenly, footsteps approached the front door. Instantly silent, they all stared at each other. Koren went to the door, opened it a crack, then flung it wide. The Halabians had dropped by for an afternoon visit. Koren graciously ushered them in and they all sank onto cushions around the table.

"I was just going to serve lunch," Seta said, when the story of the sesame seeds had been told. "Will you join us?"

"Oh, no, thank you. We've already eaten," The guests protested, though it wasn't true. To accept a meal at the first offering was rude. Guests had to be cajoled into eating, refusing twice before it was permissible to accept.

"Please join us, we have plenty," Seta urged.

"No, really, we just couldn't."

"You must join us, we really insist."

"Well, all right, if you're sure it isn't an imposition."

"No, it's no imposition at all." Seta stretched the portions so her guests all had something on their plate. She was glad to be able to feed the Halabians. They had to count every grain of wheat they ate. Poor young Martin's wrists gaped from the ends of his too-short shirt. She turned and caught Victoria making a face at him. Seta put her hands on her hips and sent Victoria a look.

After eating, John Halabian, the head of the family, pulled a letter from his shirt pocket. His eyes shone with pride. The letter was already looking worn at the creases from all the folding and unfolding.

"It's from Charles."

Seta felt better, when she thought about Charles. He would be able to help his family when he came back.

Seta cleaned up after her guests left and thought about how grateful she was to have all she did. She hated the danger of Koren's work as a courier, but it did keep them from having to rely solely on the farm.

The next day, Sunday, Victoria dashed about after church

helping her mother prepare for a visit from Margaret and the rest of the Damadian family. Victoria always liked having guests, but was especially happy to share the day with her very best friend. She was setting out a tray of cups and saucers, when footsteps approached the front door. Koren went to open it.

"Come in, come in," he said. His voice sounded surprised.

Instead of the Damadians, Cousin Rose stood in the doorway with her daughter, Fiorine.

"Cousin Rose, what an unexpected pleasure," Seta said, going to greet them. "Please sit down. The Damadians will be here any minute. Will you stay and eat with us?"

"No, thank you, we have already eaten," Rose said.

"Please join us, we insist."

"No, really we can't. We were just stopping by for a few minutes."

"You must stay. We hope you will consider it."

"No, thank you. We are on our way to town for dinner with some friends."

Victoria let out a silent breath of relief, when she heard the third and final refusal. Her pleasant afternoon would be ruined if her father's cousin stayed. Why did Aunt Rose have to be so mean?

Rose turned and smiled at Victoria.

Victoria shuddered and pulled her sweater more tightly around her.

After ten minutes Rose stood to leave.

Why had she come?

She walked to the door, hesitated, then turned to Nikol. "Weren't you in Constantinople a few years ago, when the revolutionaries took over the Ottoman Bank?" she asked casually, as if the idea had just crossed her mind.

"Yes." Nikol took out a handkerchief and wiped his forehead. Wisely, he offered no further explanation or comment.

"Well, I was wondering if you knew any of the people involved? After all, you do have the same last name as Abraham Balian, the famous revolutionary. They say most of them escaped the country, but the government is still looking for a few they suspect might be around. A few months ago, police from the capitol came here. I heard they were tracing a letter sent because of the massacre that followed it."

"What are you asking *him* for, Rose?" Koren's face was dark. "And why are you asking now? Anyway, Balian is a common name, and Constantinople is a gigantic city. Of course, he doesn't know anything about it."

There was that name Balian again. Why did the adults seem to think it so important? Victoria watched her father exchange a look with her mother. Nikol's hands were shaking. She didn't know why, but she stepped in front of him.

No one spoke.

Rose muttered something noncommittal and left.

Koren closed the door after her and shook his head. "Busybody."

The Damadians arrived and Victoria relaxed along with the rest of her family. Now they could enjoy their afternoon.

Margaret's family had brought a crock of *khashkash*, a delicious nutty spread made from ground poppy seeds. Araxie used the poppies Michael grew to prepare the delicacy, first browning the seeds in a pan, then pulverizing them on a grinding stone. The result was a kind of poppy-seed butter, a scrumptious spread on the crusty round flat bread Seta had baked.

The Damadians' visit did away with Rose's poison, and the last Sunday before the Christmas pageant passed quickly, as did the week that followed.

The Christmas eve pageant was upon them before they knew it. Victoria buttoned her heavy woolen coat. "I'll see you there."

The icy cold wind stung her cheeks and she lowered her head to protect her face from it. She hurried down the road, her feet making crunching noises on the frozen ground, as she walked. Halfway to the school, she heard the clop of a horse's hoofs. She shaded her eyes and peered ahead.

Hasan, the Kurd, was approaching from the opposite direction.

No, she wasn't in danger here on this open road, was she?

She looked back down at the ground. *Just keep walking*, she told herself. She saw the horse's hoofs clopping alongside her and felt his eyes on her head. *Just keep walking*, she said to herself again, but she looked up.

Hasan nodded to her. She nodded back and kept moving. When she had gone another thirty paces, she stopped and turned around.

Hasan was staring over his shoulder at her, as his horse plodded forward.

She turned and quickened her pace.

As soon as she arrived at the school, she rushed through the iron gate and on to her classroom, where she found Margaret waiting. Breathlessly, she told her what had happened.

"But don't tell," she said. Really, there was nothing to tell. He had done nothing wrong. It was the way he had looked at her that made her feel scared. And what could her parents do about that?

Rebecca flew through the door five minutes later, cheeks flushed with excitement. Gradually, Victoria forgot her fear, as the three angels raced about preparing themselves for their roles.

The baby Jesus was being provided by Adrienne, an older girl from a wealthy family, who owned a beautiful porcelain-faced doll. Adrienne was not there, when Victoria arrived but soon after, she hurried in.

"I'm so sorry I'm late," she said.

Victoria laid an arm on her shoulder. "It's all right. We're just glad you're safe. I'll help you get ready, if you want. Give the doll to the boys. They'll put it in the manger."

The stage was soon perfect. When the children silently

filed in, they went directly to their assigned places around a temporary stable that had been set up. The three angels stood on boxes so they were above the stable, watching over it with a seraphic presence.

Koren and Seta smiled with pride, when Victoria confidently stepped forward and raised her sweet, clear voice in the song she had practiced. And, by the close of the pageant, as the little ones exited singing their final song, a sense of peace and the holiday's importance had settled in the hearts of all the audience.

Afterward, the families who lived in the Armenian quarter of the village, hurried home to make trays of dried fruits and morsels of sweets ready for carolers who soon arrived, led by the adult choir. The singers made their way from house to house, and it was midnight before they stopped.

On Christmas morning, Victoria awoke and found her parents already up. What was in her father's hand? Mmm, something delicious. Koren smiled and handed both her and Nikol a package of sweet candies. She was lucky. Other families did not give each other presents on Christmas, as hers did. She watched Seta proudly present Koren with a sweater that she had knitted. Its intricate pattern of brightly colored, hand-dyed yarns spoke of the skill and care she had lavished on the gift.

Koren embraced Seta. "This is wonderful. I'll wear it today." He pulled the thick warm garment over his head and appreciatively ran his hands over the soft exterior. He gazed at his wife with love.

"I worked on it whenever you went out to your meetings," Seta said. "You can think of it as your *Dashnak* sweater."

"Mother hid it away every time she heard you coming," Victoria mumbled with her mouth full of sweets. She went to her parents and gave them both an affectionate hug.

"I have something for all of you, too." Nikol reached under his mattress and pulled out three items. He handed the first to Victoria. "For you," he said.

Victoria's eyes widened. "A book? For me?" She ran her hand over its cover.

"It's a story about a girl who lives in the Alpine mountains of Switzerland with her uncle. She sleds down the mountain to go to school and, well, I think you will like it."

Victoria threw her arms around Nikol. "I will love it. I–I hardly know what to say."

Nikol blushed and looked away. He went next to Seta, gave her a hug, and handed her two small silver combs to wear in her hair. He went last to Koren and held up a painting of Mount Ararat. "You once told me that this mountain stood in our midst before our lands were conquered and is a symbol of the independence we fight for now." He handed it to him. "For you."

The two men embraced.

Victoria saw how touched Koren looked and wiped a tear from her eye. Had Nikol just called her father Papa?

Nikol finished dressing and went out to the stable to tend the animals.

Koren looked dazed. "I've given him a coin or two over the years. Not much. He must have saved every one and spent them on these gifts."

After completing their chores, the family set off down the well-worn dirt road to church. They were spending the afternoon with Margaret's family and would not return until late that night.

After the morning service, families lingered on the church steps chattering until the cold began to penetrate their thick layers of clothing and they moved on. With Victoria and Margaret in the lead, their two families marched on to the Damadians' house.

By the time they all arrived at the house and burst through the door, they were chilled to the bone. The elder Mrs. Damadian, Margaret's grandmother, had steaming soup ready for them. She sprinkled each bowl with a generous measure of ground pepper to warm them up and handed them out one-by-one.

The group livened up, as they slowly began to thaw. Michael produced a deck of cards, and soon the men were arguing good-naturedly amongst themselves.

Margaret's aunt, who was a renowned story-teller, gathered the women and girls around her and entertained them with a spooky, enthralling tale. The afternoon sun went down and the lanterns began to cast long shadows on the walls. Victoria's experience on the way to the pageant the day before had left her feeling edgy and nervous. She slid closer to Margaret and clutched her hand.

"And so, we learn to watch out for the suspiciously friendly stranger. Who knows, they just might practice the evil eye!" Margaret's aunt concluded dramatically. There was a sudden crash from the kitchen. Victoria wrapped her arms around Margaret and buried her head in her shoulder.

"I'm sorry, I dropped a tray," Margaret's grandmother said, peeking through the doorway.

Margaret nudged Victoria and she looked up. Her face was still pale. She gave a small laugh and the color began to return to her cheeks. She felt her mother's puzzled stare and averted her eyes. Seta stood and started toward Victoria but just then, all the women jumped up to help Margaret's grand-mother. The moment was forgotten.

"Let us drink to our health. I'll pour everyone some more of this superb Adanalian *raki*." Michael Damadian gestured expansively and spoke loudly. The group merged together at the table, talking and laughing as Araxie and Margaret's grandmother placed large trays of succulent meat and soft, steamy rice pilaf, in front of them.

They laughed all evening long as the senior Mr. Damadian related tales of his youthful escapades. He had a quick and lively mind and had used it to plan daring deeds before, to his parent's relief, he had finally settled down and married. A spark of this pluckiness was still evident in his personality, and it made him a great favorite among both young and old.

The evening ended when Koren and Seta rose and signaled Victoria and Nikol. Victoria began putting on her many layers for the walk home. She huddled into the tight circle of her family and resolved not to let her encounter with Hasan make her afraid again. He was a Kurd, but he had lived in this village all his life. Nikol had told her some bad stories about Turks and Kurds, but he couldn't have meant someone like Hasan.

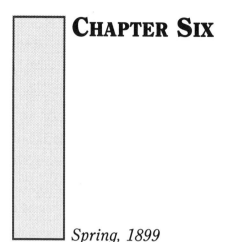

CHAPTER SIX

Spring, 1899

"**W**e'll begin planting the vegetables tomorrow," Koren said, as he led Nikol on their annual spring inspection of the farm. Their feet sank in the boggy soil as they walked. Koren drew a deep breath of its rich damp scent.

Nikol frowned. "You're not afraid of frost?"

"No. I'll tell you why. Listen to that. Do you hear it? The sound of running water? It's the melted runoff from the hills. Every year, I wait for that sound. When it gets loud enough, I know it's time to begin."

Nikol tilted his head and listened. He nodded. "Where are you going to plant the wheat this year?"

Koren smiled and laid his arm across the youth's shoulder. He was pleased that Nikol remembered. Last year, he had explained to him that every year farmers rotated their crops; keeping them in the same place robbed the soil of essential nutrients which in turn produced poorer harvests. Koren thought of Cousin Rose. If she stopped fussing and listened to his modern ideas on farming, her property would be as productive as his. No matter how often he tried to explain the benefits of crop rotation to her and her husband, they stubbornly clung to their old ways. Then they complained when their harvest was poor, blaming the inferior piece of land given to them by their grandfather. He shook his head and they walked on.

Later, at home, Victoria joined them as they thumbed through the collection of seed packets Koren had purchased. She read the label of one. Watermelons. She licked her lips. They had never grown watermelons before.

She loved this season. Just that morning, she and Seta had packed away their heavy woolen clothing in favor of the family's crisp spring cottons. And it was almost Easter, their most important holiday. Tomorrow, on the eve of the forty days of Lent, they were having a feast and were going to eat their last meat before Easter. *Shish Kebab*. Her mouth watered. Yes, she loved this season. She frowned, suddenly reminded of the part of Easter she did not like. Cousin Rose and her odious little family. Every year they came, infecting Victoria's holiday with their mean presence. Why did they have to be related to her? Rose's son, Alexan, never had anything interesting to say and her daughter, Fiorine, bland little Fiorine, never even opened her mouth. She just stood there, learning to be Rose.

Victoria colored and looked around. Her father was still plotting the vegetable garden with Nikol, her mother was preparing dinner. Thank Heavens they couldn't read her thoughts. She tried to be good and to make them proud of her, but sometimes, it was so hard.

"Seta, I've invited the Halabians to join our dinner tomorrow."

Her father's voice drew Victoria out of her reverie.

Seta looked sympathetic. "Poor dears, I heard their supply of wheat ran out two weeks ago." She gazed at her husband with love. "You knew they were hungry and invited them here."

Victoria smiled. What was it her father always said? Something about one's own good fortune being deserved only when it was shared with others.

The next afternoon, Victoria arrived home and found Seta hard at work preparing for their evening celebration with the Halabians. Yesterday, they had sent a lamb to the butcher. Seta had trimmed the fat off the fresh meat, cut it into chunks, and bathed it overnight in a marinade of onions, garlic, wine and allspice.

Victoria eyed her schoolbooks, but offered to help skewer the meat. Her end of the year exams were coming up right after Easter. She was determined to be the top student — a determination her mother didn't understand. Being the top student meant studying. She was capable but there were a lot of other bright, motivated children. Today, Martin had teased her again, boasting that he would come out ahead of her this year.

Victoria stabbed cubes of meat onto a skewer. She glanced anxiously at her pile of books. It seemed to grow higher with every look. Seta noticed and her brow furrowed in a worried frown.

When Victoria finished her part, Koren and Nikol took the rods of meat outside and arranged them side by side on a rack over a fire. Flames immediately curled up and licked at the meat. It began to crackle and drip juices into the fire. Thick spicy smoke rose and clouded the early evening air.

The Halabians ate their meal with pleasure. When they were ready to leave, Koren went to the pantry and came out with two large sacks, one containing cracked wheat, the other, flour.

He handed them to John, looked him in the eye, and said in a low voice, "I insist."

John stood without speaking for a moment. Then he grasped Koren's arm and said, "Thank you, my friend. I will remember this."

After they left, Koren poured himself a glass of *raki*, and sat beside Nikol. "What was Avedis talking to you about today? You both looked so serious."

Victoria wiped the table in front of them and listened.

"Avedis told me a terrible story. He knows an Armenian

family who lived near the mountains. The family is now ruined and destitute. A family of Kurds from the mountains settled with them for the winter. The Armenians were forced to house and feed them. The Kurds went back to the hills when the weather warmed up, but took the Armenians' food and all their valuables."

Victoria dropped the cleaning rag. "Oh, that's horrible. What will they do?"

Seta put down the pot she was scrubbing and came to Victoria's side.

"They had to move in with relatives. The Kurds left them nothing to start over with."

"But how can they do that?" Victoria said.

"The law allows them to."

Victoria looked shocked. She turned to her parents and waited for them to say this wasn't true. They remained silent.

Nikol explained that the law allowed any Kurd to winter with an Armenian family at no cost to the Kurd or his family. Robbery often followed, even murder, both without consequence. Even local land-owning Kurds were unable to control these nomadic terrorists and suffered at their hands.

"I hear stories like this and know it is time to take a different kind of action." Koren gave Nikol a serious look, which Nikol returned. Victoria caught the look. Suddenly comprehended the look. Was this what they talked about at those meetings they went to? She looked at her mother. Seta's lips were pursed with worried wrinkles. Victoria shivered. Then she picked up her pencil, spread out her books and began to study.

Throughout the forty days of Lent, Victoria and her family went to church every morning. After the service, Koren and Nikol rushed home to turn the soil, lay down the manure, and plant their crops. Seta attacked her spring cleaning. She pulled the wool out of their mattresses and comforters, washed it and re-quilted it back. Victoria studied and studied.

On the night before Easter, the family celebrated the end of Lent with another feast. Seta served meat for the first time in forty days.

Easter morning arrived. When Koren saw that Victoria was also awake, he said to her, "Christ is risen from the dead."

"Blessed be the resurrection of Christ," she said back to him. It was the traditional Easter greeting and it was customary to repeat it throughout the day to everyone one met.

Victoria waited. Her eyes sparkled greedily. Koren smiled. He reached into his pocket and dug out four coins, the customary children's Easter gift, and gave two to Victoria and two to Nikol.

Seta went to the pantry and brought out her Easter offering — *rojig*, dried grape candy and walnut roll.

Later, as they walked to church, the pocket of Victoria's pretty Easter dress bulged with a hard-boiled, dyed Easter egg. When the service ended, she planned to join her friends in a game played by children every year. They started with eggs that had been hard-boiled in water and onion skins; the onion skins turned the eggs a deep maroon color. Each child carefully selected the best egg to take to church and used it to challenge another child to a game. Each player grasped an egg in her fist with only the top showing. The challenged person repeatedly tapped her egg against her opponent's to see whose egg cracked first. Whoever held the egg that cracked, lost the round and gave her egg to the winner. The winner went on to challenge the next person and the hardest egg won its owner lots of cracked eggs to take home.

The service ended and everyone filed outside, gathering in the fenced-in courtyard of the church. The women set out refreshments on a table. Soon the area was alive with adults chatting in small groups and children playing the egg game.

Victoria ran up to her parents. "Look, my egg still hasn't cracked!" Her face was flushed with excitement.

"I challenge you."

Victoria spun around.

Martin smirked and held out a fist with the dark red tip of an egg peeking through.

Victoria's lips formed a circle. "Why, you..." She stopped and eyed her parents standing by. She drew in a breath and swung the hand holding her egg in an arc over her shoulder. She smashed it down onto Martin's egg. The egg disappeared into his palm.

Victoria laughed out loud. Arrogant pest. She had shown him. She turned her egg over to inspect it. Her eyes widened. She studied it more closely. Looked up.

Martin put his unmarred egg into his pocket and extended his empty palm. Victoria's face turned purple. She slapped her cracked egg into his hand and stomped off, muttering something under her breath.

"What? What did you say?" Martin said to her retreating back.

At home, Victoria, still smarting over the incident of the egg, helped Seta prepare for their guests. Seta tenderly unwrapped a soft cloth from her prized possession, an ornate silver tray. Victoria began to load it up with pretty piles of hors d'oeuvres. When Rose got there, she would have nothing to criticize. She would have welcomed the opportunity, but Victoria was not going to provide her with it.

Their guests arrived.

Rose stepped through the door talking. "Did you see young Michael's new wife? I couldn't help noticing her hair. It's obviously dyed, not to mention her face, which you could barely see with so much powder on it. Why he had to go outside our village for a wife, I'll never know? There are plenty of girls right here." She turned and glared at her daughter.

Fiorine blushed, furiously.

Seta looked from Fiorine's face to Rose and said, "Well, I thought she was pretty. Poor young thing, away from her family like that for the first time. It's not easy for her." She turned to the group. "Please everyone, sit and have something to eat."

Victoria sighed. It was going to be a long afternoon.

The crowning touch to dinner was *paklava*, which Seta had diligently prepared. This delicate pastry consumed so many hours to make, Seta served it only once or twice a year.

On her tabletop, Seta rolled out four or five layers of dough at a time, dusting between each with cornstarch to keep them from sticking together. A long round broom pole was her rolling pin. The dough spread out more with each stroke until it was paper-thin. Then the work of constructing the *paklava* itself began. She cut the dough into sheets the size of a cooking pan. Next, she liberally brushed each sheet with melted butter then placed one on top of another, layer upon layer, in the pan. After half the dough had been used, she sprinkled chopped nuts mixed with cinnamon and sugar on top. Then more sheets of dough followed over that. Still, the preparation was not complete. She cut it into diamond-shaped pieces, then baked it to crispy perfection. Before she served it, she dipped each piece in a sugar-syrup. The resulting confection, crisp, light and sweet, was delicious.

"It's good, but I like it with a little less syrup," Rose said.

Victoria jumped up. "I'm going for a walk." She looked at Fiorine. Fiorine was fifteen, too old to bother with her. But still, she had to be polite. "Would you like to come with me?"

Fiorine nodded, sprang up and headed for the door. Victoria's brow raised and she hurried after her cousin.

"Your dress is very pretty." Victoria could think of nothing else to say. Fiorine's plain face was already pinched and drawn, looking old before its time.

"You don't have to be polite. It's just an old dress of my mother's. She never lets me have anything new. She doesn't think I'm worth it." Suddenly, Fiorine's eyes filled with tears.

Victoria stopped. She had never thought about it before. What must it be like to have a mother like Rose, lavish with criticisms and stingy with compliments? Fiorine was now at a marriageable age and everyone knew that not one suitor's mother had approached her parents on behalf of their son. How humiliated Fiorine must feel.

Victoria took her cousin's hand. "We have a lovely piece of powder-blue material my father brought back from Mezireh. We haven't used it yet and there's more than enough for a dress. If you'd like, I'll talk to my mother. But I know she'll let you have it. You can come here and work on it. Mother and I will be glad to help."

"Oh, thank you." Fiorine brushed her wet eyes on her shoulder and sniffed. "Who knows? Maybe if I wear a new dress, a boy will actually notice me."

"I'm finished with school after this week. We'll start on it then."

At the end of the day, as the guests finally left, to Seta's surprise, Victoria turned to Fiorine and said, "Remember, I'll see you next week right after school gets out."

When they'd gone, Victoria explained. "I promised

Fiorine she could have that pretty blue material that Papa gave me. This Easter dress fits me just fine, so I don't need anything else. I feel sorry for her, because her mother never lets her have anything new, and she's worried because she thinks boys won't notice her the way she looks. I hope you don't mind."

Seta regarded her daughter with respect. "Not only do I not mind, I'm very proud of you," she said smiling. "It was very generous of you, Victoria, especially because you knew we were going to make a dress for you with it."

Victoria looked away. She felt she didn't deserve that look her mother was giving her. She had been unkind to Fiorine in the past and had judged her unfairly.

On Thursday, when exams ended, Victoria waited with her class at the door to their schoolroom for the results to be posted. Someone tapped her on the shoulder.

"I hope you do well. Really."

She looked back, then spun around to face the speaker. Martin. He smiled. She scowled. No, he did not look as if he was teasing her. But she knew him. "I hope you remember to bathe this week. Really." She turned back and missed the surprised look on his face.

The teacher came out of the door and tacked up a sheet of paper with all their names on it.

Victoria squinted through the crowd of students and found her name. She had come out at the top of her class. She whooped with glee and linked arms with Margaret and

Rebecca who had placed second and third, respectively. Martin had not even come in fourth. They started for the door and spotted Martin walking through. His shoulders sagged and his head was down. Victoria thought about her cousin, Fiorine then about what she had just said to Martin. She let go of her friends' arms and hurried to catch up to him.

"Twelfth place is still good," she said.

Martin stopped. He grinned slowly. "Really?"

Victoria laughed. "Really."

"Congratulations," he said. "I know you deserved coming out first. I'm sorry I've been so mean to you."

She would not have been so humble, if the tables were turned. "I'm sorry for what I said."

Margaret and Rebecca caught up with her and they walked out the door.

"Well, maybe he's not so bad," Victoria said, as they watched Martin walk away.

"Not so bad?" Margaret looked at her friend. "Are you crazy? He's been teasing you for years. Every chance he gets."

"I know, but I feel sorry for him now."

Margaret just shook her head. The girls rejoined arms and marched happily off, taking satisfaction in their accomplishment and anticipating the pleasant days of the summer to come. But as they walked through the village, they heard a ruckus in the marketplace. Soon they saw it.

An Armenian peddler stood with outstretched arms, blocking his vegetable cart. Two Turkish bullies were harassing him by grabbing produce from the cart. As the peddler rushed to one side of the cart, trying to stand between it and one of the men, the other reached into the unguarded space and grabbed something else. They laughed, as the man's frustration increased.

"If you want some peppers or eggplants, pay for them like everyone else," he said, advancing toward the two men.

"Don't you dare take one step closer to us, you dog." The ruffians put their hands on the curved handles of their swords, as the peddler drew close. They eyed their audience and began to posture: "These vegetables are all rotten and overpriced, anyway," one said. "He's trying to cheat people by selling them."

"I don't think he deserves to be in business," the other said. "These vegetables belong in the gutter."

One of the men nudged the other. Then both advanced toward the cart. As they did, the peddler's eyes widened with fright.

"Please don't ruin my cart. I have no other way to support my family," he said.

His pleas seemed to increase the brutes' bravado. Each grabbed a side of the cart and began to shove their shoulders against it. Two of its wheels lifted off the ground.

Without warning, the crack of a whip sounded. The bullies straightened up and the cart thudded back on all four wheels. The men looked up in surprise. Several neat piles of zucchini and lettuce tumbled. Sitting astride his horse was Hasan.

"Leave this man alone," he commanded. Technically, he had no authority over anyone else, but the gun he had unholstered and pointed at them made that a moot point.

The two agitators backed off, looking surprised. They glanced first at the Kurd on his gleaming mount, then at the Armenian peddler in his faded dusty clothes. They turned and walked away, spitting in the dirt as they did.

"Thank you," the peddler said. He squatted and began to pick up tomatoes and onions from the ground. Hasan nodded in response. He looked over at the girls, who stood staring at him, round-eyed and admiring. His eye lingered on Victoria. His handsome face broke out in a wide smile. He rode up to her and gave a mock bow.

Victoria covered her mouth and giggled. Then she looked around and her smile faded. The Turks, who had been watching, were looking at her through narrowed eyes. She backed away. This scene could so easily have disintegrated into violence. Numbing fear replaced her lighthearted mood. And something else. Something she could not define. Yet it was there.

The girls trudged home in silence. After Margaret veered off toward her house, Victoria ran all the rest of the way home. She was happy to see that Nikol was still outside tending the vegetable gardens. She ran up to him and breathlessly poured out the tale, omitting Hasan's direct exchange.

"That merchant was lucky Hasan was around," Nikol said. "He's a Kurd, but a decent man. Armenians who own shops feel safer here than in other villages."

She had told herself the same thing at Christmas time. Now she knew she had been right. She thought of something else. "Nikol, why are all the merchants Armenians?"

"Muslims think differently than we do. They consider it honorable to become soldiers. Their culture believes that in being a soldier, one is defending Islam. Turks are either soldiers, government officials, or at worst, landowners. They consider trade and finance degrading, so they leave both to the Armenians. The Armenians pursue the fields that are open to them, and they do this with diligence and great success. That's why most of the businesses you see are owned by Armenians. But the situation has made the Turks resent and look down on us even more."

"And how do the Kurds fit into this?"

"Kurds are Muslims, too, but they are not Turks. Some, like Hasan, are wealthy landowners and some are local governors or *pasha*s, as we call them. The Sultan gives the *pasha* the job of setting and collecting taxes from the Christians. We are fortunate. Our *pasha* does not set our taxes as high as others do. But he doesn't control the Turkish riffraff, who target us.

Victoria nodded and walked into the house. Her face was serious. She had learned a lot this year.

Nikol snapped a green bean from its vine and threw it into his basket. Look at him. He had promised his brother that he would continue the work they had started. And what had he done? Nothing. The letter had brought the police to their village, but it had not resulted in any new laws to protect his people. Kurds from the mountains still attacked and Turks murdered and ruined them without consequence. And, as time had gone by, the Europeans' concern had faded again.

It was time for some new action. He could tell Koren agreed. But what? And how could he be involved in anything, when it was clear from what Rose said that the police remembered him still?

CHAPTER SEVEN

Summer, 1899

"**A**ugust already! Where is the summer going?" Seta's fingers flew expertly over her fine even stitches on the delicate white material. She was letting down the hem of Victoria's Easter dress in preparation of Fiorine's upcoming wedding. "The waist will be a little short, but the overall length will be right."

Nikol and Koren had gone to Rose's house to congratulate her on Fiorine's engagement, an event that had made Victoria and Seta happy.

Victoria, true to her word, had spent almost a week helping Fiorine fashion and put together a new dress. Fiorine had hurried over each morning and worked until noon. Then she rushed back to face the drudgery of chores and her mother's jealous questioning.

As the girls sewed, they talked. Fiorine had told Victoria something she had not told anyone else. She told her about the secret crush she had on Arsen, the son of a local family. Arsen worked with his father as a goldsmith in a thriving business. He had even talked to Fiorine twice after church. Fiorine had been drawn to his quiet, gentle manner. Once, at the baths, she thought his mother had pointed to her and said something to a woman nearby. Fiorine said she had waited after that for Arsen's family to approach hers, but they hadn't.

Fiorine told Victoria how her mother had berated her these last two years, making her feel ashamed for her lack of suitors. Rose knew nothing of Arsen, nothing of her daughter's dreams. And her daughter's dreams had begun to fade with each passing month.

Victoria had felt Fiorine's pain and lived her dawning hope, as she talked that week. When the dress hung in its completed splendor, she worried that their new closeness would come to an end.

When Fiorine tried the dress on for the first time, her eyes lit up with pleasure. Nikol and Koren had just stepped in the door as she emerged from behind the screen where she was changing. "*Shad lav,*" they said, in approval.

Color crept up the sides of Fiorine's face. She beamed.

Victoria stared in surprise at the glowing cheeks set against the dark eyes sparkling with happiness. Fiorine's black hair had come unclasped and it flowed finely down her back. Why, she's actually pretty, Victoria had thought to herself, and she was not alone in her opinion.

Victoria was relieved when Fiorine continued to call on her. She noticed that Fiorine walked with her head held high. Her days with Victoria and Seta had given her much more than a new dress.

Perhaps it was her new confident bearing that made Arsen's family take a second look. One week ago, they had approached Fiorine's family about having her as a bride for their son.

Rose's criticisms turned to boasts about her daughter, and about what a great match she had made.

Arsen's family planned the wedding for the end of the summer. Most of the community was invited. It would be a huge festive outdoor occasion with music and dancing and it might last an entire week.

When Koren and Nikol returned from their trip to Rose's, they were still laughing at Rose's changed attitude toward her daughter.

"Well, Fiorine can do no wrong now, according to Rose," Koren told Seta, still chuckling.

Seta smiled, pleased that Fiorine had finally gained the acceptance she deserved. The girl had been over to visit earlier in the week and the joy she radiated was contagious.

As she did every summer night, Victoria dragged her

sleeping mat up a ladder onto the thick straw roof where she slept with her family in the cool night air. She loved the peaceful lull when she staved off sleep and gazed at the crystalline patterns in the sky. She used to feel enveloped by a protective presence, but this year, she noticed she didn't and she wondered if everyone lost that sense as they grew up.

The sweltering summer marched by. Margaret had been away, since school let out and Victoria missed her terribly. Michael Damadian owned acres of lush vineyards in the country and every summer he packed his family up and transported them there to live in huge tents erected on stationary platforms.

One day, Koren announced he had a surprise.

Both Seta and Victoria stopped what they were doing and looked at him with expectant smiles.

"I talked to Michael when he was home this week, and he invited us to the vineyards this weekend. I've already hired a carriage to take us."

Seta and Victoria hugged each other with excitement. A visit to the country was a special treat.

With Nikol, they set off three days later, their small hired carriage packed with clothing, bedding, and gifts of the lush ripe watermelons they had successfully grown in their garden. For two hours, they bumped through rolling hills. On the last thirty minutes, the horse began to strain, as the terrain ascended to the elevations that produced Michael's grapes.

At last, the carriage pulled up to a charming summer scene. Children frolicked and the fields reverberated with their voices. The Damadians' vineyard was modest, but many vineyards stood side-by-side and they stretched as far as the eye could see.

Margaret flew out of the tent, when she heard the carriage approach. Victoria spotted her, jumped up, and leapt over the side before it even came to a full stop, oblivious to her parents' alarm. An injury, they scolded, way off in the country was not easily treated, and they would be most displeased to have their little vacation spoiled by such a careless act.

Victoria reddened and apologized. But she soon had her best friend's hand in hers and the two had run into the heart of the shaded jungle of grapevines.

They sank down onto the cool moist soil.

Victoria reached up and snapped a sprig of soft purple grapes from their heavy sagging cluster. "Margaret, I have so much to tell you."

Margaret plucked a grape from Victoria's bunch and popped it into her mouth. "We haven't seen each other since school got out."

"I know and that's what I wanted to talk to you about. Do you remember that my father told me I might be able to go to college some day?"

Margaret nodded.

Victoria munched on a grape and went on. "Well, when

Papa saw how well I did this year, he told me he would definitely send me."

Margaret looked worried. "Oh Victoria, I'm happy for you, but I will miss you so."

Victoria's eyes danced with excitement. "But that's what I wanted to talk to you about. He said he would talk to your father about you going as well. He doesn't want me to go away by myself."

Margaret's brown eyes seemed to grow larger. She clasped her friend's hand in hers. "Can you imagine it? Both of us going to college, together."

Victoria's expression changed. She looked from side to side and said in a low voice, "But, you must not tell anyone. You see, my mother doesn't know yet. I told her once that he said maybe I could go and I could tell that she didn't like it. If she finds out now, she'll have two years to get him to change his mind. She never argues with my father, but trust me, she has her ways."

Margaret nodded. "I promise, I won't say a word."

The girls stayed where they were sampling the sweet ripe fruit and discussing their pact for the future. Their lips were stained purple, when they emerged from their nest an hour later and joined the others.

Margaret's entire family, her grandparents, uncle, aunt and cousin had been benefiting from the fresh country air all summer. Soon another wagon pulled up. More relatives had come. The arriving women immediately joined the others preparing the dinner. The men gathered with drinks in hand and tended the outdoor fires.

The noisy adults sat at the fireside until late that night telling stories, drinking *raki*, and laughing. Gradually, the children's eyelids grew heavy and their parents escorted them off to bed. All the children slept together on an open-air platform designated as their sleeping quarters for the night. Victoria and Margaret lay side by side, whispering about their plans for college. In the distance, they could still hear the adults' animated voices and eruptions of laughter. The girls eventually dropped off to sleep, but the grownups continued their party deep into the night.

The children awoke when the sun hit their faces early the next morning. They knew better than to disturb the adults. Nikol still slept. He had stayed up with the adults.

Victoria and Margaret, the eldest of the children, quickly assumed responsibility, leading them on an exploration of the nearby countryside. They happened upon a small bubbling stream in the woods nearby. Victoria and Margaret looked at each other and, without a word, slipped off their shoes. They waded into the cool refreshing water. The younger children followed. Then they took turns floating boats made of leaves and leaping over the narrow width of the stream. After Margaret's little cousin slipped mid-jump and sat down hard in the shallow water, Victoria announced it was time to go back.

The adults were just stirring as the children returned.

Margaret's aunt grabbed her soaking wet son and pushed him toward her tent. She looked at the older girls. "Really, I expected better of you." Victoria and Margaret slumped their shoulders and sat down to breakfast.

Seta had brought dozens of *choeregs* – enough for everyone. With luscious sliced melons, they all had a delicious morning meal. The children gobbled their *choeregs* spread thick with peach marmalade, but the adults nibbled at theirs plain, wanting only something bland after their night of drinking.

The summer morning passed pleasantly. The adults, whose heads had now cleared, led the children on a hike into the surrounding hills, but avoided any mountain streams. Bright beautiful red, yellow, and purple wild flowers dotted the landscape that they walked through. Victoria inhaled their perfumed fragrance and sighed with pleasure.

In the afternoon, while some of the group rested on mattresses, others sprawled out on the ground, and still others sat with their backs against trees, Koren turned to Michael.

"Why don't you take me on a tour of your vineyards?"

When he was sure that they were out of earshot, Koren said, "I don't know what set him off, but Nikol has been talking to me all summer about our problem with the Turks. He asks me what is the use of all we have here when the Turks can take it all away again? He's right, too."

Michael nodded. "Nikol's a smart boy. But sometimes not so smart. Has he ever told you about–?"

"No. I keep waiting. Sometimes I think he's just about to tell me, then, nothing."

"Someday he will."

"Really, what does it matter to me? I know all I need to know about him — I have from the start. But I want your advice on what Nikol wants to do."

Michael clasped Koren's shoulder. "Of course."

Koren looked from right to left. "He wants to write another letter to the *Dashnak*s in the capitol. He says he's been thinking and thinking and — " Koren looked from right to left again. "He's thought of a way to assassinate the sultan."

Michael's eyes widened. "An actual plan?"

"Yes. He says he knows the buildings in the capitol well enough to figure out how to get into the palace. Of course, he wouldn't say how he knew, but that's another story. He will need help getting the letter to the *Dashnak*s. He said he will only send the letter if I agree."

"It will be dangerous, Koren,"

"I know. That first letter of his brought the police right to our village. I have my family's safety to think about."

"I do, too, but the boy is right. What can change with Sultan Hamid on the throne? The man's a bigot and he's a liar. The Europeans tell him he must make reforms in Turkey's laws. He tells them he will. Then he does nothing but incite riots against us for complaining."

"Then you think I should let him?"

"Yes, but we must make sure the letter gets into the right

hands. We don't want the boy outsmarting himself."

"I'll take it to Mezireh myself. The *Dashnak*s there will get it into trusted hands in the capitol."

Michael stopped. "Koren, remember what happened to the last messenger?"

Koren nodded. "I do, but I know the *Dashnak*s in Mezireh. I would trust them with my life."

"And what if the police come to our village again?"

Koren shrugged. "Let them. None of our people will tell them anything."

A voice spoke. "There you are. Sorry, I didn't mean to startle you."

Michael wiped his palms on his pants. "Cousin, I could use your advice. I was showing Koren my grapes and trying to decide when to harvest them."

Michael's cousin squared his shoulders. "I know a little about grapes. Let me see them."

Michael mouthed a *whew* to Koren. "The weather this year has been perfect, just enough rain, but not too much." He grasped a grape between his thumb and index finger and held it up to the sunlight. The men drew in close and examined its translucent color.

Koren took the grape from Michael. He squeezed it. "It still feels firm. About one more week and they'll be ready for picking, I think."

Michael's cousin rolled a handful of grapes into his mouth and chewed slowly. "For wine, you want them just about ready to rot."

"They'll be as sweet as honey, the best ones around," Michael said.

Koren smiled at his friend. Michael was still facing a huge amount of work. He first had to hire local help to do the picking. Then he had to haul the grapes in large wagon-loads back to the village.

The production of wine was complex. Michael, along with Koren and any other strong men who could help, dumped the purple fruit into a huge wooden tub specifically designed for wine-making. It had a faucet on the bottom. The human part of the machinery came next. Araxie set out a wash basin and the helpers scrubbed their feet thoroughly then took turns climbing into the tub and stomping on the grapes to crush them. Within minutes, juice would begin to run out of the faucet. One-by-one, Michael set barrels under the faucet to collect the sweet nectar. As each barrel filled, he pulled it aside and stirred sugar into it. Nature took over from here; fermentation began immediately.

The Damadians made the event into a great party, and Koren's family always attended. The Damadians didn't just stomp on the grapes, they danced on them. Michael even hired musicians to keep up the tempo.

All too soon, late afternoon arrived, ending the country weekend. It was time to load the carriage and begin winding their way back to the city. When Victoria hugged Margaret good-bye, she pulled Margaret's hair aside, cupped her hands and whispered a reminder of their secret into her ear.

The wagon pulled away. Victoria and her family waved and waved until the gathered group was just a tiny dot at the top of the distant hills. The carriage had to brake, as it descended down the path.

On the ride home, Victoria thought about Fiorine's upcoming marriage. Her fiancée was from the same village so, although she was going to live with her husband's family, she would still be nearby. Victoria was very pleased to know she would not lose her cousin to another village now that they had discovered each other.

When the wagon drew up to their front door, Victoria tumbled out, tired but happy. Her brief stay in the country had been a pleasant interlude.

Nikol walked with Koren to the gardens and inspected the vegetables. The lush ripe tomatoes were nearly dropping off the weighted vines, the eggplants were shiny and plump. The squash had matured, as had the green beans, onions and carrots. Everything would have to be harvested this week. Seta and Victoria would have a lot of work putting it all up for the winter.

The men finished discussing the week's activity, but Koren did not move. A silence descended. Nikol looked at Koren with interest. Koren hesitated. He kicked the dirt, coughed then began.

"When you first came here almost three years ago, I asked you to stay because I needed help on the farm." He held his hand up, as Nikol started to speak. "I have found, to my great pleasure, that you have far surpassed all my expectations. You have learned farming quickly and enthusiastically and you have blended into our family so well that you are one of us now.

Nikol's face wrinkled with emotion. "You are my family now. I love living here and working the land. These years with you are the first peaceful ones I've known since my mother died. The other things I've been asking you about have nothing to do with my happiness here."

Koren laid his arm over Nikol's shoulder in a gesture that had become warm and familiar. "I know that. And we will send your letter. But there is something else I want to say. It's been on my mind for a long time. When I pass on, I have no one to leave my farm to."

Nikol looked distressed, but Koren went on. "Naturally, I want my daughter to benefit from everything I've built here, but of course, a woman can't own a farm or manage a business. So I am proposing to offer you my daughter's hand in marriage. In exchange, I'll promise to leave the farm to you, when I pass on."

Nikol was speechless. In a single moment his future had been outlined, even secured. And who would make a better wife for him than Victoria? It was always a pleasure to talk with her, to explore the world through her bright, intelligent eyes. But Koren was saying something else.

"This marriage could not take place for many years.

Victoria wants to go to college. I have told her that she may."
Koren smiled. "But I am young. I will be here for many years
to come. You needn't worry about your place on this farm or
in this family, while I am around. Once you are married, no
one else will dispute it either."

Nikol's heart was full. He gave his answer. "Yes," he said.

Koren embraced him warmly. "We'll keep this conversation to ourselves," he said. "Seta doesn't approve of Victoria
going to college. If I tell her about the marriage plans, I will
have to tell her about college, too. I want to give her more
time to get used to the idea as I have. In a few years, she, too,
will see Victoria's diligence in her studies and accept that she
belongs in college."

Koren and Nikol returned to the house in such good
humor that Seta glanced at them with curiosity. All evening
long, as they joked with each other and teased Victoria, she
couldn't help but wonder what had caused this sudden elat-
ed mood. Koren will explain to me later, when we are alone,
she thought. But Koren didn't offer her an explanation later.
Perplexed, she considered asking him for one. Then she
reproved herself. No, if he didn't say anything, then whatever it was didn't concern her.

Over the next few weeks, Victoria did little but work. The
Damadians returned from their country retreat, but with the
exception of the wine-making night, Victoria and Margaret
did not see each other.

Margaret's father was also busy with his poppies, which

were harvested each fall. His workers collected the milky substance in the pods and molded it into balls after drying it overnight. These balls were the true source of the Damadian's wealth. They were the raw ingredient in processing opium and Michael sold them to manufacturers throughout the country.

The day of Fiorine's wedding dawned mild, bright and clear. This last warm weather reprieve seemed like a gift from earth to the hard-working people who had cultivated her soil, tended her gardens, and harvested her bounty.

Victoria tugged at the bodice of her dress trying to get it to meet her waist and took her place in the wonderfully ornate church. She could hear the rumbling of subdued greetings from other arriving families. Suddenly, silence blanketed the parishioners and everyone turned toward the door.

Fiorine's exquisite red lace gown heightened the natural blush in her cheeks. Her dark eyes shone. Fortunately, it was the custom for the groom's family to commission the wedding gown. Arsen's mother had hired the best dressmaker around. Left up to Rose, Fiorine wouldn't have looked half so beautiful.

Victoria could hear the surprised comments from guests, who hadn't seen Fiorine all summer.

"I never realized how pretty she is."

"Arsen is lucky, he's getting a wife who is both pretty and hard working."

"How did I ever miss her for my David?"

Fiorine gave Victoria a special smile, as she passed by and took her place at the altar.

The ceremony spanned more than an hour. Father Mikayelian asked the bride three times to promise to obey her husband. Fiorine didn't hesitate. She made the promise asked of her. As a woman, she had few rights. A bad marriage, or a marriage into a difficult family, could be the ruin of her young life. It was a decision that usually took careful consideration and thought by the parents. Fiorine's parents had accepted the first and only offer made to them. She was fortunate that she was marrying a kind and gentle man.

When the service was over, the entire congregation poured out of the church and headed for Arsen's family's home, where tables sagging with food and dozens of jugs of wine awaited them.

Some people sailed regally ahead in hired carriages. Victoria's and Margaret's families sauntered along together on foot. By the time they arrived, Leon and his musicians had already begun to play. Five or six lively people had joined hands and were dancing and urging the crowd to join them. The line of dancers soon expanded to forty or more, who wove their way through the spectators in time to the music. Both the dancers and watchers applauded, when the song came to an end.

Arsen's father poured wine for the adults, who became louder and more spirited than before. Victoria and Margaret happily merged into their group of friends, who were standing nearby.

"Grace, I'm so glad you're back," Victoria said, warmly clasping the hands of her school friend. She had been away all summer. "Did your uncle return from America? I remember you said he was due back by fall."

Grace's smile instantly faded. "No, he was turned away when he came through customs."

"Why? What happened?"

"They accused him of being a revolutionary and deported him. Father's very upset. Uncle is his youngest brother, and now he may never see him again. I feel sad, too. I was only four when he left, but I still remember how he used to sing to me and chase me in the yard."

Nikol had told Victoria that any Armenian trying to return to Ottoman Turkey ran the risk of being barred re-entry, because many Armenians took out citizenship papers while in America. As a United States citizen, the Armenian was immune to arrest or punishment for political activities. In the past, the Turkish government had ignored the Armenian's new rights, jailed him, torn up his passport, and refused him the opportunity to contact American officials. But the United States government had learned of these Ottoman practices and intervened on behalf of its new citizens, reaching a compromise that allowed the Turks to refuse the return of any suspected revolutionary or anyone otherwise judged undesirable. The problem was that this law merely required suspicion, not evidence, of sedition and the Turks used it capriciously on anyone. Grace's uncle had left Turkey on a pleasure trip. He was not a *Dashnak* member, had no association with any revolutionary group, yet he would never see his home again.

Victoria thought about what Grace had just told her and about what she had witnessed on the last day of school. She realized that she still had much to learn.

Later, she danced. Eventually she put away her somber mood. But she did not forget.

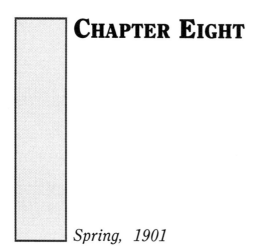

CHAPTER EIGHT

Spring, 1901

*V*ictoria stopped and wiped a pencil smudge from her face. She took a deep breath. Arm in arm, she and Margaret stepped out of the school door for the last time.

In the courtyard, the girls stopped and looked at each other. Victoria's eyes reddened. Margaret laid her head on her best friend's shoulder. They continued on. The waiting cluster of their classmates parted and enfolded them in its midst.

Martin punched Victoria lightly on her shoulder. He smiled broadly. "We did it. We graduated."

"Yes, they'll be posting the results soon. I'm not sure how I did on that last exam, so I don't know where I'll place." Victoria stopped suddenly. "Oh, what does it matter now?"

Martin nodded and laughed. "I don't know how I'll ever read another book without you to worry me into it."

Victoria had heard that another friend David, was going to school in England next year. Imagine, going to school in Europe. She looked at him. His thirteen-year-old face had abruptly paled and he looked scared. She touched his arm. "You'll be all right."

She thought about her own plans for school next year and understood how David felt. She was going to Euphrates College, in Mezireh. Her father was going to announce it to the village next week at a party. But, because the college was more than a two-hour ride from her house, she would have to board there. To be away from her parents and Nikol for months at a time: How would she stand it.? Now it was her turn to look scared.

She looked around her circle of friends. Their numbers had grown smaller over the last three years as some of her classmates, whose parents had needed their help at home, had been forced to end their education. Three of the boys who had stayed in school were going away to college next year, too. Rebecca and Grace would pass the next two years until they were married, by staying home, helping their mothers and working on their needlepoint.

The courtyard emptied of the younger children, but Victoria and her friends stayed on, reluctant to leave the school that had become so precious to them. The sun was beginning to set by the time they parted.

"What did your mother say when your father told her?" Margaret said, when they were out of earshot of the others.

Victoria fanned herself with her free hand. "*Whew.* I've never seen her get angry with him before. I feel so guilty."

Margaret grimaced. "It sounds like what went on at my house. I feel bad, too, but just think how many children we will be able to help some day when we are teachers."

"I keep reminding myself of that when I think about my mother. I know she's worried that no one will want to marry me if I go to college. My father told her not to worry about that. I guess he knows I don't care about getting married."

No, she didn't care about marriage. She had a more important mission in mind. Education. She had been given the opportunity to learn, but how many other children hadn't? Many villages didn't have schools and even when funds could be found to set them up, there weren't enough teachers to staff them. Who would she have become if she hadn't had all these years of education? Who could the others have become if they had?

This morning, her father and Nikol had been talking about something that had happened in the mountains of Turkey in the district of Sasun. Was it another massacre? She thought about the massacre that had killed Nikol's mother and about the Ottoman law that allowed the Turks and Kurds to rob and kill without punishment. Her teachers had told her that their people could change these laws if they knew how to. But for this they needed skills, the kind of skills one developed through education. And, her teachers had explained, they needed knowledge so they would know they had a right to expect better.

Yes, she would endure the pain of being away from her family to help her people, as Miss Abovian and the people who had taught her had done. She would learn to feel her parent's love across the miles. She would miss her long talks with Nikol, but she would be back someday.

It was almost dark, when Victoria reached the dirt path to her house. In the distance, she could see her mother standing in the door, silhouetted by the glowing lanterns inside. She hurried to her.

"Were you worried?" Victoria said. She wrapped her arms around her mother.

Seta held Victoria at an arm's length and looked at her sternly. "Of course, we were. You know you're not allowed out after dark. Father and Nikol were about to start out after you."

"Are we having dinner tonight or not?" Koren said.

Victoria laughed and walked into the house. "I thought you were worried about me."

"I was. You're home now, so I'm not. I'm hungry."

As the family ate, Victoria talked about her school friends and their plans for the next year. She and Margaret were the only girls who were going on with their education.

"I'm so glad you girls will be there together. I couldn't stand the thought of you going alone. I'm having enough trouble with you going at all."

Victoria looked from her mother to her father. Was her mother still angry? She thought about their college discussion. No, her mother had never really been angry. She had been worried. Worried out of love. Victoria leaned over and kissed her mother's cheek. "I know. It'll be hard for me to be away from home, too."

Seta hugged her daughter. "The other girls in your class will be getting married in a year or two and they'll be leaving home then, too." She shook her head. "I'm noticing that more and more of the parents in our village are letting their children help decide who they're going to marry. In my day, hardly any did. Most girls just married whomever their parents chose for them. I was lucky my parents weren't like that. But then, of course, the person my parents chose for me, I wanted, too." She turned and smiled at Koren.

Koren smiled back.

It was a relief to know her mother was no longer angry. But how would she react when her father made his announcement to the community?

Nikol watched Victoria as she opened the new book Koren had brought back from Mezireh. It was a book of maps that she had asked him to buy. Nikol slid to her side and gazed at the page she had open in front of her. It showed all of Europe. Her face held a serious expression.

Nikol knew God had been watching him that day five

years ago, when He had led him past Koren's house. He had everything he wanted here. Books, as many as a rich man would have. Koren bought some in Mezireh and had Michael Damadian buy others in the capitol. He had books on history, books on farming. They even had a book by a Russian writer about Napoleon's invasion of Russia.

Yes, he had everything he wanted here. He loved Koren and Seta like his own parents. He cast a quick glance at Victoria's face. It was a face that had fulfilled all the beauty hinted at in childhood. It had lost its roundness and the facial bones, now sharply defined, highlighted her delicate features and large brown eyes. It was a face that would one day belong to him.

Nikol had heard Koren telling Seta about college and knew that Koren had not told Seta about their arrangement. He understood. If Koren told Seta, he would have to tell Victoria. Why tell her about something that wouldn't happen for many years? And Nikol didn't mind waiting while Victoria went on to school and even for her to teach for a few years first. There was no hurry. He was only eighteen and his place in Koren's house was secure. And he believed in what Victoria was doing. Believed in it as one solution to their problems. But it was not his solution. His solution was a man's solution and it lay with the *Dashnak*s.

The *Dashnak*s, or federation of revolutionaries, had been established in 1890 but its roots were formed five years

before in the Armenakan Party, the first Armenian political
party. The Armenakan Party had been established in 1885
with the aim of winning, through revolution, the right of
Armenian self-rule. Its plan was to train Armenian men to
defend themselves against the Ottoman Empire's terrorism.
The party also trusted that the European powers would eventually intervene and free them from Turkish misrule.

Over the next five years, other revolutionary groups
sprang up until the *Dashnak* party was formed as an umbrel-
la organization for all the groups. One faction, the
Hunchaks, split away not long after they joined, because of
philosophical differences. The Hunchaks, the Armenian word
for bell, believed in socialism, the *Dashnak*s leaned toward
nationalism. However, both parties accepted the necessity of
using force to achieve their aims, a necessity reconfirmed by
every episode of violence.

One horrifying incident took place in 1894 in the mountainous district of Sasun. The governor, a corrupt man, had
been demanding exorbitant taxes from the men of Sasun, jail-
ing any who could not pay. In desperation, they had been
borrowing from money lenders, at three hundred percent
interest, and losing their lands when they were unable to
meet the payments. One day, the men stood up to the governor and refused to pay. In response, the governor sent
troops. But the Armenians fought back so the governor
decided to make an example out of them. He enlisted the
help of a tribe of migratory Kurds, who agreed to attack,

probably thinking it would be an easy kill and rich plunder. It wasn't. The villagers withdrew to the nearby mountains and held the Kurds off with handmade weapons. Then the governor reinforced the Kurds with three thousand soldiers, who pursued the Armenians, ruthlessly. Children were dashed against rocks, pregnant women mutilated and men bayoneted to death. In the end, nearly three thousand lay dead. A priest had negotiated and been promised safety for himself and his parishioners, if they agreed to give themselves up. He led his trusting parishioners down the mountain and they were brutally slaughtered, shortly after surrendering.

When news of these events leaked out to the world, Europeans cried out for reforms. As usual, the Turks made promises to change — as usual, they did not keep their promises. Revolutionary leaders were born and membership in revolutionary parties grew. With it, grew the people's longing for liberation.

One revolutionary leader named Serop turned his attention, in 1895, to the traumatized villages of Sasun and recruited the surviving men there to fight with him. Armenian husbands and fathers joined him, but out of desperation more than bravery. The government had promised to institute changes in the Treaty of Berlin but had not. These men had watched as their beautiful hillside pastures were seized by money lenders. They had waded their feet in cool mountain streams that flowed to the Tigris river and known that these waters would never again be theirs. They had seen their wives and children starve to death. Finally, they had witnessed the murders of their relatives and neighbors by government troops. They had nowhere to go, and nothing left to lose, so they joined the *Dashnak* guerrillas.

Serop led his bands on a series of raids, until they had ousted the Ottoman government officials in Sasun and established self-rule. But, a year ago, Serop had been poisoned and died. A new leader had been chosen and the news of it had just reached the *Dashnak*s in Kharpert. The leader's name was Andranik.

Andranik was thirty-six years old and had been battling the Turks since he was twenty-three. He had been fighting in the mountainous district of Sasun under Serop since 1895 and had commanded men from thirty-eight villages during that time. When Serop was killed last year, Andranik himself had hunted down Serop's killer and assassinated him. He was a brilliant strategist, winning battle after battle. The Turks called Andranik a *fedayi*s, an Islamic term of respect for a man so dedicated that he was prepared to die for his faith.

In a barn late that night, Koren listened with his fellow *Dashnak* members, as Nikol prepared to read the newsletter that announced Andranik's appointment.

Nikol hopped up and sat on the gate to a stall. He opened the paper. Avedis Halabian stood beside him holding a lantern. Nikol read aloud.

"The Turks had Andranik and his men trapped in a monastery, and what did they do?" He slapped his thigh with the newsletter and grinned. "They put on the uniforms of the captured Turkish officers and walked right past the soldiers."

Michael Damadian stood. "I heard when he was at the party headquarters in Tiflis last year, the party leaders all ceded to *his* opinion."

"Well, we know he knows how to use weapons. I heard he has killed over one hundred men himself," Avedis Halabian said.

"One hundred men? No, I don't believe it."

"Yes, it's true. They say in battle when the Turks have their guns pointed in one direction, he comes up behind them and *pfft*, they're gone."

"I heard the Turks have a price on his head."

Koren laughed as the men shared stories of the *Dashnak* hero, but he silently worried. He thought about what had happened in Constantinople after the revolutionaries had taken over the Ottoman bank. He shivered. Two years ago, he had carried Nikol's second letter to the *Dashnak*s in Mezireh. Thank God, it had not come back to haunt them. But what would be the price to the men in the mountains for their acts of rebellion? What would be the price to all Armenians? When you anger the Turks, they do what bullies do — they vent their anger on anyone weaker than them. No, maybe not tomorrow, but someday.

Koren looked around the barn at the roomful of men he loved like brothers. Over the last five years, their numbers had tripled as they had in every other village and city in the Armenian provinces. Levon Kalustian had joined them last year, as had his son and many of the other young men of their village. Yes, Koren would contribute what money he could toward arms for their comrades in the mountains, but he would not sleep easily at night knowing that the Turks were unlikely to forget their humiliation at the hands of the *Dashnaks*.

Seta awoke on Sunday morning sweating. Had summer come early this year? She sat up. No, it was still spring. She was just nervous. Today she and Koren were giving Victoria a big party. The entire village was invited. Outwardly, the party was Victoria's name day party — the day of the year everyone with her name celebrated. But the real purpose of the party was to announce their plans to send her to college. "We might as well tell the whole village at once," Koren had said. "They'll all be talking about it, anyway." Oh, what would her friends say? Seta's hands became clumsy and she dropped a plait of hair that she was braiding.

Koren came to her, took her chin in his hand and tilted her head upwards. "You know, Seta, a lot has changed in our village over the last five years. More of our children are going to school. Michael is sending Margaret to college, too. I even heard that the widow Filor Krikorian is running her husband's bakery."

Seta sighed. No, not everyone still clung to the old ways, but many did. She herself balanced on the edge of both groups. And sending a girl to college was an extreme idea for everyone. They were all bound to talk. Koren didn't mind what people said, but she did.

The guests were dancing at Victoria's party, when Koren stepped in front of Leon and his musicians. He signaled to Leon. The music stopped and people listened.

Seta clasped her hands in front of her and looked down. Koren stood straight.

He held up his drink. "Today we celebrate our Victoria and all others who share her name."

The guests nodded and raised their glasses back.

Koren continued. "Today, we also honor our children who just graduated from school. And today..."

He stopped.

Seta still stared at her hands. A few of the guests looked at her curiously.

Koren cleared his throat. His eyes scanned the crowd. He took a deep breath. "Seta and I are proud to announce that we are sending Victoria on to college next year."

There was a stunned silence.

Koren looked at Seta. Her cheeks were a deep red, but she straightened up, lifted her chin and stared straight ahead. He smiled at her.

"To my daughter." Koren tipped his head back and drank his *raki* in one burning shot. He remained where he was

standing, feet planted firmly apart. All around him, his
guests broke out in an uproar.

"What good is college to a girl?"

"A girl can teach. You know we need more teachers."

"Teachers, humph, let the boys do the teaching."

Levon Kalustian walked up to Koren and clapped him on
the shoulder. "Congratulations. Honestly, I can't say I would
have let Rebecca do the same, but the best of luck to your
Victoria."

Cousin Rose walked past Seta and cast her a look of
gloating outrage. Araxie went to Seta and stood beside her.
They turned as a unit to face the guests, who by now were
clustered in groups of three and four.

"Who do they think they are? They're going to give the
girl airs."

"They've spoiled her completely. I wouldn't want her for
my son now."

Mary Halabian stood with Fiorine and her mother-in-law.
They looked at each other, covered their mouths, and
laughed.

"Good for them," Mary said.

Fiorine lowered her voice and said, "Why not? She's a
smart girl. Why should they have to pretend she isn't."

"Let's go help Seta. Those old women standing in front
of her look like they're going to melt her into nothing. Look,
one of them is pointing her finger in Seta's face."

"I'm surprised my mother isn't with her." Fiorine looked

around and spotted her mother's furrowed brow and gleaming eyes in a trio of white-haired matrons. "No, never mind, that's not her way. You two go help Seta. I need to have a few words with my mother."

Mary Halabian and Fiorine's mother-in-law hurried to Seta and slid between the wall of ladies in front of her. Each took a hand. Seta smiled, softly. Mary nodded in Fiorine's direction. Seta looked and saw Fiorine approach her mother with her hands on her hips. She scowled and said something. Rose and her friends looked surprised. They looked around them. Fiorine said something more. They colored and moved off in different directions.

Mary gave a similar look to Seta's attackers and they, too, slunk away.

Seta squeezed Mary's hand. "Thank you. I told Koren this would cause quite a commotion, but he insisted. Look at him there, laughing, pouring everyone drinks. I don't think the men with him are even talking about it anymore."

"No, my Charles is with them," Mary said. "Charles will keep them talking for the rest of the day about America."

Koren refilled Charles's glass and grinned at the group of men. "I'll bet he didn't get *raki* as fine as this in America."

"No, I didn't," Charles said. "And I wasn't sure I'd be getting back home to get any more. Did you hear what happened when I tried to get off the boat?"

The men all moved closer together.

Charles looked from side to side and went on. "They pulled me into a room and started questioning me about being an enemy of the government. I thought I was done for. You know I never got my citizenship papers in America, so I had nowhere to go for help."

Nikol clenched his fist. "They knew they had you."

Charles bit his lip. "They almost did. But when they left me with a guard and went off to get their superior, I slipped the man a big bribe and he let me go. It was probably two weeks salary for him and it was a lot of money for me, too. You know I never had anything to do with the *Dashnak*s before, but I tell you, I'm going to join now."

Nikol grasped his arm. "I'm glad you're joining us and I'm glad you made it back."

Michael Damadian shook his head. "What I don't understand is why the government passed that law two years ago, forbidding us from leaving the country. If the Turks hate us so, why don't they *want* us to leave?"

Koren thought about Sasun, General Andranik, and the *Dashnak*'s overthrow of the government agents in the mountains. A scary question. Why didn't the Turks want them to leave?

In their own corner, Victoria and Margaret entertained Grace, Rebecca and David. Her friend, Adrienne, who was a year older, walked up to the group and announced her engagement to a young man whose parents owned a silk-making factory in Mezireh. She had just returned home from a visit to the city.

After congratulating her, Victoria said, "Mezireh is where I'm going to college. What is it like?"

"The city is big and the whole thing is like the center of our village, full of shops and businesses."

Margaret looked at Victoria, then said, "Did you see the college?"

"Oh yes, it's lovely." Adrienne looked at her friends and her eyes softened. "Don't worry. You won't feel like you're in the middle of the city at Euphrates College. It has its own grounds with school buildings and dormitories. It's surrounded by a tall stone fence. I peaked though the iron gate across the walkway and saw students studying together out on the lawn. They looked happy. I could see a windmill turning in the breeze. My father told me it pumps the water they use. You'll love being there. And, of course, you'll be coming home again." Adrienne stopped. Her lip quivered.

Yes, unlike Adrienne, Victoria would be coming home again.

She looked around at the rolling hills and fields. Soon the fields would be ready to be plowed and seeded. She could see them, as they looked in every season. Summer, when the wheat grew in tender and green, fall, when the sun had coaxed it into a golden sea of color and winter, when the fields lay sleeping beneath a blanket of snow. She heard the sheep baaing and could almost feel in her hands the rich oily wool sheared from their backs each spring. She saw the orchards that would bear the crisp tart apples they picked every fall and the apricots that dripped down their chins in the summer. She saw the vegetable garden and remembered the feel of its moist black soil against her bare feet. She remembered biting into a soft red tomato just plucked from its vine. She gazed at the stone house, tucked into the side of the hill. She saw the holidays they celebrated there, the parties they gave and the guests they entertained. She saw Seta and Koren laughing, and Nikol reading his book. She remembered running to the house's comforting warmth on snowy winter days and the long nights spent around the table teasing her father over games of backgammon. Suddenly, as if a picture were coming into focus, she knew that this was her home and she would never leave it. She might wander temporarily to go to college, but never would she be parted from it permanently.

Margaret looked at Victoria. Then she put her arm around her.

Victoria looked from Adrienne to Grace and Rebecca's frightened faces. Adrienne would be married a year from now. Grace and Rebecca also would soon be wives and mothers. Victoria's parents had given her many years to grow and experience her life.

A baby cried and she realized that baby might one day be her pupil. She felt the same excitement she used to experience on the first day of school. She spotted her parents' serious faces, as they talked with their friends. Her mother had once said that a good parent wants their child to be happy. Her parents had taken a daring step by allowing her to pursue her dream.

CHAPTER NINE

Spring, 1901

A knife blazed in the orange sunlight. But in whose hand was it ? Koren's? The dark turbaned man's? She struggled to see. The sun disappeared and she couldn't distinguish one from the other. She could see only their shadowy silhouettes. Another flash of a knife as it descended down, down, down. A man screamed.

Seta sat bolt upright in bed.

She looked around. Koren lay sleeping beside her. She put her hand on her chest and tried to steady her breathing.

She had had part of this dream before. But never had it ended this way. And what was the ending? Who had prevailed?

She lay back down.

And waited.

Waited for daylight to calm her beating heart.

Koren checked the girth on his horse's saddle for the last time, before he mounted.

He leaned forward and called through the open door to the house, "Well, I'm off."

Seta ran out of the door with a cloth-wrapped package in her arms. "All right, don't say it. I know it is a lot of food, but you might need it, if you don't get to the city by dinnertime."

The pallor of her skin and dark circles under her eyes were hidden for a moment in her smile.

"Seta, I'll be there before lunch time. There are plenty of food stands in the city where I can buy bread and cheese."

"How do I know how good it is? Maybe the cheese hasn't been made properly." Seta frowned. "Someone has to look out for you."

"For me?" Koren laughed. Then he squinted down at Seta's face. "Are you all right?"

Seta looked away. "Yes, I just slept poorly last night. You go. I'll be fine. But promise me you'll be careful."

Koren reached down and touched the tip of Seta's nose. "Yes, I'll be careful, my sweet."

Seta nodded and smiled again.

Victoria and Nikol stepped out of the door.

"Good-bye Papa." Victoria lifted her chin, put her fingers

to her lips and kissed them.

Nikol waved.

Seta put one arm around Victoria and the other around Nikol. She watched as Koren reached the road and turned one last time to wave good-bye.

She stood staring, until he was a tiny speck in the distance.

And sighed.

It was in God's hands now.

Victoria swept her last pile of dirt out the door. She shaded her eyes and saw Fiorine walking up the path. Eighteen-month-old Anton toddled at her side and her six-month-old daughter was in her arms. Their tapestry project. Today was the day they were going to work on it together.

"How is my little *moog*?" Victoria said.

Anton dropped his mother's hand and ran to Victoria. Victoria lifted him into the air and kissed his chubby cheeks.

Fiorine laughed. "Anton, Auntie and I are going to work on our sewing now."

Victoria drew the square of fabric from her trunk and ran her hands over its textured surface. "We've done a lot."

"It's beautiful Victoria. Your design is as good as any artist's."

The two sat on the steps. Their needles dipped in and out of the material in front of them.

Seta came out and took the baby from Fiorine's lap. She

smiled into the infant's face, then slipped Anton a wedge of *halvah*, a sweet pasty-type sesame candy.

Victoria looked at her mother letting Anton chase her around the yard. At least she didn't look pale and tired anymore. Every time her father went to the city, her mother got so nervous. And what was there to be so nervous about? He traveled to the city every week and sometimes more. He knew the roads, knew how to protect himself, too.

Victoria looked at the sun directly overhead. By now, he would have made it to the city, so really there was nothing more to worry about.

Koren had, in fact, just reached Mezireh. Wonderful Mezireh, bustling and alive with merchants. He could buy anything he wanted here, from household goods to hand-tailored clothing.

His horse clopped down narrow streets, until he reached the small inn where he planned to stay the night. The inn merely provided a place to sleep, so he pulled a rolled woolen blanket from behind his saddle and claimed a space for himself by depositing it in a corner of the large sleeping area. He flipped open his pocket watch. Time to get to the business that had brought him here. He had documents to deliver to people all over the large, spread-out city. And he had to go to the courthouse, the central post office, too.

The post office was just three blocks away. He would head there first. He meandered down streets crowded with two-story dwellings. The first floor of most were shops, whose owners lived above. He passed a dry goods store and a tobacco shop, then stepped on a sharp stone that he felt through the thin, worn soles of his boots. Time for a new pair. He detoured to his favorite leather goods store.

He opened the door, threw back his head, and inhaled the pungent scent of leather. He sighed with pleasure. The shop owner recognized his loyal customer and immediately rushed to greet Koren and lead him to a wooden bench.

Koren lowered himself down and planted his foot in front of him. This craftsman was the very best. Why just look at the way the man measured his foot over and over again. These new boots were sure to fit him perfectly. And the leather, it was like velvet.

Koren extracted a gold piece from the pouch strapped onto his belt and paid the merchant in full.

"I'll be back in two weeks. Will my boots be ready by then?"

"I'll make sure they are, my friend. It will be a pleasure to work on this fine piece of leather you selected."

Koren thanked the shoemaker and proceeded out the door. He sniffed again. This time he took in the garlic scent of falafel frying in a street vender's stand. He bought a pita-wrapped sandwich from the man and bit into its crispy mixture. Suddenly, he thought of home. Truly, he loved the city, loved the food, the busy excitement, but not enough to live here. To be able to visit a few times a month was a pleasure but, really, his heart belonged to the little stone house set among the quiet fields and peacefully grazing animals.

He stopped at a silversmith's shop and peered inside. The craftsman was meticulously tapping at a conical piece of silver with a small rounded hammer. Slowly, the malleable metal was turning into a small bowl. He glanced frequently at a sketch tacked down on the table in front of him. Koren squinted to get a better look and saw a drawing of a teapot, coffee urn, sugar bowl, and cream pitcher — all set on a large, ornate tray. The artisan worked steadily, never once glancing at his spectator. Koren looked over his shoulder, as he walked away and saw that another shopper had taken his place at the window.

He continued walking and made his way to the post office. Once inside the cool stone building, he waited his turn, then stepped up to the clerk.

"I have some letters to send out," he said in Turkish.

He stared out the window, while he waited for the postal worker to process his letters. Across from the post office, his eye lingered on a boarded-up shop. A reminder of the massacre that had swept through the provinces six years ago. There were many fine shops in Mezireh, but interspersed among them were other grim remnants of the disaster or the unfair tax system from which those merchants were unable to survive. His people had so much to contribute. Why didn't their government encourage them? Or why, at the very least, did they not end the destruction and corrupt taxation?

Unhindered, his people could make these plains into a Mecca of the Middle East.

Koren concluded his business in the post office and pushed back out through the swinging doors onto the stone steps in front. It was late afternoon. He had been in the post office more than an hour. He sighed. Why not leave the rest until tomorrow? He paused for a moment to decide and was startled by a familiar voice.

"Koren, where have you been? I haven't seen you since last fall."

Zaven, the tailor. His old friend and *Dashnak* brother.

"Zaven, it's good to see you." Koren put his arm around his friend's shoulder.

"Well, it's good to see you again, too. I'm on my way to the coffeehouse. Come with me." Zaven looked around and lowered his voice. "I'm meeting two other brothers there who have something you will want."

That settled it. Koren nodded and followed Zaven down the street.

A few minutes later, he entered the smoke-filled coffeehouse with Zaven and stared through the cloudy haze. Men sat sipping steaming hot coffee. Some leaned forward with their elbows on the table and talked to each other. Others played cards. Two men looked up and waved from their corner table. Koren and Zaven picked their way over to them.

One of the men at the table looked over his shoulder and spoke in a quiet tone. "Koren, I'm glad to see you. We have something for you to take back to the village."

Koren kept his expression neutral. He waited. Then he felt a paper pass under the table and land on his lap. He kept his eyes on the man, while he stuffed it into his saddlebag. He leaned forward. "Is it from...?"

"Yes." The other man again looked over his shoulder and leaned closer still. "It's a newsletter from the *Dashnak*s. I don't have to tell you this, but be careful There's some very sensitive information in there."

Koren looked horrified. "They wouldn't be so foolish as to print anything about the assassination plan would they?"

The man shook his head vigorously. "Oh no, no, those plans are passed on by word of mouth only, and then just in the most trusted circles. My source in the capitol tells me that they are working on it."

Koren frowned. "It has been a long time."

"And it will be longer still. Another year. Maybe even two. They have to wait until the time is right. But they like the plan. They're all still amazed at how clever it is. That's a smart boy you have there, Koren."

Koren beamed. "Yes, his brother can be very proud of him, too. So what is in this newsletter that is so--" Koren stopped and looked up at the waiter, who had arrived. He didn't know all the people in the cafe. It was smarter to be careful.

When the waiter left, all four men leaned together again.

"There's an article in there about helping out Andranik

and his men in the mountains. We are going to use the money the *Dashnak*s in America have raised to buy weapons for them."

"Good." It was good, but it was risky, too. But it was a risk worth taking and better than standing by and allowing the Turks to terrorize his people.

Koren went to bed early that night, but a few hours later was rousted from sleep by the loud voices of the other men sharing the room with him.

He sat up and slapped the floor. "Keep it down, will you?"

One of the men lit a cigarette, then he passed a flask to the man sitting next to him. "Sure, we'll keep it down." He grinned crookedly in Koren's direction.

They didn't keep it down though, and Koren was awakened two more times during the night. The next morning, he had to drag himself out of bed. He glared in the direction of his passed-out roommates and made no effort to be quiet, while he packed his belongings.

One of the men stirred, as he was leaving.

"Be careful traveling today," he said, still slurring his words. "Two days ago a merchant and his apprentice were attacked and killed by bandits."

"Thanks for the warning," Koren said. He would have liked to have told them that it was going to be hard to be careful when he was so tired, but what was the point? And he wasn't worried, not really, though he would be careful, as he always was.

The morning passed quickly as Koren went methodically about his business. He stopped last to buy gold for Mr. Sayabovian, the village jeweler. He withdrew a note from his bag and handed it to the dealer.

"Mr. Adanalian," the gold merchant said. "What a pleasure. We haven't seen you in months."

"Yes, the winter — well, you know. But my daughter is going to school here next fall, so I'll be here more often."

"Your daughter? School?"

"Yes."

"Oh...Well, then..." The merchant coughed. "Well, let me get you that gold."

Koren listened to the man's heels tap along the marble floor leading to his vault. He would have to get used to those looks people gave him when they heard he was educating his daughter. The merchant returned a few minutes later with a packet of the precious metal. Koren weighed it in his hand, nodded and slipped it into his sack. He turned to leave, but stopped and walked back to the counter.

"Who are those two men?" Koren jerked his head in the direction of the window.

The merchant looked and shook his head. "I don't know them."

"That's what I thought. I'm going to have to keep my eye on them." Koren drew out his chest and marched out the door with long firm strides.

When he was half way down the street, he glanced over

his shoulder.

The two men were following him.

He quickened his pace, zigzagged along and made sudden turns down side streets, forcing the men to reveal the fact that they were following him. But the men were not deterred. Koren ducked into a dry goods store and looked out the window. The two leaned against a lamppost and smirked back.

Koren turned to the shopkeeper. "Is there a back door out of here?"

The shopkeeper looked out at the two men. His lips compressed.

"Go through that curtain there." He gestured to the back of the store. "You will find a storeroom. On the other side is a door that opens to a back alley. Knock on the door of the building directly behind me and tell them that David sent you. They will let you go out through their front door."

Koren walked toward the back of the store.

Another clerk blocked the window with his body and began carrying on a loud, one-way conversation as if he were trying to sell Koren some goods. He continued while Koren slipped through the curtain.

"Good luck," the merchant called softly.

It was not luck that had kept Koren safe up to this point in his life.

In the alley, Koren banged on the door of the building behind him with both fists. A worried looking, heavy-set man opened it. A woman and young boy stood behind him peering over his shoulder.

"David sent me," Koren said. "Two Turks are following me. I need to lose them. Can I go out through your front door?"

The man's brow settled into a gleaming frown. He stepped aside.

Koren ran through the shop and out to the street where he continued to crisscross his way through town until he was standing in front of the inn.

He looked over his shoulder.

The men were gone.

Thank God.

He dashed into the stable, tacked up his horse and was out of town at a gallop. He didn't slow his pace until he was well out of sight of the city. He took a deep breath and smiled. Yes, he knew how to take care of himself. He yawned. A few hours ride and he would be back in the village by dinner time, then a good night's sleep.

He sensed it before he saw it, but his reaction was a beat too slow. He turned and a rock caught him full force across his forehead. The two men jumped out from behind a bush. Koren slid from his horse, seemingly in slow motion. How had they found him? He had been so sure he had eluded them.

But he hadn't grown up Armenian in a hostile empire and learned nothing about self-defense. Fully alert now, he sprang to his feet almost before he hit the ground and his hand went to his side. He pulled out his knife, spread his legs wide apart, and raised his right hand.

The two men looked from the knife in Koren's hand to the expression on his face. The grins on their faces faded. One drew a dagger from the sheath at his waist.

They had him outnumbered. Koren glanced around at the desolate surroundings. He would have no help from anyone here. It was up to him. He stood his ground. His opponent's dagger came at him. He jumped aside and as the man lunged, he lost his balance and stumbled forward. Now was Koren's chance. He plunged his own knife into the back of the stumbling man. The man's eyes widened briefly and he collapsed on the ground.

The second man didn't wait for his companion to hit the ground. He leapt at Koren and knocked the knife out of his hand. The two wrestled each other to the ground.

Koren struggled for footing and attempted to stand. His opponent was strong, as strong as he was himself. But that dagger lying in the dead man's hand could be his edge. He leapt for it. His opponent did, too. He reached it before Koren did. Koren ducked and raised his arm in defense. The knife cut into the flesh of his left forearm, drawing a deep wound. *I'm going to die*, Koren thought. The dagger came at him again. He jumped out of the way. He must reach his own knife. He backed toward it keeping his eyes on his attacker. There it was, gleaming in the sunlight beside him. He grabbed it and instantly straightened up, but not quickly enough. His assailant lunged at him, plunging his dagger deeply into Koren's abdomen and quickly withdrawing it. What harm the dagger had done was of little consequence at the moment. He was alive. Blood spurted and Koren backed away. But he tripped and fell. Looking up, he saw the dagger coming at him for the last time.

Seta straightened from the tomato plant she was weeding and shaded her eyes. Nikol was traipsing in from the fields. She brushed her hands together and the soil on them sprayed into the air. She looked up at the sun. Koren would be home soon. She must clean up in a hurry, so she could set out the late afternoon snacks he enjoyed so much.

She went to the pump with a wash basin. When she stepped back into the house, she said to Victoria and Nikol, "Why don't you two go outside and watch for Papa? The sun is starting to set. He will be home any time now."

"Don't you need me in here?" Victoria said.

"No dear. Go on out and sit. It's a lovely day. You can just about smell the sweetness of the evening breeze." Her eyes sparkled. "Let's have a picnic when Papa gets back."

Victoria clapped her hands together. "Oh, a picnic, yes."

She tapped Nikol's shoulder. "Come, I'll race you there."

"Victoria." Seta shook her head but Victoria was already off at a run.

Nikol grinned at Seta and dashed after Victoria. They

arrived at the grassy flat that overlooked the road and sat down. Victoria smiled at Nikol. "This is where I was sitting when I first met you."

"Yes, I remember that day. I was only about the age you are now." His smile faded. "That was a very bad time in my life."

"Are you thinking about your family?"

"Yes, my family and some other things."

She touched his arm.

He sighed. "It was the worst time in my life. My parents had died and I was a failure. I couldn't take care of Anna and Stephan. I had to leave them in the care of strangers. It's been almost six years, and still not a day goes by that I don't wonder what's become of them. Someday, I want to find them."

"Someday, you will."

Nikol studied Victoria's face, then he smiled.

Seta came out with a tray in her hands and a thin blanket draped over one of her arms.

"Papa's not back yet? I'm surprised. If he stopped in the village, I'm going to be most displeased."

"Mother, don't get mad yet. He's often later than this."

Seta laughed. "You're right."

The three sat chatting comfortably. As it grew later, Seta joined in less. Finally, she was silent all together. Her face settled into a worried frown and her eyes became fixed on the road.

"Mother, really, you worry all the time. And for what? I bet he ran into someone he needed to talk to in the village."

Seta frowned. "And here we are waiting for him. Well, that talk cost him his stuffed grape leaves." She popped the last one in her mouth. "I might as well go in the house and put dinner on the table. It will be too dark to eat out here by the time he gets home."

She stood, retied her apron and marched into the house.

Nikol looked at Victoria and rolled his eyes. "She's going to have a few words for him, when he gets home."

Victoria laughed. "Oh, she won't say anything to him, but he'll know."

"I bet he's doing more than talking. I bet he's having a drink with someone."

Victoria nodded. "Maybe two."

"Lets have a game of backgammon, while we're waiting."

"Wonderful. Papa can play the winner." Her eyes danced. "Me."

"Well, we'll see about that."

Nikol went into the house and returned with the Koren's backgammon board. The two rolled the dice and teased each other through a game.

It was almost dark, when Victoria squinted and spied a horse plodding down the road in the distance. It seemed to have a rider, but the rider was laying forward, arms draped about the horse's neck.

"That's him," she said. "*Ouff,* from the way he's riding, I think he did stop in the village to have some *raki*. Too much." She raised her voice and directed it at the door to the house. "Mother, Papa's home and I think he's had a little too much to drink."

Seta came to the door with her hands on her hips and a furrowed brow. She looked down the road. Suddenly, her expression changed. She gave a cry of alarm and began running toward her husband.

He was badly injured. When the dagger had come at him for the third and final time, he had rolled aside at the last second. It had planted, just momentarily, in the soil. But it was the reprieve he needed. He sat up, lunged forward with his uninjured right arm and buried his knife in and upwards, directly into his assailant's heart. The assailant screamed and collapsed, on top of Koren.

He had lain there, praying for the strength to push the dead man off his chest. Eventually, he had. Then he had bandaged his left arm with strips of cloth to slow down the bleeding. Fortunately, the wound in his abdomen was only oozing small amounts of blood. He stood up painfully, and instantly felt the world shift under him. His loyal horse had returned and was standing by, waiting for his master. Somehow, Koren dredged up the energy to climb onto the horse. He immediately fell forward, unable even to sit up.

He was too weak to direct it, but the sturdy horse steadily nosed its way home. And he wanted to make it home. He would make it home. His mount had been traveling this route for years. Koren slipped in and out of consciousness, surfacing only briefly in response to the deep pain created by occasional jostling over the uneven roads.

Strong arms lifted him down. His eyes fluttered open. He looked up the hill, saw his fields, his animals and the little stone house. He was home.

CHAPTER TEN

Spring, 1901

"**W**e need a doctor. *Now.*" Seta backed her way up the steps carrying Koren's legs.

Nikol had his shoulders. "I'll go get one as soon as we settle him inside."

Koren moaned.

"Oh, he's in pain," Seta said.

Victoria raced past them and jerked a sleeping mat off the storage shelf. The entire pile tumbled onto the floor.

"Hurry, hurry," Seta said.

Victoria climbed over the pile and dragged her father's mattress out into the middle of the room. Seta and Nikol placed him on it. Then Seta turned to Nikol.

"The nearest doctor is three villages away. You must get

him to come tonight. And tell him to hurry."

Nikol started to rush out the door, but Seta stopped him. "Here, take this gold piece with you. Make sure he knows we can afford to pay."

She watched Nikol dash out the door and jump on the horse, who still stood at the foot of the road. The horse seemed to understand the urgency of his mission because it took off at a gallop, leaving only a cloud of dust under its thundering hoof beats.

Seta ran across the room. How serious were his injuries? She tore his shirt open and inspected his wounds. Bad, very bad.

"Victoria, get the scissors from my sewing box in the corner."

Victoria riffled through the wooden box dropping spools of thread, a thimble and a tape measure on the table, until she found what she was looking for.

"Help me turn him on his side. I'm going to cut his shirt off."

Victoria did, as she was told. She knelt at Koren's right side, grasped his left arm and brought it across his chest. Then she took the left shoulder and left knee and carefully rolled him toward her. The movement brought moans of pain from her injured father. Her eyes filled with tears. She looked at her mother.

Seta quickly sliced a seam up the back of his shirt and pulled it down over his arms. She looked more closely at the wound on his abdomen and gasped. It looked worse than she had thought.

"Get me something to bathe this with."

Victoria leapt up, grabbed a bowl and began tearing strips of cloth into it. She poured water over the cloth and brought it back to Seta.

Seta gently bathed the wound. "I hope Nikol can get the doctor to come tonight. I don't like the way this looks."

"When will he be back?"

"I don't know. The village is a thirty-minute ride from here. He has to get there, then locate the doctor. We've never had to call one before. I don't even know if he'll come."

Seta finished bathing the abdominal wound and covered it with gauze. She turned her attention next to the arm and began unrolling the strips of material Koren had wrapped around it. Another wound. Maybe not so serious, but still it had to be cleaned.

Koren awoke as Seta bathed the arm wound. He shook his head. "Oh, that stings."

Seta and Victoria gazed down at him, their faces pale. He grasped Seta's hand with his good one and said, "I was attacked about thirty minutes outside of Mezireh."

"I know, darling. Don't try to talk." Seta squeezed his hand. "We're going to get help for you. Nikol went for the doctor."

"I don't know if there's anything the doctor can do for me."

Seta blinked back tears. "Don't talk that way."

Koren's eyes met hers. "Seta, we've never had any secrets from each other. I know my injuries are serious."

Seta nodded. "Yes, they are. But we must have faith because without faith, you won't have the strength to fight this. We are going to fight this. And win."

Koren's face relaxed into a thin smile and his eyelids fluttered shut. His muscles went limp, as he lapsed back into unconsciousness.

Seta finished cleaning the arm wound and then bound it tightly in clean bandages. She walked to the door and stared out into the darkness. Where was the doctor? Would he get there in time? Or was it already too late?

She rushed back to Koren's side and stared at his chest. There, she saw it, rising and falling. He was alive. She looked at Victoria, staring at her father with her hands over her mouth, wide-eyed and pale. Seta bit her lips. She had no words to reassure her daughter with.

The minutes ticked by.

At last they heard it, the sound of gravel crunching outside.

Nikol.

Seta jumped up and threw the door open. Nikol rushed in.

"Where's the doctor? What happened?"

Nikol was breathing hard. "He's coming soon. He's was with a sick patient, but said he'd come tonight."

Seta wrung her hands. She began to pace.

Victoria and Nikol exchanged worried frowns.

Victoria went to Seta and put her arm around her. "Please, Mother. Come, sit down and eat something. You're going to need your strength."

Seta nodded and stared at the plate of food she had set out earlier. She had made *kufta*. His favorite. She felt a lump form in her throat. She pushed the plate away and went back to her husband's side.

The next two hours dragged by so slowly they felt like ten. Nikol grabbed a lantern. "I'm going to the roadside to watch for him."

Another hour went by.

Just when Seta felt she couldn't stand it another minute, she heard the sound of wagon wheels. She and Victoria smiled at each other in relief. They went to the door. The doctor pulled up in his cart with Nikol running alongside lighting the way.

"Hurry, please," Seta said. "My husband is badly injured."

The young doctor leapt out of the cart and rushed into the house. He knelt down and inspected Koren's wounds.

"What happened?"

"As nearly as we can gather, he was attacked just outside of Mezireh."

"Outside of Mezireh? How did he ever get back here?" The doctor shook his head and continued his exam.

Koren's eyes flew open and he instinctively reached for his stomach.

"I'm sorry I'm causing you so much pain. I need to determine the extent of your wounds. How are you feeling? Are you in a lot of pain?"

"I feel weak and it's difficult to talk. My head hurts terribly." Koren's eye was beginning to puff out and an angry-looking bruise had appeared on his lower jaw.

The doctor felt the side of Koren's head. Koren winced. The doctor gently lowered Koren's head back onto the pillow and replaced the bandages on his arm and stomach. Then he stood.

Seta stared at him.

He shrugged. "There's not much we can do, but watch and wait. Bathe the wounds twice a day."

Seta clutched his arm. "He'll — he'll be all right, won't he?"

"His injuries are very serious. The next few days will tell. The stab wound to his stomach looks bad. If he develops a fever, that means the bowel was punctured and he probably won't make it."

Seta gasped and sank to her knees.

Victoria hovered in the corner with her hands folded in prayer. "Please don't let my Papa die, please don't let my Papa die," she said.

Nikol squeezed his eyes shut and clenched his fists.

Seta looked up at the doctor. "What can we do for him?"

"Try to get some fluids into him. Plain broth would be best." He went to his bag and removed several packets of powder. "Also, give him one of these when he gets uncomfortable or restless. Keep him as quiet as you can."

After the doctor left, Nikol and Victoria arranged their sleeping mats. They all decided to take turns sitting with Koren.

"You two must get some rest first," Seta said. "He'll need constant care over the next few days. Victoria, I'm depending on you to do all the household chores and prepare the food. Nikol, I know you want to help in here, too, but the farm chores still need to be done."

"Don't give one thought to the farm. I'll do everything." Nikol's face spasmed in a sob. "Koren has been like a father to me. I can never repay his kindness."

Seta bowed her head and settled down beside Koren. She held his hand as he dozed. If only she could will her strength to him. Toward dawn, Victoria tiptoed over to her.

"You need some rest. Go to sleep. I'll wake you in a few hours."

Seta nodded and sank down on her mattress. Fatigue overcame her anxiety and she fell into a brief, but deep sleep.

She awoke three hours later. She was at Koren's side in an instant. Was it her imagination or had his face lost a little of its pallor? She reached over and placed her hand on his forehead. It was cool. Thank God.

Koren's eyes opened at Seta's touch.

"How are you feeling this morning?" Seta said.

"I don't know, a little better maybe, but I'm thirsty."

"Oh, I'll get you some broth right away. The doctor said you could have some." At last she could do something for him. She heated the cold broth she had left over from the *kufta* she had prepared and spooned it into his mouth, bit by bit.

Nikol woke up. "How is he?"

Seta's smile reached the corners of her face. "A little better."

Koren looked at Nikol. "Before you head out to the fields, come here. I have something to say to you."

Nikol went to his side.

"I do feel a little better, but it will be a long time before I'm well enough to be up and around. You're going to have to take over all the work."

"Don't worry, you can count on me." Nikol wiped a tear from his eye. "I told Seta the same thing last night. I'll do everything."

"You just rest and get better," Seta said. And he was getting better. She could see it in his face.

Koren remained alert until late afternoon, when Nikol arrived back from the fields. Then he became restless.

Seta felt his forehead. "I don't think it's much of a fever." She looked at Victoria and Nikol. Both averted their eyes. She tried to get him to take a little broth, but he complained that he felt nauseous and stopped after a few sips.

Toward evening, he began to moan softly at the slightest touch. He became more restless. No position was comfortable for him. Seta suddenly remembered the packet the doctor had given her. She jumped up and rushed to the pantry, where she had placed it for safekeeping. She returned to Koren.

"I'm going to give you the medicine the doctor left. It will help your pain." She lifted his head and placed a dose inside his mouth. Then she carefully tilted a cup of water to his lips. He swallowed it and sank back down into the bedding. Within an hour, he seemed more comfortable.

Over the next few hours, Koren woke occasionally. Seta sat at his side with Victoria and Nikol. She felt his forehead again. He didn't seem any worse. She smiled at Victoria and Nikol. This time they smiled back.

But late that night, Koren's temperature shot up again. Bacteria was slowly leaking from his intestine into his abdominal cavity and it was multiplying unchecked. He began to shiver uncontrollably. He called for more blankets.

Seta felt like crying, as she acquiesced to the request for more blankets. She remembered the doctor's words. Koren's temperature was rising out of control. When at last the shivering was over, he suddenly started fanning himself and throwing the blankets off.

"Victoria, bring me some cool water. Quickly." Seta tried to calm Koren down.

Victoria grabbed a ceramic bowl off the shelf, splashed water into it from a large clay jug and carried it to Seta.

"Help me sit him up."

Nikol rushed to Koren's side and lifted him in his strong steady arms to a sitting position. Seta rubbed his skin vigorously with a rough cloth. She must get his temperature down. Koren seemed more comfortable, after she finished. More alert, too. She nodded to Nikol. Gently, Nikol laid him back down again and Seta covered him with a sheet.

Koren looked at Seta. "Get some rest, my dear. I'll call you when I need you."

Seta started to protest. Nikol laid a hand on her arm. "I'll sit with him."

When Seta and Victoria had fallen asleep, Nikol turned to Koren. Koren was looking at him.

"Now do you have something to tell me?" Koren said.

Nikol nodded. "Before I came here, I had been in the capitol. I became involved in something. Something terribly illegal. I want to tell you about it now."

Koren smiled. "There, that's all I wanted. Do you think I haven't known all along? What does it matter to me? I've loved you like a son. I still do. What you did was brave, and good. Remember that."

Nikol started to cry. "I should have told you myself. I should have told all of you."

Koren shook his head. "Told me, but not the women. Never the women. This is men's business." He looked over at his sleeping wife and daughter. "But you must promise me something."

Nikol wiped his eyes on his shoulder and nodded.

"You've been closer to danger than you have known. I may not be around to protect you anymore. And I need you here to take care of my women. You must stop all of your communications to the capitol. The assassination plan is under way. Really, you've done more than your share. The police have been to the village once. Surely, they will come again. I can't risk your being taken away. How would Seta and Victoria manage then?"

Nikol didn't hesitate. "I promise."

Throughout the long night, Seta, Victoria, and Nikol took turns watching. By morning, all three sat in attendance. Koren lapsed more and more frequently into delirium, awakening only briefly to periods of lucidity.

Seta dabbed at her eyes. It was in God's hands now, and it was only a question of time before He called His faithful servant back to Him.

She looked at Victoria weeping openly and at Nikol's quivering lip. They knew.

She had lived in fear of this her entire marriage, had dreamt of it at night and now that it had happened, she couldn't believe it. She had married him when she was fifteen years old. He had taken care of her since then, had managed the details of their life together. He had been so strong and look at him now – dying before her eyes. She laid her head on his chest.

Toward morning, Koren opened his eyes and sat up. He looked at Seta and smiled. Was he getting better after all?

No, the fever still burned brightly in his cheeks. He looked around the room.

"Victoria and Nikol are outside filling the water jug," Seta said.

He looked back at Seta, his eyes shining with love. "I am glad for this moment alone with you, my dear. I have something I want to say. I have loved you since that first moment I set eyes on you, a young girl coming out of the baths with your mother and sisters. When I saw you, I knew you were the woman for me and I have never regretted that decision. You have been a good wife, kept a good home and been a wonderful mother to our daughter. But you have given me more than that. You have loved me truly and completely, and for this I am grateful. I will leave this earth a rich man indeed."

They both knew the end was near and she would not betray the love and honesty they had shared by pretending otherwise. She was too overcome to respond but words were not necessary. He knew how she felt. He had just told her so.

Koren's eyes glazed with pain. He went on. "I want you to promise me something."

Seta bowed her head and nodded. "Anything."

He went on. "I want Victoria to marry Nikol."

Seta raised her head and looked at Koren in surprise.

Koren's eyes met hers. "It's the only way you'll be able to keep the farm. I love Nikol like a son, and I know Victoria will be happy with him. They both share so much, and I trust him to be good to her."

"Married? Oh Koren, she's too young."

"I see no reason why it has to be right away. Put it off as long as you can, but remember it is my wish that they be married. You must promise me this."

Exhausted with this final effort to speak, Koren fell back into the pillows for the last time. He was no longer awake, but Seta whispered her promise to him, anyway. When Victoria and Nikol returned a few minutes later, they found Koren unconscious again, with Seta sitting beside him, her eyes red with weeping.

Victoria laid her hand on her mother's shoulder and handed her a damp cloth. Seta bathed her face with it. She looked gratefully at Victoria, but said nothing.

Koren awoke only briefly one last time. One by one, he looked straight into the eyes of the three people he loved best in the world, saving until last his beloved mate. He clasped her hand in his, his eyes communicating all the love he felt. Slowly, his face relaxed and his hand grew limp. His eyes now stared unseeing. He had quietly slipped away. He was no longer in pain. He was at peace.

Seta picked up her husband's hand, pressed it to her cheek, and sobbed long and hard. Victoria waited for her to quiet down, then led her to her bed and sat at her side while she slept.

Victoria moved through the next three days in a fog. Seta

prepared Koren's body for burial, then wandered around looking lost. Victoria stayed at her side, forced her to eat, forced her to sleep, and helped her receive friends and neighbors. Then the dreaded moment arrived. It was time to bury her father.

She stood at the graveside, holding her mother up, and watched while Michael Damadian, Levon Kalustian, John Halabian and Nikol plodded toward them, each carrying a pole of the stretcher on their shoulder. The older men bowed their heads. Nikol wept openly.

The men lowered her father's body into the grave. Seta collapsed, but before turning to her, Victoria looked into the grave and said, "Good-bye, Papa." She lifted her chin, put her fingers to her lips and kissed them in a final gesture of farewell.

The entire community headed back to the house. Victoria opened the door. Where had all this food come from? Every square inch of the table was covered by food. Then she remembered all the times she had seen Seta go off to a funeral with a plate of food in hand and understood.

Throughout the afternoon, callers milled in and out. Everywhere she turned, Victoria met the sympathetic face of a family friend. She couldn't stand it another minute. She had to be alone. She ducked out the back door and snuck off through the fields. She kept walking until she came to a tree, well away from the house. At last, she was alone. She sat down, put her head on her knees and cried. Her father, oh dear, dear, Papa. How could he be gone? An image of his body lying alone in its grave flashed through her mind and she cried harder still.

After a while, she looked up.

How long had she been sitting here? And what about her mother? Who was taking care of her? She must hurry back. She had responsibilities now.

She stood, brushed her dress and wiped her eyes. A horse's hooves clopped up behind her. She spun around. Hasan. His gaze turned soft and he stared down into her eyes without speaking. A minute turned into two.

She felt as if she were being drawn into the comfort of his dark, sympathetic eyes. She took a step toward him.

He extended his hand.

She took another step.

In the distance, a door slammed.

They both started and turned toward the sound.

Victoria shook herself.

Hasan cleared his throat.

"I...heard about your father's passing. On behalf of my family, I want to tell you how sorry we are. He was a fine man, respected by all."

Victoria's eyes widened. Someone of his religion expressing sympathy to someone of hers? "Well, ah, thank you. That is kind of you to say." She stood taller. "My family accepts and appreciates your condolences."

Hasan nodded and his gaze swept down her front. His

face turned red. He fumbled with his reins, turned his horse and rode away without looking back.

Victoria ran back to the house. He had looked at her again in that way that made her feel uncomfortable. *What was it?* She stopped at the pump and splashed cold water on her face. Well, whatever it was, she knew there was no one she was going to talk to about it. No one.

She heard Seta calling for her. She took another deep breath, opened the door and went inside.

CHAPTER ELEVEN

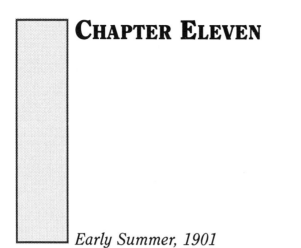

Early Summer, 1901

Nikol climbed over the north field ridge and stopped short. He stared at the pasture in front of him. It was full of grazing sheep, but his own flock still trailed behind him. What was going on? And what was Rose's son Alexan doing there?

He watched as Alexan arced a long-handled hammer in a sideways motion. It cracked against a fence post.

Nikol's jaw dropped open.

A second swing and the post was down.

Alexan moved to the one beside it.

"Just what do you think you are doing?"

Alexan ignored him, kicked the fallen post out of his way and went on to a third. He raised his hammer.

Nikol reached out and wrenched it out of his hands. "I'm talking to you. Explain yourself. Why are you taking this fence down and what are you doing in our fields?"

"*Your fields?*"

"Yes..." Nikol stopped. He let the head of the hammer drop to the ground. "Well, Seta's."

"When did women start owning land? These fields were Koren's. Now they're ours."

Nikol drew himself up and looked Alexan straight in the eye. "The man's been dead less than three weeks. Have you so little respect?"

Alexan reddened and spoke to the ground. "Well, my mother wanted me to attach these fields to ours, while the ground is still boggy enough to dig the post holes."

Nikol straightened his black armband. Rose. Now he understood. "Look, before you take down any more fences, let's talk this out."

Alexan avoided Nikol's eyes and took the sledge hammer from him. Without saying another word, he went back to his work.

Nikol clenched his fist, took a step toward him, then stopped. No, not this way.

He settled the sheep in a lower pasture and went to find Seta.

"Well, I knew she would do this eventually. But now? While we're in mourning? Shame on her."

Nikol frowned. "She knows there isn't a thing you can do

about it until the forty days are over."

Seta wiped her eyes. "And what then? How will I find the strength to fight her?" She buried her face in her hands and began to sob.

Nikol silently cursed Rose. What would they do? Rose wouldn't stop with their pastures. Once she got to their wheat fields, it was all over for them. They needed those fields to feed themselves. Whatever Koren had for savings, it wouldn't last long if they had to depend on it for all their needs. They would soon be reduced to poverty, dependent on Rose's handouts to live. No, he wouldn't let that happen. But poor Seta. So much sadness, and now this. He moved closer to her and laid his hand on her arm.

"You are not alone," he said. "I will help you."

Seta took a lace handkerchief from the pocket of her long black dress and dabbed her eyes. "Oh, you dear boy. Koren always said he had a feeling you were sent to us for a reason. And he was right."

Nikol gave a start. Koren had said something else to him two years ago. Was that the answer to their problem? It was wrong to bring it up now. But what choice did he have?

He cleared his throat.

Seta looked at him.

He looked away.

"What's on your mind, Nikol?"

Nikol took a deep breath. "I wish I didn't have to bring this up but, well, with the situation..."

"Go on, I'm listening."

"Well, a few years back, Koren talked to me about Victoria. He promised me her hand in marriage."

"I know."

Nikol raised his head. "You do?"

"Yes, it was one of the last things he spoke to me about before he died."

"And you..?"

"I promised, and I will keep that promise. But not now. She's only thirteen years old."

"It may become necessary."

"To keep the land? No. We'll find some other way."

A knock on the door ended their conversation. Nikol looked at Seta. A condolence call this early in the day? Odd. He went to the door and opened it.

"Mr. Sayabovian. Come in." The man stood looking at his shoes.

Seta rose. "Please come in."

He walked past Nikol and sat opposite Seta at the table. He briefly extended sympathy on behalf of his family, but it was clear that this was not the purpose of his visit.

Seta motioned Nikol to the table. She turned her palms up and gave a slight shrug. They both waited for Mr. Sayabovian to speak.

"I shouldn't be coming to you with a business matter, but I didn't know what else to do."

"A business matter?"

"Yes."

Nikol looked at Seta. What now?

Mr. Sayabovian looked up. "Koren was bringing gold back from Mezireh for me. A large supply. I'm expanding my business but I used up all my savings to buy the gold. I borrowed money, too. If I lose it, I'm ruined, completely ruined."

Seta put her hand over her mouth.

"I haven't been able to sleep at night. How will I feed my family? What will we do?"

"Mr. Sayabovian–"

"I have nothing but what I earn in my shop." He held his hands in front of her face. "Our home, our bread, rests in these."

"Mr. Sayabovian, please let me say something. I promise I will not let your family be ruined because of us. Give me a few days. You'll have your money back. You have my word."

Mr. Sayabovian let out a breath. "Bless you."

After he left, Nikol turned to Seta. "What are you going to do?"

Seta brushed a hair from her pale cheek. "I don't know. Perhaps I can ask about the gold when I go to the police station."

Nikol dropped the cup he held in his hands. "The police? What are you going to the police station for?"

Seta shrugged. "I don't know. A messenger came to the house this morning and said both Victoria and I were to report there this afternoon."

"I'm coming with you."

"No, Nikol. You must stay here. You know how the police are with men. If the mood suits them, they will arrest you. They don't need a reason. And if they take you away, Victoria and I will truly be lost."

"But can you face them alone?"

"I will have to. Anyway, it's different with women and the police. We're not a threat to them."

It was true, Nikol thought, but one never knew.

Victoria, who had been visiting Margaret, arrived home a few minutes later. When Seta told her about the summons, she nodded but said nothing. Her skin glowed like a white porcelain background next to her jet-black outfit.

Seta handed Victoria a black silk scarf and tied one under her own chin as well. The two set out for the village. When they arrived at the police station, a guard led them to a back room, told them to sit down, then left.

Seta licked her dry lips. What could the police want, she wondered?

The door opened and she jumped. A man strode in to the room, dressed in a stiff tunic and tailored trousers. He wore a sword tucked into a sash around his waist.

He stood before them, flipped open a shiny gold pocket watch, and studied the time.

Seta cleared her throat.

He glared down at her.

She recoiled.

"I have a few questions for you," he said after leaving Seta and Victoria in silence for a few minutes more. He walked to the desk, opened a drawer, and pulled out Koren's worn leather saddlebag.

Victoria leaned forward, her eyes filled with tears. "That's Papa's."

Seta shot Victoria a warning glance, but it was already too late.

"Aha!" The official smiled with satisfaction and turned to Seta. "Your husband was a traitor."

"A traitor? What do you mean?"

"Just what I said, a traitor. And I have the proof." He held up the *Dashnak* newsletter. "We found this inside. A traitor and a menace to our sultan."

What could that paper possibly say, Seta thought. *How did it make Koren into a traitor?* She looked at Victoria. She had her head tilted and her eyes were scanning the lines.

Seta reminded herself to ask her later what it said.

"I don't know what that is," Seta said.

The gendarme began to pace. The heels of his knee high boots clicked and echoed against the thick stone walls of the room. "Why did your husband travel to Mezireh so often?"

Seta shrugged. "He went there on business."

"We know all about his," he looked at the ceiling, "business."

"No, he was a courier."

"He was a revolutionary. And he was carrying a knife.

You people are forbidden to carry knives. With good reason, too. We found two dead men at the site."

What could she say, Seta thought? *If he carried a knife it was to defend himself. But this man didn't care about that. What did he want from her? The gold? He wanted to make sure she kept silent about the gold. No, she couldn't do that. An entire family's survival depended on that gold.*

"He was transporting supplies for one of his clients. Gold was in that bag."

A worried look crossed the official's face, but it was gone in an instant. "Get out of here before I arrest both of you." He turned to Victoria, his eyes gleaming. "Or maybe I'll keep this one here with me."

Oh dear God, no, Seta thought. No money was worth that. Her heart pounded against her chest. She rose from her chair and stood in front of Victoria.

The gendarme's eyes narrowed and he grinned. "Yes, I think I will keep her here."

Seta shook her head and stood her ground.

For a tense moment there was silence. Then, the gendarme took a step forward, and reached for Victoria.

The door to the room opened. A young officer stood in the doorway. "Sir, you are needed downstairs. Now — it's an emergency."

The gendarme's face cleared. He pulled his arm back, thrust out his chest, and swaggered to the door, shoving Seta aside as he walked past.

He could push her all he wanted, as long as he left her dear daughter alone. She looked at the empty room, grabbed Victoria by the arm, and ran from the station.

Halfway home, Seta stopped and clutched Victoria's hand.

"Victoria, from now on, do not go into the village alone. If you have to go, go only with Nikol."

"What was that man going to do to me?"

"You're too young to understand. But there's something I want to explain to you." She glanced over her shoulder. "If a man ever tries to grab you and touch you where he shouldn't, kick him hard between the legs, then run."

"Between the legs?"

"Yes, but remember, then run."

Seta was happy to get her daughter within the safety of the sturdy stone walls of their house. They did not speak of the matter again. But Seta's hands shook as she prepared dinner that night. If he had chosen to hurt Victoria, there wasn't a thing she could have done to stop him. Not a thing.

Victoria held her mother's hand through the Sunday mass that marked the end of their forty days of mourning, and stayed at her side throughout the long afternoon gathering that followed. When it was over, she sat down with her mother and Nikol, while Michael Damadian went over their finances with them.

"You must make the farm provide for you. You are dependent on the meat, vegetables, and wheat that you grow now."

Nikol exchanged a look with Seta. "Yes, Seta and I have been talking about that very issue." Victoria looked at Michael. "What about...I mean I don't want to sound selfish, but what about–" She hesitated.

Michael's eyes softened. "School?"

Victoria reddened, and looked away from Seta. "School, yes."

"Your father set aside enough money, but whether you go or not is up to your mother."

"There are some other things we need to consider," Seta said quickly. "Thank you for coming, Michael. I'll walk you to the road."

When they were outside, Seta explained to him about Mr. Sayabovian and her promise to pay him back.

"Now I understand why you couldn't answer Victoria about school."

"She thinks it's because I don't want her to go. But I'll never recover the lost gold and I have to use Koren's savings to pay Mr. Sayabovian back. I don't think I'll have enough left to send her." She stared in the direction of the village. "I wish I could get her away from here, but I just don't see how."

"I'll find out how much Mr. Sayabovian is owed, but gold is costly. If you pay him back, you won't have anything left for school or even for yourselves."

"As you pointed out, we have the farm to put food on our

table. What more do we really need? I won't have another family destroyed by this, too."

Michael patted her hand. "I understand."

The official mourning period was over. Seta and Victoria put away their black dresses, and Nikol took off his black armband. It was time for Seta to deal with Cousin Rose.

She set out for Rose's house with Nikol.

"Come in, come in." Rose opened the door wide. "We were just about to eat, will you join us?"

"No," Seta said.

"Oh please, we insist."

"Rose, you can stop this pretense right now. You know why we're here."

"Why don't you tell me?"

Seta put her hands on her hips. "You've taken all but one of my pastures."

Rose stood tall. "Now, I don't think those fields belong to you."

"Rose, they belong to us and you know it," Nikol said.

Rose pivoted around facing him and glaring. "What do you mean *us*? The land is not yours, and never has been. You're just the hired help. Who are you to interfere?"

"He was like a son to Koren." Seta laid her hand on Nikol's arm.

"Maybe he was like a son, but he wasn't Koren's son, so the land does not belong to him. It belonged to my family and I have a husband, so now it belongs to me."

The three folded their arms across their chests and stared at each other.

Maritza, Alexan's wife, stepped forward with narrowed eyes and a smile on her face. "Mother, I'm going to bring some lunch to Father and Alexan. They're in our new field putting up a fence." She glanced sidelong at Seta and Nikol and grinned at Rose.

Rose grinned back.

"Rose, I am going to say this one more time, then I'm leaving. The land belongs to us. Think about what you are doing."

Rose lifted a finger and pointed to the door. "Leave."

Seta and Nikol looked at each other. Rose ignored them. She grabbed a broom and began to sweep as if they were not there. Red-faced, they turned heel and left.

Outside, Nikol stopped and faced Seta. "Seta, you're going to have to allow Victoria to marry me. It's the only way."

"I can't, she's too young to marry now."

"Look, tomorrow you are paying Mr. Sayabovian back. You told me yourself that you have nothing left. She's not going to college. Why can't we marry now?"

"No. There must be some other way." She thought. "We'll go see Father Mikayelian. It's up to him to settle the matter, anyway."

"All right, but you'd better go soon."

"I'll talk to him this Sunday after church."

Seta didn't wait until Sunday. The next day, shortly after he left for the fields, Nikol ran back into the house. Seta took one look at his face and felt her stomach tighten. What now?

"They're out tilling one of our wheat fields. Do you understand? This is the food on our table we're talking about."

Seta compressed her lips, set down her sewing, and went to the door.

"Do you want Victoria to go with you?"

Her expression changed. "No."

Nikol looked surprised. "Shall I come with you then?"

"Oh, yes, please."

With each step that brought her closer to the village, Seta worried more. The priest's word was law, but would he decide in her favor? What would she do if he didn't? Where would she go?

Seta and Nikol reached the small parish house alongside the church. The priest's wife took one look at their faces, ushered them in, and left them alone with her husband. The priest listened to Seta's story and took notes as she talked. Then he sent for Cousin Rose and her husband.

"Father, the land belonged to my grandfather," Rose said. "My dear cousin passed away. Now there is no man to own it. I begged Koren to promise his daughter to my son. But did he?" Her voice rose. "No. Instead he made some foolish plan to send her to college." She pointed her finger at Seta. "She knows that without any other arrangements, the land goes back to me."

Seta shook her head. She looked at Father Mikayelian. "Koren was a young man." She gulped back a sob. "He didn't know he *had* to make arrangements."

Father Mikayelian looked back at Rose. "If you take her husband's land, who will take care of her?"

"We'll take care of Seta and Victoria. My husband and son can provide for all of us. After all, we're family."

"What about Nikol? Can he not take care of them?"

"Nikol." Rose rolled her eyes. "We can't count on him. What if he takes a wife? Then where would they be? On our doorstep, that's where. And we'd be stuck trying to take care of everyone on our meager little piece of land."

Nikol stepped forward. "Now wait just a moment."

Rose lifted her chin and peered down her nose at him. "Don't worry, you can stay and work for us."

Nikol gave a short laugh and didn't answer.

Seta looked at Rose sternly, but she ignored her and smiled at the priest.

Father Mikayelian asked them to sit while he thought the matter over.

Seta tried not to stare at him while he ran his finger over his notes and looked, with unfocused eyes, at the wall. She thought about the conversation she had with Koren on the morning of Victoria's party. Not everyone still clung to the old ways, but did Father Mikayelian? She tried to remember how he had reacted to the college announcement. She might have used that to measure how he would react now, but she couldn't remember seeing his face at all that day.

Father Mikayelian cleared his throat. Seta gripped her hands in her lap. Nikol looked at his feet.

"The land will go to Rose and Vahan." He looked at Rose. "I'll expect you to take care of Seta and Victoria."

Rose cast Seta and Nikol a triumphant look. Nikol turned his face away.

Seta felt her mouth go dry. She had just lost her home and was now reduced to charity.

Nikol took her arm and led her from the house in silence. When they were outside, he stopped and turned to her. "You must allow Victoria to marry me now."

"Oh Nikol, I just can't do that yet. In a few years, when she's, maybe fifteen, she can marry you. Then we'll go back to Father Mikayelian and ask him to give us back the land."

"And what if he doesn't?"

"I don't know. All I know is that I'm Victoria's mother, and I say she's too young to be married."

Nikol looked Seta in the eye. "I didn't want it to come to this, but if you don't marry Victoria to me now, I'm leaving."

Seta's eyes widened. "You'd leave us?"

"Not you — Rose and Vahan. I don't think I can work for them. In fact, I know I can't. And you know that if you lose that land now, you'll never get it back."

Seta thought it over. Nikol was right, she decided. Father

Mikayelian was unlikely to give the land back once Rose and Vahan had possession of it.

Nikol started walking. She trudged slowly behind. She thought about Victoria, confined to the house since the episode with the police.

Nikol drew further ahead.

If Victoria were married, some other man's property, the policeman would leave her alone, Seta thought.

She hurried to catch up to Nikol.

"All right, she will marry you. We'll go back inside and tell Father Mikayelian."

Rose and Vahan hadn't left yet, and on hearing the turn of events, the priest reversed his decision.

Rose's jaw dropped open. She put her hand on her hip. "Father, you can't allow this."

The priest turned to her with a look of astonishment. Then he frowned. "I can and have," he said.

Rose's face turned purple. Without a word she marched out of the house with her husband trotting at her side.

Seta and Nikol waited until they were out of sight and headed home. When they arrived, Seta said, "Let me have a few minutes alone with Victoria. She doesn't know about the gold for Mr. Sayabovian or the land problem. I have a lot to explain to her."

"I'll be out back tending the vegetables if you need me," Nikol said.

Victoria's smile of welcome faded when she saw the look on her mother's face. "What's wrong?"

Seta sat down, took both of her daughter's hands in her own and told her how their entire savings had gone to pay back Mr. Sayabovian.

Victoria shook her head. "I'm trying to understand this. Do you mean...does this mean, I can't go to college?"

Seta looked her in the eye. "It means more than that."

"Because college...I mean college is what I've always dreamed about. Papa said I could-" She stopped and frowned. "Did you say more? What more?"

Seta drew in a deep breath. "Cousin Rose believes she owns our land. I know she doesn't. But Nikol and I brought the dispute to Father Mikayelian this morning. He ruled that because there is no male heir, Rose and Vahan can have our land."

Victoria's eyes widened. "Our land? No! We can't let them take Papa's land."

Seta let go of Victoria's hands and looked down at her lap. "There is a way that we can save our land, but it involves you."

"Me?"

"Yes, you. Father Mikayelian said that if you were married, he would reverse his decision and leave the land with us."

"But who would I marry?"

"Nikol."

Victoria knitted her eyebrows. "Nikol?"

"Well...oh, this is so complicated. I have to explain something else. Papa always planned for you to marry Nikol but after college, of course. He even spoke to Nikol about it and Nikol agreed."

Victoria shook her head. "I can't believe this is happening. No college. Marriage."

Seta waited for her daughter to absorb what she had just told her.

"But Nikol is like my brother."

"Many people start off a marriage not knowing each other at all, and never even growing to like each other much. If we lose our land, you'll have to marry someone else in a few years anyway, and leave to go live with his family. If you marry Nikol, we can all stay together. You would be happy with Nikol, wouldn't you?"

Victoria was silent. Seta tried to take her hand but she pulled it away. She drew her knees up and laid her head on them.

Seta waited. What kind of mother was she to place a burden like this on a thirteen-year-old? Because of Rose, she thought. She could just...just —

Victoria spoke. "If it's what Papa wanted, then I will do it."

Seta's voice broke. "You just saved us all."

Victoria rose. "I'm going to speak to Nikol."

Instead of looking for Nikol, Victoria walked to the grassy

flat that overlooked the road. She turned in a slow circle scanning her father's fields. Then she looked down the road. Papa was not coming back. Everything had changed.

She went to find Nikol.

He stood straight when she approached and looked at her with a question in his eyes.

"I will marry you," she said.

He reached for her hand. "I know what your dreams meant to you. If there was any other way, I would find it for you. I would do anything for you, because," he paused and looked at her, "because I love you. I can't name a day when it started. It's something that just grew out of the times we talked, read together and cut the wheat in the fields. With you, I have everything I want."

Suddenly, she saw it all. She had wanted to teach so she could help her people better themselves and ensure their survival. Now she had her own family's survival to think about. But with Nikol's help, she could do it. Together, they could do it.

For the first time since her father's death, the knots in her stomach eased. Nikol had been at her side since she was a little girl. He had explained the ways of the world to her, and their problems with the Turks when no one else would. They had grown up together. And she loved him, too. Was this what Papa had seen when he made her marriage agreement with Nikol? Had he known that with Nikol, she could share the kind of love in her marriage that he had shared in his?

Nikol had been her friend and now he would be her husband. It was right. There was no one in the world she could love more than Nikol.

Later that night, while Seta sewed and Nikol read from his newspaper, Victoria got up and began to wander around the room. She lifted Koren's *raki* glass from the shelf and sniffed its interior. Next she took his sweater from the trunk and wrapped it around her shoulders. Then, she took a book of poetry from his bookshelves and ran her hand over its cover.

Nikol watched her continue to roam. "Victoria, how about a game of backgammon?"

She looked at him and smiled sadly. "No, I don't think so."

She picked up the wooden-cased game and held it to her cheek. Then she brushed a tear from her eye and put the game away.

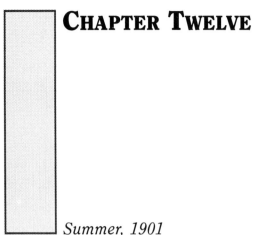

CHAPTER TWELVE

Summer, 1901

At the sound of a knock, Victoria looked up from the napkin she was embroidering.

"Honestly, the entire village is talking about it," Araxie said from the doorstep.

Seta smiled and opened the door wide. Araxie and Margaret walked into the room.

"And you should see the looks Rose is getting. She knows it, too. She doesn't say a word, but you can tell she's mad." Araxie looked at the table where Victoria sat. Every inch was covered with half-finished napkins, pillow cases waiting for lace to be sewn on the edges, and other items for Victoria's trousseau that were waiting to be completed. "We've come to help."

Seta put her hand to her chest. "Thank you. I don't know how we're going to get it all done. The wedding is in two months."

"And we have a whole farm to take care of, too," Victoria said.

In two months she would be married. *Married.* She could hardly believe it.

Since she had agreed to marry Nikol less than a week ago, each night she and her mother had sewn until their eyes were too tired to follow their stitches. She had noticed something, though. The busier Seta became, the less sad she looked. Strange.

Margaret sat down at her side and squeezed her hand. Then she said, "Mother, may Victoria and I go out for a walk?"

"Yes," Araxie said. "But only for a few minutes. We're here to help."

In the sunlight, Victoria rubbed her sore eyes. Then she hooked her arm in Margaret's. They began to walk.

"The wedding," Margaret said. "Are you nervous?"

Victoria grimaced. "Yes." She looked over her shoulder. "There's something I'm worried about. I'm not really a woman, you know. My time of month hasn't come yet."

Margaret patted her hand. "It will. It has to, doesn't it?"

Victoria shrugged. "I guess it does."

They walked in silence for a few minutes. Then Margaret said, "I've come to a decision about school. I'm not going."

Victoria stopped. "Oh, Margaret. It's because of me, isn't it?"

"I don't want to go without you. You need me here and really, school was your dream, anyway."

"But I can't have you give it up, too."

"No, I talked it over with my parents and they agreed. It's settled."

Victoria threw her arms around Margaret. "I've been worrying and worrying about what I would do without my best friend."

Margaret smiled. "We will always be here for each other. I promise."

When the girls returned to the house, Fiorine had arrived and was finishing the edge of a handkerchief. The girls picked up their needles, and began to sew. Seta and Araxie chatted, as they sewed.

"I remember the first meal I cooked after I was married." Araxie smiled and shook her head. "I was making a stew with winter vegetables for Michael's family. My mother-in-law was letting me do the whole thing myself. I wanted her to think I knew what I was doing, so I wouldn't ask her for any advice. I didn't think I needed any. After all, I had helped my mother make this same stew dozens of times when I was growing up. I knew how to cut up the vegetables and how many to use. The only problem was that my mother had always put the seasonings in herself so I didn't know that a little hot pepper goes a long way. It was a large pot of stew; I thought

I needed a lot of hot pepper."

Victoria snipped a thread and smiled. She could guess what was coming.

Araxie went on. "I placed the bowls on the table and the family gathered for dinner. Michael's father said grace, then I served the stew. I stood, like a traditional wife, waiting for the others to eat. Well, they all lifted their spoons at the same time and took a swallow. You should have seen the looks on their faces. Everyone's eyes popped open. They dropped their spoons and began calling for water. Michael's father had tears running down his cheeks. I got so nervous, I began to giggle. The more I tried to stop, the harder I laughed. Every time I got control of myself, I would think of all those eyes and it would start me up all over again."

Victoria laughed with her mother and the others. Then she stopped. She shouldn't be laughing now. Her father had been dead less than two months. What was wrong with her?

Seta looked at her and said, "Victoria, no one cries twenty-four hours a day. It's all right."

Later, after Araxie and Margaret left, she explained more fully. "You're young and even though you'll always miss Papa, you'll go on with your life. You'll have times when you're sad," her voice broke for a moment, then she went on. "But there will also be times of joy. You see, your life must continue on. It's what he wanted for you."

Victoria nodded. Her life would go on. And so would her mother's and Nikol's. It was going to be difficult without her father, though. She had taxes to pay, and no money left to pay them with.

When Nikol came in from the fields, Victoria sat down with him to go over the farm accounts.

She ran her finger down her father's ledger. "That much for taxes? How will we ever do it?"

Nikol peered over her shoulder. "And our *pasha* is supposed to be more reasonable than others. What do farmers in other villages do?"

Victoria looked at him.

"Never mind. I know. They lose their land, then they starve."

Seta began to wring her hands.

Victoria turned to Nikol and gave a slight shake of her head. She touched her mother's arm. "Don't worry. That is not going to happen to us."

"No, it isn't," Nikol said. "We have one of the largest farms around here. We just need to figure out how it will pay the taxes. Not *if*, how."

Seta's face relaxed. "I'll leave all that to the two of you, then." She rose and began to prepare dinner.

"Let's sell all the wool we sheared this spring and use the money to enlarge our flock," Victoria said.

Nikol nodded. "Yes, I like that. And I'll plant two more wheat fields. We'll sell all the extra and hope it's enough for the taxes."

Victoria flipped to the next page. "I want to start setting

money aside too. You never know when you're going to have a bad year."

Victoria continued to lay out plans with Nikol for more vegetables, more animals, more of everything. and less people to do the work. They would manage somehow, they had to.

The next morning Nikol set out for the fields with a long-handled hammer of his own. "Time to take back the fields," he said grinning.

He climbed the ridge of the same hill he had climbed three weeks ago. Alexan was on his side of the field. He had his back to Nikol and didn't turn around when Nikol approached.

Well Alexan was going to have a hard time ignoring him now. *Thwack.* A fence post was down. *Thwack, thwack,* another. Suddenly, Nikol felt a shove on his back. He stumbled forward, caught himself and spun around.

Alexan smirked.

Nikol narrowed his eyes. "Who are you pushing around?"

Alexan stuck his finger in Nikol's chest. "You."

Nikol raised his fists and went for him.

The two men struggled, each landing a few good punches until they separated and stood panting and glaring at each other.

"My mother's not through with you yet," Alexan said.

"Your mother? Your *mother*? I'm supposed to be afraid of your mother?"

"You're supposed to be afraid of us all." Alexan turned and walked off.

Nikol brushed his hair from his forehead and went back to work. What could Rose do to *him*? Rose might have her suspicions about him but what could she do? Armenians didn't inform against one another. The entire community would shun them. And how could she inform even if she wanted to? Who would she inform to? Not the local police, since someone was sure to find out. As for the police in the capitol, how would she communicate with them? She didn't read or write, nor did anyone else in her family.

He dropped another fence post. No there was no way Rose could hurt him. He took in a deep breath, then slowly let it out and continued his work.

The fences were all back in place by the end of the week.

Victoria, Seta, and Nikol labored from the first light of day until deep into the night all summer long. They planted fields, weeded the vegetable garden and put up vegetables for the upcoming winter. Every night, Victoria and Seta worked on the pieces for Victoria's trousseau. No respectable girl married without a completed one, Seta kept insisting. Still, they might not have finished it, if Fiorine, Araxie, and Margaret had not appeared at their door almost every night. And through their help, Victoria grew to know the true depth of her friendship with those women.

Three weeks before the wedding, Victoria started to rise from the dinner table when Nikol laid a restraining hand on her arm.

"I want to talk to you about something."

Victoria sat back down.

Nikol took a deep breath and began. "I want to find out what's become of Anna and Stephan."

"Your brother and sister?"

"Yes, I failed them, you see."

Victoria thought about her own circumstances. "No, Nikol, you did what you had to in order to save their lives."

"But still, they're my responsibility. They're my brother and sister."

He was looking at her, as if he expected her to know what he wanted. She thought for a moment. "No, they are our responsibility and they are welcome in our home."

The relief on Nikol's face brought tears to Victoria's eyes. More mouths to feed but if Nikol was fortunate enough to be able to bring his family back, she would help in any way she could.

"I'll write the letter for you." Victoria spread a sheet of paper in front of her, poised her pencil, and looked at Nikol.

Nikol gazed back at her with love. "Thank you," he said.

Later after Nikol had gone out, Seta leaned over and kissed Victoria's cheek.

Victoria touched her face. "What was that for?"

"For being you," Seta said.

By the end of August, Victoria's trousseau was completed and Fiorine, Araxie and Margaret's nightly visits ended.

"I'm going to miss them," Victoria said. "Even with their help, I thought we were going to have to leave a few pieces undone. The wheat is really more important. So if it came to a choice..."

Seta shook her head. "A decent girl from a decent family has a trousseau."

Victoria smiled. "And a dress."

"Yes, a dress. I wish you could have worn mine, but you're as small as I am tall. It wouldn't have worked."

"I remember all the hours I spent crocheting that lace when I was little. You used to sit and watch me. Some nights, I think I took out as many stitches as I put in."

"But you did it right in the end and now there it is – on the sleeves and hem."

"Can I see it?" Nikol said.

Seta and Victoria both turned to stare at him. "Not before the wedding," Victoria said.

Nikol held up his hands. "All right, all right."

The next morning Nikol's letter arrived from the orphanage. Stephan had been adopted three years earlier by a couple who were well-off and owned a business that he would inherit some day.

"It's not what you planned," Victoria said, when she saw his disappointed look. "But he will have a good life."

Anna was still at the orphanage. She had completed primary school and the orphanage was looking for a home to place her in. Nikol's letter had arrived just in time.

Nikol wrote back immediately, enclosing money for her trip back to the village.

When the wheat turned amber, Victoria, Seta and Nikol spent a week in the fields. They harvested, processed, and bagged their crop. Then they stored enough for their own needs and Nikol took the rest to town to sell.

"What did you get for it?" Victoria said when he returned.

"Just enough to pay the taxes. Nothing more."

She sighed. "Next year will be better."

"Yes, next year without Rose's interference, I can plant more wheat fields and plant them earlier too. We'll get a better crop and we will have more wool to sell from the lambs we bought this spring."

What would she have done without him? "We have everything we need right here."

Nikol nodded. "But what we have, you've got to make last all winter."

"Oh, I will. My mother's been teaching me how to ration food since I was a little girl. Even with the wedding, we have more than enough."

Three days before the wedding, Margaret, Araxie, and Fiorine came back to help prepare the food. They made trays and trays of *paklava*, hundreds of stuffed grape leaves, and dozens of *boregs*, baked rolls stuffed with cheese and parsley.

Michael was standing in for Koren and had generously donated the lamb meat. The women pounded it out and mixed it with seasoned vegetables, then spread it over flat, pie-sized pieces of rolled out dough and baked it into *lama-joon*s.

On the morning of her wedding, Victoria slipped into her beautiful silk gown and went with her mother to the church where Nikol stood waiting. She had heard this service before, but today it held a special meaning for her. Her life had not gone the way she planned but Nikol was a good man and she trusted him.

At the conclusion of the service, Nikol turned to Victoria and raised her veil. He looked into her large, expressive eyes and kissed her. Victoria felt a calm descend over her. This felt right. She had promised to obey him. She would do more than that. She would love him, too.

She linked arms with Nikol and the two led their guests back to their house for the reception.

Rebecca's brother, Leon, started the music for the bride and groom's first dance. Victoria knew her part. She floated a filmy silk handkerchief from her hand and approached Nikol, who sat on a chair in the middle of an open circle of people. She moved around him, snapping her fingers and swaying her hips, in a dancing attempt to entice him to join her.

Nikol also knew his part. He pretended to be unaware of Victoria, at first. Then slowly he allowed himself to be drawn in. He stood. Both raised their hands over their heads and snapped their fingers, while their feet kept pace to the music. By the end of the dance, the two had locked eyes and were dancing around each other, while their bodies never touched. The watching crowd clapped and cheered them on.

One of the guests turned to the woman standing beside her. "Do you see the way he looks at her?" she said. "He seems so happy."

"Oh, he's very happy now." Rose, the woman standing beside the guest, said. She bared her teeth in what was supposed to be a smile.

The guest took a step back, then turned and walked away.

Rose stood staring off into the distance.

It was almost midnight when the last guest left. Seta announced she was going home with Araxie and would be back the next day.

Nikol and Victoria watched the carriage carrying Seta, pull away. Victoria's heart began to beat faster. Nikol gently took her hand and led her inside. What was supposed to happen now? She had promised to be obedient to her husband, but what did that mean?

Together, they took down the sleeping mats from the shelf, then Nikol went outside to allow her time to prepare.

She couldn't stand here like a scared little girl. She was a grown-up now. She drew in a deep breath, and took a soft lace-trimmed nightgown from her trunk. The virginal white fabric billowed around her young body and enhanced her dark complexion. Her eyes were wide and her long dark lashes blinked back tears.

She stood in the same spot until Nikol returned. He

gasped when he saw her. In an instant he was at her side, kissing her and slowly, slowly lowering her to the mattress.

When it was over, Nikol lifted Victoria's chin and gazed into her face. Her soft brown eyes shone back at him. "I will love you forever," he said.

Seta came home the next day and the three went back to work.

Three days later, in the late afternoon, Victoria had her head bent over a sewing project when she heard the sound of a carriage outside. She looked at Seta. Another guest to offer congratulations? They had been appearing at their doorstep each day in groups of twos and threes.

Victoria squinted. No, the person climbing from the carriage was not from her village. Who was it? They could not have met, yet she looked familiar. With a start, Victoria realized why.

"Anna?" she said.

CHAPTER THIRTEEN

Fall, 1903

*V*ictoria took a break from kneading dough to rub her sore back.

Anna hurried to her side. "Sit down and rest. Let me do that. In your condition, you have to be careful."

Victoria lowered herself onto a cushion and sighed with relief. Twenty minutes ago, she had started mixing yeast, melted butter, eggs, and flour into a batch of *choeregs*. She thought she could do it, but there was a life growing inside of her. A life that was taking up all of her energy.

She put her hand on her stomach and felt the baby kick. Had she really only been pregnant for nine months? It seemed like she had been waiting forever for her baby to be born.

DIANE GOSHGARIAN

She had been married to Nikol for two years. The monthly period she had worried over not having, had begun three months after she was married and was soon a source of frustration to her. She wanted a baby. Everyone wanted her to have a baby. And she had not missed the worried frown her mother tried to hide when another month passed and she was not pregnant. At last the month had come when, despite the arrival of all her premenstrual symptoms, no bleeding followed. Her breasts remained tender and she found herself running to the outhouse every hour. She had lived with her secret for weeks before telling anyone and had enjoyed the private intimacy between her and her baby.

Victoria had been sick for three long months, having to lie in bed as waves of nausea had struck her, one after another. She remembered worrying over all the work that needed to be done and the burden her illness was placing on the other three. Then one day, the sickness had disappeared like magic. The color had returned to her cheeks, and her old energy came back and had stayed until a few weeks ago.

Victoria looked at Anna, up to her elbows in dough. Wasn't that just like dear sweet Anna to notice her fatigue and take over her work?

Victoria remembered the day Anna had arrived from the orphanage. Nikol had come in from the fields, taken one look at his grown-up sister, and sat down and cried. He kept telling her how sorry he was to have left her. Anna had run to him, wrapped her arms around him, and assured him of the wisdom of what he had done. She was right, too. They could never have survived the destitution of those days in their ruined village.

In the two years she had been here, Anna had worked alongside Victoria, weeding the vegetable garden, canning their food, and carding their wool. With her help, Victoria had been able to put a few coins into her jar of savings each season. Anna looked for ways to help and didn't ask for anything in return. It was easy to love her. Someone else loved her too, though she would not admit that she knew it.

Victoria's eyes twinkled. "We're having company after church tomorrow."

Anna's back stiffened. She stopped and pushed her bangs aside with her shoulder. "Oh, who?"

"The Kalustians."

Anna began to knead the dough again. "Is the entire family coming?"

"Let me think. Rebecca's coming, her mother and father, too." Victoria coughed to cover her laugh.

Anna kept her eyes on her work, but her cheeks turned bright red. "Anyone else? I mean I want to make sure we have enough food and all."

Victoria got up and put her arm around her sister-in-law. "Don't worry, Leon's coming."

For the last year, Victoria had been watching Leon watch Anna. And she had watched Anna, quietly going about her business treating him as politely as any visitor. That was another thing about Anna. It would never occur to her to think that anyone thought her special. And because she didn't, everyone thought her all the more so. Look at Leon, the handsome bachelor who could have his pick of any girl in the village. But did he want any girl in the village? No, he wanted Anna. Victoria could tell by the way his eye darted to her when he entertained at parties and by the way he managed to seat himself beside her when his family came to visit.

Victoria dampened a cloth and covered the bowl of dough Anna had finished kneading. She wondered now about this visit by the Kalustians tomorrow. Was there some special significance to it?

The door opened and Nikol strode into the room.

Victoria felt her gaze soften. Her love. Her life.

He went right to her side and crouched down. Victoria heard paper crinkle. He asked her how she was feeling and she assured him she was fine.

She touched his pocket. "What is that?"

"It's a newsletter from the *Dashnak*s. I'm going to read it now."

She braced her hand on the table and pushed herself to a standing position. "You'll have some time to read it in peace. We're going to the baths."

He caught her arm. "Save some time for me when you get back. We'll sit outside and talk. I want to tell you what this says and I want you to tell me what you think."

She would always make time for one of their talks. She

loved that he cared what she thought. She knew of no other man who asked for his wife's opinion.

She left for the baths with Seta and Anna promising to be back in time to talk.

Nikol glanced outside. No one was approaching. He withdrew the newsletter from his pocket and unfolded it. Charles Halabian had slipped it to him that morning and he had been anxious all day to learn what it said. He began to read.

The first article was about the Young Turks, a group of Turkish exiles who lived in Paris. Nikol frowned trying to remember what he knew of the Young Turks.

They were led by the sultan's own nephew, Prince Sabaheddin. But unlike his uncle, Prince Sabaheddin was a liberal who said he believed in equal rights for all Turkey's citizens. He said that if he and his group were to take power in Turkey, he would allow the provinces to govern themselves and he would put into effect a constitution drawn up in 1876 that established a liberal and democratic government in Turkey.

Nikol remembered that last February, the *Dashnak* leaders had announced they would go to Paris and meet with Turks, Arabs, Greeks, Kurds, Albanians, Circassions, and Jews in a conference with the Young Turks called, The First Congress of Ottoman Liberals.

He also remembered the arguments that had resulted from that announcement. Michael Damadian had said that it was a mistake to trust any Turk. John Halabian had supported the Armenian's participation in the congress because he believed that the Young Turks would one day overthrow the sultan and that they were sincere in what they said about equal rights. Nikol himself believed that any change to the Armenian's second-class status would come about only through their own revolutionary efforts.

He turned back to the article, read it through, then nodded grimly. He and Michael weren't the only ones who doubted the Young Turks. The writer did too.

In the article, the writer conceded that the prince and the present leadership of the Young Turks were probably being truthful when they said they believed in equality. However, the writer's source had told him that a committee had been secretly formed, called The Committee of Union and Progress, or CUP. Some, not all, members of this committee were Turkish army officers who believed in pan-Turkism, a doctrine with firm convictions in a Turkish race and a Turkish empire one day populated only by people linguistically related to Turks, which of course, the Armenians were not. The author concluded by acknowledging his inability to confirm the existence of the CUP. He said that it was even possible that his source had been lying in order to sabotage the *Dashnak*s efforts with the Young Turks.

Nikol put down the paper and rested his chin on his hand. Rumor or truth? He didn't know about the rest of the men, but he knew what he thought.

Later, when Victoria returned from the baths, he told her about the article. "Remember," he said. "If the Young Turks ever take power in Turkey, they may not be what they say they are."

The next day, Victoria walked out of church with one arm through Anna's and the other through Rebecca's and headed with them for home. Ahead, she heard Seta burst into laughter at something Levon said and heard his wife's voice rise in an apparent attempt to outdo her husband. Was it her imagination or was Leon uncharacteristically quiet today? And why did he keep putting his hands in his pockets as if he didn't know what to do with them?

She watched Anna out of the corner of her eye. Her head kept turning in the direction of Leon's handsome profile. Victoria tightened her arm on Rebecca's and nodded her head toward Anna. Rebecca looked and exchanged a smile with Victoria.

At home, Victoria seated her guests and served them food. Then she looked around. What was going on? The Kalustians had all stopped talking and were looking at Levon.

Finally, Levon cleared his throat and began, "Nikol, as your sister's guardian, we are formally making a request to you for her hand in marriage to my son, Leon."

Victoria started. So that was what this was all about? She looked at Anna. Her eyes glowed and she was smiling at Leon, who smiled back.

Levon continued, "I have known you for years and if Anna is your sister, she's a respectable girl. Leon's been working with me in my business and I can assure you, he can provide for her. We'd be honored to have her become part of our family."

Everyone, including Anna, looked expectantly at Nikol.

Nikol didn't answer right away. He looked at Victoria who nodded slightly. Then he looked at Anna. But Anna was looking at Leon who gazed back at her with eyes that told a story, the story of his feelings for her.

Nikol gave his answer. "We would be honored to accept this proposal of marriage. Anna, you may kiss the hands of our guests."

She did, and in so doing, sealed her brother's approval of the marriage. Leon's father reached into his pocket and withdrew a gold ring. He carefully slipped it on Anna's finger.

Victoria jumped up and hugged her.

Seta and Leon's mother dabbed at their eyes.

Nikol smiled and looked sad at the same time.

Levon and Nikol discussed the arrangements and decided the two would marry the following spring. Anna was only fifteen, and there was no reason to rush.

Later, after the families had sung, danced and drank to the happy couple, and Leon and his family had left, Anna sat down beside Victoria and rested her head on her shoulder.

"Are you happy Anna?"

"Oh, yes. I love him so. I just can't believe he loves me,

too."

Victoria hugged her. "Well, he does."

"I love him, but I'm glad we won't be getting married until next spring. I could never leave you now, with the baby about to be born. I think I'm as excited about it as you are."

"I know you are and what you just said means a lot to me."

Anna's smile faded. "For me, every baby born is the return of one of the lost little babies from our village."

"You remember, then?"

"Oh, yes. I was young, but not so young that I don't remember it all. Every bit." Victoria squeezed her hand. "We won't let anything happen to this baby. This baby is going to grow to be the man or woman it was meant to be.

The next morning, Victoria awoke feeling like she'd been caught under the wheels of a wagon. She would have to pay for her celebration yesterday.

She hoisted her bulk out of bed and made her way to the table.

"Where's Nikol?"

Seta put *choereg*s in front of her. "He's already eaten and gone out. We decided to let you sleep. You need your rest. How are you feeling?"

"Tired and achy. But something feels different too. I feel like I can breathe again."

Seta touched Victoria's abdomen. "Oh, the baby dropped. I think your labor will start in another day or two."

Victoria played with her earring. "Do you think it will last long?"

Seta shook her head. "The labor? I don't know. Those hips."

"My hips? Is there something wrong with my hips?"

"No, no, nothing dear."

But Victoria had caught her worried frown.

Midmorning the next day, Victoria was sweeping the carpet when she noticed a crampy tightening of her lower abdomen.

She leaned on her broom and took a deep breath. The baby was unusually active.

The feeling returned again and again as she finished sweeping and prepared lunch. So this was what contractions felt like? Still, she told no one. Her mother had told her that labor might start and stop for days. She had work to do now.

Nikol came in at noon. They all sat down to lunch, but Victoria just picked at her food.

Nikol looked at her plate. "Aren't you hungry?"

Victoria folder her arms over her stomach and sat mute.

"Victoria, why aren't you answering me?"

She looked up. "I wasn't answering you because I was having a contraction."

"What?" Seta dropped her spoon.

Nikol jumped up. "I'll get the midwife."

Anna ran to the stove. "I'll put water on to boil."

"Wait." Seta held up her hands. "It's too soon to start all

that. Victoria, when did this begin?"

"This morning. At first, I wasn't sure if it was anything more than the baby moving, but then it continued. And it got worse. Now I'm sure."

"Does it hurt very much?"

"No, not too much." She looked at Nikol. "But I can't talk while it's happening."

"Well, you're in early labor. If this keeps up, the contractions will get stronger. Just sit and rest."

"But I have grapes to put in the sun to dry and tomatoes to can."

Seta put her hands on her hips. "You have a baby about to be born."

Anna touched her hand. "Don't worry, I'll do all your work for you." She put her arm around Victoria and led her to the sleeping mat Seta had pulled from the shelf.

Seta chatted with Victoria as she sat propped up in bed, but she was worried. How would this labor go? Would her daughter be able to pass a baby through those narrow hips? She had been worrying about this through Victoria's entire pregnancy. She had told no one, thinking, what good would it do? Nature was going to take its course no matter how many people worried.

By late afternoon, Victoria's contractions had become intense. Seta sent Nikol off to fetch the midwife. She and Anna sat and talked to Victoria to distract her from the mounting pain.

When Nikol returned and announced that the midwife was on her way, Seta met him at the door but did not allow him in. This was women's work. She tried to reassure him with a smile, but she could see him through the window pacing back and forth and casting anxious glances at the house. Minutes later, she looked back out and saw him shade his eyes and scan the road. He frowned, took out his pocket watch, and looked at it with a puzzled expression. He tapped the watch, held it to his ear, then resumed his pacing.

Seta turned back to Victoria. Her contractions were making her moan.

"Squeeze my hand. It will help you get through the pain," she said. Where was the midwife?

Nikol tapped on the window and pointed down the road.

A few minutes later, Seta held the door open and Shakar Mama, the midwife, came in.

"How is she?"

Seta lowered her voice. "I don't know. She's awfully tiny."

The midwife's wrinkled face was serious. "Yes, but don't worry. I delivered most of the children in this village. I'll deliver Victoria's baby, too."

Seta told herself to relax. Shakar Mama had been trained by her mother. She had been delivering babies since she was a young woman. And it was in God's hands now.

Throughout the evening, Victoria's contractions intensified and became closer together, but each time the midwife examined her, she shook her head. The baby was no closer to being born than the last time.

Anna went outside to Nikol. Her face was pale as she handed him a plate of food. "You need to get something in your stomach."

"What's going on in there? Is she all right?"

"I guess. I don't know. The midwife said it's going to be slow. Maybe even tomorrow before the baby's born."

"Tomorrow?" He shook his head.

Anna nodded and hurried back inside.

By six in the morning, Victoria's face was drenched in perspiration. "I can't do it any longer."

The midwife wiped her forehead. "There, there, just a few more hours and your baby will be born."

"A few more hours?" Anna burst into tears. "She's tired and in pain. Can't you do something?"

"There's nothing any of us can do. Nature has to take its course." She exchanged a look with Seta. Seta wrung her hands.

The hours crept slowly by. Morning turned to noon.

Suddenly Victoria cried out. "I think the baby is coming."

The midwife, who was pouring herself a glass of water, rushed to Victoria's side. She felt her stomach. "Yes, the baby's coming."

The words were barely out of her mouth when the next contraction began.

"I want you to push now," the midwife said.

Victoria pushed with each contraction and as she did, the worried frowns on the midwife and Seta's faces deepened. Finally, they pulled her to a squatting position and braced her on either side.

Victoria took a deep breath. Something was happening. She felt it--a slowly spreading warmth. She gathered the last of her strength and pushed. There, at last. The pressure was gone. Her baby had been born.

The midwife cleaned and wrapped the baby in a bundle. Then she turned to Victoria. "Your son," she said.

"It's a boy? Oh, he's beautiful. Mother, look at his tiny little hands."

Seta wiped her eyes. "What a precious darling."

Anna gazed in wonder and touched his toes.

The midwife helped Victoria put the baby to her breast, then stood.

Victoria looked up and smiled. "Thank you, Shakar Mama."

The midwife looked at her feet.

Victoria looked at Seta and raised her eyebrows.

"Is something wrong?" Seta said.

"No, no, she's all right now. But she's small. Having babies is going to be risky for her. Think about it."

Victoria looked down at the infant in her arms. Babies were too dear to say no to more. She had gotten through a pregnancy once. She could do it again.

The midwife left and Nikol stepped into the room. He looked at Victoria who sat propped up on lacy white pillows. Her long dark tendrils of hair cascaded down her exposed chest while the baby peacefully nursed.

He rushed to her side. Her lashes rose and she met his eyes.

He brushed her face with his hand. "I love you so much."

"What are you going to name him?" Anna said.

Victoria looked at Nikol.

"Koren," he said.

Seta's face lit up with a smile and her eyes filled with tears. "Thank you." Then her expression changed. She crossed the room and opened the lid to a wooden box. A blue glass bead sparkled in her hand and she pinned it to the baby's nightgown.

Victoria stroked her baby's head. Now he was protected from the evil eye. She wasn't sure she really believed in the evil eye, but one never knew. Babies did occasionally take sick and die. Maybe their deaths were caused by a malevolent look. She pulled her son closer to her chest. Let her mother put the bead on him. Why take chances?

Victoria touched little Koren's ear. If the baby had been a girl, the midwife would have sterilized a needle on a clove of garlic and pierced her ear with a silk thread. Thank goodness, she didn't have to put him through that.

Victoria and Nikol celebrated their baby's birth for forty days. Friends and relatives dropped by daily with gifts. On the fifth day, they hosted a party to honor little Koren's first bath and Nikol nearly committed an unpardonable social crime of throwing away the bath water instead of sprinkling it on the vegetable garden.

On the fortieth day, Victoria got up and prepared her son for his christening. Nikol had asked Fiorine and her husband, Arsen, to be Koren's godparents, an honor they had gladly accepted.

When they appeared at the door before church that morning, Fiorine carried a package in her arms. "For the baby," she said.

Victoria opened it and took out Koren's christening outfit. "Oh, it's just beautiful!" She ran her hands over the thousands of stitches Fiorine had embroidered onto it. She must have worked on it for months. And, as was traditional for godparents, she and Arsen were paying for all of the christening expenses.

Victoria reached over and kissed her cousin's cheek. "Thank you."

At the church, Victoria and Nikol stepped back, while Fiorine and Arsen stood at the altar holding the baby. Little Koren lay like an angel in his godmother's experienced hands until it was time to be bathed in the purifying waters. Fiorine handed the serene infant to the priest, who gently lowered him into the cool water. A startled Koren let out a howl of indignation.

Victoria searched for her mother's eyes in the parishioners. Several of the women were smiling knowingly at each other. Seta looked at her with sympathy.

Victoria tried to pay attention to the priest's words. She hated to cause her baby any discomfort. But the bathing was as much a part of the ritual as was her and Nikol's secondary role.

Koren was still wailing, but Father Mikayelian appeared unperturbed. He placed Koren gently on the towel spread across Fiorine's waiting arms. Arsen folded it around the infant. The service was over.

Victoria filed out of the church, carrying her now-quiet baby. All at once, exhaustion hit her. She still had the christening party to get though this afternoon. How would she do it?

Margaret hurried to her side, took one look at her face and said, "Let me carry the baby for you, Victoria."

Victoria handed him to her and sighed with relief. She longed to support her tired frame against Margaret's shoulder on the walk back home. But Margaret was carrying her baby for her now, holding her up in another way. Later today, she would tell Margaret how much she appreciated her friendship. But no, that was not necessary. Margaret knew. With her, there was no need to explain why Victoria felt as she did about anything. Margaret had been at her side for as long as she could remember. She was a part of her thoughts, hopes and dreams.

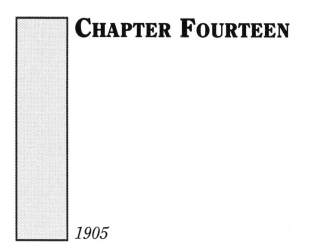

CHAPTER FOURTEEN

1905

"**K**oren, stay away from that stove. It's hot." Victoria's arm shook with fatigue but she lifted it and pointed to the other side of the room. "Go play where I don't have to watch you so closely. I have work to do."

Koren trotted to the other side of the room, picked up a block, and stacked it on top of another one.

"Where Grandma?"

"She went into the village this morning. Remember, you waved good-bye to her?"

"Papa?"

"He's outside in the fields, but he'll be in for lunch soon."

At the mention of his papa, Koren's blue eyes lit up with a smile. Lately, Nikol had been taking him out in the fields in the afternoons. Someday this farm would be his and Nikol insisted that even a two-year-old could learn something from watching.

Victoria finished pounding out the meat she was going to make into *kufta*. She had just set it aside, when Anna arrived at the door for a visit.

"How are you feeling? You look pale." Anna laid her hand on Victoria's arm.

"Then I guess you heard?"

"That you are pregnant? Yes."

Victoria shook her head. "I just told my mother yesterday."

"Well, that gave her time enough to tell the whole village."

"So I see." Victoria laughed then looked serious. "I didn't tell her or Nikol right away." She lowered her voice. "I keep thinking about what the midwife said when Koren was born. It took me a long time to get pregnant both with Koren and this time. I didn't want to disappoint anyone with false hopes. I hope nothing goes wrong."

"Oh Victoria, nothing will go wrong."

"I don't know. Having babies is dangerous."

Anna paled and put her hand on her own swollen abdomen.

"Forgive me, Anna. What was I thinking? Saying something like that when you're due for your baby, when? In another month?"

Anna nodded. "Five or six weeks."

"Well, you look as healthy as can be."

Anna's face relaxed into a smile. "I'm doing fine. Leon's mother doesn't let me lift a finger. This is her first grandchild. In fact, she told me today to stay home after this week. Sometimes babies come sooner than you think. But I wanted to get out today to tell you how happy I was about your news."

"Two babies on the way." Seta stood in the doorway and grinned.

When Koren heard her voice, he dropped his playthings and, with a wide smile, rushed to greet his grandmother.

"Little *moog*." Seta scooped him into her arms.

Victoria looked from her mother's unusual blue eyes and wide smile to the mirror image in her arms. There was no doubt about it: Koren looked more like his grandmother than either of his parents. He seemed to have even inherited her height.

"You bring candy?" His eyes searched hers, hopefully.

Seta kissed the top of his head. "Yes, but first, lunch for you." She led him to the table and Victoria served the group their meal.

After lunch, Nikol took Koren into the fields for the afternoon. They returned as Victoria was lifting her pan of *kufta* from the oven.

Nikol sniffed. "Mmm, that smells wonderful." He laid his hand on Koren's shoulder. "We men are hungry."

Victoria smiled. "Did you men remember to wash your hands?"

Nikol opened his mouth, closed it, and went to the pump with Koren.

When they returned, Victoria sat everyone down. She helped herself to a large serving of meat. "Well, at least my appetite hasn't been affected this time."

Seta took a helping of meat herself. "No, not yet, but it's bound to be soon. Remember how sick you were for the first three months with Koren?"

"Mother, I'm eleven weeks now. I think I'm past being sick now."

"But I thought..."

"You thought I was early because I just told you about it. But no, I've known for a while." She studied Seta's face. There was that worried look she used to see so much. "What is it?"

Seta shook her head. "Nothing, dear. Nothing at all."

Nikol looked from one to the other. "Is something wrong?"

Victoria frowned. "No."

"Because I was going to a meeting tonight, but if there is..."

"Please, I don't want anyone worrying about me," Victoria said. She worried enough herself. She didn't need them doing it, too. She looked at Nikol. "You go to your meeting."

Nikol felt his way down the dark road. Michael Damadian had called this meeting tonight because he had news to give them about Andranik, the revolutionary leader in the mountain villages of Sasun.

Nikol thought about Andranik, a hero to so many Armenian men. For more than two years, he and his troops had kept the government officials out of the entire mountainous region he defended. Had something happened to end the self-rule Andranik had established?

At the meeting, Michael gave them the sad news. "Andranik has fled to Persia. Self-rule is over for our people in the mountains."

Nikol made a fist and punched his other palm. "What happened?"

"The government has been unhappy about the independence of that area since it began," Michael said.

One of the men laughed. "They're probably afraid it will give the rest of us ideas."

Michael nodded. "From what I hear, the government sent troops to attack the villages. Andranik and his troops moved in to defend them. The villagers would have been slaughtered if he hadn't. He saved the villagers but got trapped in the process. He escaped by fleeing the country."

There was silence in the room. The men all bowed their heads. Finally, John Halabian spoke.

"Our dream of equal rights and governing ourselves does

not have to leave the country with Andranik. The Young Turks in Paris. There's our answer."

Levon Kalustian sat up straight. "John is right. Andranik was successful in the mountains because the villages were remote, cut off by the terrain. Here on the plains, we couldn't have defended ourselves that way."

Later, after the meeting ended, Nikol walked home. He stopped and kicked a stone. To trust a Turk, any Turk, was a mistake. And what about the secret committee within the Young Turks ranks, The Committee of Union and Progress rumored about two years ago? No, they had heard nothing more about it, but that didn't mean that it didn't exist.

He reached home and climbed into bed, but lay awake thinking about the meeting. A mistake, definitely a mistake, he decided. He rolled onto his side and went to sleep.

Two nights later, Victoria awoke with a start. Something was wrong. There, she felt it again, a deep gripping pain in her lower abdomen. She sat up. She was bleeding too. Cold fingers of apprehension tightened around her heart and she began to perspire. Soon she had doubled over and was moaning in pain.

Seta jumped up. "Victoria, what's wrong?"

"Something's wrong with the baby," she said through clenched teeth.

"You're having pain?"

"Pain and bleeding."

"Oh, darling, I've been worried about you since you told me you still had your appetite. Really, nausea is a sign of a strong pregnancy."

"And I thought I was lucky. I'm miscarrying, aren't I?"

Seta's silence answered her question.

Nikol was already awake. "What can I do?" He put his arm around Victoria and drew her close.

Seta pointed to Koren. "I think you'd better get him over to Fiorine's."

Nikol woke Koren, who was delighted to hear he was going to play with his cousins. Nikol kept his tone light, picked up a lantern, and the two went out the door.

Victoria moaned, again. It was all so painful. And what was going to happen to her? She rocked back and forth and tried to keep from crying out.

Nikol ran back in the door. "Shall I go for the midwife, or maybe the doctor?"

"No, there's nothing either can do," Seta said. "It's in God's hands."

Nikol kneeled down at Victoria's side.

She burst into tears. "I'm so scared."

He kissed her forehead, and looked into her eyes. "Listen to me: You're going to be all right. And we're going to be right here with you through the whole thing."

As the night dragged by, Victoria continued to have a steady, searing pain in her lower stomach. She bled heavily until, at last, toward morning, it was over and she lay weakly against the pillows. Her face was as white as the sheets. Her enormous dark eyes shadowed her tired, drawn face. She tried to sit, but became so lightheaded that she fell back again.

Seta looked at her and grew ashen herself. She turned to Nikol. "Get the midwife. Quick."

The midwife took one look at Victoria and dropped her bag. "Liquids. She needs liquids. She's lost a lot of blood." She tapped Victoria's arm. "Can you hear me?"

Victoria's eyes blinked open. "Yes, but I feel so funny. Like I can't quite wake up."

The midwife exchanged a worried look with Seta. She gently put her hand under Victoria's head and tilted it forward. With her other hand, she dribbled spoonfuls of water into Victoria's mouth. When she had done all she could, the midwife left with instructions for Seta to make tea out of dried parsley. "It will build up her blood," she said.

For the next two days, Victoria woke only to the gentle but insistent prodding of Seta who fed her nourishing broth and teas until, at last, the crisis had passed.

Victoria opened her eyes and propped herself up on her elbows. Finally she could sit up without passing out.

Seta brought her a cup of tea. "Oh, darling, are you feeling better?"

"I think so. I can sit up."

"And that's all you should try for now. It's going to take time to get your strength back."

"Where is Koren?"

"With Fiorine. But don't worry about him. Nikol says he's having fun with his cousins. Naturally, he doesn't understand anything that's going on."

Victoria's eyes filled with tears. "Poor little thing. I wanted him to have a brother or sister to play with here."

"Don't be sad. You'll have another one some day."

Victoria turned away. Those words would hardly have comforted her mother when she was having her miscarriages, and they didn't comfort Victoria now. She lay down and turned on her side. She was well enough now to feel the pain of her loss. A loss even her mother didn't seem to understand. Suddenly, she felt very lonely.

Victoria was sitting up again, when Nikol returned from the village an hour later. His pleased smile instantly turned to concern, when Victoria took one look at him and burst into tears.

"I'm sorry." She rested her head on her knees and sobbed.

"Sorry? Why? You've done nothing wrong."

"But I feel like I have."

Nikol crossed the room and took her hand in his. He looked like he didn't know what to say but when he spoke, his words were exactly what she needed to hear.

"Feel sad, darling. You have a right to. We've lost something we wanted very much."

Although Victoria cried anew, this time they were tears

of healing. She was not alone.

When she had dried her eyes, she turned to Nikol. "I want to see Koren."

Seta shook her head. "Oh, honey, no. You're too sick."

Nikol stood. "No, I think he should come home now." He looked at Seta and nodded toward the door. She followed him to it. "I think she needs him," he said.

Seta looked uncertain. "Well, if you think it best."

"I do."

When Nikol reached Fiorine's house, she met him at he door. "How is she?" She gripped his arm. "Tell me truthfully. I need to know."

Nikol looked at Fiorine with affection. "She's better. Truly she is. She's even sitting up now."

"Oh, thank God. I've been awake nights worrying.

Nikol followed Fiorine into the main room of her house. Then he stopped short.

"How is my darling niece? I've been worried sick about her. Of course, seventeen is too young to be having a baby." Rose's eyebrows formed a valley and she smiled.

Fiorine stepped between them. "Nikol was just telling me that Victoria is better."

Nikol focused on the empty room. "Where is Koren?"

"He's outside playing with Anton and Marie," Fiorine said.

Rose took a step sideways. "Because she was really too young when she married. I'm surprised she even carried one to term."

Fiorine threw up her hands.

Her mother-in-law stared at Rose from the table where she sat.

Rose just looked at Nikol and smiled.

The back door flew open and the children stampeded in led by eight-year-old, Anton. Koren's adoring eyes left his cousin long enough to spot his father.

"Papa." He dashed to Nikol and jumped up into his arms.

"Will you stay with us for lunch?" Fiorine said.

Nikol had no trouble giving his three refusals for food. "I really just came to get Koren. It's time for him to go home."

"Oh, so soon? I hope it's not because," Fiorine looked at her mother, "of anything that was said here."

"No, not at all." Nikol shifted Koren to one arm and took Fiorine's hand. "You have helped us so much. I'm taking Koren home because Victoria needs him. I appreciate everything you've done for us. Truly."

Fiorine shook her head. "Victoria has done more for me than I'll ever be able to do for her. There are some acts of kindness that you can never repay."

They embraced and Nikol left with his son still in his arms.

Rose went to the window and watched him walk away. How dare he turn her own daughter against her. She could see the anger, the accusation, in Fiorine's eyes. As if what had happened was *her* fault.

Who was Nikol anyway, she thought? Just some stranger who had arrived in their village from who knew where? Oh, everyone liked him so much. The men of the village listened to what he said. Her cousin had trusted him like a son. He had walked into all their lives and now he had taken the land that should rightfully have been hers. Well, she would fix him. He had been running from something when he came here nine years ago. *What?* Well, whatever it was, she would find out. How she would do that she didn't know, but of the eventuality that she would do it, she was sure.

CHAPTER FIFTEEN

Late spring, 1908

*V*ictoria covered the packed picnic hamper with a cloth. Today she would visit her father's grave. The entire community was going to the cemetery for the annual commemoration of their loved ones. She and Seta had cooked for days to prepare the food they were bringing and Nikol had hired a carriage.

"Koren, come here and let me comb your hair," Victoria said. "Then I want you to sit out front and stop getting in everyone's way."

Victoria combed her five-year-old son's hair neatly to one side. His face had lost all its baby roundness and its sharp lines made him look all the more like his grandmother.

Seta held out her hand. "Come, darling, we'll both go

outside and sit together. We don't want those nice clothes mussed up."

Victoria watched the two chat with each other on the doorstep, while she folded a blanket. Really, her mother babied him so. But he was starting school in the fall and he would mature there as she had. She was not worried about how Seta would fill those empty hours either. She patted her stomach. She was pregnant again, though she hadn't told anyone yet. Soon she would have to tell them. The familiar nausea had started already and she wouldn't be able to hide it from them for long.

Victoria untied her apron and smoothed her black dress. Her father had been dead for seven years, but this day had not become any easier for her with the passing years. Why did he have to die so young?

She looked at Seta again through the open door. How did she stand it, losing the love of her life? If something were to happen to Nikol... No. Victoria shuddered. She mustn't even think it.

Wagon wheels crunched up the hill. Time to go. She gathered an armload of blankets and went outside.

Nikol went into the house and came out, bent under the weight of the picnic hamper. He carried it to the driver who hoisted it into the wagon.

No one spoke on the way to the cemetery. Victoria and Seta folded their hands in their laps. Nikol stared into the distance. Even Koren was solemn.

When the driver pulled up to the cemetery, Victoria noticed Margaret climbing out of her carriage with her husband, Solomon, and her two-year-old son, Diran. A dozen or so others were already parked and more were pulling in behind her. Nikol jumped down and slid the picnic hamper to the edge. He balanced it on his shoulder, carried it to Koren's grave, and went back to help Seta and Victoria down.

At the grave site, Seta and Victoria spread a rug out on the ground and layered blankets on top of it. Then they all stood and folded their hands in prayer.

Seta began to cry. Soon her whole body shook.

Victoria looked at Nikol.

"I loved him like my own father," he said.

The two collapsed in each other's arms.

Little Koren looked at the adults in astonishment. What was wrong? Even his father was crying. He felt his own eyes fill, but what were they crying about? One thing he was sure of, picnic or not, he didn't like it here.

Finally Seta dried her eyes and Victoria and Nikol separated.

"Come, Koren, it's time to pay our respects to our friends," Victoria said.

Koren reached for his grandmother's hand. They'd better not cry again. That was scary. But at their first stop, Aunt Fiorine started to cry and his parents did, too. He looked at his seven-year-old cousin, Marie. Her hair was braided with black ribbons. Then he looked at his eleven-year-old cousin, Anton. Anton looked back at him without smiling. Where was the picnic his mother had promised him?

Eventually, after many other stops, the adults began to talk. Laugh even. Other children began to play. He asked for permission to go find his cousins.

When he found them, Koren walked up to Anton, grinned, and gave him a shove. Anton recovered his balance, stuck his index fingers in his ears, and waggled the rest of them at Koren. Then Anton turned heel and fled. Koren looked at Marie and jerked his head in Anton's direction. She nodded and they both took off at a run.

They followed Anton, until he disappeared down a row of deserted graves. Koren squeezed Marie's hand. His heart thumped. After all, dead people lived here. The two crept down the grassy lane. Where was Anton?

Suddenly, Anton popped up from behind a gravestone. Koren and Marie screamed. Anton laughed and ran off. Koren frowned, grabbed Marie's hand again, and chased after him.

The children continued to play, until a regal looking carriage pulled up and Father Mikayelian stepped down. The entire cemetery grew silent. Koren looked around and saw his mother gesturing to him. He walked back and waited for the priest to visit his family.

Once Father Mikayelian had blessed all of the family's loved ones, they began to eat and the party began.

"Here's to the memory of the man who took me in when I had no where to go." Nikol tipped his glass of *raki* and swallowed it in one gulp.

Two children raced by squealing with laughter.

Leon refilled both glasses. "Now we'll drink to the memory of my dear grandfather."

Nikol slung his arm around Leon and they stumbled off to find Arsen.

Marie waggled her braids at Koren and he chased her down a dirt path.

The day drew to a close when the sun began to set and a chill descended. Victoria called to Koren, gathered up their belongings, and helped her mother into the carriage. Nikol climbed up after them and slumped into a seat.

The next morning Nikol lingered at the breakfast table, holding his head in his hands. Finally he raised himself up, stretched, and plodded to the door.

"I'm going out to the fields. I may be in for lunch, I may not, depending on how I feel."

Victoria nodded and hid a smile.

She and Seta cleaned all morning. Toward noontime, John Halabian appeared at their door. He waved a worn-looking envelope in the air.

"It's for Nikol. From America."

Victoria drew in a breath. "For Nikol? Are you sure?"

"Yes. It arrived in the village this morning."

Victoria took the envelope and read the front. "It just

says, the province of Kharpert. It doesn't even have our village on it."

"From the looks of it, it traveled around a while before it reached you."

"Well, I'd better take it to him right away."

Victoria headed for the fields. Who did Nikol know in America? She reached him just as he was heading back.

"Nikol, this letter came for you from America."

"From America? For me?" He took the envelope from her and studied the handwriting on the cover. His eyes widened. He took out a handkerchief and wiped his forehead.

"Nikol, who is it from?"

"My brother."

"Stephan?"

"No, Abraham."

"You never told me you had a brother named Abraham."

Nikol looked at her. "No, I didn't. And there are other things I can't tell you about even now."

What was he talking about? And why did he look so nervous? She wanted to ask him, but he had walked away. She turned and went back to the house.

Abraham had written to him. Why? When they had parted, they had agreed not to contact each other unless it was an emergency. If the government ever connected him to Abraham, it was all over for him. So what had happened to make Abraham take that risk?

Nikol sat down and opened the letter. It began:

Dearest Brother,

I can only hope this letter reaches you in time. I knew when we parted that you said you were going home to Kharpert, but you know why I haven't tried to reach you. I've also heard through our brothers, that you had a home and were safe. You are no longer safe. Someone has betrayed you. You must leave Turkey at once.

Years ago, the police raided a *Dashnak* office and found a letter with detailed plans about assassinating the sultan. They knew from its contents that it was written by someone involved in the Ottoman Bank incident but they had no idea who it was or where they were. Then someone tipped them off that you were in the provinces. They're going from village to village, searching for you. They will hang you if they find you.

The letter went on to explain that Nikol was to go to America and gave instructions on how he was to get out of the country. After finishing it, Nikol sat lost in memories of the event that had precipitated his need to flee...

They had spent months planning it. They'd worked out

every detail, and if it failed, they had been prepared to die for it.

He remembered the exact date, Wednesday, August 26, 1896. He had watched it all from the street. At 1:15 in the afternoon, two of their men had strolled into the bank, dressed in business suits. They had scanned the large open area which was surrounded by offices, and found it empty of customers, as they'd expected it to be at that hour. One man went to the gold counter, the other to the silver. As planned, each made requests to change money. The clerks nodded their agreement and the men hurried back to the door and signaled. Two men, dressed as porters, entered. Each had a large sack slung over their shoulders. They set them down. As soon as they did, Nikol blew a whistle outside. Twenty-five armed men stepped out of alleyways and dashed toward the bank, firing as they ran.

As the men were running, the porters were untying the drawstrings on their sacks. They carefully took out bombs and rifles and laid them on the floor.

Once everyone was in, the men sealed the doors shut. Abraham told Nikol the rest of the story later that day. The men erected barricades out of bags of silver coins. Everyone had rehearsed their parts. They were orderly and calm. Initially, nothing went wrong.

The leader, Abraham, stepped up to the terrified clerks. He had been seventeen at the time. "We have come to present our demands to the European powers," he said. "They are to send a representative to the sultan and force him to end the injustice for our people. No more massacres, and we want the same rights as the Muslim citizens of Turkey."

The silver clerk nodded rapidly.

Abraham stepped closer. "We'll remain here for forty-eight hours only. If our demands are not met by then, we're going to blow this place up. Everyone — you, the executives, and ourselves — will go with it."

"But we're just clerks," the silver clerk said.

Abraham looked up the stairway. "Take me to the director's office."

"Sir Edgar Vincent?"

"Yes. And don't try anything along the way."

The clerk looked at the grim determined faces of the armed men. "Come this way."

In his office, Sir Edgar Vincent climbed up on his desk and looked at the skylight above him. Five minutes ago, he had heard gunshots outside. He had looked over the railing and what he saw convinced him to get out fast. But he couldn't reach the skylight. He leaned down and pulled his desk chair up. A man in his position, having to climb out of his own bank like a thief, he thought. He climbed up on the chair and stuck his head through the skylight. He was eye-level with the roof. How could he climb the rest of the way? Then he heard more noise downstairs and he began clawing at the roof, trying to pull the rest of his substantial bulk through. The chair toppled over and his legs swung wildly. Sweat poured down his face. Finally, he managed to inch his way up and he flopped onto the roof with a thump.

The building directly to the right of the bank housed the offices for the Tobacco Exchange, but it was separated from the bank by a three-foot alleyway. He stood up and saw the street below. His knees wobbled and he felt like he couldn't breathe. He tried to force his shaky legs to move but they wouldn't budge. He tried to keep from looking down, but the more he did, the more his eyes were drawn in that direction. It was undignified for a man in his position, but what could he do? He dropped to his hands and knees and crawled to the edge of the roof. He looked at the span and knew he couldn't do it. But then, he heard footsteps marching up the stairs and pulling himself up to a crouch, he sprang over the gap. He landed on his belly, scraping his chin on the gravel roof, but he had made it. He crawled to the nearest skylight.

The inhabitant of the office below sat at his desk, his head bent over a stack of papers. Sir Edgar rapped on the glass. The clerk looked up. Startled, he ran for the door to his office and opened it.

A guard came in. The clerk pointed in Sir Edgar's direction and the guard raised his gun.

"No, no! It's me, Sir Edgar." He wiped soot and blood from his face and watched as recognition dawned on their faces.

The guard lowered his gun. "What are you doing up

there?"

"Never mind, help me down." He glanced over his shoulder. "Now. Hurry."

Abraham reached the director's office and saw the disarray. "Damn." He jumped up onto the desk, righted the chair, and climbed up. He peered through the skylight in time to see the bank director's head disappear through the neighboring skylight.

He turned to the clerk. "Who's next in line?"

The clerk raised his shaking arm and pointed it down the hall. "Mr. Auboyneau."

"Take me to him."

Abraham explained the situation to Mr. Auboyneau and said, "We've drawn up papers spelling out our demands. We want you to convince the sultan to agree to the terms."

"But these are your quarrels with your government. Why involve us? The Ottoman Bank is a European institution."

"We are aware of that and we chose this bank for precisely that reason. Your employees here are European, and most of the bank's money is from European investments. Europe has a lot to lose if you don't do what we say."

Mr. Auboyneau rested his chin on his palm. Then he spoke: "I will help you. And not just because I am afraid. You see, I want to help. I have lived in Turkey for six years now. I would have to be blind not to see how your people suffer. Everything they do to you is legal, too. What kind of a country treats its own citizens that way?"

Abraham grasped his shoulder. "I will make sure you get to the Porte safely. You have my word." He went back to Sir Edgar's office and pulled the shutters.

Nikol leaned against the wall of a store but kept his eyes on the third window of the top floor of the Ottoman Bank. His brother had told him that no one would suspect a thirteen year old. He hoped that was right because the shutters had just closed.

He put his hands in his pockets and strolled down an alley. Could everyone see the fear he felt inside? No, his brother had told him he was the best. And he was. He pulled down the brim of his hat and went around to the back of the bank.

A basement window opened and a lookout gestured to him. Inside, he found Abraham waiting for him. Abraham handed him the papers and explained where he wanted them taken. Nikol nodded, slipped back outside, and walked directly to the government offices.

"I am the messenger for the revolutionaries," he said to the guard at the door.

The guard glared at Nikol and brought him into a room where Sir Edgar sat conferring with other worried-looking men. Nikol handed him the papers.

Sir Edgar tore the envelopes open and read the letters. The *Dashnak*s had written three letters to the government.

The first was a position paper criticizing the lack of representation for Armenians in the government. The second listed twelve specific demands, including judicial reforms, tax reforms, and equal treatment under the law. The third letter detailed their intentions in the bank: they would stay there for forty-eight hours, during which no money would be taken and nothing in the bank touched. After the time was up, if their demands had not been met, the men would detonate the bombs and destroy the bank's money and business papers. The employees would die along with the revolutionaries themselves.

Sir Edgar ran his hand through his hair. "Send for my deputy, Mr. Auboyneau, immediately. The *Dashnak*s have agreed to let him go unharmed so he can vouch for what's going on inside the bank. And you warn the police not to start shooting when the bank doors open."

"I'll take care of it personally, sir," a police captain said.

Mr. Auboyneau reached the group a short time later and confirmed that no harm had been done yet. The men talked and finalized a plan that Sir Edgar had been working on since he arrived.

"Someone must bring our offer back to the *Dashnak*s," Sir Edgar said.

A short silence ensued. Then Maximov, a representative from the Russian embassy, spoke. "I will go."

"Before you do, I want someone to go to the sultan and get his personal word that the men involved will be pardoned, and that they will be allowed to leave the country with me."

The sultan agreed to Sir Edgar's request and Maximov set out for the bank saying that he was more worried about the police outside the bank than he was about the men inside. But the police had been given their orders and despite the gathering crowds, he reached his destination safely.

Once inside the bank, he sat down with Abraham and the rest of the men. He told them that bank or no bank, the *Dashnak*s did not have the following to influence a change of the magnitude they were asking. What he could offer them was a safe escort from the bank to Sir Edgar's yacht, in which, Sir Edgar would personally transport them out of the county. They could keep their weapons but had to leave the bombs behind. When Abraham asked him about their demands, Maximov assured him that the foreign powers were sympathetic and would begin talks with the Turkish government on the Armenian's behalf.

Nikol rubbed his eyes. Why had they agreed to leave the bank? Twelve years later, and nothing had changed. But he was glad they had left because his brother would not be alive, if they hadn't.

Nikol had been allowed aboard Sir Edgar's yacht before it set sail. On the yacht, Abraham told him what had gone on in the bank and Sir Edgar told him about his escape from it.

Really, once they had lost Sir Edgar as a hostage, their bargaining power had been drastically reduced and Abraham had had no choice but to abandon their mission and flee the country.

Nikol shook his head. It was too bad, though. The Ottoman Bank had been only the first in a series of plans their group had made. Had Abraham stayed, they would have held a demonstration in the center of the city, occupied a second bank, and bombed a police station. But without Abraham, their plans had come to ruin.

Nikol had left Abraham at the boat and walked through the city. As he walked, he began to notice that men in long robes and turbans were gathering. He became alarmed, knowing that the presence of these religious fanatics meant trouble. Some of the fanatics carried wooden clubs, some iron bars. They did not try to hide their weapons from the police and the police did not try to take their weapons away.

Nikol had begun to run. He ran out of the city and kept going until he had gotten to Kharpert and the dirt road in front of Koren's house.

Later, he had learned how the Turks had done their killing right in front of the police. In fact, some of the police joined them. Any Armenian became their target and the streets had run red with the blood of children, poor laborers, and dock workers, most of whom had never even heard about the revolutionaries. The massacres had gone on for two days. Then the British Marines had landed and the Turkish police realized they had to either end the violence, or risk the wrath of European military power. But more than five thousand people were already dead.

The massacres were reported in newspapers throughout Europe. Ambassadors of the six great powers met and drew up another reform scheme, but couldn't agree how to enforce it. So like every other reform scheme, it was never implemented.

Armenian men joined the *Dashnak*s in larger numbers that year than ever before.

And now someone had betrayed him to the government. Who? Then he remembered Alexan's words. *My mother is not through with you yet.* How had Rose done it?

He had to leave. The police might be on their way to the village that very minute. And every minute he was in the village, his entire family was in danger. But it was him the police wanted, not them. Once he was gone, they would leave his family alone.

Nikol got up and started walking back to the house. What could he possibly say to Victoria to explain his leaving? He couldn't tell her the truth. Koren had told him not to. There was too much danger in her knowing. If the police questioned her, they would see it in her eyes. She would be arrested, tortured even. No, he couldn't tell her.

Victoria ran to him when he stepped through the door. "What did the letter say?"

He couldn't meet her eyes. "I never told you about

Abraham because... because I thought he was dead."

Victoria frowned. "Why couldn't you tell me he was dead?"

"I just...well, never mind. He isn't. In fact, he's in America and wants me to come see him."

"But you won't, will you?"

He didn't answer her. Instead he watched her eyes slowly widen with surprise.

"You're going, aren't you?"

He couldn't stand to see the hurt in her face. The hurt he had caused. He spoke to the wall. "I haven't seen Abraham in years. I'll go to America and see him. I'll get a job so when I come back, we'll be able to have everything we want."

"I thought you had everything you wanted already."

Couldn't he have thought of something better than that? "Well, I have, but I may not get this chance again."

Victoria grasped his arm. "Nikol, don't go. I wish I didn't have to tell you this way, but I'm pregnant. Do you remember what the midwife told me? What if I die?"

He mustn't look at her. If he did, he would tell her and she would be in danger. He looked at the ceiling. He looked at the floor. He walked to the window and stared out. "Victoria, my brother arranged passage now. It will be wasted, if I don't go."

She looked at him like she no longer knew him. Then her eyes narrowed and her lips compressed. "I see you've made up your mind about this."

"Well, I... "

"Never mind. I'm going to find my mother."

He watched her walk out the door with her chin up and her back stiff. He felt like a monster.

Seta came running in, wiping dirt from the vegetable garden from her hands. "Nikol, have you thought about this? If you leave, you may never be able to come back."

"Well, I might not have this chance again."

Seta put her hands on her hips. "What did that letter say? Did it say something bad about our family? Is that why you're leaving?"

"No, no. Nothing like that." Nikol turned and began throwing clothes into a duffel bag.

In less than two hours, he was ready. He turned to Victoria and saw a world of hurt reflected in her large brown eyes. He fell into her arms. He didn't want to let go of her but he had to. Had to get out before he endangered them all.

Victoria stood on the hill and watched until she could no longer see him. How long would he be gone?

A year?

Two?

Forever?

And how would they all survive without him?

CHAPTER SIXTEEN

July, 1908

Victoria felt as dry as the sun-scorched grass. She picked up her embroidery, looked at its intricate pattern of threads, and put it down. How could she concentrate on something so meaningless? Nikol was gone. Had been gone for two months. It was all she could do to crawl out of her bed each morning. Yet she must make herself get going, and not on her embroidery, either. She had a farm to run, alone and the summer was drumming by. When fall came, how was she going to do it all — to harvest the wheat, pick the vegetables, process, store, sell? She leaned on the table and put her head in her hands.

Seta swept the floor around Victoria. The bristles of the broom tickled her leg.

"Mother, can you buy some bread in the village this afternoon?"

"What? Buy bread when we can make it?"

"Well, I don't know. It seems like too much trouble. Anyway, if you don't want to go today, you can go tomorrow."

Seta put her hands on her hips.

Victoria's gaze swept past her, then came quickly back. Oh, she hadn't seen that in two months.

"Now, you listen to me," Seta said. "It's time for you to start taking some responsibility around here. We can't go on like this. I've been cleaning the house, tending the vegetables, and taking care of Koren. It's too much."

"Mother, I'll make the bread if that's what you want."

"I'm not talking about bread and you know it."

Victoria's eyes filled with tears.

Seta sat down and put her arm over Victoria's shoulder. "Darling, I know the pain you are in. But you must come back to us now. Koren needs you. I need you."

She had been telling herself the same thing, over and over, but she had not been able to make herself take the laundry basin from her mother, or answer Koren's calls for help. She sighed. "I'll try Mother."

"No."

Victoria raised her brow. "No?"

"No, the less you do, the less you want to do. Get up."

Seta led her to the door, handed her a scarf, and kissed her cheek. "Go into the village and buy the bread, dear. And stop in to see Margaret at the same time. You haven't seen her in weeks."

She felt her dark mood fade a bit, as she began to walk. The fresh air, the hot sun on her back — they felt good. Maybe she would go to Margaret's house. In fact, she would stop there first and invite her to walk to the village together the way they used to when they were still girls. She quickened her step.

Nikol had left. Well, she would have to learn to live without him. Her step became more firm. Who needed him anyway? But her farm — all that wheat, how would she ever do it without him? She had to think. There must be a way.

When Margaret saw who was on the other side of the door, she threw her arms around Victoria. "You look better than you have in months."

"And I feel better, too. My mother finally let me have it today. I've been sitting around doing nothing, while she's been tiptoeing around me. She hasn't said anything, but I know she felt sorry for me."

"Everyone in the village does."

"I know that. I can see it in their eyes. But I'm not going to let my mother, or anyone else feel that way anymore."

"Good for you. That's the Victoria I know."

"I'm not saying I don't have problems. I have a mother, a son, and another one on the way."

"You're pregnant? I didn't know that."

"No, my mother didn't run around the village telling

everyone this time. But it is good news, isn't it?"

Margaret looked at Victoria fondly. "Yes. Babies are always good news." She grinned. "I hope they are because I'm pregnant, too."

Victoria smiled. "Maybe our babies will be best friends like we are."

Margaret walked her son, Diran, to her mother's house and left him in her care. The two strolled, arm in arm, toward the village.

When they reached its outskirts, they stopped and looked at each other. A crowd of Turkish and Armenian people had gathered in the square. Was something wrong?

Victoria pulled Margaret back. "Let's stand where we can get away if we need to."

Margaret nodded.

A crier climbed up on a box, and held up his hands.

The village grew quiet.

"The revolution has come! The power of Sultan Abdul Hamid had been destroyed and the Young Turks are in control!"

Everyone began to talk. The crier held up his hands again. "The constitution of 1876 has been implemented. The Young Turks have declared all citizens of Turkey equal under the law."

Victoria looked at Margaret. Just like that? Was it possible? And what did the Turkish villagers think about it?

Margaret nodded in the direction of three Turkish

women. They had joined hands with two Armenian women and were cheering. Soon the entire crowd was, too, Turks and Armenians alike. Someone began knocking on doors. Leon came running into the village with his guitar and began to play.

Fiorine's husband, Arsen, grabbed Victoria's hand and pulled her into the street to join the rest of her dancing neighbors.

More musicians joined Leon and more people poured into the teeming village.

Victoria looked over her shoulder as Arsen spun her around and saw Seta arrive, holding Koren's hand. Michael Damadian rushed up to her and said something. Seta pointed to Koren and shook her head.

Victoria elbowed her way over to them.

"Mother, have you heard the news?"

Seta nodded. "About the Young Turks? Yes."

Victoria squatted down, so she was eye level with Koren. "I want you to remember this day as the day the Armenians became equal with the Turks. This is something that your grandfather and father worked very hard for."

Seta looked around. "I'm afraid I don't understand it very well."

Victoria jumped up and began to twirl Koren around. "I'll explain it to you later, Mother."

At home that night, Victoria told Seta what the constitution meant to them as Armenians. "We will have representatives in parliament for the first time who will present our grievances, and work out solutions. And it's not just the Armenians who benefit. Other non-Muslim groups do too, the Greeks, the Jews, the Slavs, to name a few."

Seta shrugged. "Well, the government is one thing. Here in our village we have other things to worry about. Like massacres — have we seen the last of those?"

"Well..." Victoria stopped. *If the Young Turks ever take power in Turkey, they may not be what they say they are.* She thought about Nikol's words. Then she bit her lip. Nikol. What did he know? She turned to Seta. "I believe we have. The Young Turks will not tolerate violence against us any more than they would tolerate it against Muslims."

Seta folded her arms. "I don't know. Where will the government be if our Turkish neighbors decide to turn against us?"

"But just look how they celebrated right alongside us today."

"They did, didn't they? Maybe you're right. You know more about this than I do, dear. And it's so good to see you smiling again."

Despite her optimism, Nikol's warning continued to nag Victoria, until she learned of an event that took place in the capitol ten days later. In a demonstration of sympathy, several thousand people, both Turks and Armenians, gathered at an Armenian cemetery where victims of the 1895 and 1896 massacres lay buried. Christian priests and Muslim *imam*s attended and each led their people in prayers for the victims. Turks expressing sympathy for something they had done? Nothing like that had ever happened before. Victoria drew a breath of relief and Nikol's words receded to the back of her mind.

Victoria continued to wait for news from the capitol, but her immediate concern was the food on their table and how she was going to harvest the wheat. Fall was drawing near.

One morning, she got up and admitted to herself that she needed help. She was almost six months pregnant and she simply could not harvest the wheat with just her mother and five-year-old son.

She walked to the Halabian's house and knocked on their door.

Mary Halabian opened the door.

"Why, Victoria, come in. What a pleasant surprise. We were just sitting down to lunch. Will you join us?"

"No, thank you. I've already eaten."

"Please join us, we have plenty."

They did not have plenty and Victoria stayed firm throughout her three polite refusals. Then she said, "I've come to ask for help."

John Halabian wiped his mouth and stood. "What can we do for you?"

Victoria looked past him. "Actually, I came to speak to Martin."

"Oh?" John gestured to Martin, who got up and joined

them.

She saw Martin exchange a sympathetic glance with his father. When would everyone stop feeling sorry for her? She raised her chin.

"Martin, I want to hire you to help me cut my wheat. I'll pay you one-third of our crop."

"I'd be glad to help out." Martin looked at his father. "If you and Avedis can manage without me."

John touched Victoria's upturned chin. "Don't ever be ashamed to ask us for help. Your father once helped my family when we needed it. I don't forget a kindness like that."

Martin smiled and lightly punched her arm. Victoria walked home past the Halabians' fields. They were half the size of her own. She thought about the food she had seen on their table. She herself rationed food so she could add to her savings each year. Martin's family rationed food because it was all they had to eat. Really, she was helping them as much as they were helping her. She lowered her chin and walked the rest of the way home.

On the morning she was going to harvest the wheat, Victoria rose early, dressed in old clothes, and covered her skirt with an apron. Seta looked at her bulging waist and clucked her tongue. But there was nothing Victoria could do about it. Pregnant or not, she had to work in those fields.

Martin arrived just as she finished setting up the screens she used to separate the stalks of wheat from their kernels.

All morning long, Martin slashed the wheat with his

scythe and Koren dragged it on a hand cart to Victoria and Seta, who thrashed it against the screens. By midmorning, Victoria's muscles were burning. She had to force herself to go back to work after lunch. But each *sssk* of the stalks against the screen brought her an increasing feeling of satisfaction and she mopped her brow and went on. At the end of three days, their task was complete.

"Your farm is so beautiful," Martin said.

Victoria followed his eyes, as they swept over the upwardly ascending fields, across the rows and rows of shiny red tomatoes in the vegetable garden, and on to the grape arbor standing beside her stone house.

"This farm was my father's pride and joy. Now it is mine. It's funny isn't it, how the threat of loss makes you realize the strength you have to fight?"

Martin studied her face. "How very true."

With the wheat harvest complete, Victoria and Seta turned to the rest of their winter's food supply. Any spare moments Victoria had, she spent reading about what was going on in the capitol.

She learned that Sultan Abdul Hamid still officially retained his position but he had been stripped of his power by the Young Turks' Committee of Union and Progress. A parliament was being formed that would include Armenian representatives who would help identify injustices in the law and work on reforms. Each time Victoria read about the changes going on, she would think of Nikol and all he had missed by leaving when he did. He had struggled for so many years and had missed the revolution by two months.

One afternoon, Fiorine visited and the two talked about how the changes in government had changed their own outlook for the future.

"I used to think about those massacres and worry that my son would lose me the way Nikol lost his mother," Victoria said.

"And what about the taxes? It's no better to starve to death because you lost your land to the tax collector."

Victoria gave a short laugh. "After my father died, I learned about taxes. It hasn't been easy."

A knock on the door interrupted their conversation. Victoria went to the door. It was Rose. What did she want?

Victoria called Seta in from the garden. When Seta saw Rose, she looked at Victoria, who shrugged.

Fiorine looked at her mother and blushed.

"I just came by to see how you were." Rose looked around the tidy living room. A look of surprise crossed her face.

Victoria straightened her back. What had Rose been expecting to see — a house in shambles?

Rose sighed deeply. "I suppose we're going to have to help you get your crops in."

"No, we did that weeks ago," Victoria said.

"You did? How?"

"I hired Martin Halabian."

"You did *what*? I mean, I'm glad you were able to get by,

dear. Especially after the way Nikol left you."

Fiorine set her cup down firmly on the table. "Mother, Nikol is just away visiting his brother."

"Well, yes, if you say so."

Fiorine jumped up and took her mother firmly by the arm. "It's time to go now."

Victoria grinned at her cousin. "Thank you, Fiorine. Come again soon."

When they had left, Seta turned to Victoria. "Well, that's probably the worst of what you'll have to face."

"I don't know. I sort of like the way she comes out and says it. No one else in the village does, but I can tell what they think, just the same."

Seta looked Victoria in the eye. "It doesn't matter what anyone else thinks. You know Nikol is a good man. Papa thought so, too. Nikol loves you. He'll be back someday."

Victoria turned away. Love? He had left her pregnant, knowing she might die. What did love mean to him? And how would she feel even if he came back tomorrow? Would she ever trust him again?

CHAPTER SEVENTEEN

Fall, 1908

*K*oren started school the next week. Victoria leaned on her broom and watched him get ready to go. She remembered her own school days and her dream of college, so long ago. She felt her lips turn up in a wistful smile.

Koren pulled a sweater over his head, touched her arm, and walked off.

She didn't know why, but the gesture made her think of Nikol and she blinked back tears. Why had he left her?

Nikol had half-walked, half-run the day he left. If only there was a way to outpace the guilt. He thought about the hurt look on his wife's face. The hurt he had caused.

No, he must force himself not to think. He had to watch

instead for a raised patch of dust, listen for hoof beats, anything that signaled the police were catching up with him. He had villages to cross through, villages where he would have to walk right past the police and fade into the scenery by eliminating any look, expression, or gesture that made him stand out.

How much did the police know? Would they guess the direction he was headed in?

He stopped and forced himself to take a deep breath. Then he slowly let it out, feeling the tension in his muscles ease. There, that was better. Now he could use his senses for what lay immediately ahead of him — slipping out of Turkey without getting caught and hanged.

He reached his first village, stuck his hands in his pockets and reminded himself to slow his pace.

Two women walked toward him. Uncovered heads, wide brown eyes, Armenian, he thought.

"*Paree gesor,*" he said in greeting.

"Good afternoon to you," they answered and kept walking.

He went another ten feet. A man dressed like him crossed in front of him.

The man nodded to Nikol. "*Eench keghetseeg or eh.*"

"Yes, it is a beautiful day," Nikol said.

He reached the village square. Just a few more steps and he would be through it. A policeman came out of a bakery, eating a *beoreg.*

Nikol resisted the urge to run. Instead, he stared straight ahead and continued on.

The policeman glanced at him and went back to his pastry.

Nikol passed through two more villages without incident. He was on the road when he heard hoof beats pounding in the distance.

He looked to his right. Open fields. He looked to his left and ran for the shelter of a boulder.

He flattened himself on the ground behind the rock and pulled grass over his legs. He lay still while the horses came closer, were in front, then passed by. He peeked out and saw the backs of police uniforms.

They were looking for him.

He was in as much danger as he had been twelve years ago. Twelve years ago, he had escaped. He would this time, too. He would get out of Turkey, establish himself in America, and send for Victoria, his love. He would survive for her.

With that in mind, Nikol got up, brushed dried grass from his pants and walked westward to the city of Smyrna.

He was overwhelmed, when he reached the teeming coastal city. Where should he go? The police might be here already, looking for him.

He found his way to the Armenian quarter and walked into a coffeehouse.

"I'm looking for Marderos Ermanian," he said to the proprietor.

"You are?"

Nikol lowered his voice. "Nikol Balian."

The proprietor's eyes widened. He stepped up to the window and looked down the street. Then he grabbed Nikol's elbow. "Come this way."

The proprietor led Nikol through the smoky room filled with men drinking coffee, men playing cards. Dark-haired men like himself. Men laughing and leaning together talking. It was all so familiar. A lump formed in Nikol's throat. Then he reminded himself of the danger he was in and the necessity to stay focused on his escape.

The proprietor pulled aside a curtain leading to a back room. "In here."

Nikol sat down on a packing crate. "You've heard of me then?"

"We all have. Police from the capitol are all over the city. They're asking questions about you. We're going to have to get you out on the next boat."

"Marderos is supposed to be making arrangements for that."

"Yes, Marderos is a brother *Dashnak*. I'll go get him now."

Fifteen minutes later, he was back with a man of medium height and black hair.

The man extended his hand. "I knew your brother."

"Thank you for helping me. I hope I haven't put anyone

else in danger."

"We're all brothers in the fight." Marderos pulled up another box and sat down. "Here are the plans. We're putting you on a French liner that's sailing in two days. Until then, stay here."

Nikol nodded.

Marderos clasped Nikol's shoulders with both hands. "I mean right here. Don't go out into the alley. Don't go out into the shop. Stay where you are."

This was serious. And he still had to get to the boat without being spotted.

As if reading his mind, Marderos pulled Nikol's chin to the side. "You've got a few days growth. Keep it. You'll be surprised how much a beard alters one's appearance. We'll part your hair in the middle and put spectacles on you."

"I'm traveling on a French ship?"

"Yes. And you're going as a Frenchman. We're sending a young girl with you who will pretend to be your wife. She was educated in the capitol and speaks fluent French. If anything happens, let her do the talking."

Nikol took off his sweater. "What will I do with her in America?"

"She has relatives there. And if all goes well, your brother said he will marry her."

"Marry her? I don't want him to get married just for me."

"No, he said he would have been sending for a wife soon anyway."

Nikol spent two long days hiding out in the back room of the coffeehouse and worrying that the police would storm through the curtain and arrest him. But Smyrna was a large city and the morning he was due to set sail arrived without incident.

He put on a jacket and pants, tailored in a style he remembered the Europeans wearing when he was in the capitol. The coffee shop owner walked him to the dock where Marderos stood with a frightened young girl.

"This is Marig Tumanian," he said.

Nikol tipped his hat and the two climbed aboard the ship.

Nikol looked at Marig's threadbare clothes that bore a look of faded elegance and felt sorry for her. He had learned that until last year, Marig had been wealthy. Then her parents had both died of influenza. Her father's wealth had gone to his cousin who, instead of taking Marig in as he should have, had placed her in an orphanage. Now she was leaving to start a new life in America and marry his brother, if she met with his approval. She seemed to be trying to make the best of her situation and he admired her for that.

Nikol had just deposited Marig's large trunk in the cabin she was going to share with another woman, when a whistle sounded. The ship was going to be searched.

This was it.

Nikol jumped into the top bunk. "When they come in here, tell them I'm sick."

Marig pulled the blanket over him with shaking fingers

and nodded.

They listened. Boot steps pounded up the stairs and down the hallway. Eventually they heard a knock at their door.

"We're searching all rooms," a man in a dock policeman's uniform, said in Turkish.

Marig shrugged and answered in French pointing to Nikol.

Nikol coughed.

The policeman leaned into the hallway and called out.

One of the ship's officers came in.

Marig spoke to him in French.

The officer turned to the policeman. "She said her husband is sick with a cough and a fever."

Nikol coughed again, trying to make it sound as phlegmy as possible.

The ship officer wrinkled his nose and directed the policeman out by the elbow.

"We're looking for an Armenian man, anyway," the policeman said. He turned to walk away.

The ship officer pulled the door shut and gave Nikol a wink as he did.

For the first week of the trip, Marig was seasick and Nikol brought broth to her bunk. She assured him that she didn't mind being sick if it meant she was going to America and to an easier life. There was nothing left for her in Turkey. Eventually her nausea eased and she was able to go out on the deck and chat with some of the other women.

One day, Nikol heard footsteps clattering down the hallway.

"Land ahead," a young boy shouted.

Nikol and Marig went outside and stood at the ship's railing. America. They waited there until the ship docked.

Nikol slung his duffel bag over his shoulder and picked up Marig's trunk. "It's called Ellis Island."

Marig looked as pale as she had on the first few days of their trip. She hung onto the railing as if to steady herself and followed Nikol off the boat.

They exited into a fenced-in area so congested with people, they could barely squeeze themselves through. More ships were pulling in with hundreds more people crowded on their decks. The midmorning sun bore down heavily on them. Nikol and Marig joined a line that was slowly inching its way up the steps leading to a huge building.

A vendor wheeled a pushcart by filled with tubes that looked like they were stuffed with meat. Nikol sniffed. He was hungry, but unsure how to negotiate anything in this foreign language so he stayed in line. By the time they entered the great hallway of the massive building, he was too nervous to think about his stomach or anything besides getting through the gate on the other side of the building.

Nikol looked around. A soldier in uniform said something Nikol couldn't understand and gestured in the direction of a man Nikol could see was a doctor. Nikol lowered his head and went where he was told. He must avoid eye contact with the soldier. One never knew with soldiers.

Marig's hands were shaking by the time their turn came. Nikol patted her arm and went first. The exam was brief. The doctor asked Nikol to open his mouth and looked inside. Apparently satisfied, he pointed Nikol down the line to another doctor who held a scary looking hooked metal object. He was using it to examine people's eyes. Nikol tensed. This was going to hurt. But it was part of his entrance into America, so he stood still while the doctor inverted his eyelid and looked underneath. It was painful but Nikol gave Marig a reassuring smile and moved to the next station.

Both Nikol and Marig passed their physical exams, but some others did not. To come all this way and not be permitted to enter America? What would he have done?

Nikol stepped up to the final station and broke out into a sweat. A soldier sat behind a desk looking at him.

"Do you speak English?"

"A little," Nikol said in a heavily accented voice.

"What is your name?"

"Nikol..." What was his name supposed to be? "Kalousdian."

The inspector wrote the name down. "And your wife?" He looked at Marig.

"Marig."

"Do you have a job here?"

What was the man asking him?

The inspector caught the eye of the man sitting next to him and rolled his eyes. The man sitting next to him grinned back.

Nikol looked around.

A voice said in Armenian, "He's asking you if you have a job here."

Nikol turned to the source of help. "You speak English?"

"Yes."

"Thank you. Tell him my brother lives here and will help me get one."

Nikol's interpreter answered for him, and at the mention of his brother, the inspector's face relaxed. "Ah, so you have a sponsor then?"

Nikol answered through the interpreter. The inspector took his rubber stamp and pressed it onto Nikol's immigration papers giving Mr. and Mrs. Kalousdian the right to enter the United States.

Nikol and Marig walked down a ramp and outside to a ferry which took them to Manhattan.

He had made it.

He scanned the sidewalks looking for Abraham. Where was he?

Someone was walking toward him. A little older and a little more mature – Abraham, his idol. Nikol pushed his way through the people remaining between them and embraced his brother.

Abraham hugged him back then held him at arm's length. "I didn't think I would ever see you again, Brother."

"Nor me, you." Nikol squeezed his brother's arm, then turned and introduced Marig.

Abraham smiled at Marig, but she did not smile back. She looked scared and her lip quivered.

Abraham's eyes softened. He took her arm in his. "Don't worry. I will get you to your uncle's house. You are safe with me."

For the first time since she had stepped off the boat, Marig's lips turned up in her lovely smile.

Abraham instantly assumed command, when they arrived at the train station. He bought three tickets to Boston and led his group to a bench to wait.

Nikol was impressed. Abraham seemed to speak this new language with ease. And he walked around this big city as though he didn't even see the buildings that stood as tall as the mountains of home.

Nikol sat and watched street vendors holding up bags of peanuts and shouting for customers. Fancy horse-drawn carriages rolled by him, carrying people dressed in velvets and silks. Smyrna was like a country village compared to this.

At last the night train to Boston pulled in and the three boarded. As the train glided along the tracks on the long ride, Nikol and Abraham stayed awake talking. Abraham told him that in America, the *Dashnak*s were actively raising money to send to their brothers in the old country. He told him about the life he had made for himself in this country and about his plans for the future. Neither mentioned their defeat at the Ottoman Bank and Abraham's necessity to flee. The memory of it was still painful, even after all these years.

The big engine screeched to a stop in Boston the next morning and the two men clambered down the heavy iron steps with the trunk between them and Marig close behind. They hopped on a trolley, which clicked and clacked its way out of town. When the trolley driver announced they were in Watertown Square, Abraham indicated that this was their stop.

The three marched down block after block of neatly kept houses, until Abraham stopped in front of a white, two-story structure.

"This is where Marig's relatives live. It's called a two-family house."

A smiling man opened the door and shook Abraham's hand vigorously. Then he loudly ushered them in. Marig's aunt laid her arm across Marig's shoulder, murmured a few words in her ear, and led her off. Nikol had heard that Marig's relatives had been appalled by their cousin's behavior in placing Marig in an orphanage.

Nikol looked around. What splendor these people lived in. They had many rooms. One was for cooking and eating in and it had a table as high as his thighs with stools to sit on made of wood. They even had a box-like structure with food inside that they kept cold with a large block of ice in a compartment above it.

Marig came back looking freshly scrubbed and her uncle seated his guests at the table.

"I'm taking Nikol out to Whitinsville tomorrow," Abraham said. He worked in a shoe factory and had told Nikol he would get him a job there or in one of the woolen mills. Abraham addressed himself to Marig's uncle. "I've saved just about enough money to set up an apartment and open a shop, a grocery shop."

Marig's uncle nodded in approval. *"Shad lav."*

The next morning, Sunday, Abraham roused Nikol early and without stopping to eat, the two set out for Whitinsville. Abraham negotiated a bed and meals for Nikol which his landlady agreed to, for three dollars a week. Three dollars. Imagine being able to afford that. But Abraham explained to him that he would be earning seven dollars a week at the factory.

After Nikol settled his belongings in his room, Abraham took him to visit a friend, Sarkis, who worked in the shoe factory with Abraham. In the seven years that Sarkis had been in America, he had brought over his parents and three brothers who all lived with him in a small apartment.

The family was from Kharpert and they welcomed Nikol warmly.

"We are about to eat, " Sarkis said. "Will you join us?"

Nikol had not eaten in more than eighteen hours. His stomach was crying for food but still, one had to be polite.

"Oh no, really, I'm not hungry."

Sarkis sat down at the table. "If you're sure, then." He turned to Abraham. "Will you eat with us?"

"Yes, thank you. I'm starved." Abraham pulled up a chair and sat down.

Nikol watched his brother put a forkful of steamy rice pilaf in his mouth. Where were his manners? And why hadn't his hosts pleaded with Nikol to join them? His stomach growled. He would forget that custom. If anyone offered him food again, he was accepting it on the first offer.

Nikol watched Sarkis joke with his father, while his mother put a plate of *manti*, dough stuffed with meat, on the table. He missed Victoria. No, he could not go home, but he would save every penny he earned and bring her here to him.

Nikol rose at five the next morning and was at the landlady's table in minutes, satisfying his considerable hunger. Then he and Abraham wiped the crumbs from their faces and walked to the shoe factory where Abraham worked. Nikol waited while Abraham spoke to his supervisor about a job. Abraham had told Nikol that if he couldn't get a job here, there were textile, rubber and steel factories and they liked to hire Armenians, because they knew how hard they worked.

Abraham's supervisor hired Nikol and led him to a room filled with massive machines. The noise from them hurt Nikol's ears. He watched his supervisor's lips move without sound. It didn't matter, anyway. He wouldn't have understood, even if he could have heard. The supervisor gestured and Nikol understood he was being assigned a place between two other men in a production line where the final stages of shoe construction were completed.

He looked at the men on either side of him and did what they did. He worked steadily throughout the day, breaking only for a hasty lunch at the boarding house. When the final whistle blew, he left the factory and found Abraham outside.

Back at the boarding house, Nikol sat on his bed and opened and closed his hands to relieve the ache. The day had been long and tedious.

Abraham said something.

Nikol pulled on his earlobes and stretched his jaw. "What did you say?"

Abraham raised his voice. "I said, you should think about taking out your citizenship papers."

"Here? Why, I didn't need them to get a job."

"No, but," Abraham looked at him, "you know you can never go back."

Nikol sighed. No, he could not go back; he could never return to his home or family. "I'll think about it."

Abraham looked sympathetic. "It takes time, Nikol."

He had to stop feeling sorry for himself and accept it. This was his new home. He would learn English, so he could take the oath of allegiance to his new country. He straightened his back. "I'll do it. From now on, I want you to speak to me only in English."

"Good for you," Abraham said.

A simple meal was waiting in the dining room were the ten other boarders, all men, all Armenian immigrants, were seated. Nikol noticed that most of them spoke English. If they could, he could.

Nikol's resolve to assimilate into his new culture stayed with him until he climbed into bed that night where, without the distractions of the day, his longing for Victoria and the family he left behind, became acute. He had hurt her. She might even be angry with him. But someday she would understand, he promised himself.

He laid his head on the pillow. The narrow cot he slept on was up off the floor. He had so much to get used to in his strange new country. But he fell asleep dreaming of home, of the rolling hills that met the mountains, of the quiet peace of his little farm, and of the love he felt for Victoria. As he slept, his lashes became moist with the emotion he would not allow himself to feel in the sunlight of day.

CHAPTER EIGHTEEN

Winter, 1909

Victoria wrapped her three-month-old son, Paul, in a blanket and went to answer the door.

Solomon, Margaret's husband, stood on her doorstep. "Margaret had the baby. It's a girl. Miriam."

"Is she all right?"

"Yes, she and the baby are both fine. Araxie is with them."

"Thank God! We'll go see them now."

Solomon left to continue spreading the news and Victoria turned to Koren. "Put your coat on quickly."

Seta put her own coat on and held out her arms. "Let me carry the baby for you."

"No, I can do it." Victoria alternated Paul in either arm,

while she slipped into her coat.

She walked to her trunk and pulled out the blanket she had knit for Margaret's baby. "I'll give her this today and save the nightgown I made for the christening. We can't stay long; I have to go over the accounts later."

Spring, taxes, they would all be here before she knew it.

Seta packed rolls and a crock of apricot preserves to bring along.

Victoria wrapped Paul in an additional thick woolen blanket and the group started on the cold walk to the village.

Paul had been born a week after Christmas. Victoria had gone into labor in the middle of the night but she had not told Seta until she couldn't manage on her own anymore. She had found herself doing that a lot since Nikol left, handling everything herself, avoiding help unless it was absolutely necessary.

Her labor had been long again and had left her so weak, she had been unable to hold the crying infant to her breast. But she had made it, no thanks to Nikol, and now she was slowly regaining her strength. She would need it for the upcoming spring.

The farm was a lot of work, but it was hers. No matter who came and went in her life, she was still married to Nikol so no one could dispute her right to be there. Father Mikayelian would only give it to Rose now, if he thought Victoria couldn't manage on her own. She had only her mother and two sons to take care of. She could manage just fine.

In the village, Victoria nodded to a Turkish woman carrying a baby, too.

The woman smiled and pointed to Paul. "How old?"

"Three months. And yours?"

"Four months."

"He's beautiful."

The woman smiled again and walked on.

A year ago, Victoria would have avoided the woman's eyes and walked on, but now things were different. Nikol had been so wrong in his mistrust of the Young Turks. It had been nine months since the coup and the Committee of Union and Progress was continuing to work with *Dashnak* representatives in parliament. Of course, all the Armenians had been disappointed when the membership of the parliament was announced and only fourteen were Armenian. To be representative of the population of Turkey, there should have been sixty-two, but everyone agreed that prejudices developed over lifetimes did not disappear overnight.

That business about pan-Turkism that Nikol had told her about had clearly been a rumor, too. All members of the Committee of Union and Progress continued to publicly support equality for all Turkey's citizens and their message was making life in the villages much more peaceful. And because of this, Armenian families who, years ago, had fled to Russia to escape persecution in the more turbulent areas, were coming home.

When Victoria arrived at Margaret's house, she went right to the cradle. "Oh Margaret, she's beautiful."

The baby opened her eyes and peered around with an unfocused gaze. Her little legs began kicking and her arms motioned in the rhythmic dance of a newborn.

"Let me wrap her more tightly in her blanket." Victoria squatted over the little wooden cradle and expertly criss-crossed the corners of the blanket over the baby. The infant's eyes closed and she dropped off to sleep.

"Koren, look what the baby has for you in her crib," Margaret said.

Koren stepped to the cradle and peered in. His eyes lit up. He reached in and took out a small bag of hard red candy, the baby's gift to him.

Someone knocked on the door and Araxie opened it. Anna stepped in with her three children, Lucin, Kenarie and one-year-old Haig.

Victoria hugged her. "How are you, Sister?"

Anna held out her finger to Paul and he grasped it in his palm. "I'm fine. How is my little godson?"

"He's wonderful, and really, I can't thank you enough for all you did for me after he was born. I didn't want you to have to do anything."

Anna made a dismissive gesture with her hand. "I only did what any sister would do."

Anna's girls took their bags of candy from the cradle and soon all the children were red, sticky, and rambunctious from their treats.

Victoria opened the door. "Outside. Koren, you're the oldest, so watch out for the others."

Victoria closed the door and blew on her hands. "It's cold out there."

Araxie passed her a cup of coffee. "You must be looking forward to spring."

"Well, yes and no. I have so much work to do on the farm."

Araxie looked sympathetic. "Will you get Martin Halabian again?"

There they all were, looking like they felt sorry for her. Victoria raised her chin. "Yes, he's a hard worker and he knows the land. I know enough about farming and rotating crops. I'll do all right."

Anna changed the subject. "You know when I came through the village today, I stopped in the bakery. When I was leaving, my hands were full and Lehman, the wife of one of the Turkish landowners, held the door open for me. I almost forgot to thank her I was so surprised."

Margaret leaned forward. "I heard two of the wealthy aghas enrolled their children in our Armenian school."

"Imagine, Turks and Armenians going to school together," Seta said.

Araxie shook her head. "I always thought all those meetings the men went to were foolishness, but I was wrong."

Seta rested her chin on her hand. "I'm not sure I believe

things will stay the way they are. People don't change that easily."

Victoria caught Margaret's eye and looked at the ceiling. What could she say? Perhaps changes took time for everyone to accept, Armenians and Turks alike.

There was another knock on the door.

Victoria rose. "Stay where you are. I'll get it." Solomon was certainly doing his job.

But when she opened the door she did not find another well-wisher; instead she found Anna's mother-in-law.

"I've come for Anna. Leon is sick."

Anna dropped her cup and jumped up. "What happened?"

"He came home and said he didn't feel well. He's hot like he has a fever."

Anna paled. "What do you think it is?"

Her mother-in-law lowered her voice. "Pneumonia."

Victoria drew in her breath. Pneumonia. People died from pneumonia.

"Let us keep the children for you," she said to Anna.

Anna accepted Victoria's offer for the girls but took the baby, who was still nursing, with her.

Victoria walked home with Seta, her three and four-year-old nieces and her sons. She tried to keep her tone light and a smile on her face for the girls sake but she was worried and ashamed of herself for what she was worrying about. If Leon died, she would have to take Anna and the children in. How would she ever do that now? She was struggling hard enough to feed her family and pay her taxes. She thought of her savings jar. Yes, she was continuing to put a few coins aside each year, but that savings was like her armor against the disasters that life seemed to keep bringing her. To be without it — well, she just couldn't.

The next day, Victoria heard that Anna had called in a doctor. Leon must be seriously ill. She rushed to Anna's door.

"It was just a cold last week," Anna said. "I begged him not to go out, but he went anyway. Now look what's happened."

Leon thrashed around in his bed.

Anna wrung her hands. "He doesn't know where he is half the time." Her face wrinkled into a sob. "He is the only man I have ever loved. What will I do if I lose him?"

Victoria drew Anna into her arms. "You mustn't think that way."

Anna straightened her spine. "You are right."

"I'll pray for him," Victoria said and left.

At home, Victoria found that the fire had shrunk to a few glowing embers. Seta had her hands full with the four children. Victoria piled wood into the heating chamber of the stove and stoked up the fire. Then she prepared dinner, nursed Paul, and put all the children to bed.

As soon as they were settled, Koren began whispering to the girls, who were snuggled together under a thick quilt.

They began to giggle.

"It's time to go to sleep now," Victoria said.

They were quiet for a few minutes more. Then Koren started making noises and they all began giggling again.

Victoria snapped her ledger closed. "Koren, this is your last warning."

"Yes, Mother." Koren sounded surprised.

Victoria seldom reprimanded him, but her patience was short tonight. She kept thinking about Leon's illness and how she would ever support so many people if he didn't make it. Then she thought about Anna and the loss she faced and felt guilty over the selfish nature of her thoughts.

The next morning, Victoria sent for Martin Halabian. "I'm anxious to talk to you about the spring planting," she said. "Will you work for me again this year?"

Martin nodded. "Of course."

Victoria told him how she wanted the crops laid out, when she wanted the manure spread, and what fields she wanted left fallow.

"You leave some of your fields unplanted?"

"Yes, it's called crop rotation. My father taught me about it. Your wheat produces more kernels and is less susceptible to blight when you give the soil a chance to rest."

"I've heard of that, but my father thinks it's foolish to leave whole fields unplanted."

"Maybe someday you'll be able to convince him."

"Maybe, but in a few years he'll turn the farm over to

Avedis and me, so we will be able to do what we want then."

In a few years. What if Nikol didn't come back? What would she do then? Victoria mentally admonished herself. She would drive herself crazy if she thought that way. Whatever happened, she would deal with it.

Martin stood to leave. "Well, you certainly know a lot about farming for, well, you know."

Victoria smiled. "For a woman?"

Martin regarded her with admiration. "Yes."

"Well, I do what I have to do."

For the next week, Koren kept his cousins entertained while their father fought for his life. Victoria watched Koren set up a play school, sing songs, and read to the girls. She was grateful that they were too young to know the precarious position their lives hung in. She tried not to think about the impact on her own family if Leon lost his battle but she wasn't always successful.

One morning, Martin knocked on the door. "I stopped by because I know you've been waiting to hear. Leon is better."

She hoped no one could read the relief on her face and know why it was there. What would they think of her?

"He's still very weak and the doctor said it will be months before he recovers, but he will recover."

Lucin tapped Victoria on the arm. "Is Papa better?"

Victoria bent down and drew both girls to her side. "Yes, darlings, and he wants to see you very soon."

Victoria brought the girls home two days later and her

life returned to normal.

Spring arrived and with it, Martin's daily presence. Victoria worked alongside him planting the vegetables and turning the fields and, as she did, she became aware of the way he looked at her, when he thought she wasn't looking. She was twenty-one years old and she knew when she walked through the village men noticed her. But there was only one man she cared about and he was gone so she kept her own attention on the farm.

In mid-April, shocking news reached the village. When Victoria heard it, she ran to Margaret. All around the village, other Armenians clustered in small groups and discussed it in low worried tones, while their Turkish neighbors walked past them with smiles on their faces. Massacres had broken out in Adana and from the looks of it, they were going to be as bad as the massacres of 1895 and 1896.

CHAPTER NINETEEN

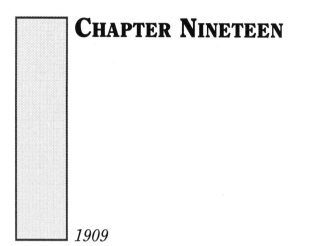

1909

*V*ictoria pressed on home. Her brow was furrowed and she was breathing fast. The Turks had done it again. What a fool she had been to believe they wouldn't.

Another massacre to the south in Adana. What had happened to their newly formed peace with the Young Turks? She was sure from what she had heard in the village that the government had a hand in the cruelty. Violence of this dimension could never take hold unless the government allowed it to. But how direct a hand did it have? Nikol had warned her about the Young Turks. She had dismissed his warning because she was angry with him. But was he right? The Young Turks could have been lying to gain power and support in Turkey and now that they had it, may have ordered the murder of the people they no longer needed.

Victoria reached home. Seta was preparing lunch. She looked at Victoria's face. "So it's true, then?"

Victoria nodded. "Armenian people are being slaughtered as we speak. Half the city of Adana has already been wiped out."

Seta sank down on a cushion. "Does anyone know what started it?"

"No. Only that it started two days ago."

"We should stay in."

"Mother, Adana is a two-day journey from here."

"Victoria, you were a little girl when it happened but massacres once very nearly reached our doorstep. And they started in the capitol, further away than Adana."

Victoria remembered. Her father had been here to protect her. Now it was up to her to protect her family. Suddenly, she remembered Koren and jumped up.

"Koren is in school. I should have brought him home."

She started out the door, then turned back to Seta. "Margaret said her father is away on business. What if he gets caught up in the violence?"

Seta looked worried. "We can only pray he doesn't."

Victoria hurried out the door. Martin was on his way in. "What's wrong?" he said seeing the look on her face.

Victoria told him about Adana. Quickly he brushed soil from his hand. "Let me go with you to get Koren."

"No, I..." she began then stopped. Why was she thinking

about her pride at a time like this? "Yes, thank you."

They were halfway to the village when Martin suddenly stopped. "I have relatives who live in Adana. My father's cousin. At this time of year, hundreds of Armenians who live in outlying villages are in Adana to harvest the barley."

"Then the timing couldn't have been worse."

"Or better, depending on whether you are a Turk or an Armenian."

Victoria looked at him. He was frowning. All the men in the village had read the same newsletter that Nikol had. She wondered if Martin was thinking about that now.

In the village, Victoria and Martin learned that the situation in Adana had been tense since the Young Turks' revolution last summer and that the violence was no surprise to anyone who knew the area.

Adana was a large city flanked by rich fertile farms where wheat, corn, and barley were grown. Armenians made up more than half its population.

Adana's governor, Bahri Pasha, was a corrupt official whose appointed staff were no better than criminals. All of the governor's local administrators were men who thought like he did; they liked their entitled positions and saw no reason to give them up. They had been angry when the Young Turks declared the Armenians their equals.

The Armenians of Adana had been talking openly in cafés and stores about their new status. Since the revolution, the ruling Turks had listened to these conversations, and resented them deeply.

Their animosity had continued to grow throughout the year.

Several days ago, a group of Armenians were found murdered. The shop owners had taken a good look at their Turkish neighbors, and locked their doors. But to no avail; shortly after they did, the violence broke out. The Turkish villagers were soon joined by police and once again the streets ran with blood.

The word in the village was that it showed no sign of stopping.

With Martin's help, Victoria retrieved her son from school, brought him home, and kept him there.

Two days later, Martin went into the village for news. He stopped at Victoria's on his way home.

"Have you heard anything from your relatives?"

"No and I don't think we are going to for weeks."

"And the massacres?"

"All we know is that Adana is still in chaos. The British vice consul is on his way, but even he will have trouble restoring peace."

"The British vice consul? Well, eventually he will."

"Let us hope."

The British vice consul, Doughty Whylie, arrived in Adana and was horrified. Hysterical people were running from the city and dead bodies lay everywhere. Why wasn't anyone trying to stop this?

He stormed to the government building and found the provincial governor and commandant hiding in a back room.

Cowards, he thought. No one was doing anything to help the victims. It was up to him. "I need troops," he told the governor.

The governor made a face and assigned him six soldiers and no officers. Whylie took his tiny regiment out into the streets, but was unable to stop the melee that day.

The next morning, he telegraphed Britain for a warship, then went back to the government building. This time, he demanded fifty soldiers and an officer. He marched up one street and down another with his men, capturing the rioters' attention by first firing over their heads, then shouting at them to go home. Each time he did, the fighting stopped but as soon as he rounded the next corner, it started back up again. By noon, the town's bazaar was on fire and the Turks and Armenians were caught up in hand-to-hand fighting.

He was only one man, but still he had to try. He quieted down another street but this time, posted a guard to maintain order. Then he walked on.

The guard waited until Whylie was just out of earshot. Then he grinned, raised his rifle, and fired directly into the back of an Armenian man, who was stepping into his house. The guard looked at a turban-clad Turk and nodded in the direction of a young woman carrying a baby. The woman began to run. The soldier fixed his sights on her, and fired.

Slaughter in the streets began anew.

Whylie brought his troops to the tobacco factory where hundreds of people lay wounded. Suddenly, he reeled. An Armenian man had shot him. He watched recognition dawn on the man's face. From a distance, the man must have mistaken him for a Turkish soldier. But if the Turkish officials learned of Whylie's injury, they would have the excuse they had been waiting for. They would storm the Armenian quarter and there would be no survivors.

The massacre must be stopped today. He sent the governor a message saying that no blame would come to him personally, if he ended the violence now. Whylie told him to do this by using reliable soldiers and good officers to seal off the Armenian quarter. He also told him to order the entire city to stay indoors, and to authorize patrols to shoot any offenders.

The governor implemented Whylie's plan and by the next morning, the streets were quiet. Whylie drew a breath of relief. The governor had either seen the sense in his plan, or had seen the British warship Whylie had requested arrive that morning with several other foreign warships. In either case, the carnage had stopped but two thousand people in the city of Adana, and more than twenty thousand from the surrounding villages, lay dead.

Victoria stood in the Halabians' doorway. "Have you heard from your relatives? Did they make it?"

John Halabian nodded. "We just received a telegram."

"Then they..."

"Yes, they are safe. But they say the city is in shock."

Victoria's lips tightened. "I trusted the Young Turks."

"We all did," John said.

Victoria thought about Nikol. Well, maybe not everyone.

But she didn't know what to think about the Young Turks when the following week she learned that, while the massacre had been going on in Adana, the Young Turks had been ousted from power by the sultan and the men loyal to him. The Young Turks had just ended the sultan's ten day regime by storming the capitol with their Action Army, taking back power, and sending the sultan to Salonika in exile.

Perhaps the violence in Adana had been a result of the sultan's coup; perhaps the Young Turks really did believe in what they said they did. Victoria wanted to think that but two days later, when Turkish soldiers sent by the Young Turks arrived in Adana, another massacre broke out.

The soldiers had been met by Turkish agitators who were dressed as Armenian revolutionaries. The agitators opened fire on the soldiers, and screamed that the revolution had begun.

The shocked troops fired back. Soon Armenian residents were again being dragged from their homes and murdered in the streets. But the resulting slaughter was even worse this time because it was being done by men trained in the art of killing.

A woman huddled in terror beside her daughter-in-law and grandchildren in her living quarters behind her husband's tobacco shop. She listened to the screams coming from the street. She had cabled her cousin in Kharpert, saying that they were all right. But that was before the killing had begun again. Now her husband's and son's bodies lay with the other casualties near the railroad tracks and she could not even get out to give them a proper Christian burial.

The noise drew close to her door. Then she heard the door to the shop slam open in a splintering of wood. Who was out there? She crept to the curtain and peeked into the shop. A soldier was stuffing hand-carved pipes and bags of tobacco down his shirt.

The soldier looked up and stared at the crack in the curtain. His eyes narrowed. He advanced across the shop and tore the curtain aside.

The woman pushed her daughter-in-law and grandchildren behind her and met the soldier's eyes.

The soldier turned as if to leave, but pulled out his sword instead and, in one slash, the woman lay dead. He raised his sword again and brought it across the throat of the younger woman. She fell to the floor drowning in her own blood. The soldier made quick work of the children, all but one ten-year-old boy, whom he missed in the pile of dead bodies. As he walked away, the young boy's face remained frozen in a silent scream.

The soldier wiped his victims' blood off his hands, helped himself to two boxes of cigars, then swaggered out the door and on to the next shop.

Outside, other soldiers were similarly loaded down with booty of their own. The cracked wooden door to the tobacco shop tilted on its broken hinges, inviting anyone to come in and help himself.

In another part of town, thirty soldiers assembled in the house of a Turkish bey and opened fire on an Armenian school next door. Two thousand people, made homeless in the massacres ten days before, were crammed inside. Windows shattered, some people fell and the rest ran for shelter in the Armenian church beside it. But within minutes, the soldiers were firing on them again and the church erupted in flames.

In an Armenian section of the city, a group of Turkish men marched down a street of crowded wooden houses carrying cans of kerosene. One of the men sprinkled the contents of his can in the doorway of each house. At the end of the block, the leader struck a match and the house in front of him exploded in flames. The fire spread, domino fashion, down the block.

As each house caught fire, its occupants leapt out and

soldiers standing nearby shot them.

Adana's surrounding villages fell prey to the marauders, too. In some, the entire Armenian population was wiped out.

Then the violence began to spread outside of Adana.

Northeast of Adana, a Turkish officer led his band of irregulars up a mountain toward Hadjin, a town populated by twenty thousand Armenians.

The officer licked his lips. This would be easy. He had missed the excitement in Adana by two days, but had had no trouble forming a new regiment. Some of his band were soldiers, the rest, willing new recruits. His superiors had told him that if anyone asked, he was acting on his own. But he wasn't expecting anyone to ask.

The sun was just coming up. The Armenians of Hadjin would be asleep in their beds. Their village was far too remote for news of Adana to have reached them yet. He would kill them all.

He signaled his aide who blew forcefully into a bugle. His band of irregulars drew out rifles and ran at Hadjin. But as they entered the village, the attackers halted. In front of them, every able bodied man in Hadjin stood aiming a hand-made weapon at their chests.

The men of Hadjin had been defending their families for hundreds of years. They were smart, tough, and their homes in the hills afforded them a clear view of the area. When, the day before, they had heard what was going on in Adana, they had hidden scouts all along the mountainous pass.

This morning, the scouts had seen the soldiers' approach and, running up secret trails, had alerted the rest of the men.

Many of the aggressors took one look at the grim expressions on the Hadjinites' faces, and ran.

The officer watched them and his face turned beet-red. He screamed orders for his remaining soldiers to branch out and attack. But everywhere his troops went, the men of Hadjin stopped them short.

For ten days, the officer continued to lead advances on Hadjin, and for ten days, he continued to get beaten back.

His last attempt was to destroy the city by fire. But when his men set bushes on the outskirts of the city ablaze, the wind changed direction and the fire died out.

In Hadjin, the officer's mission was a complete failure.

But other towns and villages were not as fortunate.

When Victoria heard of the renewed trouble in Adana, she locked her doors and kept her family inside. She gathered news at night, as her father had once done. From Margaret, she learned that Michael Damadian was still missing, and that the devastation was continuing to spread.

One afternoon in Mezireh, a gang of Turkish men appeared on the street carrying weapons. The Armenians locked their doors. The men's first act of destruction was to overturn a peddler's cart and steal all his wares.

Police hastened to the scene and a crowd of local Turks assembled.

The police had been on alert for an outbreak of violence, but were unclear whether they were supposed to encourage or discourage it. They asked their commander for guidance. Their commander asked his superior and the question eventually landed in the hands of the local governor.

The governor issued an order for peace.

The police ordered the crowd to disperse and it did. Then they kept the entire city in their houses for two days. Mezireh had no deaths.

Victoria dropped her needlework. Someone was knocking on her door. She looked at Seta who put her face in her hands.

Victoria called through the side stop of the door. "Who is there?"

"Victoria, it's me, Margaret."

Victoria flung open the door.

Margaret fell in hugging her. "He's home. My father is home. It's all over."

Victoria stepped out into the sunlight of day and inhaled the sweet spring air. "What happened?"

Margaret told her how Michael had been trying to get home for weeks. He had gotten as far as Mezireh, when the second massacre had broken out in Adana. He knew that travel would be unsafe so he had stayed where he was until it was safe to leave.

Later that night, Victoria gathered with other friends at the Damadians' house to welcome Michael home and find out what he knew about Adana.

"The massacres are over," Victoria said. "But what are the Young Turks going to do about them? They promised us peace."

Michael nodded. "They did. And if we're going to continue to work with them, we want to know what happened. Mezireh proves that when the police want to stop a disturbance, they can."

"What will the Young Turks do?" Victoria asked.

Michael turned his palms up. "I don't know. I heard that they sent a military tribunal to Adana but what we will learn from that, I can't say."

Victoria pushed her hair back. She wasn't sure how she felt about the Young Turks. The sultan would never have sent a tribunal to investigate a massacre. The Young Turks had. But did that prove their sincerity?

Michael had no answer for her.

Victoria sent Koren back to school the next day and turned her attention to her farm. Her wheat should have been planted weeks ago. She could not risk using her savings this year when she might need it even more some other time.

Three weeks later, Victoria learned the results of the military tribunal's investigation into Adana. Three weeks, she thought? The investigation should have taken months and its results were as disappointing as its length: Three Armenian revolutionaries were the cause of the entire massacre. Not one Turk was held responsible. Outrageous.

Victoria, along with thousands of other Armenians, began an intense letter writing campaign. European newspapers carried the story, too, and eventually, the government had the good sense to be embarrassed by their shoddy work. They ordered another investigation headed by two members of the newly formed parliament, Hagop Babikian and Yusuf Kemal. Both set out for Adana the same day.

Hagop Babikian knew how devastated the Armenians in Turkey were by Adana. They had become victims once again. As their representative, he was determined to get to the truth of how that had happened. He intended to conduct a proper investigation and told Yusuf Kemal as much as the train bumped along to Adana.

Yusuf Kemal listened to him and nodded politely.

When they reached Adana, Babikian, with Kemal's help, set up a court and called in community leaders and surviving eyewitnesses to give testimony. But by the end of the first week, Babikian was frustrated. Witnesses had failed to show up. Those who did looked frightened and refused to tell what they saw. Someone was scaring these people. Who?

Babikian discussed the problem with Kemal one afternoon in a coffee shop. "I won't give up. I owe it to my people. I'm going to the European newspapers and telling them what's happening."

Kemal's eyes widened. "Oh, you mustn't..."

Babikian looked at him. "Mustn't what?"

Kemal reddened. "Well, you know. The government wants us to do what we can, but what are we to do if people don't want to talk?"

Babikian set his coffee cup down. "Now look here," he began.

"No, no. You misunderstand me."

Babikian waited.

"You are right," Kemal said. "Tomorrow, we'll wire the capitol. But relax now and finish your coffee."

Babikian squinted at Kemal, then his face relaxed. "Tomorrow, then."

Kemal turned and caught the waiter's eye. A look passed between them. A minute later, the waiter brushed by their table and upset Babikian's coffee.

Kemal slapped the table with his palm. "You clumsy oaf."

"It's just a cup of coffee," Babikian said. "I wasn't even going to finish it."

"No, these people have to learn to be more careful. Waiter, bring this man another cup."

Babikian decided it was easier to accept the fresh cup than argue. He raised it to his lips but put it down suddenly as another thought struck him. "The government might very well be behind our witnesses' reluctance to come forward. Maybe I should go to the newspapers, after all."

"No, why would the government send us here if they didn't want to get to the truth?"

Babikian smiled. "I can tell you never grew up an Armenian." He drained his cup, got up and said, "I'll see you in the morning."

But by morning Babikian was too sick to get out of bed. His lower abdomen spasmed and he lay retching in agony. He continued to deteriorate throughout the day. His aide sent for the doctor that evening, but by the time the doctor arrived, Babikian was dead.

"What happened?" Babikian's aide said.

The doctor held up his finger. "I can't prove it, but all the signs point to poisoning."

Kemal took the first morning train back to the capitol. Regrettable, that business with Babikian. But his orders had come from the highest echelons of the government and he dared not disobey.

The government appointed another investigative team. This time with two Turks and one Armenian. By early autumn, their report was ready. Nine Turks and six Armenians were executed for their parts in the disturbances. The governor was removed from office and the commandant sentenced to three months in jail. The central government was cleared of any culpability.

The investigative team had done exactly what it was supposed to do. It had concluded the investigation but made little attempt to uncover the whole truth.

Victoria read the report and discussed it at Margaret and Solomon's house one Sunday after church. "I wonder how thorough that investigation was."

Solomon nodded. "I heard that some of the people they convicted weren't the guilty ones."

"And the idea that the Young Turks had nothing to do with it," Victoria shook her head. "I just don't believe it."

"Neither do a lot of other people," Michael said. "And I'll tell you why. The Turkish editor of a newspaper put out by the Young Turks was expelled from the country. The reason he was expelled is that he was telling people that certain members of the Young Turks Committee of Union and Progress were forcing him to publish articles they wrote to deliberately inflame the Turks against the Armenians."

"Do you believe him?" Margaret said.

Michael thought for a moment. "I believe it is possible the Young Turks wanted the massacre to happen. The first outbreak of violence occurred on the day the Young Turks were forced out by the sultan, but they didn't know that was going to happen. If they had planned the massacre months before, they wouldn't have had any way to stop it that day."

Solomon leaned forward. "They could have even ordered

the governor and commandant to pretend to be afraid so they wouldn't try to stop it."

Victoria nodded. "I wondered why they were given such light sentences."

"But it is possible," Michael said, "that the sultan's reactionary regime ordered the massacre as a way of re-establishing the Muslim's superior position."

"And the second massacre?" Victoria asked.

"The soldiers arrived at dark and were fired on. They may have believed it really was Armenian revolutionaries who were doing it so they took their outrage out on all the Armenians. But that doesn't necessarily mean that they had orders to do it. I don't think we'll ever know."

Victoria thought about what Michael said. She supposed it was possible that the Young Turks had nothing to do with the massacre. The sultan had never punished a Turk for murdering Armenians, the Young Turks had. Perhaps she should not give up on them just yet.

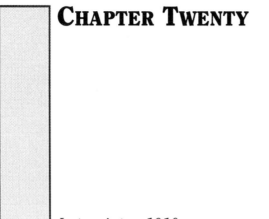

CHAPTER TWENTY

Late winter, 1910

Six-year-old Koren ran into the house waving a travel-worn envelope. "A letter, a letter. From America."

Victoria turned the envelope over and studied the handwriting. It was from Nikol.

"Uncle Leon gave it to me this afternoon when I was coming out of school. He told me to go right home with it and not to lose it. And I came right home and I didn't lose it."

Seta looked at Victoria's trembling hands and turned to Koren. "Darling, will you come out to the well with me and help me fill the water jug?"

Victoria mouthed a thank-you to her mother. She waited until they were gone then turned the letter over once again and examined the outside. She didn't want to open it. She didn't want to be pulled to the edge of the emotional abyss she had faced two years ago when he left.

She clutched the letter to her chest and closed her eyes. Then she felt a surge of energy, a reminder of the strength she had gained over the time she had been on her own. She opened the letter.

Dear Victoria,

I hope this letter finds you well. I did not write to you sooner for reasons I still can't tell you about but I think about you every day. I miss you and Koren and pray that everything went all right with the birth of our baby. He or she must be a year and a half by now.

I'm living in Massachusetts, in a small town called Whitinsville and working in a factory. I have to move around when the factories lay me off but I always find work again. I'm boarding now with my brother. He bought a building last year and opened a store on the first floor. He and his wife, Marig, live above it with their baby.

Last year, I heard about the Adana massacres. I thanked God they weren't in Kharpert, but when will it stop?

In America, things are different. The factories pay a man enough to live. That's all we ask from life, isn't it? No, on second thought, that's not all we ask. We also want to be safe. And here we are. You don't have to be afraid all the time. The police don't arrest people unless they have a reason, and I mean a real reason. And there is so much opportunity here. Just look at all my brother has done for himself since he's been here.

I like it in America and I want you to come. Turkey will never change. From this distance, I can see that. I am saving for your passage and will send it to you in a few months. Until then, write to me at my brother's house and tell me everything. I count the days until we can be together again.

Your loving husband,

Nikol

Victoria crumpled up the letter and flung it across the room. What kind of a husband leaves on a few hours notice, doesn't write in two years, then – *whist* – expects her to give up everything she's struggled so hard to keep?

She wouldn't do it. She belonged here. He did, too. Someday he would know that.

When Seta peeked back in the door, she found Victoria crouched at the table, furiously scribbling away on a sheet of paper.

Seta cleared her throat.

Victoria did not stop writing. "He's not coming back."

She looked up. "That's what you wanted to know, isn't it?"

"Yes, well I..." Seta raised her eyebrows. "You mean never?"

"He wants us to go to America."

"To America, but that's so far away."

Koren walked in and set down the water jug. "To America? That would be exciting."

Victoria stood and put her arm around her son. "Come here." She led him to the door. "Look out there. What do you see?"

He tilted his head. "The farm?"

"*Our* farm. And when you go to the village, what do you find there?"

He looked at her.

"I'll tell you what," she said. "You find our church. You find our bakeries, our shoe maker, and our jeweler. You eat meals with our friends, people who speak the same language we do. Everything you see and find would be lost to us if we left."

"Everything?"

"Yes."

"Then I don't want to leave."

She kissed the top of his head. "I don't either. This is our home. This is where we'll stay."

When Nikol received Victoria's reply, he sat down and put his head in his hands. His dear, sweet Victoria. Everything he had, everything he accomplished was meaningless without her. She had said she wouldn't come. Never. But he could not go to her. And he could not live without her. He had to find a way. But how? The new government in Turkey allowed the *Dashnak*s to meet openly now, but they would not pardon the crime he had committed. No, his brother had been right. He could never go back. He would just have to convince her to come here.

Victoria had told Nikol she wouldn't leave Turkey, but she wondered about her answer to him when, that spring, she learned that the membership to the Young Turks' Committee of Union and Progress had changed. Now men who were quite public in their beliefs in pan-Turkism were a dominant voice. She asked Michael Damadian about it. He explained that after the massacres in Adana, the *Dashnak*s had reluctantly agreed to continue working with the Young Turks, but were considering breaking with them now. Because of this, Armenian representatives had gone to the Europeans looking for support for their cause. And they had been successful. The Europeans had begun work on a reform plan for Turkey that would guarantee the Armenians' rights to fair treatment under the law.

Victoria felt much more optimistic after her talk with Michael.

One afternoon, while she stood in her wheat field waiting for Martin who was coming to discuss the spring planting, she saw Koren on his way home from school. He climbed up the hill to the house. She called to him and he went to her side.

"How was school?"

"Wonderful. The teacher said that I'm the best math student in the class." He turned to go back to the house. "I'm going inside to study."

He was so like her. She had loved school and he did, too. She wondered if she would be able to give him the college education she had not been able to have. She remembered what her teacher had once said to her. Education brought opportunity. With Martin's help, the farm was flourishing. Perhaps she could.

Victoria shaded her eyes. Someone else was coming up the hill. Martin. But he was walking fast, and he looked scared. Something was wrong.

He reached her side. "I was just served with a draft notice."

"A draft notice. When did the Turks start wanting Armenian men in their army?"

"After the Young Turks came into power. And the *Dashnak*s did sign that agreement to continue working with the Young Turks, so what can I do?"

Victoria reminded Martin of the *Dashnak*s impending break with the Young Turks then said, "Can you buy your way out of the draft?"

Martin shook his head. "The fee used to be nominal but

now it's more than my family earns in a year."

"We have to think of something." Victoria reached out and touched his arm. "And I'm not just saying that because you work for me. Truly, you are my friend."

Martin looked like he wanted to say something, but he remained silent.

Victoria went on. "Let's go to Michael Damadian. He'll know what to do."

Michael's face was grave. "I heard this was happening and I understand why you don't want to go, especially with this idea of pan-Turkism taking hold in the government."

"But what can Martin do? His notice says he has to report to duty in one month."

Michael rested his chin on his hand. "He has four choices, but he won't like the first three."

Martin folded his arms. "They are?"

"To join the military, to pay the exemption fee, or to go to America."

"All impossible, of course," Martin said.

"You said four choices," Victoria said.

Yes, the fourth choice is to marry an orphan. You can get an exemption if you do that."

Martin glanced at Victoria. "Marriage? I don't know."

Michael looked from Martin to Victoria. "Listen, Martin. This is an important decision. Life and death. Think about it."

Martin sighed. "I'll talk it over with my father."

"Good, and if you decide on marriage, come to me. I'm going to Diyarbekir on business later this week. If your father wants me to act as his agent, I can bring a girl home from an orphanage there."

Victoria looked at Martin's troubled face, as they walked away from Michael's house. "I know how you feel."

He stopped and took her hand. "Do you really know how I feel?"

She looked at the ground. "I meant the marriage. Having to get married."

"But I meant-"

She gently pulled her hand away. "You mustn't think that way. You must think of saving yourself. The other, well, you know, is impossible."

Now it was Martin's turn to look at the ground.

"We won't speak of it again," Victoria said.

Martin nodded and parted for his own house.

At home, Martin told his parents about Michael's sugges-tion and offer.

"Thank God for Michael," John said. "It's the only way. We'll go to him tonight and accept."

Mary looked at her son. "Is something wrong Martin?"

"No ."

"Because you can't let yourself go into the Turkish army. The Turks are violent people. The soldiers even worse." She put her arm around her ten-year-old nephew.

Martin looked at the boy. Their only surviving relative from Adana. The boy no longer spoke at all. Victoria was right. He had to save himself.

Martin went with his family to the Damadians' house, where Michael and John discussed the specifics of the sort of girl they had in mind. Someone from a good family, reasonably pretty, not too tall.

"And educated," Martin said. *Like Victoria*, he thought.

Victoria stood with Margaret in front of the Damadians' house on the afternoon Michael was due back from his trip. Half of the village waited with her.

Aunt Rose stood shoulder-to-shoulder with one of her cronies. "What are those noisy Tevrizians doing here? What business is it of theirs?"

"Who knows?" her friend said. "Bunch of people with nothing better to do. Well, I might as well sit down. Not that this matters to me in the least."

"Me either." Rose picked a spot where she had the best view.

Victoria looked at Margaret who covered her mouth and giggled.

The Damadian carriage appeared over the hill and came to a stop in front of the house.

Everyone stopped talking. The door to the carriage opened and Araxie stepped out, followed by a proudly beaming Michael. He stood at the carriage door, held up his arm, and a blushing young girl stepped out.

Victoria studied the girl who was pretty in a quiet sort of way. She carried a book in her hand. Martin would like that. Victoria looked around. Martin was hidden in the crowd.

John and Mary Halabian stepped forward and greeted the girl whose name, Michael announced, was Sona.

Sona bowed her head and kissed John's hand. John slipped a ring on Sona's finger. Martin was now engaged. But he hadn't laid eyes on his wife-to-be. Someone nudged him forward. He greeted the girl, looking like he didn't know what to do with his hands. Sona, too, looked everywhere but at Martin.

Michael invited everyone into his house to celebrate the engagement.

Victoria linked her arm through Margaret's. "She seems nice."

"She does," Margaret said. "But can you imagine having to meet the man you're marrying in front of the entire village?" She leaned closer to Victoria's ear. "While we're on the subject of the entire village knowing, my mother told me you got a letter from Nikol."

Victoria told her about Nikol's letter and her reply.

"Good for you," Margaret said. "Why should you give up your farm after what he did?"

"That's what I say. I was pregnant and he knew how dangerous that was. And what if I went and he found another brother in Brazil? What would I do alone in America?"

"Another country, another language. No, you are right. Stay where you are. Let him come back to you."

"And another thing–" Victoria stopped. "Why, Auntie Rose. How are you?"

"Oh, as well as can be expected. So, what do you think? Kind of plain-looking isn't she?"

"No, I think she's pretty."

"Well, yes, put enough powder on a face and you can hide anything, I suppose."

Victoria sighed. What was the point?

"I heard you got a letter from Nikol," Rose said.

"Yes, Auntie."

"Well, when is he coming back?"

"I don't know yet."

"Did he say anything else?"

"No," Victoria said. Was it her imagination or did Aunt Rose look worried? Why should she look worried?

Her thoughts were interrupted by Anna and Leon's arrival. Where Leon appeared, music followed and it wasn't long before every guest was dancing.

The party didn't break up until late that night. Before she left, Victoria congratulated Martin. "She seems like a very nice girl. Really, it's all for the best."

Martin nodded.

Ten days later, Victoria rose and dressed for Martin's wedding. She dipped the paklava she was bringing in syrup, while Seta arranged stuffed grape leaves on a platter. Koren entertained his toddling little brother, who happily followed him everywhere with adoring eyes.

Victoria thought about Martin. She had fought and competed with him when she was a child. She had come to like him when she was an adolescent. And, in the years he had been working for her, she had grown to love him. But she loved him in the way she loved her friends, not in the way she loved Nikol. *Had* loved Nikol. Now her feelings for Nikol were confused by her mistrust of him.

She sighed and walked to the church.

Martin stood at the altar listening to Father Mikayelian, but thinking about Sona. She had been orphaned since she was twelve. She had no family. No one else in the world. She needed him.

He glanced out at the parishioners. Victoria was seated with her mother and sons. She was sitting too far away for him to get a good look at her face.

Sona had lost everyone who had been important to her. She needed him to do more than put food on her table.

He looked back at Victoria. She was even harder to see now. He could not have her. Could never have her.

Father Mikayelian completed the service by asking Martin, if he accepted Sona as his wife.

He said he did and meant it.

Victoria took her sons' hands and left the church for the reception. Anna caught up with her and they strolled along together.

Victoria looked up at the sky and smiled. "I hope Leon is setting up the band because I want to dance. When I dance, I feel happy."

"I'm glad, Sister," Anna laid her hand on Victoria's arm. "You're so good. You try to spare my feelings because Nikol is my brother, but I know how you feel about him leaving."

"But that's just it. Why did he leave?"

"I don't know but Abraham, he was always..."

"Always what?"

Anna brushed a wrinkle from her skirt. "You know, I was quite young when Abraham left home. I don't remember him at all. But Nikol was older. He used to talk about him all the time."

Victoria waited.

Anna seemed to be choosing her words. "It was like Abraham was his hero. He would have done anything Abraham said. I think they got into some kind of trouble together."

"But after all these years, why would that matter?"

Anna shrugged helplessly. "I don't know. I just don't know."

Victoria heard the distant swell of music. She looked at Anna and smiled. Whatever Nikol had done, wherever he had gone, Anna was still her sister and she was grateful for that.

The music was closer now and beckoning her. She walked into the Halabians' yard, edged her way into the dancers' midst and forgot her worries for one day.

CHAPTER TWENTY-ONE

Spring, 1914

*V*ictoria re-read the letter she had just received from Nikol. Then she folded it and slipped it back into the envelope. She took a deep breath in and let it slowly out.

Seta sat at the table opposite her, cutting up cheese for the boys' lunch. She looked at Victoria, bit her lip, then went back to her task.

Victoria smiled. "He's coming home, Mother."

Seta dropped her knife, walked to Victoria, and hugged her. "Thank God."

Victoria gestured with the envelope. "He says he'll be home by the end of the summer."

"As soon as that?"

"Yes."

"Then our prayers have been answered."

Since Victoria's first letter from Nikol four years ago, she had continued to hear from him. At first, his letters urged her to make a home with him in America. But she had remained adamant. She was in the only home she wanted to be in.

Then, a year ago, the tone of Nikol's letters had changed. He wanted to come back. Life in America remained good, he assured her; still, it wasn't the same. This was the man she knew and loved. He had told her he didn't know if he *could* come back, he had details to work out, but if he could, he would. And now she knew that he had found a way.

"He's bringing back America's modern farming methods, too," Victoria said. "He's been visiting farms in Whitinsville, Andover, and other towns on Sundays to learn more. He's going to teach the men of our village what he knows."

Seta went back to preparing the boys' lunch. "Martin will appreciate that."

Victoria thought about Martin. Nikol owed him a lot. Martin had continued to work for her every season. Her savings had increased bit by bit, due in large part to his help. Other young men from the village could have worked for her, but none had the farming experience that Martin had.

Nikol was coming home just in time because John Halabian had announced last week, that he was turning his farm over to Martin next year.

Eleven-year-old Koren walked in the door, followed by

five-year-old Paul. Victoria told them about Nikol's impending return.

Koren's face broke out in a wide smile. He turned to his brother. "Did you hear that Paul? Papa is coming home."

Paul's smile was not quite as broad as Koren's. "What is he like?"

Koren laid his hand on his brother's shoulder. "Oh, you'll like him. You'll see."

Victoria saw the trusting look on her youngest son's face, as he listened to his brother tell him about his father. Everything was working out. Their lives were going to be easier, too, because Nikol was bringing back all the money he had saved. Really, she could use her own savings for a few comforts now. No, she decided, spending money was just not in her nature.

She put Nikol's letter back in her trunk with the other ones. Nikol was coming back to be a part of the family and the community. She had been wise to refuse to leave Turkey.

Nikol would be glad he came back, too, because the Europeans had just completed their reform plan. When it was implemented, the Armenians in Turkey would be treated very differently and because the Europeans were going to administer the plan themselves, its chances of success were good.

Victoria knew if it weren't for the European's plan, she would have felt compelled to leave for her sons' sakes. The Young Turks Committee of Union and Progress was still dominated by men who were fanatic pan-Turks and everyone said that the Armenians were no better off now than they had been in the days of Sultan Hamid's reign.

Michael Damadian had kept Victoria, and everyone else who wanted to know, informed of changes in the government so she had known when the *Dashnak*s had broken with the Committee because of their racist membership. She had agreed with the *Dashnak*'s decision because Michael had also told her that a terrible fanatic, named Zia Gokalp, had become the Committee's chief theoretician.

Zia Gokalp, Michael explained, was one of pan-Turkism's most vocal promoters. Zia wanted Turkey to one day be a giant nation, populated solely by Turkish-speaking Muslims. To accomplish this, he was urging Turkey to expand eastward into Russian Azerbaijan and north-west into Persia, reminding his followers that the Azerbaijanis were close relatives of the Ottoman Turks and that Persia had a northeastern population of Turkish people.

But for Turkey to do what Zia wanted, Armenians, Greeks and Jews, both in Turkey and in the coveted new territories, would have to be ridden from the land.

Russia had a large population of Armenians, who lived between Turkey and Azerbaijan. Russia was known for protecting its Armenian population and it did not give up territory easily. Victoria knew that Zia's goals were not going to be easily attained, but she was still very concerned when she heard about them. And she was not reassured by his claim that Armenians could become Turks by being forced to convert to Islam. Zia's ideas implied the destruction of their culture and their national identity, something she would resist despite the consequences, as her people had for centuries.

Michael had also kept Victoria informed about the rise to power of Enver, Taalat and Djemal, three racist embracers of pan-Turkism and now the Young Turk's three most important men. Secret decisions of the Committee of Union and Progress were translated into policy by these men. As the membership of the Committee continued to remain firmly committed to pan-Turkism, Victoria had begun to despair. But two challenges to the power of the Committee of Union and Progress had occurred over the last three years. They had given Victoria reason to hope that the government would return to its politics of 1908.

The first occurred in 1911, when a liberal opposition party formed and won a by-election in the capitol. But the Committee dissolved the parliament and held a corrupt election that won their successful return to power.

The second challenge occurred in July of 1912, when a group of army officers, called the Savior Officers, forced the Committee to give up power. Then the Balkan wars, which drove Turkey out of Europe, gave the Committee a pretext to declare a national emergency. Enver stormed the government building, shot the Minister of War, forced the opposition leader to resign and established a military dictatorship.

Victoria would have given up hope, but Michael reminded her that ambassadors from Britain, France, Russia, Germany, and Austria-Hungary had convened in Constantinople and were working on a reform plan. For three decades, mutual suspicion and jealousy had prevented these countries from reaching agreement on a reform plan. But two months ago, Victoria had learned that these nations, in particular the two most directly involved, Russia and Great Britain, had endorsed a specific plan.

The plan divided the six provinces of Turkish Armenia into two administrative districts. Each one was to be administered by a European inspector-general who was appointed by the Turks, but also approved by the Great Powers. The job of each inspector-general was to supervise all levels of government in the provinces. As supervisors, they would eradicate bribery, uphold justice, promote harmony between the races and establish a fair tax collection system.

So with the impending help from the Europeans, which Turkey had reluctantly agreed to, Victoria knew she had been right to stay where she was.

One spring morning, Victoria learned that two inspector-generals had been appointed, Westenenk, a Dutch colonial administrator, and Major Hoff from the Norwegian army. Both would be in their positions in three months.

Victoria waited impatiently for her sons to return home from school so she could go to Michael's house and discuss its impact.

"Calm down Victoria," Seta said after she had gone to the

door for the third time in fifteen minutes.

"The boy's afternoon snack, is it — ?"

"It's all laid out. They'll come in, eat, and we'll go to Michael's house. Now sit."

Victoria pulled too hard on the needle she was working through her piece of embroidery and it slipped off the thread. She put it away. "I'm too excited. This is the first time in years that our people have had something positive to celebrate."

Seta folded her arms. "Let's wait and see."

"I don't think you understand, Mother. The Turks won't be administering this reform plan. The Europeans will."

"Well, maybe. I don't understand these things very well. I didn't go to school like you did." She frowned. "Honestly, Victoria, you and Margaret insist on talking about politics like men. I don't like it. It's very unfeminine."

"Well, we're all affected by politics and we're especially affected by this reform."

"*If* anything comes of it."

Victoria looked out the door again. Her mother had expressed doubt after the Young Turks revolution and she had been right. But this reform was different. It wasn't dependent on the Turks doing what they agreed to do. It was dependent on the Europeans and she knew the Armenians could trust the Europeans.

Later, at Michael's house, she discussed it with Margaret, Solomon, Anna, and Leon.

"It will work won't it?" Victoria asked.

"Well," Michael said, "it does have the backing of all the foreign powers. I think it will."

Victoria eyed Seta. She had one brow raised.

"Will our Turkish neighbors let these changes happen?" Victoria said. "I mean, remember Adana?"

Solomon nodded. "None of us will ever forget it. But you must keep in mind the military power the Europeans have to back the inspector-generals."

"Then our lives are going to be different now," Victoria said. "New court systems, taxes that are reasonable. I feel very grateful to the Europeans."

"Now I've been listening to all of you talk about this for months," Seta said.

Everyone stopped talking and turned to her.

Seta played with her fingers. "Well, I know I don't know much about politics, but something doesn't make sense to me."

"What is that?" Michael said.

Seta looked at him. "Why did the Turks agree to this plan of the Europeans?"

"Oh Mother, why does it matter? The point is they did."

"No," Michael said. "Seta has a good point. And I'm not sure either, but my best guess is that they want to keep the Russians happy because of Zia Gokalp's plan about expanding into Azerbaijan. They would need Russia's cooperation for that."

"Oh, I see," Seta said and got up to help Araxie prepare coffee for her guests.

Victoria labored hard for the next three months and by early summer, the neat little rows of her vegetable garden were defined by immature versions of the vegetables that she and Nikol would harvest in the fall. Martin had taught Koren how to mend fences and herd the sheep. When Koren completed the school year, he went out into the fields to work, often taking Paul with him.

When Victoria learned that Major Hoff had arrived in Van, and Westenenk was due in Erzerum in a matter of days, she knew that her people's place in Turkey was truly assured. Thinking about that, and knowing that Nikol would be home in four more weeks, she went to bed on August 3, 1914, happy and secure.

She woke up to one of the bleakest days of her life.

The Europeans had declared war.

Major Hoff left for home at the end of the week and Westenenk turned back.

Victoria was worried about their loss of Europe's aid and even more so by her rapidly emerging awareness that Turkey was preparing itself for war.

She learned that two days before the war had broken out, Enver had signed an agreement to align Turkey with Austria and Germany. She was not surprised. She remembered studying the roots of that alliance in school. Sultan Hamid had allowed a German bank to finance the building of a railway that would span from Baghdad to Berlin. He had also allowed the German military to train the Ottoman army. The Young Turks continued the alliance in secret. Enver had even gone to Germany in 1908 to study their military.

As the day for Turkey's inevitable involvement in the war drew near, Victoria also learned, through Michael, what the *Dashnak*s knew. Leaders of the Committee of Union and Progress had approached the *Dashnak*s a month ago and tried to get them to convince the Armenians of Russia to rise against the Tsar, if war broke out. The *Dashnak*s had known about Zia Gokalp's plans to expand into Russian Azerbaijan and had known why the Committee leaders were asking, so they wisely refused.

Victoria thought about her mother. Seta had wondered why the Turks would agree to the European's reform plan. Now Victoria knew. The Turks had known this war was coming and that the reform plan would never be implemented. Seta was ignorant to the ways of the world. She could not read or write. Yet she had sensed something they had all missed.

Victoria began to hear Enver's name mentioned with increasing frequency. He was the Minister of War. He had also set up a group called the Special Organization and given them an assignment to prepare Southern Russia, including Azerbaijan, for Ottoman conquest. His Special Organization was led by two men, Dr. Nazim and Behaeddin Shakir, who believed as passionately in pan-Turkism as Enver himself did.

August turned into September and September into October, while the villagers waited daily for news that Turkey had joined the war.

On the next to the last day of October, Victoria walked into the village and found a sixteen-year-old boy holding a stack of newspapers, while he announced the headlines.

"Turkey joins the war!" he said.

He raced past Victoria. She reached out and caught his arm. "I'll take one of those."

She stood where she was and read the article. *Our participation in the World War represents vindication of our national ideal. The ideal of our nation and people leads us toward the destruction of our Muscovite enemy, in order to obtain thereby a natural frontier to our empire, which should include and unite all branches of our race.* Victoria looked up. Solomon stood nearby. He was unsmiling and pale.

Victoria pointed to the paper. "Muscovite enemy?"

Solomon grimaced. "Russia. An excuse, of course, to enlarge Turkey's empire." He pointed further down the page. "Did you read that?"

Victoria looked. It was a poem by Zia Gokalp. She read the last lines aloud. *"The land of the enemy shall be devastated. Turkey shall be enlarged and become Turan."*

Solomon shook his head. "I don't like it. All of Russia's Armenian population lives in the area they are talking about."

"And a war. What will become of our own young men? Will they be drafted into the Turkish army?"

"I'm sure they will."

Solomon nodded in the direction of his house. "Let's go inside and talk where it is warm."

Margaret stood at the door. When Victoria walked in, they fell into each other's arms.

"If Turkey wins the war, what will become of us?" Margaret said.

"If Turkey wins the war, we must all leave," Victoria said. "I believe they will destroy us to complete their plans for a Turkish empire. I don't believe now that they ever had any intention of allowing the European reforms."

Solomon nodded. "I don't, either." He lowered his voice. "Let's hope Turkey doesn't win the war."

Later that afternoon, Father Mikayelian held a special church service. Victoria walked into the churchyard and saw two turban-clad men standing near the open back door. Spies. Earlier, Solomon had privately hoped for Turkey's defeat. Victoria knew that most of the Armenian community shared his sentiments. But if Father Mikayelian voiced it in his service, they might all be in trouble.

She was relieved when the priest's fine resonant voice prayed only for Ottoman victory. When the service was over, Victoria noticed him peek around to where the men had been standing, and smile.

All of the single young men from the village were drafted

in the first week of November. Victoria followed the news of the war daily. In late December, Enver marched 95,000 soldiers into Russia. He announced that first he would capture a Russian military base in Sarikamish, next a fortress in Kars, and last the city of Baku, located on the Caspian sea in Azerbaijan. With the capture of Baku, half of Zia Gokalp's expansion would be complete.

But within two weeks, eighty percent of Enver's men were dead, most by means of Russia's most powerful weapon. A weapon that had defeated other great men throughout history — the Russian winter.

Entire divisions froze to death and the few who didn't were easy targets for Russian guns. But Victoria could not celebrate Enver's ineptness, because many of the soldiers who died were Armenian.

Enver scurried back to Constantinople from Sarikamish. How was he going to cover up the reality that thousands upon thousands of men had died as a result of his poor planning? Everyone thought him a great man. A man of action. He could not lose his standing in Turkey. He would blame the Armenians. Not publicly. No, publicly he would say that the Armenian soldiers had proved themselves. But privately, in the right circles, he could whisper that the Armenian soldiers had acted as spies and caused his defeat. Behaeddin Shakir would appreciate any story that inflamed hatred of the Armenians. He was, after all, still gathering support for the plans he had made to deal with them. Talaat, too, would make sure the story was spread where it would be the most useful. Neither man would care whether it was true or not.

The bitter winter winds swept across the frozen fields and stung the exposed part of Victoria's face. She made this trip to Margaret's house every day to get news of the war. News she both dreaded and needed to hear.

She reached Margaret's door and stopped. Someone was crying inside. Wailing.

Victoria banged on the door. Margaret opened it with tears streaming down her cheeks.

"Margaret, what's wrong?"

Margaret gulped back her sobs. "Solomon has been drafted."

Victoria looked past Margaret and saw Solomon sitting at the table with his head in his hands.

"I thought they only called single men."

"I don't understand it," Solomon said. "They're not honoring any previous exemptions. And they're only calling *Armenian* men. None of the married Turks were called."

Victoria drew in a breath. "Other Armenian men have been called, too?"

"Yes. Every man under the age of fifty." He turned to Margaret. "We'd better go talk to your father."

Victoria went from Margaret's to Anna's house. One look at Anna's face confirmed what Victoria feared. "Leon was drafted?"

She went next to Fiorine's house and found that Arsen, too, had been drafted.

Michael was able to raise enough money to pay Solomon's way out of the army. But none of the other families in the village could afford the exemption fee, which was now more than most earned in ten years.

Leon left with his guitar in his hand. Arsen with a pack strapped to his back. And Martin, dear Martin, wiped tears from his eyes and walked away from the soil he had spent his life tilling.

Victoria looked around the empty village. Women, children, and old men. How would they live? Who would plant their wheat? Who would protect them if the Turks turned on them again?

CHAPTER TWENTY-TWO

January, 1915

*V*ictoria leafed through Nikol's letters. She should have left when she could. Or Nikol should have come home sooner. He wouldn't have been drafted into the Turkish army. He was a United States citizen. He could have helped her on the farm. If only they had known. Now no one was allowed in or out of Turkey.

The schools had been closed down.

She no longer walked into the village every day. She didn't like the deserted feel to it. She didn't like the way the muscles of her back felt so prominent. As if they were protecting her from something. But what?

She tied Nikol's letters back together again and held the stack against her cheek. If she could touch him again, sleep beside him, feel the nearness of his devotion, she would feel safe.

But they had missed each other by a cruel and random act of fate.

What was Nikol doing in America now? Did he miss her as much as she missed him?

Nikol woke, stretched, and swung his aching feet onto the cold floor. Outside, the darkness of the winter sky had begun to lighten. He sniffed. Marig was brewing coffee. In anticipation of its stimulating effect, he walked to the kitchen.

Marig flipped two sizzling eggs onto a plate and set them down on the table in front of him.

Nikol broke off a piece of crisp cracker bread and dipped it into the yoke. "Good morning, Marig."

Marig nodded without smiling and went back to her frying pan.

Abraham spread a wedge of cream cheese on his *choeregs*. "Sarkis invited us over to play pinocle tonight.

Nikol shook his head. "I don't think so."

Abraham set down his fork. "Brother, you have to start getting out again. Staying home like this, its not getting you any closer to her."

Nikol sighed. "Why didn't I go home sooner?"

"You couldn't have known."

"But now she's alone, in the middle of a war. I can't get letters into Turkey anymore. I don't even know if she's safe."

"There is nothing you can do about it except make yourself crazy. And that wouldn't do either of you any good. Come play cards with us tonight. Get your mind off of it. Today is Saturday. You don't have to work tomorrow."

Saturday, the end of fifty-seven hours of work. Maybe his brother was right. It was foolish to sit here night after night worrying. "I will go."

Marig banged her spatula into the sink.

Nikol looked at Abraham. Abraham's shoulders twitched.

"Marig, is something wrong?" Abraham said.

She looked at him, shook her head, and walked from the room.

Abraham turned the key to the door of his downstairs grocery shop. His two sons, five-year-old John, and two-year-old Stephan, stood at his side.

"You may choose one treat. Then go outside to play. John, you watch Stephan and don't bother your mother. She doesn't feel well today."

Inside his shop, Abraham inhaled the smell of cumin, *sumac, chaiman*, and nutmeg, the spices of home. He lifted the lid to a tub and popped a salty black olive in his mouth. Wooden barrels filled with cracked wheat, flour and pistachio nuts lined the walls. *Basterma*, Armenian sausage, that he and Marig had made on their table top, hung from the ceiling, drying in muslin bags. All of the Armenians in the neighborhood came to him for their food. He did a good business here. He was a fortunate man.

He thought about Marig. What did his wife have to be so unhappy about? Every day couldn't be a wedding, could it?

Nikol, now had something to be unhappy about. He wanted to go home. And he couldn't. He had to leave the woman he loved to escape the trouble Abraham had gotten him into. Now it was up to Abraham to distract him from his worries. He wished Marig would understand.

Marig walked into the store an hour later, her hands still wet from the laundry tub. He could use her help today. Saturday was his busiest day.

He handed her a sheet of paper. "The priest asked us to post this notice about the church bazaar."

Marig tacked it to a wall. "Can we go?"

"Well, I'll talk to Nikol. We'll see."

Marig turned from him and picked up a broom.

"Marig, I-"

The door to the shop opened and interrupted Abraham. A dark-haired young man walked in.

"*Bon jour.*"

Marig's face brightened with a smile. "*Parlez vous Francais?*"

"*Oui.*"

Abraham watched the young man converse with his wife in the foreign language. It was unusual for anyone not Armenian to come into his store. But a customer was a customer, and Marig looked happy. She hadn't looked happy in a while. This was what she needed. To socialize with other people. Not with an *odar*, but with other Armenians, like herself. He would take her to Watertown as soon as he got his brother settled down.

Nikol threaded a shuttle through his loom making sure the thread stayed smooth. Forty other men sat in front of similar looms. The noise pounded in his head.

He thought about the fences he used to mend and the fields he used to spend his days walking through. He sighed. This tedium had been his life six days a week, for seven years. By the end of each day, his eyes ached from the poor lighting. The giant machine vibrated from its powerful motor. He was lucky he had never lost his hand in one of the gears. He would be fired on the spot.

One day he would go back. Back to the open air and the woman he loved. He'd deal with Cousin Rose when he got there. Walk right up to her and tell her what he knew, tell her everyone else would, too, if she went to the authorities again.

The thread broke and he stopped to retie it. He hadn't been laid off in months. He was grateful for that, at least. President Wilson was claiming America wouldn't join the war, but ask any factory worker. They would tell the people to get ready.

The monotonous day droned on until at last, the final whistle blew and the mammoth machines all ground to a halt.

Nikol walked into Abraham's store and stepped behind the counter. A customer asked him something. He saw her lips move but after a week behind the loom, he couldn't hear what she was saying.

She pointed to a barrel of sesame seeds. He nodded. By the time his hearing came back, it would be Monday and time to go to work.

Abraham locked the door on his last customer of the day. He picked up a rag and wiped down the counter in silence.

Nikol began putting covers over the barrels. He looked at Abraham. His brother looked worried.

"Is something wrong?"

Abraham looked up. "No, not really."

Nikol waited.

"Its Marig," Abraham said. "She seems unhappy."

Nikol nodded "She's young. She wasn't really raised for this kind of life." Nikol saw the look on Abraham's face. He was making him feel worse. "But she was a orphan and you've given her a home, children and food on her table."

Abraham straightened his back. "I have, haven't I?"

"Yes. Just don't forget. She doesn't have a mother or anyone else to keep her company. Take her out sometime. Encourage her to get friendly with some of the other women around here." Nikol laid his hand on Abraham's arm. "And stop worrying about me."

Before they left for the card game, Abraham turned to

Marig. "I'm taking you to the bazaar next month."

He was rewarded by her pretty smile.

Nikol and Abraham stepped into Sarkis's noisy, smoke-filled kitchen and took their place at a table with three other men.

The others had already started playing and Nikol waited with Abraham to play the winners.

Pinocle was a centuries-old game. It was played by three people at a time who rotated after each hand. The first person to accrue a thousand points, won. Nikol was glad Abraham had insisted he come. The game required strategy and a good memory of the cards. The concentration would help him forget his worry about Victoria. Abraham was right. He wasn't doing himself or Victoria any good staying in the way he had. He picked up the beer Sarkis had poured him and took a large gulp.

By one o'clock in the morning, the men had abandoned the cards and Sarkis was pouring everyone *raki*.

One of the card players turned to Nikol. "I'm sorry you couldn't go home."

"The war won't last forever," Nikol said. "When it's over, I'll go."

Another player took a sip from his glass. "My folks are back there, too. We're all worried."

Sarkis leaned heavily on Nikol's shoulder and stood. He refilled everyone's glass, then raised his own. "To our people in the old country."

Nikol and Abraham lurched home an hour later, singing off-key ballads as they walked.

In the kitchen, Abraham whispered something and they both roared with laughter. Marig appeared in the doorway blinking sleep from her eyes. She looked at them, frowned, and turned back into the bedroom.

Nikol fell, still clothed, onto the made-up couch in the living room. He belched, rolled over and was soon asleep.

He woke four hours later and sat up. His temples throbbed and he had to shade his eyes from the painful light. It was foolish for him to have drunk so much. Now, he would spend his only day off fighting a headache. He took an aspirin, got dressed, and went out for the paper.

The cold January air revived him and he decided to walk into town for the New York Times. He had become adept enough at speaking his new language and enjoyed the challenge of reading it.

At the newsstand, Nikol paid for his paper and sat down on the curb and read. *Turks advise Christians to Flee.* His body grew rigid. He read on.

...the German ambassador has warned the Minister of a Balkan state in Constantinople that in the event of the allied fleet's forcing the straits, the Turks will vent their wrath by a massacre of the Christian population. In Constantinople no endeavor is any longer made by the Ministers to hide their feelings toward their Christian subjects.

To the Greek Patriarch, who was sent to Talaat Pasha to remonstrate against the excesses committed by the organs of his Ministry, he unequivocally replied that there was no room for Christians in Turkey, and that the best the Patriarch could do for his flock would be to advise them to clear out of the country and make room for the Moslem refugees.

Taalat was advising the Greeks to leave. But the Greeks had citizenship in Greece. What about the Armenians, Turkey's largest Christian population? They were not allowed out.

Nikol thought about Talaat, the Minister of the Interior, and Turkey's most important leader. More important even than Enver. Talaat was a religious zealot, a dangerous man. The newspaper article had said that Turkey would begin exterminating the Christians if the Allies tried to gain control of the Straights of Dardanelles. Nikol knew the Turks would use the Straights as an excuse to rid themselves of the Christians but he also knew, that Germany, Turkey's ally, would let them, if it kept the Europeans from capturing the Straights.

The Straights of Dardanelles were a narrow waterway connecting the Mediterranean to the Black Sea. The mouth of the Danube River was on the Black Sea. If Turkey and Germany's enemies had access to the Danube River, they could bypass the German front by sailing all the way up the river into Germany.

The Allies were bound to try to gain control of the Straights and thereby the Black Sea and the Danube, because the German front was looking impenetrable and the river was a back door into Germany.

He had to get Victoria and his sons out of Turkey. But how?

He ran all the way home and showed Abraham the newspaper article.

"Right there for the world to see. Talaat said it. The German ambassador confirmed it."

Nikol gripped Abraham's arm. "What am I going to do?"

"You and I both know the Turks won't wait for the Allies to attack the Straights," Abraham said. "Why should they? War is the Young Turks shield to do what they have wanted to do from the start."

"Then I must find a way to get her out."

Abraham read the article again. "We can't help all of our people, but we can get your family out of Turkey. We have friends who will help us."

"But Turkey and the United States are enemies. Victoria is a Turkish citizen."

"Yes, but she's also your wife. And you are an *American* citizen."

Abraham made plans to go to the immigration office in the morning and meet Nikol at the factory at the end of the day.

The next day, Nikol struggled to keep his mind on his

work. Once, his hand slipped when he was pulling his shuttle through the loom and almost caught on the gear beneath it. He pulled it back in time but let it serve as a warning. He had enough problems without getting Victoria over here and being too crippled to take care of her.

Abraham was waiting when Nikol walked out of work. He looked at Abraham's face. Abraham was not smiling.

"We have a problem," Abraham said.

Nikol felt his heart accelerate. "A problem?"

Abraham looked at the ground. "Your immigration papers say you came into this country in 1908 with a wife."

"What? How can that..." Nikol stopped. He thought back. The inspector at the immigration office had asked him something about Marig. He hadn't known what the inspector was saying at the time, but he must have asked if Marig was his wife.

"I explained to my friend at the immigration office that it was *my* wife you brought through customs, but he said it was not a problem easily fixed."

"But Victoria. They're going to kill her — I know it."

Abraham called on and wrote to everyone he knew, but everyone said the same thing.

Nikol banged his fist on the kitchen table. "If I can't get my family away from the Turks, I'll fight them."

"How are you going to do that?" Abraham asked.

"I'm joining the United States army."

Nikol was at the recruitment desk in the morning.

"Your name please?"

"Nikol Kalousdian."

"Where were you born?"

"Turkey."

The recruiter put down his pencil. "You can't join the United States army."

"But I am an American citizen."

"You are, but you were born on foreign soil. If America goes to war, Turkey will be our enemy."

Nikol looked him in the eye. "If this country doesn't go to war, Turkey will still be my enemy."

The recruiter's face softened. "I know. I've read the papers too. But really, there is nothing I can do."

Four weeks later, the New York Times published another article based on an interview with Talaat Bey, who had just been made the Minister of War in addition to his other Ministries. Talaat confirmed that Turkey considered the war a holy war and as such, Christians were their enemy.

Nikol could not leave the war to others to fight. But what could he do if America would not let him join their army?

The solution came to him from a friend.

"The French Foreign Legion requires only that you swear loyalty to the Legion. You need not be born in France."

Four days later, Nikol was on a boat to France.

CHAPTER TWENTY-THREE

February, 1915

*V*ictoria hurried down the frozen road toward home. She had gone to the village that morning despite her resolve not to. She wanted to see the notice for herself.

It had been tacked up in the village square, just as she had been told it would be. An order for every Armenian household to turn in their weapons.

What weapons?

Since the Young Turks had come to power in 1908, Armenians were allowed to own weapons, but hers was a household with two women and two boys. What would they be doing with weapons?

The Turks were up to something.

Last week, Michael Damadian had told her that the

*Dashnak*s had learned that Armenian men had been pulled from their positions as soldiers. They had been stripped of their coats and were being forced to carry supplies on their backs like pack animals while the Turks whipped and prodded them with bayonets.

Martin, Leon, and Arsen — she couldn't bear to think of how they must be suffering.

Something was going on, but what could it be? She thought about the notice. It had been specific. It said *every* household must turn in two rifles and a sword. But what if she didn't own either?

She had gone from the village square to Margaret's house. Margaret had shrugged. "If we don't own any weapons, how can we turn them in?"

"Well, of course we can't, but there was something about that notice."

Margaret looked at her.

"Something, I don't know."

"Threatening?"

"Yes, threatening. That's it."

"I'll talk to my father," Margaret said.

Margaret sat in her mother's living room. Araxie had insisted she and the children stay until Michael and Solomon returned from the police station with instructions on how to respond to the demand. But her father and Solomon had been gone for four hours now. Something was wrong.

Someone banged on the door. "Police. Open up."

Margaret looked at her mother.

Araxie began to shake.

Margaret's grandfather looked up from the cushion where he sat. "You might as well open it, they'll just kick it down if you don't."

Margaret pushed eight-year-old Diran and six-year-old Miriam behind her.

Araxie went to the door, but it crashed open just as she reached it.

A heavy-set man in a police uniform stepped into the room. "Hand over your weapons."

Three other men in uniforms walked in behind him pointing guns at Araxie. Araxie gave Margaret a look and she understood she was being told to stay seated.

Margaret noticed the policemen's uniforms all looked new. She had heard that the police were increasing their forces.

Araxie ran her hand through her hair. "But we have no guns of any kind."

The leader caught one of the other policeman's eye and laughed. He pointed to Araxie. "These people are all liars."

Araxie looked him in the eye. "I can't give you what I don't have."

The laugh disappeared from the leader's face. He crossed the room, took the butt of his rifle and smashed Margaret's grandfather across the face. He fell on his side, unconscious.

Araxie screamed. Margaret clutched her children.

The leader turned to the other men. "Search the house."

The men ripped open sacks of wheat, overturned jars of dried beans and smashed glass containers of poppy seed butter to the floor. Next, they slit open Araxie's mattresses and cushions.

The leader grabbed Araxie by the shoulders. "Where have you hidden them?"

"I, I..."

The leader gave her a violent shove and she fell to the floor. Then he raised his foot and kicked her.

Margaret put a restraining hand on Diran's arm. She cold feel the fury building in him. But he was just a little boy and these men were barbarians.

When Victoria found Margaret at her parent's house, it was late at night. Araxie was awake but her eye was swollen shut and her arm in a sling. Margaret held a cold cloth to her grandfather's face.

Victoria felt like she was going to be sick.

Margaret looked up at her and began to cry. "The police were here searching for weapons."

Victoria ran to her and drew her into her arms. "Where is your father?"

"He and Solomon have been gone since this afternoon."

Victoria stayed with Margaret. She helped her clean up and tend Araxie and her grandfather. Hours later, Michael and Solomon returned. Their clothes were wrinkled and their faces bruised.

"We were arrested," Michael said, after Margaret told him what happened. "They let us out but said if we don't turn in our weapons tomorrow, they will send us away. They told us, bragged really, that they are doing this in every village."

Araxie's hands flew to her face. "What will we do?"

"I'm going to buy what they want from our Turkish neighbors."

Victoria frowned. "Will they sell them?"

The corners of Michael's lips turned down. "Oh yes, for a price, of course."

"But isn't your money in the city?" Margaret asked.

"Most of it, yes. But I have enough to buy what I need." He looked at Victoria. "I'd advise you to do the same. I'll bring the weapons you buy to the police station for you. That is if you have the money to pay for them."

Victoria thought about her savings jar. "Yes, I do."

The next morning, Michael, Solomon, and every other Armenian who had either bought or owned weapons, laid them on the steps of the police station and stood waiting to be dismissed.

The leader of the raids, eyed the gleaming guns and swords. "Here is our proof."

He signaled a man standing behind a cloth draped camera who snapped a picture of the men, standing before a stockpile of weapons. "Develop it and send it to the capitol."

After the weapons search, Victoria had no difficulty getting information. The Turks bragged about their cruelty now. And why not? They had nothing to fear from the Armenians anymore.

In late March, Victoria heard that Turkish soldiers were on their way to Zeitun.

Zeitun, like Hadjin, was set in a remote mountainous area accessible only by a narrow pass. Also like Hadjin, Zeitun's population was almost without exception, Armenian. The Armenians of Zeitun were both shepherds and warriors. They manufactured their own weapons, and ruled themselves. For Armenians throughout Turkey, Zeitun was a symbol of an independence that had endured despite waves of attempted Turkish domination. Episodes of their defiant stands had become legend.

More than fifty years ago, the Turkish governor of near-by Marash had dispatched troops into the mountains of Zeitun in an attempt to end the people's resistance and force them to pay the higher taxes he was demanding. But his soldiers proved to be no match for the brave men of Zeitun.

The governor had lived with his failure for two years, then he had called for reinforcements. Ten thousand soldiers surrounded Zeitun. They set fire to several of the outlying villages and raped many of the young girls living there. But their actions so enraged the men of Zeitun, that it wasn't long before the Turkish troops were again in retreat.

Throughout the ensuing years, the men of Zeitun continued to fight the Ottoman government as it made repeated,
unsuccessful attempts to steal Zeitun's land, and impoverish
its people with an unfair tax system. When the first political
parties were being established and a collective spirit of defi-
ance was awakening in Armenians in other parts of Turkey,
the Zeitunites readiness and willingness to defend themselves, became a model for Armenians everywhere.

During the Massacre of 1895, when every other province
was under attack, the men of Zeitun took the offensive and
ambushed the Turkish troops as they marched up the mountain pass. Then they dressed in the uniforms of their Turkish
prisoners and retaliated by attacking some of the nearby
Turkish towns. Their ferocity grew with each town they
attacked until the entire battle had deteriorated into a race
war.

The British ambassador became concerned knowing that
Turkish reinforcements were on their way with orders to
cover every road leading to Zeitun. If they prevailed, every
man, woman, and child of Zeitun would be killed. The ambassador was able to persuade the government to call off the
reinforcements only by threatening British military action.
Then the Zeitunites sat down with the Turks and worked out
the terms of a peace agreement.

What better place to pilot Turkey's solution to their
Christian problem than Zeitun, the very area that had given
the government so much trouble with their independent

ways?

A twelve-year-old Armenian boy, a lookout for the fighting men of Zeitun, stood on a hillside and watched General Fakhri Pasha pause astride his horse. The general sat tall in his saddle. He adjusted his reins. Then he raised a sword. Thousands of soldiers began to climb the mountain toward Zeitun. The boy noticed movement beyond the soldiers. He shaded his eyes and looked. Hundreds of Turks were camped in a field.

The boy ran ahead to Zeitun and waited. General Fakhri soon galloped into town flanked by his soldiers. He dismounted at the government building and strode inside. His men stood at attention outside. The boy tried to catch the eye of one of the soldiers, but the soldier stared straight ahead. The boy ran around to the back of the building and peeked in. The general was gesturing at the mayor, while several other important leaders of Zeitun stood frowning. The boy inched the window up, and listened.

"Not one of the men from Zeitun enlisted in the Ottoman Army," the general said.

The mayor folded his arms. "Why? So they can be treated like animals?"

The general drew himself up. "I demand that every man fit for service report for duty."

"No," the mayor said. "Our men are needed here to defend our women and children."

The boy listened, as the men continued to argue. Then he heard something he never thought he would hear from any man of Zeitun. The mayor was agreeing to send the young men to war.

The boy ran to his uncle who was waiting for him and told him what he had overheard.

His uncle turned to the group of muscular young men waiting with him and frowned. "No. The old man can make all the promises he wants, but *we're* not going."

The men nodded and walked off.

By evening, every man of military age had fled to the mountains where they knew the terrain and could survive indefinitely.

Emissaries went to talk to them and eventually persuaded forty men to enlist.

At his uncle's urging, the young boy followed the draftees first to a newly erected barracks in a nearby Turkish town, then to another village. The boy heard an officer tell the men that they were going to get fitted for their uniforms, but when they reached the center of town, he saw the officer give a signal to the Turkish soldiers with him. The soldiers drew their guns and pushed the Zeitun men into a jail.

The boy ran back to the mountains and told his uncle what he had seen.

His uncle nodded. "Just what I thought."

He gathered a group of twenty-five men and took them to a monastery set on a hill above the road. He waited for the

Turks to approach. When they did, the Zeitun men attacked. The battle lasted twenty-four hours, at the end of which three hundred Turkish soldiers lay dead. The Zeitun survivors withdrew back into the mountains.

Thousands more Turkish soldiers ascended on Zeitun. With all their able-bodied men gone, the villagers were unable to defend themselves and after decades of resistance, Zeitun was defeated.

General Fakhri marched into town, glaring. He hammered up a notice demanding that the villagers evacuate their homes. The first to go were the town's leading families. The rest followed within days. As each house emptied, the general's men tacked an official seal across its door, announcing that the house was being held by the Turkish government.

General Fakhri Pasha himself led the last villagers out. When one old woman stopped to wipe a tear from her eye, he strode up to her and said with a sneer, "You're a disloyal citizen. But even though you don't deserve it, our government is going to be benevolent. You will be allowed to return at the end of the war."

The woman nodded and walked away from her home.

The general turned the villagers over to his soldiers who led them on a long, roundabout route out of the mountains and then on through the searing plains. With each passing day, the Zeitunites became increasingly starved and ragged. The first to die were the very old and the very young. They were left where they fell.

The general rode to the field the young boy had spotted from the mountain. The Turks camped there had been made homeless two years before when Turkey was defeated in the Balkan wars. The general waited while they took down their tents and packed up their household goods. Then he took them up the mountain to Zeitun.

When they arrived and spotted the sturdy stone houses waiting for them, they looked at each other and smiled. The general gestured and each family pulled the seal from their house of choice. Zeitun, for Armenians, had ceased to exist.

The general, and others like him, went from Zeitun to the surrounding towns and villages, then on toward the provinces.

CHAPTER TWENTY-FOUR

Summer, 1915

*T*he church bells tolled loudly, their metallic ring echoing all the way to the outskirts of the village. Victoria heard it. The feeling of dread that had been with her since the weapons search made sense now. She dropped the weeds she had been pulling and raced toward the house.

Seta stood in the doorway. Her face was lined with worry.

"What is it, Victoria? Why are they ringing the bells in the middle of the week?"

"I'm going into town to find out," Victoria said. But she knew why. She'd seen the Turks in the village pointing at the Armenian homes and heard them saying that the Armenians had been marched out of other towns and villages in the provinces.

"Do you think the village is safe?"

Victoria turned her palms up. "What does it matter now?"

The village square was full of people, who wore the same worried expressions that Victoria knew was on her own face. Public buildings, each with a poster nailed to it, loomed all around her.

Margaret had just walked up to one. Her lips formed a circle and her hand flew to her mouth as she read.

Victoria hurried over to her and gripped her arm. "Does it say what I think it does?"

Margaret turned to her. "I know we've been expecting it, but I just didn't believe it until now."

"Then it does say — "

"That we're being deported? Yes."

"When?"

"The men are ordered to report here in two days. We will get our instructions after they leave." Margaret put her head on Victoria's shoulder and wept. "This is too horrible for words. My father and Solomon have to leave in two days. In two days."

The village had become quiet, except for a sudden wailing coming from one of the houses.

Victoria looked around. "We must hide them. Hide all of us."

Margaret looked up. "You're right. Let's go talk to my father."

Solomon and Michael were both waiting at Margaret's

house. Their faces were pale, their expressions grave.

Margaret laid her hand on her chest. "What are we to do?"

She looked across the room. Diran and Miriam sat staring at her.

Diran looked from his mother to his father. "Why? Why do the Turks hate us so?"

Margaret knelt down in front of her children. "I can't tell you. We don't understand it ourselves. Maybe the Turks blame us for their problems in the war."

"But can't we just tell them that it's not our fault?" Diran said.

Margaret stroked her son's face. "No, darling, I'm afraid it's not that simple."

"What about our vineyards?" Michael said. "We could all hide out there."

Victoria thought about the vineyards. They were remote. The Turks who lived there were simple country folk. Many of them had worked for Michael for years. With sufficient compensation, they might be persuaded to hide them all.

"But our money?" Solomon said.

Michael nodded. "Yes, it's still in the city. Impossible to get to. But we have jewelry to sell, and silver."

Margaret ran her foot along her thick oriental carpet. "We can sell this, too."

"And I have money," Victoria said. "Gold." Her savings. She had used some of it to buy the guns, but she still had money left.

She left, after they had finished making their plans. Michael and Solomon would sell everything they owned tomorrow. Then they would leave for the country the next day, where they would make preparations for them all to go into hiding.

Victoria hurried down the dirt road. Surely Seta and her sons had heard the news by now and must be frightened. She had to get to them and tell them there was hope yet.

Someone was coming toward her on horseback. Someone she knew. But who? He drew closer. It was Hasan the Kurd. She hadn't spoken to him since the day of her father's funeral but she had seen him in the village. Seen the way he looked at her.

Hasan stopped and flashed her a smile.

With his white even teeth, his dark skin, he was more handsome than ever. But she couldn't be thinking about that now.

"The Armenians have been ordered to leave," he said.

She nodded. He was looking at her in the way he had looked at her in the village.

"You don't have to go. I will take you in, if you are willing to work in my house and be one of my wives."

Wife to another man? A Muslim? No, she was married. Michael's plan was risky, but if it failed, she would leave with her reputation intact.

She shook her head. "No. Thank you, but I can't."

Hasan nodded. "I thought you would say that but think about it. Think what will happen if you leave."

"I know what I am facing," Victoria said and began to walk away.

"Wait," Hasan said.

She turned.

"I will send a messenger to your house in one week. Give me your answer then."

"It will be the same." In one week, she and her family would be in hiding anyway.

Seta met her in the door with tears streaming down her face.

Victoria went to her sons. She remembered the Massacre of 1895, and how as a child she had watched the adults murmur together in low worried tones. She remembered the looks on her parents' faces and the conversations that had stopped when they saw her edging near. Yet she had still managed to find out what was going on.

"Darlings, I can't pretend that the news isn't bad, very bad indeed. But I can promise you that we will stay together. God will protect us."

The next day, Victoria heard that General Fakhri Pasha was in Mezireh saying that all Armenians must leave because of their disloyalty to the government.

She heard the Turks in the village say that the governor in Mezireh had asked the general to spare the Armenians of his province since none had given him cause to doubt their loyalty. But the general had reminded the governor of Talaat's reply to a German correspondent who asked him how they would distinguish between the Armenians who were guilty of treason and those who were innocent. Talaat had said that no distinction was to be made between the innocent and guilty, because after all, those who were innocent today might be guilty tomorrow.

The general had also warned the Muslims not to shield the Armenians and said that any who did, would suffer the same fate.

Victoria ran to Margaret and was relieved to hear that Michael and Solomon had settled their affairs and were leaving once it grew dark. It was unlikely that the Turks in the country would have heard the general's warning.

Victoria left Margaret promising to come back in the morning.

Margaret took her children to her parent's house early that evening to wait until it was safe for the men to slip out of the village.

But they had barely sat down when there was a knock on the door.

Margaret thought about the last knock on this door. Her mother still limped from what had happened. Her heart pounded but she signaled the family and rose to answer the door herself. She opened it and two Turkish soldiers pushed past her. They walked straight to Michael and Solomon and grabbed them by the arms.

"What do you want with us?" Michael said.

"Don't ask questions. Just come with us."

"Wait. Let me get my shoes on."

"You don't need shoes where you are going." The soldier laughed and prodded him toward the door. His comrade followed with Solomon.

Margaret ran ahead and stood in front of one of them. "Please don't take them away."

But the soldier would not even look at her.

Victoria went with Margaret to the police station in the morning. Solomon, Michael, John Halabian, Levon Kalustian, and all the village's thirty-five remaining Armenian men stood surrounded by soldiers on the stone steps.

The soldiers raised their rifles and marched their prisoners out of town.

Victoria waited with Margaret until long after the men were out of sight. Then she turned and silently trudged back to her house. All hope of escape was gone. She and her family were next.

Solomon marched along the deserted dirt road. The flat plains offered no hiding places. He was powerless to escape. He should have left weeks ago, when he heard about Zeitun.

"Where are you taking us?" he asked the soldier nearest him.

The soldier's eyes narrowed and he pointed his gun at Solomon's head. "Just keep walking."

Michael tapped Solomon's arm and shook his head.

Solomon kept walking.

The sun grew high in the sky. Solomon was tired and thirsty, but still they kept marching.

At last they stopped. Solomon sat beside Michael. Michael was trying to catch his breath.

"Are you all right?" Solomon asked.

Michael opened his mouth but his reply was cut off by a gunshot. He fell backward.

All the soldiers opened fire and one by one, the men around Solomon fell.

But Solomon was younger than the rest. He leapt to his feet and began to run. He made it across the field before a bullet pierced his thigh. He fell, clutching his leg and looked up into the face of death.

"Tell me, soldier," he said through gritted teeth. "Are you planning to deport our women and children this way, too?"

The soldier stared at him for a moment, then said, "No, we don't waste valuable lead on women and children." He spat in the dust, turned around and marched away.

Solomon lay bleeding on the ground. Soon it would be dark. And the jackals would be out.

The next day, Victoria went into the village and found a new notice ordering the women and children to be ready to leave in a week. The notice said that they could return when the war was over and that they would be treated kindly.

Victoria turned around and walked home. The notice had said "kindly." What was kind about driving people from their homes? And there wasn't anything she could do about it. The men were gone. Whatever was going to happen would happen.

Two days later, Victoria sat in her living room and watched Koren and Paul. The boys no longer read books. They seldom even spoke. They just sat. Sat and stared into the distance.

Koren was twelve-years-old. She was glad the Turks hadn't marched him out with the men. But what would happen when they left the village? Would he be separated from her then?

The stillness of the house made her feel like she couldn't breath. She stood and went to the door. Someone was walking up the path. Sona, Martin Halabian's wife. She was out of breath and looked frightened.

"The fields outside of town are filled with Armenian refugees."

"Refugees?"

Sona burst into tears. "They're all in rags and they look like they're starving."

Victoria headed for her pantry.

"Don't bother. The Turks aren't letting anyone get near them."

Victoria pivoted so she was facing Sona. "Show me where they are."

When Victoria saw the hundreds of women and children laying in the open field, she felt sick. Most of them had no blankets. All were filthy and emaciated.

Who did the Turks think they were?

She marched up to the nearest soldier. "These people need food and water."

The soldier's eyebrows formed valleys. "Get out of here, you infidel."

Victoria stood her ground.

He pushed her toward the road and she stumbled.

"We have our orders. You're not getting near them."

He could push her all he wanted, but she was coming back with food. Still, she had to think of a way to get it past the guards.

By the time it was dark, Victoria had a plan.

Seta put dried chick peas into Victoria's basket. "What you are doing is very brave. I'm proud of you."

"I am helping them because I must." Victoria lowered her voice. "Those people could be us."

Seta added three loaves of bread to what Victoria was bringing.

Victoria was almost ready to leave for the fields when she heard a knock on the door. She answered it and found Hasan's messenger. When he announced why he had come Seta turned to Victoria in surprise.

"When did — ?"

Victoria shrugged. "It doesn't matter." She turned to the messenger. "Tell him I said no."

Seta laid her hand on Victoria's arm. "What is going to happen to us, is very serious. Save yourself. I will take care of the boys."

Victoria smiled softly. "Do you think I would leave you and the boys? No, I promised them that wherever we go, we will go together, and we will."

Margaret, Sona, Anna, and Fiorine went with Victoria to the fields. They stood at a distance and saw that the guards had built a fire. Victoria took a deep breath, picked up a heavy jug and walked toward them.

Liquor was forbidden to Muslims, but Victoria knew that soldiers did not always keep the laws of their religion. She hoped these men would drink her *raki*, because it was all she had.

She crept near their campsite and set the heavy ceramic jug down along the path she had seen them take to gather wood. Then she ran back to Margaret and the protective circle of her friends. They all wrapped their arms around each other and waited.

Within an hour their patience was rewarded. The guards had gathered at the campfire and were passing the jug around.

Victoria signaled her friends and they tiptoed down the path into the field.

The women lying on the ground spotted Victoria's group approach and rose to their feet. Margaret, Anna, Sona, and Fiorine had all brought cracker bread and cheese, which they handed out to as many of them as they could.

"Bless you," one of the women said.

Victoria gave away her last loaf of bread. "Tell us what happened."

The woman nearest her spoke. "We're all from different villages and we all have different stories. In my village, only the young men were arrested and marched out of town. The Turks took them to a field and shot them all."

Victoria gasped. "But how do you – ?"

"How do I know this? The Turks came back and told us what they did."

Margaret clapped her hands over her mouth. "Oh God, oh God."

Victoria wrapped her arm around Margaret's shoulder. "Remember, every village has a different story."

The woman nodded. "Yes, it does."

"What happened after the young men left?" Victoria said.

"We set out with our fathers, mothers, and children. Some of us were on foot, some were in carts. The Turks made us go all day without eating."

Victoria thought about her sons. "No food?"

"Or water. By evening the children were crying."

Victoria felt Anna grip her arm.

Victoria looked at the woman telling the story. Her

cheekbones stood out and her eyes were huge.

The woman went on. "We were only allowed to bring a little food. But we've been walking for weeks. Eventually, we ran out. My mother passed out once. A guard galloped up to her and whipped her until she got up again. They tell us we're going all the way to Syria."

"Walking to Syria? That will take weeks."

"Still," another woman said, "they've made no attempt to give us more food."

"Thank God, we've been able to find water at night," the first woman said.

But Victoria knew that to get to Syria they would have to cross the plains where there was no water.

The woman continued her story. "On the third night of the march, we were attacked by bandits. They demanded we give them our money and jewelry, then they ransacked our belongings and beat us. My father tried to defend me. He died right in front of my eyes. I had to leave him there in the field." She buried her face in her hands. "I couldn't even give him a decent Christian burial."

"Tell them about the young girls," another voice said.

Victoria began to shiver.

A woman with gray streaked hair stepped forward. "One night, my daughter was dragged off with four other girls. I could hear her screaming, but the guards held me down and I couldn't get to her. After a while, I heard gunshots. Then silence."

She began to cry. "If it weren't for my other children, well..."

The first woman took her hand and continued. "We have been attacked every few days. The gendarmes won't help us. In fact, I know they are arranging the brutality because just before it happens, they disappear into the hills and bandits come from the same direction a few hours later."

Margaret looked around the dark field. "How many people are in your group?"

The woman looked at her. "Do you mean now, or when we started out?"

Margaret hesitated. "Both, I guess."

"We started out with three times what we have now. Our parents have fallen down dead as we marched along. All the older folks are dead now. And each time they fall, we've had to just leave them where they are."

"As we go along, we meet other convoys and join with them. I see them and think that they look like a bunch of ragged skeletons, then I realize they look like we do. Lately, I've been wishing I would fall down dead now and get it over with. I don't believe the Turks are going to let us live anyway."

"I'm from one of the convoys that joined them along the way," another woman said. "The Turks told us we could bring as much as we could carry. I sold everything I had to the Turks in my village. I didn't get anything close to what it was worth, but when I started out, I had gold in my pocket.

The guards told me that if I paid them, they would protect my family from the locals when we passed through villages. I paid them everything I had. Then they stood by and watched, while the locals beat my parents and took my blankets and food."

A tiny woman with a kerchief over her head said, "The Kurds are attacking us, too."

"The Kurds?" Victoria said.

"Yes, the Kurds that live in the mountains. They don't even want anything from us. I think they kill for pleasure." She looked at her feet. "I don't know why I've been spared when so many others haven't."

Several of the other women murmured in agreement.

By the time Victoria left, she felt sick. She had done what she could for the poor women but they had a long way to go before they reached Syria.

Victoria tried not to think about her own family who were next.

When she arrived home, Seta was standing in the door. "What happened? I've been so worried."

Victoria told her what she had seen and heard.

Seta became weak and had to sit down. "You must accept Hasan's offer," she said. "Tell him that the boys know how to work. Insist that he take them, too."

Victoria shook her head. "I can't live with another man."

"Listen to me Victoria. The Turks are not going to let any of us live. Save yourself and the boys."

The next morning Victoria went to Margaret and told her about Hasan's offer.

"Accept it," Margaret said.

"But my reputation. What would Nikol say if he found out?"

"Who is going to tell him?" Margaret put her hands on Victoria's face. "You are beautiful. Use what you have. Anyway, better one man than many."

Victoria walked home, thinking. Margaret thought she should do it. Seta had said the Turks were not going to let them live. Seta had been right about the Young Turks, she had been right about the European's reform plan.

"But I can't leave you," Victoria said to her mother, when she arrived home.

"Victoria, what will happen to me, will happen anyway. There is nothing you can do."

But there was something she could do. She sent a note to Hasan listing her conditions for coming to live with him.

The next day she received his reply.

He had agreed to her terms. Her sons *and* mother could come to his house.

The night before the women and children left, Anna, Fiorine, Araxie, and Margaret gathered at Victoria's house.

Victoria looked around the room. She had eaten in their homes. She had danced at their weddings. She had cooked in their kitchens. She had held their babies in her arms. She had mourned their losses. They were her family. And now they were leaving. She might never see them again.

"My dearest ones, I have known and loved you most of my life. You are a part of me, I am a part of you. Wherever you go, whatever happens, nothing can change that. We have existed in each other's pasts, we will exist in each other's future. If only one of us survives, the others will live on in her."

With tears in their eyes, the women moved together and embraced.

Victoria held on tightly. With their love, these women had given her strength. The Turks could take her home. They could take her church and her community. But they could not take that strength away.

CHAPTER TWENTY-FIVE

The next day

*V*ictoria turned from the village square with a heavy heart. They were gone. The Turks had marched them off like they said they would.

She ran her hand over her rich red-and-green skirt and studied how the interwoven gold threads sparkled in the sunlight. She should not have risked coming. She was dressed as a Kurdish woman but still, one of the Turks might recognize her. The village was dangerous. She hurried away.

Last night, after the others had left, Victoria had spoken to Seta and the boys.

"I have no idea how long we'll be gone or if we'll ever be allowed to return to our home. We can only pray the war will end and we will be allowed to practice our own religion again." She looked at the boys. "For now, we'll do what we must to save ourselves."

She had said it as though she had no misgivings. But she did. She, a married woman, a Christian, was turning her back on her husband and her church. If it were not for her mother and sons, she would have gone with Margaret, Anna and Fiorine. Taken her chances with the deportations. But her mother had said that if they went, they would die. She could not sacrifice her family to her morals. She would go to Hasan.

Hasan lived on a huge farm with his large, extended family. He was a Kurd. Victoria thought about the Kurds and the instances when the government had encouraged their violence against the Armenians.

When she was a little girl she had heard about the Kurds from the mountains settling with Armenians for the winter. This had begun during Abdul Hamid's reign and the Young Turks had never completely done away with it.

Kurds had participated in the massacre of Armenians during periods of violence.

And, the *Hamidiye*, the Kurdish cavalry, formed by and named after Sultan Hamid. The *Hamidiye* were supposed to defend Turkey's borders against Russian expansionism, but in practice what they did was to butcher without consequence the Armenians, the infidels as the *Hamidiye* were encouraged to think of them, living near the border.

Victoria knew these stories. She knew her sons did, too.

But she also knew that she couldn't blame an entire ethnic group for the actions of some.

Last night, she had told her sons that within any larger group, were individuals who had chosen not to adopt the ideas and beliefs of the group to which they belong. She had told them that Hasan and his family were an example of this. She had also told them about his bravery in defending the peddler against the unscrupulous Turks. Hasan had given them an opportunity that no one else in the village had and they must be grateful for that.

Hasan had been happy to take Victoria's boys in. He had seen them working in the fields last summer. The older one mending fences, the younger one tilling the soil. They would be useful to him. But the mother, what use was she? And there was the matter of meals. Elders always ate first but he couldn't give an Armenian woman the same respect he gave one of his own.

He had almost refused Victoria's conditions. Told her to go with the Turks, to what he knew was her certain death. Then he had thought about her shining black hair. The eyes that made him want to step inside her head. And the firm young body that her married clothes did not hide.

He decided to put the mother in a small cottage away from the main house where she could take her meals apart from him.

Satisfied that he had made the right decision, Hasan

climbed on his horse the day the Armenian women left the village and went to fetch Victoria.

Alone on her doorstep, Victoria watched Hasan's horse climb the hill. She looked around. She had done her best. The house was as secure as she could make it. Koren had nailed boards across the windows, Seta had packed Victoria's hand-sewn tapestries into her trunk, and Victoria had thought of a way to hide their silver and gold.

First, she had sewn four gold pieces into the hem of the thick woolen coat she was bringing. Then she had put the rest of her coins with her mother's silver tray, tea set, and her twelve patterned silver coffee spoons, and taken it to the back yard. She had buried all but two silver spoons and one gold piece deep under a tomato plant in the corner of her garden. The rest she had placed in a shallow hole hear the water pump and covered it loosely with dirt. She may never be back, but she would rather let the earth have her treasures than her Turkish neighbors.

Hasan reached the house and dismounted.

Victoria stood.

He motioned her to his side and leaned close.

He was so handsome. She stared at the ground.

He pulled her hair aside and whispered in her ear. "You are mine until the war is over and your husband comes for you."

He caressed her shoulder.

Her body felt warm. She kept her eyes on the ground.

"You are so beautiful."

She looked at him, then lowered her lashes again.

He cleared his throat. "Well, enough of that until later. I just want you to know that in my house, you will be treated fairly and with kindness."

He was such a nice man.

"I told you your mother and sons could come and they can, but I am putting them in a small house on my property."

He was so thoughtful, sparing her the awkwardness that her nights with him would bring. She looked up into his warm dark eyes and hazarded a smile.

Then she thought about his wife. How would she react to Victoria?

Hasan looked concerned. "What's wrong?"

Victoria rolled a stone with her foot. "Well..."

"Yes?"

"I am worried that..." She turned her head away. "That some of your family will resent me."

He shook his head. "You will be treated with respect."

"By everyone?"

"*Everyone.*"

Hasan pulled Victoria up on his horse and held her in place with his arm. She could feel his warm breath on her back.

She called for Seta and the boys. They had packed as

much as they could carry and they followed on foot as she rode down the hill with Hasan.

She did not look back at her sturdy stone house or at her sheep bleating in their pasture or her wheat rising up from the soil, but she knew it was all there, behind her.

Hasan brought them first to Seta's and the boys' house. Victoria opened the door and looked inside.

It had a dirt floor and she could see daylight through the boards on the wall. But Seta had brought bedding and blankets along, and there was a small stove in the corner. She thought about the women she had seen sleeping on the bare ground and was grateful for what they had.

Hasan explained that Victoria would bring food to them each morning and Seta nodded in understanding. Victoria knew Seta would keep busy knitting socks and sweaters from the wool she had brought and the boys would be out in the fields all day.

"Victoria left with Hasan and walked toward the main house. With each step, she grew more nervous. Hasan had told her she would be treated with respect, but he couldn't make his family like her.

Hasan noticed the look on her face and smiled. "I told you not to worry."

She smiled back. Such a kind, thoughtful man. She planned to work hard in Hasan's house. Perhaps, in time, his family would find her easier to accept.

Hasan pointed to the house. "I'm giving you the key to

the panty. Armenians know how to budget. There is a war going on and I can't risk running out of food before the winter is over."

Victoria began to worry again. In a Kurdish household, the most important woman was the one who held the key to the pantry.

"Will your wife mind?"

"Fadime? She and my mother have been squabbling over that key for years. And neither have been able to make the food last the winter."

Victoria adjusted the collar on her blouse and stepped into Hasan's house. So many people. Hasan had told her that he lived with his mother, wife, aunts, cousins and their families. Twenty people in all. Hasan's back was to her, but Victoria could see that one woman was staring at her with hatred in her eyes.

Hasan turned and introduced her. "My wife, Fadime." Then he introduced Victoria to his mother, Amine, and the rest of his clan.

He gestured toward Victoria. "As I told you this morning, I'm giving her the key to the pantry." He looked directly at his wife. "I'll be angry if she's given any trouble. I expect everyone to cooperate."

Fadime's expression stayed neutral, but Victoria could see her white knuckles.

Hasan turned his hand palm up. "Fadime, the key."

Fadime hesitated. She put her hand in her pocket, but

withdrew it without the key.

Hasan shifted to the other foot.

She put her hand back in her pocket and pulled out a key. But instead of putting it in Hasan's outstretched hand, she slammed it on the table.

Hasan's face darkened. He reached Fadime in one step, raised his hand, and slapped her across the face. "How dare you be so insolent."

Fadime's hand flew to her cheek, which was already turning red. The other women stepped forward, so they stood between Fadime and her husband. Hasan's mother, Amine, nudged Fadime.

Fadime lowered her eyes. "I'm sorry."

Hasan threw out his chest. "See that it doesn't happen again." He turned heel and strutted out of the house with the rest of the men following him.

Everywhere Victoria looked, someone was staring back at her through narrowed eyes. How would she ever survive in this house? And Hasan. She had seen nothing but acts of kindness in the years she had known him. This quick temper of his was a surprise. She would have to be very careful never to anger him.

She touched Fadime's arm. "Would you show me around?"

But Fadime jerked her arm away and walked out of the room, flanked by Amine, and two other women.

"I'll help you," a friendly voice said.

Victoria turned and found that the voice belonged to a dark-haired young woman with straight bangs and a turned-up nose. "I'm Milan," she said. "I'm married to Hasan's cousin, Jalal."

Victoria's shoulders relaxed. "I didn't know what I was going to do. I want to have a look at the pantry, so I can take inventory of what we have."

"Be careful. Fadime will steal supplies from there just so you'll run out early and look bad."

"But then, we'll all go hungry."

"She doesn't care. She did it when Amine was in charge. She really doesn't understand that the war means Hasan can't go to the city to buy supplies. All she knows is that she wants her status back."

"I was afraid of that."

"She and Amine used to fight over that key. Now..."

"Now they have their resentment of me in common."

"Well, yes."

"What did she say when Hasan told her I was coming?"

"To Hasan? Not much. No one says much to Hasan."

Victoria looked out the window to where the men were standing talking. "Does he lose his temper often?"

"No. Not often. Really just if someone talks back or embarrasses him in any way."

Then it was simple. She would make sure she never contradicted, or made him feel belittled in any way.

Victoria was happy to see that Hasan's household spoke

Turkish. She supposed it was because they had lived in a Turkish village for so many generations. Turkish was a language she was entirely comfortable with. The Kurds had several dialects, each vastly different, and she didn't speak any of them.

Milan showed Victoria around the pantry and she did some quick calculating. This was a large household and seeing they all stayed fed was a big responsibility. Victoria was relieved to hear that Hasan had cows and goats to supply milk and cheese.

Milan walked Victoria back to the kitchen.

"Thank you," Victoria said. "You've been very kind to me."

"I want to learn to manage a house like you. Jalal works for the government and someday when he is promoted, we will have our own house."

"I'll be glad to teach you whatever I know," Victoria said. "Let me begin with the wheat."

Milan listened to the exotic-looking newcomer explain how to calculate food supplies and divide them over a year. Victoria was small and delicate looking, but somehow she exuded a certain strength. Fadime may think she could bully her around as she had Milan, but Milan suspected Fadime's job would not be so easy with this one.

Milan didn't mind Victoria being in Hasan's house. She had nothing against Armenians. Not like some of the other people here. She would help Victoria and Victoria would help her learn what she needed to know to run her own house.

Milan did feel sorry for Fadime. She knew that Hasan seldom called for her at night. Hadn't for years. Kurdish men were allowed more than one wife, but not many exercised his right. As Hasan's first wife, Fadime had higher status, and this second wife was really not a wife at all, but still, it must be a blow to Fadime's pride.

Yes she felt sorry for Fadime, but that was as far as it went. She owed her no loyalty. After all, Fadime had shown Milan nothing but hostility and rivalry since she had come to this house when she married Jalal.

Victoria and Milan spent the afternoon preparing dinner and making plans to boil down tomatoes the next day and put them up in glass jars for the winter. In the late afternoon, they walked out to the garden to pick fresh green beans for dinner. But Victoria had just snapped her first pod from its stem, when she thought of the pantry and ran back inside. She turned the key in the lock and caught the disappointed look on Fadime's face, as she did.

Victoria cooked the green beans in scrambled eggs and the leftover meat she picked off a leg of lamb. She served it with steamed wheat. The household ate in shifts with the elders going first.

When it was Fadime's turn to eat, she pointed to her plate and said, "Is this all we get?"

Victoria noticed that a bruise had formed on her cheek where the red mark had been. "I have a lot of people to feed and the winter will be long."

Fadime raised one brow. "You're worrying about winter when it's summer?"

"Well yes, with the war and all."

Fadime looked at her mother-in-law and shook her head. "She's worried about war, like a man."

Amine laughed with Fadime.

Victoria felt her cheeks grow warm, but she wisely said nothing.

Hasan had gone to the village, so Victoria set aside a plate for herself and him then left the house with a plate for her mother and sons.

Fadime waited until the door closed behind Victoria, then said, "Did you see how much food she took to the others? We all starve while the Armenians eat."

Amine nodded in the direction of the closed door. "She should have gotten marched out with the rest of her kind. Now she's taking food from us."

Milan stood. "How do you know how much was on that plate? It was covered. I was there when she portioned it out. She gave them less than us."

Fadime looked up. "Traitor."

Victoria walked into the cottage and looked around. Seta

had spread blankets on the dirt floor. She was sitting in front of a table, knitting. Victoria wished they could have carried Seta's thick carpet here but still, her mother and boys had a roof over their heads. Whatever she had to do to keep it there, she would.

The cottage was rough, but with the boys reading and Seta's needles clicking, it felt quite homey. Victoria hated to leave its peacefulness and go back to the big, noisy house, but she still had work to do.

Victoria's stomach rumbled as she walked back. She had been too upset to eat since noontime the day before and she was looking forward to her plate of food.

Hasan met her in front of the house. "I'm afraid I have bad news for you. The villagers are already looting the Armenian homes."

"And I suppose no one is stopping them?"

Hasan shook his head. "I'm sorry, Victoria."

"I'm not surprised."

"If I had any way of stopping them, I would. But I'm just one man."

He was a nice man, too. Victoria could see that now. The incident with Fadime, well, she supposed Fadime would try anyone's patience.

"Has anyone broken into my house?"

"No. But, of course, your house is outside of the village. It may take longer before anyone discovers it."

Victoria thought about her gold and her mother's silver

service. She could only hope that if anyone looked, they would discover the shallow hole and not look any further. But there was no reason her wheat and animals should go to a stranger, when they could be used right here so she suggested Hasan send someone over to get them.

Hasan liked her idea and agreed to send someone the next day.

When Victoria walked into the kitchen with Hasan, she discovered that the plate of food she had set aside for herself was gone.

Fadime wandered into the kitchen and smiled at Victoria.

Better to be hungry than to stir up trouble. Victoria handed Hasan his plate and began cleaning the dishes without a word. Maybe now Fadime would see that she could be her friend.

The hour grew late and one by one, people said good night to each other and went off to sleep. Hasan's house was large enough to have more than one sleeping room and Hasan slept in a small cottage adjacent to the main house.

When he was ready, Hasan motioned for Victoria to follow him.

Victoria thought about her mother and sons and followed him silently. But she kept her eyes on the floor, too ashamed of herself to look at anyone else.

They entered the cottage and Victoria stood at the door.

Hasan set down the lantern he was holding, strode across the room, and gathered her into his arms. He drew her chin up and kissed her fully on the mouth.

Victoria felt her body respond. She was no better than the lowest class girl she knew. Hasan's probing hand tantalized her. She thought about his tenderness, his thoughtfulness and how attractive they made him to her. Still, this should be her duty, not her pleasure.

When it was over, Hasan sighed in contentment, rolled over and fell asleep.

Victoria lay awake crying into her pillow. How would she ever live with her shame when this was over?

If it was ever over.

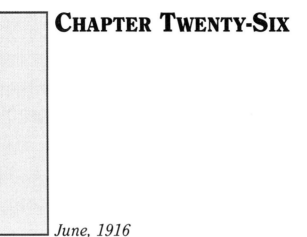

CHAPTER TWENTY-SIX

June, 1916

Nikol shivered in the drizzling rain. He had been in a trench, elbow-to-elbow with the other men in his battalion for six days now. Tomorrow, they would go to headquarters in the village and after that to the reserves in the woods. Six days in the trenches, six days in the village, and six days in the woods. A tedious pattern that had been going on for months. He hoped this period of inactivity would end soon. He had joined the Legion to fight. Germany and Turkey must be defeated.

He had been in the Legion for a year, a year that had alternated between active combat and months of waiting. But he was proud to be a Legionnaire and proud of the part the Legion was playing in the war.

The French Foreign Legion had been established in 1831 by the king of France. Any foreigner could join the Legion and fight for France. One had only to swear loyalty to the Legion, not the country. When the Legion was first established, its men could only fight outside of France. But when the war began two years ago, the rules had changed and the Legionnaires were allowed to fight within the country as well.

Nikol had first trained in Rouen, then he had been assigned to a battalion made up of a combination of seasoned fighting men and new recruits like himself. Over the last year he had become good friends with an American named Alan Seeger, who was a graduate of Harvard University and a poet. Seeger had told Nikol that he had joined the Legion, when the war first broke out in Europe, because he hadn't wanted to wait for America to become involved.

During their periods of inactivity in the trenches, Nikol and Seeger had gotten to know each other. Seeger had been in the Legion a year longer than Nikol. He told Nikol that he had spent his first months in the Legion, battling the scorn of the veteran Legionnaires, who had repeatedly told him and the other new recruits that they would never make good soldiers.

Nikol could understand their scorn, when Seeger told him about his first march out of training camp. The march had been going on for three endless weeks when one day, two soldiers, who had been college students at Yale, decided they'd had enough. They put down their guns and lay down on the ground. Their colonel rode up and asked them what they thought they were doing. One explained, in formal college French, that he was tired and needed a nap. The colonel looked at him, drew out his revolver and screamed, "March!"

They marched.

Seeger also told Nikol about twelve Cossacks, who had come to their training camp and enlisted. With each passing day, they appeared to grow more dissatisfied, but none of them spoke French and none of the Legionnaires spoke the Cossacks' dialect of Russian. No one knew what was wrong. Eventually, the Cossacks began a hunger strike and their superiors grew desperate. They pleaded in a tongue the Cossacks could not understand to be told what was wrong. Finally, the Legionnaires located a soldier, who could communicate with the Cossacks. The soldier told his officers that the Cossacks had come to join the Foreign Legion Cavalry and they didn't like being common foot soldiers. The Legion released them from service and explained that the Legion had no cavalry.

Seeger's stories distracted Nikol from his worry about Victoria and his family, alone and unprotected on the farm. He had heard about the deportations and deaths, and was desperate at the thought something might have happened to her. Seeger's stories also allowed Nikol to push away the guilt he felt for not being home to protect his family. He wished he could be on Turkish soil, battling the Turks himself but he knew that he would have to content himself with fighting Turkey's ally, Germany.

Nikol wished he could have been with the corps of Legionnaires who had landed in Turkey a year ago and fought hand-to-hand with the Turks. He learned that the plans to attack Turkey had been drawn up earlier in the war by two different men. One, a leader in the French army, Gallieni, and the other, First Lord of the British Admiralty, Winston Churchill. Both men had seen the importance of finding a way around the strong German line in France.

The first step of both men's plans was to seize Constantinople and gain control of the Straits of Dardanelles. But when Turkey's leaders threatened to massacre its Christian population if the Straits were attacked, the commander on the Western Front put the plans aside. No one wanted the blood of innocent people on their hands. Then, Turkey began its system of extermination anyway, so the commander dispatched a Legion regiment to Turkey. The Legionnaires managed to land on Turkish soil at a strategic point on the Straits, but the commander had sent far fewer troops than either Churchill or Gallieni had proposed. Without adequate forces, the mission failed. Every commissioned officer was killed and only one in one hundred foot soldiers survived.

But Nikol was certain that even if he had known the risk, he would have volunteered for the opportunity to face the

Turks with a gun in his hand. He often thought about it and regretted that the troops had been called for while he was still in training.

Nikol had been in the Legion for five months when France announced that Americans in the Legion could join a regular French regiment if they wished. Although many Americans left the Legion, Nikol, Seeger, and a core group of their comrades had taken the loyalty they had sworn to the Legion seriously, and stayed on.

Soon after his decision to stay, in September of 1915, Nikol went to combat for the first time. His unit was a reinforcement for an ongoing battle to capture back the Vimy Ridge in France near the border of Belgium. France had begun the offensive months earlier in order to cut off German supplies that were being transported across the nearby plain of Douai. Despite heavy losses, France had announced that they would retreat only when every last reinforcement was gone.

Nikol's regiment fought bravely, but the fight was bloody. Nikol had watched in horror as his friends fell to the ground screaming in agony, their bodies ripped apart by machine guns. By the time they retreated, Nikol's regiment had lost over half of its men and they hadn't reached their objective.

After Vimy Ridge, Nikol had spent most of the winter in the trenches with Seeger and the rest of his surviving comrades. By June, they were all anxiously hoping to go back to battle.

From the rumors Nikol had been hearing, they would soon have their wish.

Seeger dropped into the trench beside Nikol. "We just got orders to report to headquarters. I think we're pulling out."

Nikol brushed caked dirt from his blue uniform. "At last."

He stuffed what remained from his daily ration of a half loaf of bread, a piece of cheese, a tin of sardines and a candy bar into his shirt and crept back to the woods with Seeger and the rest of his regiment. This could only mean that they were being sent back to the front lines, though to what battle, he could only guess.

When Nikol reached headquarters he learned that they were being sent to recapture to Somme Canal. This was an important battle. If they won, it would significantly weaken the German forces and bring the war closer to an end. But, Nikol learned, the Germans were fighting back hard and it would not be a battle easily won.

When they arrived at the Somme Canal, Nikol initially found himself again marking time in the trenches. But something was in the air — a tension, a feeling of expectancy — and he knew it wouldn't be long before he was called to action.

"This waiting is worse when you can hear the guns," Seeger said on their ninth day in the trenches.

Nikol nodded. "But it won't be long. I heard that the French and British have lost half of their troops. They need us."

Seeger pulled a pencil from his pocket. "The corporal said we're waiting for the rest of the Legionnaires to arrive. Then we're going in."

"Then we're going in soon because they just arrived."

Nikol watched Seeger begin writing on one of his ever-present scraps of paper. Seeger had once explained to Nikol that he wrote because his poetry made him see the beauty of the world around him. Tomorrow or the next day they were going to battle. What beauty did Seeger see in the war? Or did he see instead the importance of what they were fighting for?

Early that evening, while gunfire erupted overhead, the new arrivals began edging their way into the trenches. Nikol had heard that the Legion had just merged all the surviving troops in France into one large regiment.

He moved closer to Seeger to make room for a soldier, who had just jumped into the trench on the other side of him. He glanced at the man and saw him staring back in surprise.

"Nikol," the man said.

Nikol looked closely. The soldier's face seemed familiar. Who was he? Nikol looked again. The man had the expressive brown eyes of an Armenian. Then Nikol knew.

"Solomon," he said.

He clasped Solomon in as much of an embrace as their crowded quarters allowed. Then he took a closer look at

Solomon. Time and the war had taken their toll. Solomon's face was creased with worry and fatigue. He had a certain look, too — a set of his jaw, a rigidity of his shoulders — that made Nikol certain Solomon could fight back now in a way that he couldn't have seven years ago, when Nikol last saw him.

Nikol wanted to ask Solomon about Victoria. Then again, he didn't want to because that hardness he saw in Solomon had come from something beyond the war. What? What did Solomon know about their women?

Nikol couldn't face what Solomon had to tell him, so instead he told Solomon how he had come to be where he was.

When it was Solomon's turn, he was quiet.

The silence hung between them, until it began to cut off Nikol's air.

"Tell me about her," he said.

Solomon took off his helmet. "I'll tell you what I know."

Nikol bowed his head.

Solomon began. "The women and children were marched out of the village one week after the men and the Turks killed them all. Not with their bullets, but by marching them across the desert without food or water. The Turks are proud of what they did."

"But our own wives, too? Are you sure?"

Solomon grasped Nikol's arm. "No one could have survived that route the Turks took them on. No one was meant to."

"But are you sure that our women were taken?"

"Yes, I'm absolutely sure."

Nikol could not speak. The Turks had done it. It was over. The only woman he had ever loved. The only woman he could love, gone. His sons too. And he was an American citizen; he could have gotten them out. Now they were all dead and it was his fault. He had caused her pain, and ultimately, her death. What good was he?

Seeger tapped Nikol's shoulder. "Remember why you are here. You are fighting the oppressors. With Germany's defeat, will come Turkey's."

Nikol took out his rifle and began to clean it. "I didn't save her, but I'll die making sure Turkey is the loser in this war."

"I feel that way, too," Solomon said. "I've lost everyone, Margaret, Diran, Miriam. I'll make them pay."

"But how did you ever get out of Turkey?"

"Its a long story."

"We have all night."

Solomon slid his back along the wall of the trench and sat. "Michael and I were going to take our family and yours into hiding, but we were arrested before we could leave. The next morning, the Turks marched us out of town, while our women watched. Victoria was with Margaret. I hope they stayed together. It gives me comfort to think they did."

Nikol closed his eyes and forced himself not to think about her.

Solomon continued. "We marched for hours. I was worried about Michael going that long without water or rest. He was weak by the time we stopped. All the men were. We sat and the Turks opened fire on us."

"The Turks killed them all?" Nikol said.

"All," Solomon said. "Michael, Levon, John, the entire village. I saw it with my own eyes."

"How did you get away?"

"I was the only one young enough to run. They shot me, but they only got my leg. Then a soldier came after me with his bayonet, but he let me go. Maybe in the end he couldn't face what he was doing when he had to look me in the eye. I don't know, but I don't think he expected me to live long."

"But you did."

"Oh, yes. I don't know how, but I did. I couldn't move from the spot where they left me, until the next morning. Then I knew if I didn't, I would surely die.

"I tore my shirt into strips and bandaged the wound. I had to find shelter but I was weak. I didn't know where to go either. The Turks were marching the Armenians out of every city and village in Kharpert. I decided to go home, because Michael and I had hidden money in the barn and I thought I could use it to escape.

"I found water the next day at the foot of a nearby hill and I stayed near it, until I got my strength back. But that bullet wound hurt and the day I tried to start walking again, it began to fester. I stopped and removed the bullet myself. I lost another day doing it. I have a big scar where it was, but the medics tell me I'm fortunate to have a leg at all.

"I reached the village at night. I waited until it seemed like the whole village was asleep, then I snuck into a barn and slept with the horses and cows. I ate the horse's oats and felt like I had eaten a feast.

"I stayed in that barn, buried under the hay. One day I heard the Turks talking, saying that the soldiers had left and taken our women and children out to the desert.

"I waited until it was late again and went to my house. I climbed over the wall and looked in a window. Margaret and the children were gone. Turks were living there but they were asleep, so I went inside and stole a turban, a shirt and a pair of pants. When I put them on, I looked like a Turk. I walked past your house on my way out of the village. It was boarded up. She is gone."

Nikol nodded and accepted the finality of Victoria's death. He would never forgive himself.

"I left Turkey by way of Adana," Solomon said. "I bribed a dock policeman. I think he knew I wasn't really a Turk, but he let me go anyway. You know, not all Turks agree with what the government is doing. I think they just don't know how to stop it."

Nikol clasped Solomon's shoulder. "Well, perhaps we've been spared for a reason. Maybe we'll find out tomorrow."

"Maybe we will."

Nikol dozed fitfully dreaming about his family and the

woman he loved. She had been his whole world. Now all that remained of that world was the empty dusty edges of his village.

Nikol woke up before the sun rose knowing today was the day. He listened to the artillery roll out and begin its ear-splitting clamor. He heard the bugles call the French army into battle. He picked up his rifle and waited for the Legion signal, the Legion's unique call to action. Then he heard it: the scream of a trumpet. He jumped out of the trench and ran forward with the rest of the Legionnaires at his side.

He was determined to prevail, but the Germans were equally determined and on the first hill, machine gun fire erupted all around him.

Nikol flung himself face down and tasted dirt in his dry mouth. The machine guns pelted the air above him.

"Seeger, Solomon, are you all right?"

His two best friends lay face down.

"Seeger, Solomon," he said, again.

Seeger put his thumb and forefinger together in a circle. Solomon looked up.

All around Nikol lay men bleeding into the soil of a country not their own from the guns of an enemy whose face they had yet to see.

When the machine gun fire changed direction, Nikol and his surviving comrades began advancing by sprinting a few paces, then flinging themselves on their stomachs again. Slowly, foot by foot, his unit moved toward their objective that day, a small village named Belloy-en-Santerre.

Nikol could taste the fear in his mouth and he could see it in the faces of his buddies around him. But he was unhurt, a trained soldier. He thought of Victoria. He had not fought in Turkey, but he would fight here.

The dust cleared for a moment and Nikol looked ahead. A machine gun station loomed in front of him. He had gotten further than he thought.

He turned to Seeger. "Cover me."

Seeger elbowed Solomon and pointed to Nikol. Solomon nodded and passed the message on to the next man. Nikol jumped up and ran straight ahead. The rest of the men split into two groups and took off to the right and left.

The dust became dense again and hid Nikol's approach. He unpinned his grenade, said a prayer, and threw it. Germans spilled out of their dugout and the two groups of men surged forward, brandishing their bayonets.

He should have felt sickened by what he was doing, but they were the enemy and if he didn't kill them, they would kill him.

They were down to six men, but they had done it. They had captured a machine gun station and the German blockhouse behind it.

Their captain had been shot on the first hill and Nikol realized that he had become the men's officer now. He gave a signal and they pressed on, At the outskirts of Belloy-en-Santerre, he joined forces with men from other battalions who had gotten through. Twenty men in all. Twenty men to capture an entire village. It wasn't enough.

Nikol waited as long as he could for reinforcements, but none came. It was up to them.

He gestured toward the village and his men moved in.

The village was a shell of what it had been. All of the people who had once lived there were gone and inside every crumbling stone building, German soldiers lay in wait.

Nikol signaled for the men to split up. Then he crept forward himself, until he reached the remnants of an old stone wall that surrounded a partially collapsed house. He leapt up, lobbed a grenade in the window and flung himself face down in the sand. The grenade detonated and the rest of the building slid into a pile of stones. As it did, two German soldiers stumbled out of the rubble, swung their rifles around and looked for their enemy. But Nikol came at them from behind and knocked out first one, then the other, before either had a chance to react.

He continued on to the next ruined house, then to the next. His companions did the same until every last German had been driven out. Nikol looked around. They had done it. They had captured the village of Belloy-en-Santerre and, for the first time since the war began, had penetrated the thick German line.

But the twenty men Nikol had started with were not here. Who was missing? Nikol looked around. Solomon stood nearby, his face blackened with smoke, his eyes drooping with fatigue.

Where was Seeger?

Nikol ran in search of his friend. He found him lying on the ground, near a pile of stones that had once been a house.

Nikol dropped to his knees. His friend, the gentle poet, was dead. The world would never know the verses he might have written. His words had been stopped in a battlefield in France.

It was time to move out, but Nikol sat with his friend and brushed a tear from his eye. The rest of the men caught up with him and stood with their hats off and heads bowed.

Nikol knew he had to go. He stood and started to walk away. But then, he thought of something and ran back. He reached into Seeger's pocket and pulled out a tattered scrap of paper. On it were the very last lines Seeger ever wrote. Nikol read it and it was then that he truly understood what Seeger meant, when he talked about his need to write. The poem spoke to Nikol, and to every man who had gone into combat, knowing the gravity of what stood before him.

> I have a rendezvous with Death.
> At some disputed barricade,
> When Spring comes back with rustling shade
> And apple blossoms fill the air.
> I have a rendezvous with Death.
> When Spring brings back blue days and fair.
> It may be he shall take my hand
> And lead me into his dark land
> And close my eyes and quench my breath.

It may be I shall pass him still.

I have a rendezvous with Death

On some scarred slope of battered hill,

When Spring comes round again this year

And the first meadow flowers appear.

  God knows 'twere better to be deep

Pillowed in silk and scented down,

Where Love throbs out in blissful sleep,

Pulse nigh to pulse, and breath to breath,

Where hushed awakenings are dear...

But I've a rendezvous with Death

At midnight in some flaming town,

When Spring trips north again this year,

And I to my pledged word am true,

I shall not fail that rendezvous.

Nikol folded the piece of paper and tucked it in his pocket. He slung his rifle over his shoulder and trudged out with his company. Death had taken the poet who still had so much left to give. Why hadn't it taken him?

Day after day, Nikol fought alongside his comrades. As time went by, he found himself less and less affected by each death. But he still mourned the loss of his friend, Seeger. Nikol knew he would never forget those long months in the trenches and knew that Seeger's poetry would stay with him always.

Eventually, Solomon was transferred to another unit, and Nikol lost contact with him. As the months went by, Nikol marveled at how he continued to survive each battle. He supposed it was because, though he woke each morning caring little whether he lived or died, during the heat of battle, something took over and made him fight his hardest. Each night, he thought about Victoria and wondered when the war ended what would be left for him without her or his family. But another day would dawn, another battle, and he went on.

The months gave way to years, as the war slowly progressed. The French remained determined to break down the defenses of the German line, knowing it was their only route to victory, but their objective necessitated the sacrifice of lives. Slowly, the French gained ground and with the help of the Legionnaires, the attackers became the defenders. For their efforts, the Legionnaires were awarded the *Medaille Militaire* and became the most decorated unit in the French army.

CHAPTER TWENTY-SEVEN

Fall, 1916

Victoria crawled out of her blanket into the chill of the early autumn morning. She dressed and slipped into her thin leather shoes. She could feel the cold floor through the holes in the soles but she would have to live with them or eventually go barefoot because she could not go into the village for new ones. And even if she could have, the Armenians were gone. Who would make them?

She searched under her pillow and pulled out the key to the pantry. She looked up. Fadime was watching her from her bed across the room.

Victoria slipped the key over her wrist.

Fadime folded her arms and looked away.

Victoria lit the stove and pulled a block of cheese, dripping with brine, from a crock. Milan heard her and hurried to slice the crusty bread Victoria had baked the day before.

Hasan's mother, Amine, and his two aunts sat down and ate without a word. Victoria brought Amine coffee, hot the way she liked it. Amine took it from her, sipped and nodded.

Victoria walked back to the kitchen. She was working as hard as she could, but Amine had not grown to like her as she had hoped. She cracked an egg into a pan for Hasan. He was out looking over his fields, but he liked an egg when he came in. At least Amine tolerated her. If his mother didn't want her there, Hasan might throw her out. She couldn't let that happen.

Hasan walked in the door with Jalal. "We're cutting the wheat next week."

Victoria put his egg in front of him and walked back to the stove. She felt his eyes follow her. He did that a lot, lately. She wished he wouldn't. It made her feel as though she couldn't think a thought by herself. He called for her almost every night now, too. She thought about her mother and sons. Well, as long as he was happy with her. The war couldn't last forever.

Hasan held up the heel from the loaf of bread. "Wonderful. It weighs almost nothing and the taste, well... Fadime, did you try this?"

Fadime's eyes narrowed.

Victoria busied herself with the dishes.

Fadime sat down. "Bread and cheese, bread and cheese. What do you think we are, a bunch of peasants?"

Victoria looked at Milan, her only friend in the house.

Milan went to the table. "Don't you remember the dinner Victoria cooked for us last night? She made *keshkeg*, chicken with wheat and spices."

"Well, it wasn't enough."

"I'm doing my best," Victoria said. "But I have to make the food last."

Fadime sneered and opened her mouth to retort, but she looked at Hasan and stopped. Victoria looked at Hasan, too. His back was rigid and his fists were clenched. Fadime looked at her plate and began eating.

Hasan's back slowly relaxed. He finished his breakfast and left.

Fadime waited until the door banged shut behind him. Then she turned to Victoria. "We're hungry, but you take what is ours and give it to your own."

Victoria sighed and made no answer. She had fed twenty people all winter long and not a meal had gone by that she hadn't put food on the table. She looked at Fadime's thick waistline. The woman was not hungry. But that was really not why she was complaining anyway.

Hasan's nephew, Talib, came into the house with a crate full of fresh green peppers. She would stuff them with rice and lamb for dinner and the rest she would pickle in brine, vinegar, hot pepper, and garlic.

So much work.

Milan saw the look on her face and squeezed her arm.

What would she have done this past year without Milan? Milan was the only person in the house she could talk to. The only one she trusted. Victoria thought about Margaret, Fiorine and Anna and she had to bite the inside of her cheek to keep from weeping. What had become of them? And why had she been spared?

Victoria put thinner slices of bread and smaller pieces of cheese onto a plate for her mother and the boys. She kept the plate uncovered and walked past Fadime with it.

Fadime said nothing until Victoria got out the door. Then, she said, in a voice loud enough for Victoria to hear, "See what I mean? They get plenty. I go hungry. Me, the wife of a rich man."

Victoria's eyes stung. It was so unfair. And there wasn't a thing she could do about it.

Koren looked up when the door opened and his mother walked in. He seldom got to see her anymore. Usually he was out in the fields when she got here. He and Paul were the first ones out there in the mornings. He made sure Hasan saw it, too. Today he had come in to check on his grand-mother, because he thought he had heard her moaning in her sleep last night.

"Hello, Mother," he said.

"Oh, Koren, you're not outside. Is everything all right?

Hasan didn't send you in, did he?"

Koren looked at his mother's anxious face. He wouldn't burden her with worries about his grandmother. "No, Hasan said he likes the way I mend the fences. He hasn't lost a single sheep since I've been here."

She stood on her toes to kiss his forehead. "Good. You remember what I told you about being here?"

Koren remembered. She had said they would all do what they had to do to save themselves. He ran his foot over the thick oriental carpet. Hasan had brought it from their house after their first night here. Koren didn't mind working in the fields, but he wished his mother didn't have to be where she was.

When Koren had left, Victoria turned to her mother. "Aren't you going to eat?"

"Later. I'm not hungry now."

"Well, you need something in your stomach."

"Don't worry about me." Seta's forehead wrinkled. "You look tired. Are you getting enough sleep?"

"As much as I can, but I have a lot of work to do. Especially now in the fall."

"You're not... you know?"

"Pregnant? No, thank God. I'm doing what you said and it's working. I don't know what I would do if it didn't. I can't have a half-Armenian, half-Muslim baby."

"No, you can't," Seta said. "Neither culture would accept it."

"Well, you know I don't get pregnant easily. Even when I want to. So I don't think I have anything to worry about now."

Seta clutched her arm. "If it happens, Shakar mamma, the midwife, used to know what to do. The Muslim midwife will, too."

"I'll pray that won't be necessary."

"But if it is and I'm not here, remember."

Victoria frowned. "What do you mean, not here? Where else would you be?"

Seta did not answer.

Victoria left for the main house. She would have liked to ask her mother more, but she had stayed as long as she could. She had work to do. Another meal was coming, then another.

Hasan watched Victoria enter the house ahead of him. She was lovely. Lean, firm, eyes that made him want to stare at her all day. A beautiful flower. His beautiful flower. Forever. The war might end, but he had promised only to release her to her husband. The man hadn't come for her before the war, why should he come now?

He knew, also, that the end of the war would not bring her people back. He had heard things, terrible things about what had happened on the marches. And he knew that what he had heard was true, because he had heard it from his friend, General Fakhri Pasha.

The general had told him what happened to the convoy that had passed through their village just before Victoria came to live with him. He said that as soon as the convoy had reached the plains, Kurds from the nearby hills attacked again and carried off all the rest of the young girls. Then the remaining convoy started across the plains. They had marched for half a day, when the guards blew a whistle and everyone stopped.

The guards rode through the lines and rounded up all the young boys and the surviving old men. Then, in front of their families, the guards took out their guns and started shooting. One by one, the undefended males fell. The women screamed hysterically until the guards swung their guns in the women's direction. When the guards were finished, they forced the rest of the group to go on.

They caught up with another convoy and merged, swelling their numbers to eighteen thousand. This time they let the males live. But no one had eaten or drunk water since they had left Kharpert. They marched across the plains for forty days. The further they went, the more rapidly people died.

Eventually, they reached the eastern Euphrates River, but hundreds of torn-apart bodies clogged its flow and the water had turned red with their blood.

The guards laughed and called for the head of the nearby village. The man demanded money and threatened to kill anyone who did not pay him. The ragged group frantically dug out their remaining coins and tossed them on the ground. The head of the village counted it, nodded, and allowed them to leave.

The hot summer sun continued to bear down and more people were overcome. When the convoy reached a Kurdish village, the residents took everything the people still had, including the clothes they were wearing.

Naked, they walked for five more days.

They came to a village that had a fountain with running water. The people looked at each other with relief and stumbled toward it. But when they reached it, a policeman stepped in front of it.

"You must pay for the water," he said.

Fifty-two days from the outset of their journey, three hundred half-dead, men, women and children limped into the last city standing between Turkey and Syria. Before allowing them to cross the border, the guards rounded up all the men and any of the women or children they decided were sick, and burned them to death. The remaining people went over the border into the city of Ras-ul-Ain, then on to Aleppo. Out of the original eighteen thousand people, only one hundred and fifty women and children lived to reach their destination.

Hasan thought that what the Turks were doing was horrifying, but the general had made it clear that he was acting on orders from the government and there was nothing anyone could do to stop it.

Hasan knew also that the Turks' actions meant that

Victoria would remain his forever.

Or for as long as he wanted her.

The following week, Victoria had a reprieve from Fadime's snipping remarks because they were all busy harvesting the wheat and even Fadime was too worn at the end of the day to bother.

On the last morning of the wheat harvest, Victoria stopped while she was dressing and held her stomach. She felt nauseous. Odd. She sat down and took a deep breath. It passed. She wiped perspiration from her forehead and went out to join the women waiting for the first cartload of wheat to appear.

She forgot about the episode but two days later, it happened again. Again, it passed quickly, but she still felt tired for the rest of the day.

When it happened the next day, she admitted the truth to herself. She hurried to Seta and found her alone.

Seta looked up from her knitting. "Victoria, you look pale. Are you getting enough rest?"

"I'm afraid that is not the problem."

"What is it then? Food? Are you eating enough?"

"It's not that either." Victoria looked at her mother. "Remember what we were talking about a few weeks ago?"

Seta dropped her knitting needles. "You're pregnant?"

Victoria nodded.

"Oh, dear." Seta looked at her lap. Then her chin swept

up. "You'll have to see the midwife."

"And how will I do that?"

"We must find a way."

"I've been thinking and thinking. If I leave Hasan's property, one of the village Turks might recognize me."

"I'll go get the midwife."

Victoria jumped. "No, Mother. It would be just as dangerous for you."

"But if it would help you, I don't care."

Victoria took her hand. "*I* care. If I lost you, I would have one less reason to make myself stay with Hasan."

"Then we must think of something else."

"I suppose I could tell Hasan. Ask for his help."

Now it was Seta's turn to look alarmed. "No. He will forbid it. And if you have his baby, he won't let you leave. Ever."

Her mother was right. Hasan favored her too much as it was. He would never let her take his child and go back to her home when the war was over. And she could never leave her child behind.

"You have one friend in the house," Seta said. "Will she help?"

"Milan? She might. I'll ask her." Victoria studied her mother's bony wrist. "Mother, you look terribly thin."

"Now don't you worry about me. You have enough to think about."

Victoria went back to the crowded house and thought about her problem, as she did her morning chores. She knew just when it had happened. Six weeks ago, Hasan had come back from town earlier than she expected and wanted her right away. She'd had no time to prepare herself with the square of sponge her mother had told her to use. She had been skipping months since she had been in Hasan's house and eating so little in an effort to please Fadime, so until she had the signs, she had not thought she was pregnant.

She wanted to talk to Milan, but every time she tried, Fadime was hovering nearby.

Just before lunch, Victoria picked up a basket and said to Milan, "I'm going out to pick apricots. Will you come with me?" She gave Milan a look.

Milan took hold of the basket. "Oh, yes."

They walked past Fadime, who narrowed her eyes but stayed where she was.

Milan put a handful of apricots into the basket. "What's wrong?"

Victoria's hand shook. "I need your help. I'm pregnant."

Milan looked concerned. "Don't have it. He'll never let you go if you do."

"My mother said the same. But I need you to do something for me."

"Tell me."

"Get the midwife your women use."

Milan thought for a moment.

Victoria waited. What she was asking Milan to do was dangerous for her, too. If Hasan found out, he would be angry. Milan and Jalal were dependent on Hasan, until Jalal got the promotion he was waiting for.

"I'll do it."

"I won't forget this," Victoria said. She thought about the hem of her coat. "Tell the midwife I can pay."

Milan left shortly after lunch, giving no one an explanation to where she was going.

Victoria worried about her the whole time she was gone. What if Hasan discovered where she had gone? Hasan's anger was dangerous. And if anything went wrong, the midwife would be thrown in jail for her actions. The midwife might very well refuse to help. She might even tell Hasan herself. Then where would they all be?

Milan came back later that afternoon, but Victoria was busy preparing supper and the house was full of people.

Victoria forced her hand to stay steady, when she chopped up onions with a knife. She had to talk to Milan, but how?

Finally, Milan asked Victoria to let her into the pantry. Victoria followed her in.

"Tonight," Milan whispered.

Victoria felt both relief and fear. "Tonight?"

"Yes, we will meet her in the barn."

"We? You're coming with me?"

Milan smiled. "I won't let you go through this alone."

Victoria was touched. "Milan-"

Milan suddenly looked past Victoria.

Victoria followed her gaze. Fadime was standing in the doorway.

Victoria let her sentence drop. Milan was her friend. She understood how much what she was doing meant to Victoria.

Victoria knew that if she looked at Hasan, he would read her nervousness in her eyes. He was always looking into her eyes, too. So that evening she kept her sewing on her lap.

One by one, the household went to bed.

Hasan stood.

Victoria pulled her needle through the fabric.

He tapped her shoulder.

Surely if she slept with him, he would hear her leave.

She rose, put her hand on his shoulder and whispered in his ear.

He nodded and went off to his bed alone.

Fadime watched him leave, then looked back at Victoria.

Victoria quickly averted her eyes. She pulled out her mattress and went to bed.

When the entire household was taking the slow deep breaths of sleep, Victoria slipped out from under her blankets and crept out the front door.

But where was Milan? Had she fallen asleep?

The door creaked open.

Victoria searched for a face in the moonlight. It was Milan.

The two made their way to the barn. Victoria gently closed the door and lit a lantern.

"What did you say to Hasan?" Milan asked.

"I told him it was my time of month."

Victoria and Milan sat and waited for the midwife.

An hour ticked by.

Footsteps approached the door. It opened.

Victoria raised the lantern.

"I knew you two were up to something." Fadime folded her arms.

How had she known?

Fadime's eyes gloated. "What is it?"

Victoria stood. "Fadime, I'm pregnant and I am asking you, woman to woman, not to tell anyone."

Fadime walked into the barn. "Why should I keep secrets for you?"

"Because a baby would be a disaster for us all."

"For you maybe, not me."

"No, for all of us. It would keep me here forever."

Fadime unfolded her arms.

Victoria held her eyes in a steady gaze.

Fadime rested her chin on her palm.

A shadow appeared in the door. Victoria, Fadime, and Milan turned.

The midwife stepped into the barn and closed the door behind her.

Fadime looked at her, then at Victoria. She shrugged her shoulders. "What do I care what you do?" She turned and walked out of the barn.

Victoria's knees felt weak. But her relief lasted only a moment. The midwife spread a dingy blanket on the straw and gestured for Victoria to lie down.

Victoria's heart beat faster. She lay down. The midwife reached into a leather bag and withdrew a sharp metallic hook-like instrument. She wiped it on her skirt.

With growing horror, Victoria watched the object come at her. She clung to Milan's hand and clenched her jaws to keep from screaming. An almost unbearable pain tore through her body.

"Oh, God," she prayed. "Give me strength."

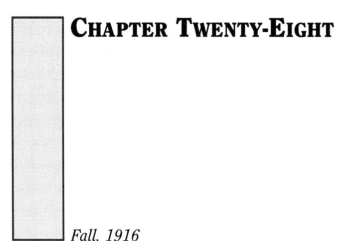

CHAPTER TWENTY-EIGHT

Fall, 1916

Seta hurried to the main house frantic with worry. Victoria hadn't come to the cottage that morning. Something must be terribly wrong. If the midwife had come and something had happened...

She quickened her pace. She had once heard a story about a young girl who had been raped by a Turkish soldier. The midwife had visited her and the girl had died. Seta felt her stomach flop. She thought about last night when she had woken knowing that something was wrong. She had told herself that she was worrying needlessly, but now, she knew she had been right.

The main house loomed in the distance. Seta had never been inside. The thought of going where she wasn't welcome had always made her uncomfortable. But her daughter was in there and today she had no other choice but to go in.

She reached the door, but, too winded to climb the steps, she sat down and caught her breath. Then she stood, grabbed hold of the railing and pulled herself up.

Victoria lay on her mattress, whiter than the sheets. Her breathing was shallow and she was moaning. Hasan paced around her.

Milan rushed to face Seta. "Victoria took sick during the night."

Milan was sending her a signal. Seta forced herself to smile. "Let me take care of her." She shrugged. "Why should you all be bothered?"

Hasan stopped pacing. He gestured toward Victoria. "If she's sick, I'll send for a doctor."

Seta drew in her breath. "A doctor, no." She had said it too quickly. Now his eyes were narrowed with suspicion. She pushed her hair off her forehead. "I mean, a doctor," she turned her palms up. "We can't waste a doctor's time with this."

Hasan shifted his weight. "I want to know what's wrong." He looked around.

Fadime bit into a slice of bread.

Milan knelt and wiped Victoria's face.

Seta gave Hasan a half smile. "I think it's one of those women's things. You have more important things to think about. Let me nurse her for a few days, then send her back to you."

Hasan watched Victoria draw her knees up. "Well, I suppose, until she's better."

Hasan sent for Koren and Paul to carry Victoria to the cottage.

When Koren saw his mother, he looked scared. "What happened?"

Seta put her hands on her hips. "Now, never mind and do as you're told. Grab hold of that mattress."

Koren easily picked up one end, but Paul could not lift the other. Seta looked at Paul. She couldn't possibly help him and she wanted to get away from Hasan as quickly as possible.

She signaled Milan.

Milan stepped forward. "I can help."

Hasan straightened and waved his hand at one of his nephews. "Talib, help them carry her."

When they reached the cottage, Seta shooed Koren and Paul off to the fields and thanked Talib. She waited until Talib had left, then hurried to Victoria's side.

Victoria rocked back and forth. "Oh Mother, it was awful. I'm bleeding and my stomach aches. I don't know how I ever got back to the house last night."

Seta grasped her hand. "Don't worry, darling. I'm going to get you better."

She lit her small stove and heated some broth. She wished she had more to give Victoria, but she hadn't had the strength to plant a full garden this year. She had planted parsley though, and she added it to the broth as the midwife had once instructed her to do.

Seta raised Victoria's head and fed her the broth. When Victoria had finished it, she started to fall back asleep but suddenly looked alarmed. "The pantry key. I must get it." She sat up, but quickly collapsed back on the pillow.

Seta pulled the blanket over her. "You're too weak to stand up, let alone walk."

"But if Fadime gets in there, she'll throw the food away just to make me look bad."

"It's out of your hands. You just have to hope she doesn't."

For the next week, Victoria fought a fever and the pain in her stomach. At the end of it, she was strong enough to stand.

"I'm going back," she said.

Seta's hand flew to her chest. "No, you're too weak."

She wanted to stay with her mother and sons until the war was over and they could all go home but her place in Hasan's house was keeping them all alive now. "If I can stand, I can work."

"But you'll get sick again."

"I won't let myself." She took her mother's hand. "I have to go back. You know that, don't you?"

Seta looked at the floor. "Yes."

Victoria walked to the door, then looked back at her mother. Seta's cheekbones stood out and her eyes had dark circles. "Mother, you have exhausted yourself taking care of me."

"Oh, don't worry about me. You just do what you can to get your strength back."

Victoria held onto the door frame. "I don't think I can walk back here with your food for a while."

"No, don't even try. I'll send the boys down for it."

Victoria trudged slowly back to the main house. She hoped she would never have to go through anything like this again. But, thinking about it, she realized that she couldn't anyway. She had spent all her gold coins. She would have to be very careful.

Milan met her at the door. "I'm so glad you're back." She took the pantry key from her wrist and handed it to Victoria.

"Then you've had it?"

"Yes, but I don't know how much longer Hasan would have let me keep it."

Victoria felt lightheaded. She waited for it to pass. "Has Fadime been difficult?"

"Yes," Milan said. "I caught her turning up the stove, so the wheat would burn. I think she watered down the yogurt, too, and I'm sure she added too much salt to the rolls. Of course, she told Hasan that I made it wrong. By tomorrow, he would have given the key to her."

"Then I came back just in time."

Victoria stepped into the house and saw dirty dishes, dust-covered tables, and bedding still lying on the floor. She wiped her forehead. She couldn't do it.

But she got herself through the day by promising herself that each new task she took on was her last. Milan helped her and by the end of the day, Amine and Hasan's aunts did too. As soon as the last supper dish was washed, Victoria pulled out her mattress and lay down. Hasan thankfully made no demands on her that night. In fact, he left her alone for three weeks by which time she was essentially back to normal.

Victoria enjoyed seeing her sons, who alternated coming to the house each morning for the day's ration of food. She wished she could spend more time talking to them. She had seen so little of them in the year they all had been here. But they, too, had work to get to. Work that kept them important to Hasan. So she handed them the plate and sent them on their way. Then she turned to face the daily arguments and complaints of Fadime and her cronies.

One morning, Koren stood in the doorway after Victoria had given him the food.

"You'd better get back to the house with that, then out to the fields."

Koren hesitated, then walked down the steps. He stopped and turned to face her. "I think you'd better go see Grandmother."

"Why? Is something wrong?"

"Well, just go see her."

Victoria ran down the stairs. "Koren, if something is wrong, you must tell me."

He looked at the ground. "She made me promise not to tell you."

"Tell me what?"

"She's not eating. I think she's sick."

Victoria thought about her mother's gaunt look the last time she had seen her. She had to get to the cottage and see what was wrong. Koren left with his head bowed and his shoulders sagging. Victoria ran into the house to finish her morning chores.

"Look at the way she folds that bedding," Fadime said from where she sat. "It's a mess."

Victoria arranged a neat stack of folded quilts in the corner. She didn't look in Fadime's direction. She put a pot of water on the stove.

Fadime raised her voice. "I suppose we're having wheat for lunch again. And of course she'll give most of it to her own."

Victoria stepped out of the pantry but kept her eyes on her work.

Hasan walked in the door.

Fadime's eyes darted askance, then she said, "Look at that table. She hasn't even wiped it down."

Victoria stopped sweeping and stirred the wheat into the boiling water. She retied her apron and picked up her broom again.

Hasan's eyes went from his wife to Victoria.

"And look how she..." Fadime stopped.

Hasan's hands had turned into fists. He started toward Fadime.

She cowered. Amine walked in front of her.

Hasan veered past Fadime and went out the door.

Fadime flushed and glared at Victoria. She picked up her sewing and stabbed her needle up through the fabric. The thread snapped. She knotted it and began again.

Victoria finished cleaning the dishes then ran to the cottage. "Mother, Koren said you're not eating."

Seta looked up from the sock she was darning. "Don't worry about me, Victoria. But stay with me, just for today."

"Stay with you? I can't. I have work to do." She knelt down by her mother. "When the war is over, we'll go home and everything will go back to the way it was."

"No, I won't be going home. I'm afraid this is the end for me."

"The end? What are you talking about?" Victoria said. Then she took a good look at her mother. Seta was breathing rapidly. Her face was gray, emaciated-looking, and her flesh hung in folds on the sharp, protruding bones of her arms. But she couldn't mean...

Victoria jumped up and pulled Seta's mattress out. "Here, lie down."

Seta winced in pain as she tried to stand.

Victoria assisted her to bed and covered her with her

quilt. "You've made yourself sick caring for me. I'll make you better. I know I can."

Seta closed her eyes then opened them. "My time has come. I can feel it."

Victoria gulped. "This is all my fault."

Seta grasped her arm "No. Don't feel bad. This is something that started a long time ago. Something in my stomach... I don't know what. I haven't told you because you have too much to worry about as it is."

"But what I am doing there – " Victoria gestured toward the main house, " – is for you."

Seta shook her head. "For the boys. And yourself. I would not have let you do that for me." She gripped Victoria's arm again. "Victoria, tomorrow I won't be here but I will leave in peace, if you promise me one thing."

Victoria wiped her eyes. "Yes. Yes."

"That you will keep yourself and your sons safe. Someday, you might feel bad about what you have done. But don't. You have saved us all and you have been very brave. Remember that."

Victoria nodded and covered Seta's arm with the blanket. She sat with her mother all afternoon, knowing it was the last time she would.

Seta dropped off to sleep waking for brief periods until, as the fiery ball of sunlight dipped low in the sky, she simply stopped breathing. Victoria had been watching the sun, but she felt a gentle tap on her shoulder and when she looked, she saw that her mother had gone. She was alone. She began to cry. Without her mother, who was she? A twenty-six-year-old orphan wandering alone in the hostile desert that her world had disintegrated into.

Koren and Paul found her still sitting beside Seta, when they returned from the fields.

She looked up. "Grandmother is gone."

Koren and Paul looked at each other. "Gone?" Koren said. "But how can that be?"

Victoria explained about the illness Seta had been battling for months.

Seven-year-old Paul cried openly. Thirteen-year-old Koren cleared his throat, coughed and turned his head to the side.

Victoria stood and went to him. "Even grown men cry."

Koren broke down. "I didn't know she was that sick."

"You didn't know because she didn't want you to know."

"But I should have. I should have told you, too."

"Even if you had, there was nothing any of us could have done for her."

With her words to her son, Victoria accepted the truth. Her mother's death was something apart from the Turks. Something apart from herself, too. It had been inevitable.

Victoria buried her mother the next morning in the unfrozen ground of a hill tall enough to overlook the rolling pastures and wheat fields that had once been her home.

Victoria returned to the main house later that day. Her sons followed, carrying their bedding on their backs. She had sent word to Hasan the day before by way of Koren, and Hasan had told her she could stay at the cottage until today.

Even Fadime was sensitive enough to cease her complaints for the day, but Victoria moved through the afternoon feeling as frail as she had three weeks ago when she had returned from her mother's care.

As the months passed and fall turned to winter, Victoria fought her sadness by reminding herself that her mother had died beside her daughter and had been attended by the family who loved her. When Victoria thought about what the women in the fields had told her about their parents' deaths, she was grateful for that, at least. And she was grateful that she and her sons remained under Hasan's roof, protected from the dangers that those gentle women had struggled with.

But her protection came at a price — the price of Fadime's continuing harassment and Hasan's nightly demands.

One winter afternoon, Hasan returned from the village uncharacteristically subdued. He sat on a cushion and watched Victoria spoon rice into dried squashes. She walked to the pantry. His eyes followed her there. When she came out, he was still watching her.

Had she done something wrong? She looked up from the chick peas she was rinsing. He quickly looked away.

He said nothing to her when she was alone with him that night, but he slept holding her to his chest.

The next day, she realized he was watching her again. She looked around the room. Everyone she looked at, looked away.

She invited Milan out to the barn to gather eggs. "Something is wrong, I can feel it."

Milan clasped her hands. "Well...that is..."

"Milan, please."

Milan looked up at the rafters. A bird flew by and landed in a nest.

Victoria felt like a scarf had been pulled too tightly around her neck. "It's about me, isn't it."

Milan sighed. "Jalal told me that the Turks have ordered all Muslim households to turn out any Armenians they have living there."

"But they said that at the beginning of the war."

"Yes, but now they're arresting people who disobey."

Victoria tried to inhale. She couldn't. "What will happen to my sons?"

"Listen, Victoria, Hasan wouldn't turn you out. What he feels for you grows stronger every day. And no one knows you're here."

Victoria found she could breath again. "You're right. No one does."

But still, she jumped every time someone entered the house and worried for an entire week when Koren and Paul went outside to work. Then, when one week turned into three and nothing happened, her anxiety slowly slipped away.

The rest of the household relaxed, also.

But two months later, in the late afternoon, Hasan's nephew, Talib, came running in the door, flushed and out of breath. "Soldiers. They're headed up the road."

Victoria dropped the spoon she was stirring a pot of soup with. It fell to the floor with a loud clatter. She spun around. "Koren and Paul."

Milan ran to her. "You must hide."

"No, my sons."

"Jalal will warn them. Hide. If the Turks find you, they will find them as well."

Victoria began to perspire. She looked around the room. Her eyes lit on the pantry. Yes, the pantry. She yanked the key from her wrist. An angry welt appeared on her skin. Her hands shook. She fumbled with the lock.

Heavy footsteps clomped up the stairs.

She opened the pantry door and ran in.

Someone pounded on the door. Milan held her shoulder to the pantry door and turned the key in the lock.

Hasan sailed regally to the door. He opened it, smiled benignly, and gestured the soldiers in. He straightened his shoulders, raised his chin, and looked at the leader.

"Lord – " The leader stopped and looked around the room.

Jalal picked up a steamy cup of coffee and sipped.

Milan stirred the soup.

Fadime pulled her needle through a piece of cloth and

stared thoughtfully back.

The leader cleared his throat. "I'm sorry to disturb you, Lord, but I have orders to search every house."

Hasan humphed. "Go ahead and search but remember, I'll be very displeased if anything's broken."

"Oh, yes, sir." The leader folded his arms and watched, while his men spread out around the room. When one picked up a flowered porcelain vase and turned it over, the leader hurried to him, smacked his shoulder, and pointed to the shelf. The soldier reddened and gently put it back where it belonged.

Milan stirred the soup again.

Fadime put down her sewing and stood.

The soldiers continued their search.

Milan looked at Fadime and jerked her head in the direction of the stove. Fadime frowned and walked to her side.

Milan lowered her voice to a whisper. "I'm afraid for you."

Fadime raised her brow. "For me? Why?"

"Sssh." Milan looked toward the soldiers. "For the harm that will come to you if you go."

Fadime lowered her voice. "What are you talking about? Why should *I* go anywhere?"

"Then you don't know?"

"Know what?"

"That Muslims who are caught hiding Armenians are punished, even hanged." Milan shook her head. "You're Hasan's wife. They'll think you're as guilty as he is."

Fadime's face changed expression.

Milan patted her arm. "Don't worry, I'm sure they won't find them." She looked up. A soldier was trying the door to the pantry.

The leader said something to Hasan.

Hasan looked at Milan and pointed to the lock. "Open it."

Milan fumbled with the lock, tried the door, then fumbled again. The soldier frowned and tapped his foot. Milan turned the key and opened the door. The soldier stepped inside the small space and Milan followed close on his heels. He whipped around and gave her an irritated look, but she remained just short of touching him. He walked to a shelf, turned back and bumped into Milan. He glared and stomped to another shelf. She stayed at his side. He let out a breath, then walked back to the door of the pantry, stepping on Milan's toe as he did.

"Oh, excuse me, sir," Milan said. She smiled a fool's smile. "I was standing too close to you, wasn't I?"

The soldier stared at her as one looks at a good copy of a well-known painting — with the knowledge that the details are correct, but the sense that something is amiss.

The soldier narrowed his eyes and rested his chin on his hand.

Milan stared back with a blank face.

The soldier paused, then shrugged. "No one in there."

The leader took an ivory whistle from his pocket and blew into it. The search was over.

Jalal stood at the door watching, as the soldiers filed past him and down the dirt road. He closed the door with a bang. "They're gone."

Milan was the first to react. She rushed to the pantry door, unlocked it, and stepped inside. "You can come out now."

A burlap sack of wheat began to tremble, then fell over. Victoria crawled out and collapsed in Milan's arms, both laughing and crying at the same time.

"I thought I would die when I heard you opening the door."

"I took as long as I could."

"I didn't know where to hide. I was lucky that empty sack was there."

The two stepped out of the pantry, arm-in-arm. Hasan gave Victoria a wide smile. Jalal congratulated her on her clever hiding place. Even Fadime could say with complete sincerity that she was glad Victoria had not been discovered.

Koren and Paul strode into the house grinning. They had bits of straw stuck in their hair and clinging to their clothes. Hasan looked at them and laughed. Victoria followed suit. The rest of the household soon did, too.

Victoria set a stack of bowls on the table. "Let's eat." She spooned an extra large portion of soup into Fadime's bowl and smiled.

Amine helped the boys brush the straw from their clothing. Hasan's aunt held the bowls for Victoria to fill.

Perhaps the mutual danger had brought them all closer together.

But it hadn't. By the next day, Fadime was complaining again. Amine had sided with her and Hasan's aunts were leaving all the cooking and serving to Victoria. Victoria sighed, picked up her broom and went on. Someday the war would be over and she would take her sons and leave.

The war drummed on for another year and a half. Then, through snatches of the men's conversations, Victoria began to hear that the Ottoman Empire was losing the war. She silently cheered, knowing this meant she could go home soon. But the end of the war made her think of Margaret, Anna, and Fiorine. What had become of them? Had they survived the terrible marches? The thought that they might not have filled her with despair. They were her friends, her family. What would she do without them?

By the fall of 1918, the men in Hasan's house were talking openly about the Empire's imminent defeat. Victoria noticed that the more they talked about it, the more strangely Hasan acted. He followed her everywhere, to the barn, to the garden. In the evening, he sat and stared at her while she cleaned the dishes and wiped down the table. And every night, he kept her in his bed. She hated it. He made her feel smothered. And now that she knew she was leaving soon, she could admit to herself how much she felt like a slave in his house and how tired she was of Fadime and the other women in the house. She cooked for them, cleaned their dirty dishes, and all they did was find something to complain about. If it weren't for her friendship with Milan, dear Milan, she would have snapped long ago.

One afternoon, in early October, Fadime complained that Victoria had buttered the roll she was eating with rancid butter.

Victoria put her hand on her hip. "It is perfectly fresh and you know it." Why was she arguing with Fadime? The woman complained every day. Victoria knew she was just playing into Fadime's hand.

Fadime's eyes gleamed. "You keep all that food in the pantry and dole out crumbs to us."

It was best to ignore her. But Victoria's mouth was opening and she didn't seem to be able to stop it. "How do you know what I keep in there?"

"Oh, I know." Fadime looked around the room.

Hasan was watching. He rose and walked toward them. He looked from Victoria to Fadime.

Victoria took her hand off her hip. She ought to smile sweetly at him like she usually did. Shrug and walk away, like she usually did. But she didn't. She stood and stared back.

"Victoria, if Fadime wants another roll, give it to her."

The corners of Fadime's lips turned up. "She should give everyone more. For three years now she's been starving us."

For three years she had fed twenty people and made the food from Hasan's farm last the winter. She ripped the pantry key from her wrist and flung it at Hasan. "Take it.

Why should I care when I'm leaving anyway?"

An ominous silence descended on the room.

Had she really said that?

She covered her mouth. "Oh, forgive me." She bent down to pick up the key from where it had landed after it struck Hasan's chest.

Hasan's face had turned icy white.

She fingered the key. She tried to smile at him. He stared back. What should she do? She turned to walk away.

The blow landed on her right cheek. Hasan grabbed her shoulder, spun her around, and landed another closed fisted punch on her chin. Her head snapped back. She couldn't see. She tried to protect her face, but before she could raise her hands, he hit her again and again until she fell to the floor. And still he didn't stop. She tried to crawl away, but there was no escaping his rage. He raised his booted foot and kicked. She heard her bones crack. He kicked her again and again, until she mercifully slipped into unconsciousness. His abuse continued, even then. Fadime tried to grab his waist and pull him away. He shook her off. Milan ran to the door and screamed for Jalal. Jalal came running in and wrapped his powerful arms around Hasan. He murmured soothing words into Hasan's ear and gently coaxed him to the door.

On the doorstep, Hasan broke free of Jalal and ran back to Victoria. He kicked her unmoving body one last time. "Get her out of here. I never want to see her face again."

CHAPTER TWENTY-NINE

Fall, 1918

*V*ictoria opened her eyes. Shadows and blurs danced across her vision. Was she dreaming? The wall in front of her seemed to be the wall of her own house. And whose hands were wiping her forehead? Whose voice was urging her back to the world?

But the pain gripped her head like a cinch and she could not stay. She floated back to the place where she didn't hurt.

Time passed.

She tried to open her eyes again. Only the left lid would raise. She tilted her head and squinted. Koren and Paul hovered at the foot of her mattress watching.

A woman bathed her face. "Lie still. You're safe now."

Victoria's lips formed a question.

The woman answered. "You are home. You've been here since the Kurd beat you up three weeks ago."

Victoria struggled to move. She wanted to grasp the woman's hand, touch her face.

The woman smiled. "Yes, it's me. I'm back. The war is over. I don't know why God spared me, but He did."

The tears that sprang to Victoria's injured eyes were as conversely painful as her sense of happiness. She drifted back to sleep. Margaret was here.

Victoria awoke again the following day. Margaret sat beside her, crocheting a small square. Victoria's voice was hoarse, almost a whisper. "Is it really you?"

Margaret jumped at the sound of her voice. "Yes, it's me."

"But how..?"

Margaret looked at her with eyes darkened by sorrow. "You will need all your strength for me to tell you what happened."

Victoria's fingers brushed Margaret's hand. "No, tell me now."

"I can't talk about it yet."

Victoria tried to focus with her left eye. Margaret's hair was gray, but her hands were steady. "I understand, but tell me, did you come here from Syria?"

"Yes, I was in Aleppo working in an orphanage during the day and taking in sewing at night, when we heard that the war had ended and we could go home." Margaret hesitated. "After all that happened I didn't know if I could face coming home. I thought about staying where I was but something told me to come home, so I did."

Koren appeared in Victoria's field of vision. "I found her in the village. I had gone there looking for help."

Victoria looked at him. "You went into the village?"

"Yes. Talib and Bayram had helped me carry you home. They told me that the war had ended a week ago."

"I had just arrived when Koren found me," Margaret said.

"I am so lucky you were here. How did you know I needed you?"

"God guided me here."

How could Margaret have kept her faith after all she had apparently been through?

As if she could read Victoria's thoughts, Margaret answered. "It has been my faith that has kept me going."

Victoria tried to reach for her friend's hand, but the pain prevented her from moving.

Margaret arranged Victoria's arm at her side. "Lie still. You will not be able to get up for weeks, maybe months."

Victoria shuddered. "I'm just glad I can't see how I look. I remember him punching me, over and over again. I couldn't get away. I thought he was going to kill me and I remember thinking how senseless it was for me to have made it so far, only to have it end anyway."

Koren edged closer. "Talib came to the fields and told Paul and I what happened. When we got to the house, Hasan was gone. Fadime was cleaning the blood off your face and wrapping your arm in a bandage."

"Fadime helped *me*?"

Lines appeared on Margaret's forehead. "I think she was ashamed of her husband's behavior."

Koren clenched his fists. "I should have been there. I would have stopped him."

"Hush, now," Victoria said. "He would have turned on you, too. And you don't have the right to defend yourself, even now."

"Victoria, you mustn't get excited." Margaret gave Koren a meaningful look. He bowed his head and fell silent.

Over the next few weeks, Victoria slowly began to gain back her strength. One day, she braved a look in the mirror. The right side of her face had taken the brunt of the beating. It was battered and misshapen. Her right eye remained swollen shut.

Margaret put her arm around Victoria. "You'll be surprised to see how much time will heal it."

"Don't feel bad for me Margaret. I know what you went through was far worse."

Another month went by. The bruises and swelling slowly receded. As Victoria gained mobility in her limbs, her hand flew frequently to the right side of her face, examining by touch its marred surface. Eventually she could open her right eye but unfortunately to no avail. The eye remained sightless, her reminder of Hasan. She would never forget him and she would never escape the guilt she felt for having lived with him while her friends suffered on the marches.

One night, after Koren and Paul had gone to sleep, Victoria turned to Margaret. "Do you think you can tell me your story now?"

Margaret met her eye. "Are you ready to hear it?"

Victoria nodded.

Margaret began. "When we left the village, I kept Diran and Miriam close to my side. My mother walked with us, too. Each village we came to drew more women into our caravan. Soon we were thousands. I became separated from Anna and Fiorine. I don't know what happened to them.

"I was terrified because I remembered the stories we had heard from the women in the fields about the attacks, so I told everyone around me to keep their heads covered. I smeared my face with mud so I would look dirty and ugly. I did the same to Miriam, because you just never know.

"We lost some of the old folks on the first day. Then each day after that we lost more. Mother, God bless her, kept going for weeks. I don't know how she did it. I lost her in the desert when we ran out of water."

Victoria covered her face with her hands. "Poor Araxie. I can't bear to think how she must have suffered."

Margaret nodded. "The sun was scorching. One day, she just collapsed. Diran and Miriam saw her fall and were hysterical. I tried to stop, I wanted to stay with her, but a guard rode up to me and lashed me with his whip. I had to leave my mother where she fell in the sand."

Victoria thought about her own mother's death. Seta had died because it was her time. Victoria had been able to bury Seta near the fields of home. Hasan and her time with him had given her that, at least.

Margaret took out a handkerchief and dabbed her eyes. I went on for my children's sake."

Victoria's own eyes filled.

Margaret continued. "One day we came to a puddle outside of a village. I was so happy. I grabbed Diran and Miriam and ran for it. We fell on our stomachs and lapped it with our tongues. I can't tell you how good it tasted after all those days of nothing. But the Turks wouldn't even let us have that muddy slop. They whipped us until we got up. I still have scars on my back to prove it.

"Diran was only nine, Miriam only seven. But they never complained. They just kept on walking. They almost made it, too. Almost." Margaret stared into space.

Victoria took her hand. "Tell me what happened to them."

"My baby was the first to go. She had become so weak she couldn't walk so I was carrying her. She died in my arms. Diran went two days later. I truly didn't want to go on after my Diran died. I laid down beside him, but the other women forced me to get up. We did that for each other. When one wanted to give up, the others made her go on.

"Thirty-five people from our convoy reached the camps along the Euphrates, where all the surviving Armenians were staying. Thousands of us were crowded into fenced-in areas like animals. And our suffering didn't end there. The Turks made us sleep out in the open and only gave us one slice of bread a day. Then dysentery hit and hundreds more people died each day.

"I don't know why but I never took sick, so I helped take care of the ones who did. When some English missionaries set up a tent for sick children, I worked there taking care of them. I knew that if I had died, my children could have been any one of these. We had four hundred children in our care.

"Some days we didn't get our bread and we had nothing at all to give the children. At least ten died each day. I could only stand it because we were able to save some, too. My mother once told me that you could prevent dysentery by boiling water before you drink it, so I told the missionaries that and we tried it. Of course, many of the children were too far gone already, but I like to think I did some good for the rest.

"The missionaries liked the work I did, so they asked me to go with them to Aleppo where they had set up a school for orphans. I stayed with the children until the war was over. I hated to leave them even then, but many had relatives who were sending for them so they were leaving, too."

Victoria was silent. What could she say to Margaret? She rubbed the right side of her face. Hasan had nearly killed her, but it was worth saving her mother and sons from what Margaret had gone through.

Margaret spoke at last. "Don't dwell on it, Victoria. I'm alive and will go on from here because I have to. Because I was chosen to. We have all suffered. I don't know why I survived, but I did. I didn't asked to be spared but I was."

Victoria lay awake that night, haunted by the images of Margaret's story. She thought about Miriam and the day she had been born. She had lain in her cradle and trusted the world to take care of her. What had a seven-year-old girl done to make the Turks treated her so cruelly? Victoria couldn't help Miriam or any of the others who had died, but she could help the survivors when they returned home. Perhaps Anna and Fiorine would be back. She wanted to be ready to help them, if she could. And she had a plan about how she was going to do it, too.

The next morning, she was up with the sun. She went to Koren and shook his shoulder. "You must get up. We have work to do."

Koren sat up and rubbed sleep from his eyes. "What do you want me to do?"

"I want you to dig up the vegetable garden."

Koren frowned. "We can't plant the vegetables yet."

"No, we can't, but in a way, we have food in the ground. Before we went to Hasan's, I buried our gold and my mother's silver service. If it's still there, we can use it to get through the winter."

Koren nudged Paul awake, then slipped on his pants. "If it's there, Paul and I will find it."

Victoria hoped that anyone who had come to loot her house while she was gone, and she knew they had because almost everything inside had been taken, had looked only as far as the superficial hole near the water pump. She needed the rest for her plan and said as much to Margaret.

"You'll have your mother's silver back and enough money to get through the winter," Margaret said.

"Oh no, I'm not keeping the silver. I'm selling it."

"That lovely silver service? Why?"

Victoria told Margaret about her intention to help the returning survivors.

"But Victoria, you were never a rich woman. Even with the silver service, how much can you hope to do?"

"I'm not giving them that money. I'm using it to set up a business."

"What sort of business?"

"I'll tell you about it when the boys come back. *If* they find what I buried."

Margaret went to the door and looked out. "They are still digging."

Victoria waited for the boys to return, praying the gold and silver had not been discovered. She needed it for her own family as well as the survivors.

An hour went by. Then Koren opened the door. His face was dirt-stained, but he was grinning. He held up a dirt-encrusted earthenware jar. Paul came in with the silver pieces.

Victoria smiled. "Thank God." She counted the coins in the jar. "Take the silver to the village and sell it."

Koren nodded.

"Get as much as you can for it."

Koren nodded again.

She handed him the gold. "Then put it all together and buy as many raisins as you can."

Koren's eyes widened. "Raisins?"

"Yes, raisins. I'll explain why when you come back."

Koren and Paul left for the village. Victoria could feel Margaret staring at her.

Victoria turned and smiled. "You must think I'm crazy."

"I think you're too smart to be crazy. But what are you going to do with all those raisins?"

"I'm going to make *raki* and sell it."

"I changed my mind. Yes, I do think you're crazy. Who are you going to sell it to? None of our people are going to have money to buy *raki*."

"I'm not going to sell it to Armenians. I going to sell it to the Turks."

The Turks? But their religion forbids liquor."

"Remember the soldiers in the field?"

Margaret's expression cleared. "Oh."

Victoria went on. "And plenty of other Turks drink, too. They might as well buy from me. My mother's *raki* recipe was the best around."

With her sons' help, Victoria built a still far larger than

anything her parents had ever had. She checked it every day. After three weeks, when she lifted the lid she smelled fumes. Three weeks after that, the fumes began to burn her eyes and nostrils. She knew the fermentation process was almost complete.

"How are you going to sell it?" Margaret said. "You can't just set up a cart in the street."

"Oh, don't worry. I have a plan." Victoria slipped on her coat, tied a scarf under her chin, and headed out the door.

Sad, broken houses dotted the route to the village. But she could not think about the people she had lost. She had to think about the people she could help.

When Victoria returned home from the village an hour later, she was delighted. She had her first customer.

Over the next weeks and months, Victoria's cache of gold grew, as her bootlegging business prospered. She even sold her *raki* to the important village officials. If anyone tried to cheat her, they quickly learned it wouldn't be easy. One customer threatened to turn her in to the authorities unless she gave him free liquor. She just smiled and handed him a jug. He strutted away with a smug grin on his face.

He hurried back to her the next day and handed her some coins, apologizing for the misunderstanding. Victoria had set up her network well. Among the people on her payroll was the chief of police, who had told her he wasn't going to be cheated out of his commission by anyone.

But the police chief wasn't always nearby when Victoria

needed him.

One afternoon, when Victoria was walking home from the village, she noticed a man following her.

Her purse held the gold coin she had just earned. She clutched it to her side and quickened her pace.

She heard the man's footsteps on the dirt road behind her. And she was alone. She could run, but so could he. What did he want? Her money or her? She clenched her jaw. She would not let him have either.

She spun around and faced him.

His brow raised, he hesitated. Then he looked at the empty landscape around him and started for her.

She waited. He was ten paces from her, an arm's length. He was reaching for her.

She raised her foot and used the rage she had suppressed for three years to kick him between the legs.

Now she could run and he could not.

She had to wrap her foot with strips of muslin to bring down the swelling that came on that night, but she smiled right through the pain, happy that no one would ever take advantage of her again.

Victoria's business continued to grow. Soon she was drawing customers from other villages as well. She set up two more stills and kept all three operating at once. She sold each batch within days of it being ready. But her supply of gold sat in its jar. She knew from her business that a few Armenians had returned to nearby villages, but none of the people from hers had. She thought about Anna and Fiorine. The war had been over for six months. Where were they?

Spring arrived. She planted her wheat and waited.

Victoria went into the village on business two or three times a week, but she managed to avoid seeing Hasan. She was glad. He was one person she couldn't defend herself from and she knew she could never look at him again without being frightened. She was thankful he seemed to want to avoid her, too.

One day, when Victoria was sweeping her floor, someone knocked on the door. "Milan, what a surprise."

Milan stepped in the door and quickly closed it behind her. "I don't want anyone to see me. You know how people talk."

Victoria nodded. "I'm glad you've come. I've missed you."

Milan brushed the right side of Victoria's face. "It's almost healed."

"Yes, but I'm afraid the injuries will always be apparent."

"They will, but you are still very beautiful, you know."

Victoria led Milan to the table and the two women sat.

"I can stay for only a few minutes." Milan blushed. "I've come to ask for your help."

Victoria grasped her hand. "You were my only friend in Hasan's house. I will do anything you ask."

Milan hesitated, then began. "Jalal has been offered the promotion he has been waiting for. It would mean that we could leave Hasan's house and move to Mezireh. I don't want to take advantage, but I don't know what else to do."

"Milan, a true friend asks for help when she needs it. How much do you want?"

Milan sighed with relief and told her the amount. Victoria emptied out half of her savings and handed it to Milan.

"I won't forget this," Milan said.

"And I won't forget how you got the midwife for me, kept my secret, and hid me from the Turks."

"You can't imagine how dreadful Hasan's house has been since you left. Hasan is in a constant temper. We all try to stay out of his way, Fadime especially. She gets the brunt of it."

"Before I knew him, I thought he was the kindest man I'd ever met. Even after I saw him go after Fadime that first day, I never thought he was capable of doing what he did to me."

"I thought he had killed you. I'm afraid of him now. We all are." Milan stared at the wall. "You know, he never mentions you. No one else does, either. But still your presence in that house is stronger than ever. Be careful, Victoria."

Victoria's hand flew to the damaged right side of her face. "I'm trying to forget him and even if I do, I will never forget you or our friendship."

The two women embraced. Then Milan gathered her things and left.

Victoria wiped down the table. Milan was moving away. She would never see her again, but she would carry with her the bonds of their friendship.

Margaret arrived back from the village out of breath and frowning. "I just found two Armenian children in an abandoned house. I don't know how they got there and they were too frightened to tell me."

Victoria grabbed her kerchief and covered her head. "Show me where they are."

Margaret led Victoria through a gate to a house in the village. What had once been a front door hung on one hinge. The only two windows were broken and shards of glass struck up from rotted-looking frames. Inside a boy of about six and a girl of about four huddled in a corner. Flies swarmed over their heads.

Victoria knelt before them. "What happened to you?"

The children said nothing.

She tried again. "Where are your parents?"

The boy shrugged. The girl bit her finger.

Victoria took the boy's hand. "You must tell me how you got here if I am to help you."

The boy's eyes were wide with fear. "My mother and father brought us here, but I don't know where they are."

The only other Armenians to return to the village were missing. But they were supposed to be allowed to come home. What had happened?

Victoria left Margaret with the children and went to the police station. The guard at the door recognized her and brought her to the chief. She told him why she was there.

"Because of our — " the police chief looked from side to

side, "business arrangement, I'll let them go."

But why had he arrested them in the first place, she wondered?

The chief called an order to the guard and a few minutes later, he returned with a pale-looking man and woman. Victoria looked at them closely. She remembered them from church, but had known them only slightly.

She thanked the chief and left with the couple.

As soon as they were out of the building, the woman turned to Victoria. "My children."

"They are safe. Scared, but safe."

"Oh, thank God. They've been alone for two days. I've been frantic. We came back because we were told we could. But when we got here, the police arrested us after we insisted that the Turks who were living in our house leave."

The man scowled. "I'm writing to my brother for money. As soon as we can, we're leaving. There is nothing for Armenians in Turkey anymore."

Victoria was silent. Was that true? But she was thriving. And what if she left and Fiorine or Anna came home? What would they do without her? No, she would stay.

The children ran to their parents, when they saw them. Victoria pressed gold coins into the man's hand. "You needn't wait for your brother to send money. Take this and leave if you think it best."

The couple left the village that same afternoon. Victoria and Margaret waved good-bye and walked home.

Three weeks later, a letter arrived at Victoria's door. "It's for you, Margaret."

Margaret pointed to herself. "For me?"

She took the envelope from Victoria and gasped. "It's from Solomon."

"From Solomon?" Victoria said. "He's alive?"

Margaret tore open the envelope and read. Her eyes filled with tears. "Yes, he is alive, but the Turks shot my father and all the other men of our village."

Victoria bowed her head. Michael had been her father's friend. He had entertained her family at his vineyards. She had spent afternoons in his house drinking coffee and discussing the changing political situation. He had helped so many people. And now he was dead.

"I'm sorry, Margaret."

"I knew really. But hearing it, well." She wiped her eyes, "You understand."

Victoria nodded. Then she touched the envelope. "Where is Solomon now? And how did he ever survive the violence?"

Margaret told her how Solomon had gotten out of the country and fought in the war. She said he was writing in hopes that Margaret was alive. "Now he's in the East. In the Republic of Armenia."

"Armenia. I've heard something about it, but we get so little news here."

"I'll tell you what I learned about it while I was in Syria."

Margaret went on to explain that during the war, the

Russian army advanced into Turkey and captured the Armenian provinces on the border uniting the Turkish Armenians with their brethren in Russia. The Armenians in the Russian-occupied provinces had heard about what was happening to their people in other parts of Turkey and were happy to be under Russian protection. In March of 1917, the Russian revolution took place and the new government announced that it would continue to protect the Armenians. But a second revolt in October of that year brought Lenin and the Bolsheviks to power. To remain true to Socialism, Lenin said, Russians could not continue to occupy the provinces. To do so would be imperialistic, and Lenin abhorred imperialism. Lenin withdrew all Russian troops and announced that Southern Russia, Armenian, Georgia and Azerbaijan, were under self-rule. The Armenians wanted independence, but Lenin withdrew his troops before the country had a chance to establish an army of its own. Turkey quickly struck, gained back the territory it had lost, and continued to advance across Southern Russia. By May of 1918, Turkey had conquered most of the territory that was supposed to be the Republic of Armenia. Most, but not all. The Armenians surprised the Turks by halting them before they had finished. The small piece of territory that had not been conquered by the Turks was now the Republic of Armenia.

Margaret explained that the country's future was still very uncertain, because Turkey had not given up panTurkism and its plan to unite with Azerbaijan. She also explained that the Allies had not disarmed the Ottoman army upon its defeat so Turkey might very well make another attempt at overpowering the tiny, inadequately defended country. But she said that Solomon knew the risk and thought it was worth taking. He told her, too, that the Allies had promised restitution to the Armenians for what they had suffered and as part of the armistice, they were negotiating the lost territory back.

Victoria watched Margaret write back to her husband. Margaret's face was flushed. A little smile played at the corners of her mouth. Victoria knew that it was just a matter of time, before Margaret left to join Solomon. He had written that he had won an important position in the government. He needed Margaret at his side. Victoria knew that Margaret wanted to be part of the fight and wanted to be with her husband. And Victoria understood this. What was there here for Margaret now? Empty houses, unplowed fields? She waited daily with Victoria, but still, none of their friends returned.

Solomon's reply arrived in May with the money for Margaret's travel.

"Margaret, are you sure? The journey will be dangerous."

"I'm sure."

"You will have to cross over the mountains on foot."

Margaret took her hand. "I'm sure."

"Kurds live in the mountains. You might be attacked."

Margaret put her arm around Victoria. "I have to go. I know the risk I am taking. I know what I am leaving behind.

But I must go, anyway."

Margaret left a week later.

Victoria stood watching her climb onto the horse-drawn cart that would take her away from the village. Away from Victoria. Victoria ran to the cart. Margaret leaned over the side and wrapped her arms around Victoria. They sobbed in each other's arms.

Then the cart pulled away and took with it the last friend Victoria had. What would she do now?

CHAPTER THIRTY

July, 1919

*V*ictoria closed the cover to her ledger. Her money jar was full, her wheat was growing, she had bought a new flock of sheep, but what good was any of it without her friends and family? Anna and Fiorine had still not come back. She was beginning to despair.

None of the Armenians from her village had come home. But Margaret had told her how impoverished the survivors in Syria were and Victoria still hoped that in time, when they had the resources, they would return.

Victoria walked to the door and watched Koren disentangle a tomato plant that had fallen in the garden. He was fifteen years old now, a man, and under his capable hands, her farm would flourish.

She saw him turn to Paul and watched him guide Paul's hand, as he hammered a stake into the ground. Koren read with Paul every night. The Turks who had robbed her house had left her father's books and Koren used them to make up for the education his brother had missed out on. Victoria herself was reviewing and teaching Paul math skills.

Really, they were doing quite well. She just needed to be patient. Eventually her community would return.

One afternoon, Koren flew into the house tracking in dirt on shoes that he didn't stop to wipe. "I just saw some people moving into the Halabian's house."

Now Turks were taking over her neighbor's house. "Oh, dear," Victoria said.

"No, you don't understand. The people are Armenian."

Victoria jumped up. "Armenians?"

She ran down the old familiar path leading to the Halabian's house. Pebbles rolled out of her way as she went. Who was there? Koren hadn't been able to tell her. He had only known from their dress that they were Armenian.

The woman who answered the door had lines on her face that shouldn't have appeared for years. Her shirt was patched and faded. It gapped at her waist and was held up only by her protruding hip bones.

"Sona," Victoria said.

Sona squinted in the sunlight. "Victoria?"

Victoria embraced Sona. She could feel her ribs through her muslin blouse. "I have been waiting and waiting for someone to come back. What happened to you? Where is everyone else?"

Sona's face changed expression. She sat down on the steps to the house. "We can talk here."

Victoria looked at Sona. Her face looked pained. "Are you able to tell me about it, Sona?"

Sona nodded. "But it is a long story and not a happy one."

Victoria drew in a shaky breath.

Sona began. "We walked out of the village and kept on walking. Mary died first. Then Charles's wife. And Martin's nephew who survived Adana? A guard noticed his height, he had grown a lot over the past year, and shot him in front of me.

"I don't know how, but I made it to the camps in Aleppo. I was very sick there, with a high fever. I thought I was going to die. In a way, I wanted to. But then, maybe I didn't because I got better.

"I found out later that I had had typhus. We had a big outbreak of it in the camps. I stayed in Aleppo until the war was over. I didn't know what to do, when I heard we could go home. I asked myself what was here for me? And how would I get back? I had no money. No one else in the camps did either."

Victoria straightened up. Then it might be true. Anna and Fiorine might be alive but without the money for travel. She could help, if she only knew how to find them.

Sona continued. "I have a distant cousin, Haig, and eventually he found me in the camps. He and his wife, Marnos, had left Turkey before the war. We had boards in the camps, where people who were looking for their relatives, posted their names. I saw his and remembered him so I told one of the camp officials and he brought Haig to me."

Victoria started thinking. She could write to the officials in the camps herself and tell them who she was looking for. If Sona could travel back here, Anna and Fiorine could too. "And you didn't have a problem getting back here?"

"No, not really. Haig had a little money, not much. I told him about the farm here and we decided to come back and run it together. He and his wife have a little baby girl and they had to leave everything behind when they left Turkey. This farm can take care of us all."

"Yes, it can," Victoria said. "And I will help too."

Sona looked at her and smiled. "The closer I got to our village, the more I heard about you and the help you have given to the Armenians who returned to their villages around here."

Victoria turned her palm up. "I have a little business. I hear things and I do what I can."

"You are so kind."

Victoria turned her head away. "It's nothing, really." She hesitated. "Sona, what happened to Martin?"

Sona's eyes filled with tears. "The Turks said he died in action, but I heard things about the Armenian soldiers, how the Turks took away their guns, made them carry supplies like animals, then shot them."

"He was a wonderful man."

"And he died with a lot of other wonderful men. I believed what I heard about the Turks, because I saw what they did to the women and children of our village."

Victoria played with a blade of grass. Sona might know. Victoria had to ask. "Do you know what happened to Anna and Fiorine?"

Sona stared at her hands. "Yes, Victoria, I do know."

"Are they — "

"They didn't make it."

"Neither of them?"

Sona shook her head. "Anna gave in to the heat of the desert. What happened to Fiorine was worse."

Victoria began to weep. "Tell me."

"She made it to the Euphrates river. Then the Turks took her and thirty other women, tied their hands behind their backs, and pushed them in. They made the rest of us watch and laughed at our horror."

Victoria walked back to her house and sat on the grassy rise above her fields. The Turks had killed two dear, gentle women. She had been waiting for them to come back to her. They would not return. Sona had told her that even Rose had died. The Turks hadn't cared who the person was. If they were Armenian, they killed them. She thought about the couple she had rescued from the police station. The Turks' cruelty had not stopped. The couple had said there was nothing in Turkey for them anymore. They were right. Without her community, the village was no longer home.

But where was home now? She was sure to hear from Nikol soon. He would ask her to go to America. She didn't know what she would do. Could she live with him as his wife after what she had done? And what would she tell him?

She sighed and put her head down on her knees.

Hasan watched Victoria from where he lay concealed behind a rock. Was she crying? He couldn't tell. Perhaps she missed him, was sorry for what she had said. She was still beautiful. Her face had healed but it bore his mark. He liked that.

She stood and walked into the house. He waited until the door closed behind her then he climbed down the hill and climbed on his horse. He must get her back. She belonged to him.

He jerked the reins and the horse reversed direction. He would go to the village and talk to the police chief. Hasan kicked his horse to a trot. If he wanted her back, he would have her. She had no rights here. The police chief would do his usual hedging, insist that Hasan give him time to think it over, but with enough money, Hasan knew he would get his way.

Victoria carefully filled a clay jug with her *raki* for the police chief. She looked up. He was looking at her with a strange expression. She hoped she hadn't done anything wrong. She paid him a commission on every jug of *raki* she sold. He seemed to even like her now. She had noticed that in the months they had been in business, he had gone from treating her with a certain arrogant disdain, to what seemed like respect.

But today it appeared that he had something on his mind. She waited.

He opened his mouth, looked as though he was going to say something, then closed it again and left.

She supposed that if he had any complaints about their business arrangement, he would tell her eventually.

One day, Koren returned from the village out of breath and flushed. He held up an envelope. "A letter. From America."

Victoria paled. He had written at last. Now what would she say to him in reply?

Koren studied her face. "Aren't you going to open it?"

"Yes, of course."

Victoria took the envelope from him and opened it with shaking fingers. She read aloud.

> My Darling Wife and Sons,
>
> Solomon wrote and told me that you are alive. I am so happy. How did you ever survive? When I thought you had been killed in the massacres, I wanted to die too. I even prayed to God

to take me in battle, but now I understand His reason for sparing me. I was in Syria after the war, but I came back to America a few months ago. Imagine, I was so near to you. I could have come and gotten you, but I didn't know.

I want you to come to America. Turkey is the wrong place for Armenians to be now. I've heard rumors that more trouble is coming. In fact, I want you to leave as soon as I send money for your passage.

Nikol's letter went on to give Victoria details of how she would leave Turkey and described Nikol's plans for their future. The last part Victoria read to herself.

"... So many of our people died. I hear more tales of horror every day. Whatever you did to survive was right because you saved our sons and yourself."

Victoria folded the letter. He was right. She had done what she had to do.

He wanted her to go to America. Should she leave Turkey and go to him?

She watched Koren wash his hands in the basin. He kept his eyes on the water. Paul held a book in front of his face, but Victoria could see him peering up over the top of it. She thought about Anna and Fiorine and the terrible deaths they had suffered. Nikol said more trouble was coming. Her sons had a right to a future. She could not put them in peril. And she could not condemn them to life in a country that treated them as inferiors, because they might just begin to believe that they were.

"Your father wants us to go to America. We will do it."

Koren dried his hands. "Are you sure Mother?"

"Yes."

Victoria decided she could be ready to leave in three weeks. She owned almost nothing. Nothing except the farm. Her father's farm.

She knew she had to sell it. She had told her sons she would leave. But how could she do it? How could any other place ever be home? She walked through her wheat fields and pulled the maturing kernels from their stalks. She brought them to her face and inhaled their nutty fragrance. She would leave, but she would carry with her this smell of home.

She looked up and saw Koren mending a fence in the far north pasture. She had to take him from the open air and rolling hills. She could promise him only safety in exchange.

She looked down the hill. Paul was leading her sheep to the village to sell. He was nine years old. He would never know the joy of racing to the grassy flat overlooking the road and eating grape leaves and cheese in the setting sun.

But he had spent a good part of his life hiding from people who hated him simply because he was not one of them, and she must take him from here because of it.

A week passed. Then two. Finally, she sat down and wrote

a notice putting her farm up for sale. She brought it to the board in the village, where public announcements were posted. But before she could tack it up, another announcement caught her eye.

She read it and felt her chest pull the air from her throat.

The announcement was from the governor and it forbade Armenians from leaving Kharpert. Nikol had said more trouble was coming. He was right. Now she had waited too long. She had escaped death once, but where would she go this time?

She ran to the police station.

The police chief looked at her in surprise. "We don't do business here."

Victoria brushed a strand of hair from her face. "No, I've come for another reason."

"And that is?"

"I need an exit visa."

The police chief shook his head. "All exit visas have been denied."

"Perhaps you can help me." Victoria met the police chief's eye. He was looking at her again like he wanted to say something.

He frowned and bit his lip. Then his expression changed. He moistened his finger and used it to riffle through some papers on his desk. "Perhaps I can."

"You know I can pay you whatever you ask."

"No, I don't want money. I want to make a trade with you."

"A trade?"

"You need something from me. I need something from you."

Hasan paced up and down the path from his house to his barn. Tomorrow he would have her back. He had paid that greedy chief, and he had promised to send three men to Hasan at dawn. The men would accompany Hasan to Victoria's house and use their guns to force her back.

Hasan kicked at a rock. He would make her leave her sons where they were. They would have to take care of themselves. And in Hasan's house, things were going to be different this time. He had been too lenient with her before. He had indulged her and she had lost her respect for him. If she forgot this time, he need only touch her face to remind her.

He was up and dressed the next morning when the three policemen galloped up to his door. He climbed on his horse, wishing Jalal was with him. But Jalal had moved away. Hasan eyed the policemen's rifles. There was nothing to stop him. By nightfall, she would again be his.

Hasan trotted up to Victoria's door, just as the sun came up over the horizon. He signaled the policemen, swung from his horse, and strode to her door.

The policemen pointed their guns and followed.

He raised his fist and banged on the door. No one answered.

He banged again. Still no answer.

He clenched his jaw, drew back his foot, and splintered the door open.

No one was there. Her bedding was gone, the stove was cold. She had left.

He turned to the policemen. They stared back at him, impassively.

He would kill her when he found her. He grabbed a ceramic vase glazed in a leaf design and smashed it to the floor. He picked up a crystal glass that smelled like the liquor she made and threw it against the wall. He kicked at a sack of wheat and it spit its contents across the floor. He eyed a kerosene lantern hanging on the wall. Yes, he would destroy her house, too. He sprinkled the fuel onto the floor, lit a match and ran from the house. *Prroom.* It exploded into flames.

He stood on a grassy rise with the policemen and watched as the flames spread through the straw roof and reached for the sky.

He turned and ran for his horse. "I'm going to see the chief. Follow me."

The police chief answered his door himself.

"She's not there," Hasan said.

The chief sighed and threw his hands in the air. "Oh, you know these Armenians. What can you do?"

"Where would she have gone?"

"To the north. Where else?"

Hasan jumped back on his horse, gestured to the chief's

men, and galloped off. The men looked at their superior. He winked. They nodded and spurred their horses in Hasan's direction.

The police chief stood at his door until the dust had settled. Then he walked out to a shed behind his house. He would be a rich man soon. Richer than the woman could have made him, if she had stayed. Inside the shed was her still and she had given him her recipe for making *raki*. She said it had been her mothers and that it had been a secret that had remained in her family for generations. Now it was his.

In a city to the southwest, Victoria handed a driver coins to take her and her sons to Adana, where they would board a ship that would take them first to Marseilles, France, then to America and away from the only home they had ever known. She tossed her wool quilt into the cart and climbed up. The driver picked up his reins. She looked back in the direction from which they had come and noticed a red-orange glow in the sky.

She pointed to it. "Look, a red sky. A sign of good luck."

Koren and Paul climbed into the cart. The driver clucked and it began to roll. Victoria brushed a tear from her eye and forced herself not to look back again.

The End